To Tony S.,
Who is without
a doubt the best
"Devil's Advocate" I've
ever known. Thanks for
all your help this past
year and best wishes to you
and yours in '87

Mike Reynolds
Xmas 86

RULES OF THE KNIFE FIGHT

Other Novels by Walter Walker

A DIME TO DANCE BY
THE TWO DUDE DEFENSE

RULES OF THE KNIFE FIGHT

Walter Walker

1817

HARPER & ROW, PUBLISHERS, NEW YORK

Cambridge, Philadelphia, San Francisco, Washington
London, Mexico City, São Paulo, Singapore, Sydney

The author extends his grateful appreciation to Dr. John Manwaring of Marin County for his invaluable assistance in the preparation of this book.

FIRST EDITION

Designer: Jénine Holmes

Library of Congress Cataloging-in-Publication Data

Walker, Walter.
  Rules of the knife fight.

  I. Title.
PS3573.A425417R85   1986   813'.54   86-45160
ISBN 0-06-015646-5

86 87 88 89 90 HC 10 9 8 7 6 5 4 3 2 1

To Brett, my joy

There are no rules in a knife fight.

—*Butch Cassidy and the Sundance Kid*

_____

RULES OF THE KNIFE FIGHT

Bobby O'Berry

CHAPTER ONE

The cash register in the Greek's diner was an army-green NCR model that had been there when the Greek bought the place. The Greek would shove down the price keys, numbers would pop into a window for the customer to see, and the drawer would fly open—usually hitting the Greek in his ample stomach. The Greek didn't care. Every hit in the stomach was money in the bank, he liked to say.

On the back of the cash register were two postcard-size signs. One of them was supposed to read "No Personal Checks," but someone had marked it up with a pen so that now it read "No Fat Chicks." The second sign had been defaced to read "We Reserve the Right to Refuse Service to Louie." The Greek didn't care about that, either.

He also didn't care that the former Mrs. Gallagher (he had no idea what name she was going by now) was sitting in the very last booth with her hand inside the zipper of her equally drunken companion. He would have cared if anybody else had noticed, but as long as nobody did he was not going to make a scene out of it.

What the Greek did care about was closing his place by midnight and getting home before one. It had been a problem these past couple of Friday nights because some of the high school boys kept wanting to order things right up until the last minute. Four of them were in tonight, including Bobby O'Berry, who had been the last to leave for two or three weeks in a row.

The Greek's plan was simple. At quarter of twelve he had shut down the grill and told the cook to go home. He had told the waitress she could leave at twelve o'clock, regardless of who was still there. But it was ten to now, and the boys were talking so much they weren't half done with their food. The Greek tuned his ear to their conversation.

3

"What I'd really like to do," Julie Sabatini was saying, "is kill someone."

Julie was the smallest of the four boys. His nose was long, his ears stuck out of his curly brown hair and he was wearing a gray T-shirt with a drawing of Mickey Mouse on the front. He was holding a giant cheeseburger, a Greekburger, as he talked, and ketchup was dribbling over his fingers. From the tone of his voice he might have been telling everyone how much he would like to go in to town to see a baseball game.

"Just for the experience," he said. "Just to see how it feels."

Linehan, the thick-armed boy next to him, was wearing a red T-shirt with a "Welcome to Miller Time" slogan on it. He didn't seem particularly distraught that Julie Sabatini wanted to kill someone. "You should have been born ten years earlier, Julie," he said. "Then you could have gone to 'Nam and killed gooks."

"I still been thinking about the Marines," Julie told him. "But my old man says I oughtta go in the Navy 'cause the food's better."

Mullaney, the redhead with the scar across the bridge of his nose, said, "My brother was in Vietnam. He didn't get to kill no gooks, though." Then, after a moment, he added, "I think he got to cut off some ears."

"What?" exclaimed Linehan, who lived across the street from the Mullaneys. "I never heard that one before."

Mullaney shrugged. "He don't like to talk about all the stuff he did over there."

Julie shook his head in commiseration. "They did some wicked shit, those guys."

But Linehan wasn't listening to Julie. He was saying to Mullaney, "You mean he don't like to talk about all the stuff he used to type for that Protestant chaplain he worked for?"

Mullaney said, "He was doing other stuff, too. He just don't like to talk about it. . . . Hey, Julie, if you could kill anyone and get away with it, who would it be?"

Julie chewed the last of his burger thoughtfully before answering. "Liver-archie," he said.

"How come?"

Julie grinned and promptly lost an onion and a piece of tomato from the corner of his mouth. "He's the only fag whose name I can think of right now."

"I don't know," said Mullaney. "He's supposed to be a real nice guy."

"Who told you that?" asked Linehan. "Your brother?"

"Fuck you, Linehan."

From his position at the cash register the Greek called out, "Hey, watch the language down there." One other thing the Greek cared about, and that was anything that disturbed his customers; and loud swearing, he knew, was liable to do just that. "The food's bad enough," he liked to say. "The people don't gotta put up with a lot of horseshit, too."

Mullaney lowered his voice and turned back to the others. "Guys like Liberace, you don't know if they're really fags or not. A lot of them guys just pretend like they are so they can get on television. Like— who's that guy? Wayne Newton. You hear him sing, you think he's a fag, but he's not. He raises horses and everything."

"Oh, well, that settles it," Linehan said. "He can't be a fag if he raises horses."

The Greek stopped listening long enough to ring out some customers. The roar of a motorcycle sounded in the parking lot and the Greek looked up in time to see Vinnie Carelli squeeze his Honda 750 between two parked cars rather than use an open space some twenty feet away. The boys all called Carelli "Loogie," but the Greek didn't know why and so he called him by his given name.

"Vinnie," the Greek said when Carelli bounced in with his helmet under his arm, "I no gonna feed you, that's what you think. You want Coke, that's all right, but I close up the grill now. No frappes, no nothin'."

"It's okay, Greek," Carelli said as he blew past him. He went straight to the stool next to Mullaney and began picking fries off Mullaney's plate.

"Hey, get your own, Loogie," Mullaney said, trying to slap Carelli's hand away.

Carelli ignored him, his hand flashing in and out, over and around Mullaney's arm until Mullaney gave up and pushed the plate of fries to a spot in front of Carelli.

"What are you guys doin'?" Carelli asked with his mouth full.

"Talkin' about what's gonna happen when school's over. Linehan says he's gonna spend all summer workin' out—"

"Figure I might as well, you know? I mean, it's gonna be my last chance to do something like that and I can look for a job in the fall, same as now."

"Julie, here, says he's gonna join the Marines and kill people."

"I was just saying that's something I'd like to experience, that's all."

Carelli nodded. "Sure," he said. "What's Bobby gonna do?"

Bobby O'Berry, who hadn't spoken in some time, said, "I'm gonna steal your bike and drive it across country."

Carelli said, "What the heck? I won't have time to use it once I start going out with Katie McClennon."

"Katie 'Large Mounds of Joy' McClennon?" crooned Linehan.

"You're gonna have to get rid of Jeff Knight first," said Mullaney.

"Maybe you can get Julie to help you," Linehan said.

And Julie, who hadn't caught Linehan's remark, said, "Jees, I didn't know Katie McClennon was one of the options. I'd rather do her than join the service."

Carelli said, "I'm not going to have to worry about Jeff Knight. He's going to Notre Dame, isn't he? You know where that is?"

"Illinois," offered someone.

Someone else said Ohio.

"Well, it's not around here," said Carelli. "That's for sure. Katie's gonna be at Stonehill, he's gonna be at Notre Dame, and I'm gonna be at UMass. So who do you think's gonna get more chance to see her? I'll just be a couple of hours away, for Chrissake. He'll be in the middle of nowhere."

"Fuckin' Notre Dame," said Linehan morosely. Then he brightened. "So where you been all night, anyhow, Loogie?"

Carelli shrugged. "I just come from Brady's house. Him and Lynch are playing knuckles in Brady's kitchen."

"Last time I played knuckles with Brady I didn't have no skin on my hand for a week."

"They're doing it different this time. This time if you flinch you gotta take off your shirt and stand in front of the door while the other guy shoots you in the back with a BB gun."

"Bullshit."

"No, really. You flinch then, winner gets to shoot you again."

The Greek could hear the boys hooting and howling about how crazy Brady and Lynch were. He glanced at the clock over the door and saw that it was now midnight. "C'mon boys," he said. "Time to go."

They looked up in unison, as though they had been caught cheating on an examination. Then they went back to laughing. They laughed until Bobby O'Berry proposed that everybody go over to Brady's and then all the laughter stopped abruptly.

6

"Brady," said Linehan, "is nuts. I wouldn't go anywhere near that guy with any kind of gun in his hand."

Mullaney shook his head. "No way I'm goin' over there. Fuckin' Brady would miss you on purpose just so's he could shoot you in the head."

Linehan said, "Yeah. Then he'd laugh about it. Think it was funny."

Bobby O'Berry looked at Carelli and Carelli said, "Don't look at me. I been there. I wanted to get shot with a BB gun, you think I woulda come here?"

Bobby looked at Julie Sabatini.

"Ah, I gotta go home. The old man's making me and my brothers get up early and go down the Cape, fix up my grandmother's cottage." He looked apologetic. "The old man gets the place one crummy week a summer and we gotta spend half the spring workin' on the stupid thing."

At approximately the same time everyone reached for his check and stood up. Everyone except Bobby.

"You want a ride, Bobby?" Linehan asked.

"I'll go on Loogie's bike if he lets me."

Carelli hesitated. "I can't, Bobby. I only got one helmet and I can't risk gitting stopped again."

"That's all right. I'll stay here and talk to the Greek for a while."

"No problem to take you home," said Linehan. But Bobby said no, he wanted to talk.

Soon the only people left in the diner were Bobby, the Greek, Mrs. Gallagher and her companion. " 'Scoose me," called the Greek, and Bobby looked over his shoulder. Mrs. Gallagher, or whatever her name was now, was asleep. So was her friend.

Bobby got up and shook Mrs. Gallagher by the shoulder. She slid to the floor and that was when Bobby saw that her hand was caught in the man's zipper. It rested there as though it were in an overhead strap on a subway car. Bobby glanced up in embarrassment. The Greek shrugged.

"Hey," Bobby said, and the man jerked awake.

There was a moment of fright when he first looked at Bobby, and it made Bobby grin. The man tried to sit up straight, noticed Mrs. Gallagher's hand and pulled it out of his pants. He held it in the air as if it were a fish he had just caught, and then he threw it away. The motion made Mrs. Gallagher go face first onto the tile.

Pushing himself up onto the seat, the man stepped over her and got out to the aisle, next to Bobby. He was about five feet ten and a hundred and eighty pounds. He had black oily hair, he wore a short-sleeved shirt and khaki pants, and his zipper was down. He took one look at the woman lying on the floor and he headed for the door.

"What about her?" Bobby said, grabbing his arm.

"Fuck her," the man said.

"You got to take your trash with you," Bobby told him.

"Mind your own goddamn business," the man said, and tried to pull his arm away.

Bobby jerked him back. The man pushed him. Bobby punched him in the side of the head. It was that fast.

The Greek was there in an instant as Bobby, pumped up, stood over the fallen man, daring him to get back to his feet. The Greek steered him to a stool at the counter, talking every inch of the way. "Bobby, Bobby, a Chrissake, goddamn you."

Somehow the Greek had Mrs. Gallagher awake and on her feet. He had the battered man standing up next to her. He had the bill under the man's nose and was even managing to collect his money. And then the Greek was ushering them out the door, shutting it behind them; pulling the shade and turning the lock. "Yes, yes, thank you very much. That's right. Everything okay now. Yes, yes."

The Greek walked back and picked up the dishes and cups that had been left in Mrs. Gallagher's booth. He took them behind the counter, thrust them into a sink full of water and left them there. Only then did he walk to the end of the counter and look at Bobby.

"I got him pretty good, huh, Greek?"

"Yeah. You got good sucker punch, Bobby."

Bobby looked crestfallen. "Hey, he started the pushin'. He was lookin' at me. It wasn't no sucker punch."

"Boy, you good just like your father, you know that?"

"I'm nothing like my father."

"Sure. Toughest guy in Portshead, Massachusetts." The Greek's tone changed. "He still drive the fork truck, don't he? You keep on punchin' like I just seen, who knows, maybe you get to drive fork truck, too."

Bobby took the soda glass that Mullaney had left on the counter and began spinning it on its edge, letting it wobble from side to side. He was holding his hands out to catch it in case it fell over, but the Greek snatched it anyway.

"You know, I seen your father fight one time when he just about your age. He fight this truckdriver down the carnival. Truckdriver twice his size, twice as old, maybe; and every time he knock your father down, your father get up again. About ten times this happen. Then the truckdriver start to laugh. He hold out his hand to help your father up. He say, 'Kid, you're all right. Let me buy you a beer.' Your father, he smile. He take the man's hand, he get up. Then, still holding the man's hand, he hit him right in the face. He stick his leg behind the man and trip him. With the man on the ground, your father, he pick up a chair and hit him over the head. He pick up a cement block and try to hit him with that, too, but all the people jump in then and take it away from him before he kill the guy." The Greek paused. "Your father, he one tough bastard. But that don't mean nobody like him."

"He beat the guy, didn't he?"

The Greek nodded. "Yeah, he beat him. So now what?"

"So now maybe next time people won't try to push him around."

The Greek nodded again, his eyes fixed on Bobby's. "Nobody ever try to push your father around."

"Sometimes you just gotta stand up and be a man, Greek. Sometimes you gotta do things to show you're not just one of them puppets on a string." As if to demonstrate, Bobby got to his feet. He stood about six two, and his narrow waist and flat stomach gave his torso a classical V shape. It had been natural to begin with, but it had been honed by hundreds of hours of working out with weights. His black T-shirt with the Harley-Davidson insignia clung to his chest like an extra skin, but the short sleeves flared at the shoulders, where they had been stretched beyond the capacity of the material.

The Greek said, "Here you are. You eighteen years old. I fifty-six and you telling me what life is all about. It's like the paperboy say: I got news for you, kid."

Still, he looked at Bobby admiringly. "Jesus, Bobby, with your build you shoulda been on the football team, trying to get a scholarship to college, not trying to beat people up alla time."

The boy threw back his blond head and laughed sharply. "What? Be out there with all them glory boys? Who needs it?" He dug some crumpled and folded dollar bills out of the pocket of his dungarees and threw them up in the air as if they were confetti. They all landed on the counter, but not in any one place. "Besides," he said, "I'm not what you call college material. The old man told me so himself."

He laughed again and sauntered to the door, delighted with what he had seen in the Greek's eyes.

9

CHAPTER TWO

Leaving the Greek's, he crossed Webster and walked in front of the old Howard Johnson's, the one that had been driven out of business by the McDonald's on the other side of the Artery. The McDonald's was closed at this hour, as was almost everything Bobby passed: the Stop & Shop, the fried clam stand, the factory shoe outlet, the Leaning Tower of Pizza. There was a light on at the Leaning Tower, but it was an outside light and it was only to show passing motorists the mural that had been painted on the wall. The mural had been done by the daughter of the guy who owned the Leaning Tower. It depicted a group of happy Italians stomping on grapes at a hillside vineyard. Someone had come along after the artist was done and had drawn mustaches on the women, put hair under their arms, sketched in genitals on the men.

Just past the Leaning Tower was a Dunkin' Donuts that stayed open all night. There had once been a bronze plaque on the wall saying that it was the world's first Dunkin' Donuts, but Brady had stolen it and the shop had never put up another one.

Bobby stopped and looked through the plate-glass window. There were two cops inside, their backs to him, drinking coffee out of white ceramic mugs. The only other person Bobby could see was the waitress, and she was an old lady, somebody Bobby didn't recognize. Bobby craned his neck to look past her, trying to see if Beaver Brown's older brother was in the back of the shop making donuts, but just then one of the cops turned around and stared at him. It was enough to make Bobby walk on. He never had anything to say to Beaver Brown's older brother anyhow.

He cut through the Shell gas station and crossed over Warring Road, where Gene Petrini had been killed the summer before when he lost control of his cherry Mustang. Mullaney had been in that car. He had gone through the windshield and walked away with nothing but stitches, but Gino had eaten the steering wheel. For no reason he could ever explain, Mullaney had told the police the car was going thirty-five when it went off the roadway. Accident reconstruction had determined the car was going seventy, perhaps even eighty, and the discrepancy had given Gino's mother the idea that the accident had somehow been Mullaney's fault. At the funeral she had taken the dirt she was supposed to throw on her son's coffin and had thrown it at Mullaney instead.

Warring Road intersected the Artery at a twenty-degree angle. On the other side of it was the parking lot to the Bowl-A-Rama. The lot was empty except for three cars clustered near the darkened entrance. People were standing around the cars, smoking and laughing, but they cut off all talk when they saw Bobby. He saw them, too, saw their shapes and the orange glow of their cigarettes; but he couldn't tell who they were. So he kept walking, not fast, but as though he had somewhere to go.

A horn beeped. He slowed down, turned his head. A hand was sticking out the window of an unfamiliar car and waving frantically at him.

"Hey, Bobby," a voice called. "Bob-bee."

It was Butchie Keane and Bobby quickly veered his course to go over to see him. Turning his head, looking off toward the emptiness of Warring Road, he strolled across the parking lot as though his feet were pulling him along and he didn't much care whether he went with them or not.

"Yo, Bobby," one of the people standing in the dark said, and Bobby gave a half wave because he wasn't sure who it was. "How's it goin'?" he said.

Butchie Keane was with a girl, although Bobby didn't see that until he was nearly to the car. She was slouched against Butchie's side, her head tucked against his chest. Butchie's right arm was draped over her shoulder and hanging down so that his fingers could play in the space where her blouse had pulled out of her skirt. His left arm was resting on the sill of the open driver's window and in his left hand he held a quart bottle of Schaefer beer.

Bobby leaned in the passenger's window and looked around. It was a red Dodge Coronet with bench seats and a column shift. The only interior light came from the radio, and that didn't show much. "Whose wheels?"

11

Butchie cocked his head at the girl and handed the Schaefer across her body to Bobby. "Barbra's."

Bobby stood upright long enough to bubble the beer, then he ducked his head inside the car again and handed the bottle back. The girl had not moved. She was staring at Bobby through partially closed lids. Bobby was surprised to see that he knew who she was.

"You know Bobby O'Berry?" Butchie said, gesturing at his friend. She didn't answer.

"Bobby, this is Barbara Cochrane."

"How's it goin'?"

"Okay," she said. She sat up. "I seen you in detention."

"Yeah?" The two boys exchanged smiles. "When was that?"

"Plenty of times," she said. She took the bottle from Butchie's hand and drank from it without taking her eyes off Bobby. She had big eyes and a pouting mouth that turned south at the corners.

Bobby looked her up and down. It was hard to tell with her sitting in the dark, but he knew she was overweight. Large-breasted, heavy in the hips and the legs. "Yeah," he said, "well, I seen you plenty of times, too. Hey, Butchie, come on out here and let me talk to you for a minute, wouldja?"

Butchie got out, taking the bottle with him. Together, he and Bobby walked into the nearby shadows of the bowling alley. They looked back at the car. Barbara appeared to be brushing her hair.

"Hey, Keane," Bobby whispered, "what the fuck are you doin' with that pig?"

Butchie looked surprised. "Don't you know who she is? Barbara Cochrane, man." He tucked the bottle between his arm and his chest, raised his left hand with his fingers curled in a tube, and began sliding his right index finger in and out of the tube as he grinned from ear to ear.

Bobby slapped him on the shoulder to make him stop. "What about her brothers, Butch? You gonna screw around with them, too?"

"What? You think her brothers don't want her to go out, have a good time? They bought her the car, didn't they? That wasn't so she could go into the Common, ride the swan boats. Besides" —he huffed his shoulders—"it's Friday night. They gotta be out breakin' legs."

"Maybe they get a day off tomorrow. Maybe they'll come see you just to stay in practice."

"What do you think I'm gonna do, rape her? I'm tellin' you, this

---

12

broad loves it." Butchie grinned again. "Anyhow, them brothers of hers aren't gonna know where I live. I got her to pick me up and let me off right here."

"That's good thinking, Butch. You don't suppose they could look you up in the phone book or anything?"

Butchie hesitated. "Look, there are plenty of Keanes in this city. My father's got five brothers. She don't know which one is him. She don't even know my real first name." He glanced back at the car just in time to catch Barbara with her nose in her armpit. "Look at that. She's getting ready for me."

Bobby looked as Barbara, perhaps knowing she had been caught, pretended she was scratching the back of her head. "Jesus," he said. "You get anything yet?"

"Not yet. But she's already kind of brushed up against it a couple of times."

"It?"

"*It*-it. The magic wand. The happy twanger. My mighty oak. As soon as we finish this beer here I'm gonna take her up Watch Hill, see if she wants to brush up against it some more." He tried to keep Bobby from taking the bottle. "Hey, leave me some, man. I gotta make sure she gets drunk."

"You gotta make sure you get drunk, by the looks of her."

"I guess. I get Timmy Callahan to buy for me and I goes to him, 'Timmy, make sure you get the beer in two bags.' He goes, 'How come?' I go, 'In case hers falls off.' "

Butchie waited for Bobby to laugh, but Bobby only screwed up his brow. "I don't get it," he said.

Butchie, his mouth twitching, said, "You know, she's so ugly I gotta make her wear one bag and I gotta— Ah, fuck you, Bobby, you get it."

The two of them roared with laughter until Barbara leaned across the seat of her car and yelled, "Hey, we goin' someplace or what?"

The parking lot of the Bowl-A-Rama bled into the parking lot of Mr. Joe's, a restaurant known primarily for the fact that its waiters wore white gloves. Bobby had never eaten there, but he thought it might be a good place to take a date. He made a mental note to take somebody to Mr. Joe's someday. He'd do it when he got a car.

There was a car parked behind the restaurant now. It was a red Cadillac with huge whitewalls and Bobby suspected it belonged to Mr. Joe himself. That would be the thing to have, Bobby thought. You could get all kinds of broads with a car like that.

The parking lot of Mr. Joe's was separated from the vast lot of the A&P by a three-foot-high tin barrier. The lot of the A&P was so huge that even in its best days, before the Stop & Shop had come to the Artery, it had been too big for the store. The CYO used it for car washes. A children's circus was held there once a year. On spring Sundays tables were set up and it was used for rummage sales.

In the middle of the lot was an A&P sign that stood thirty feet in the air, supported by twin pillars. Bobby was passing underneath it when something splattered on the pavement next to his feet. Tilting his head back so that he could peer into the darkness, he saw two figures looking down at him.

"Hey, assholes," he said.

"Eat shit, asshole," one of the figures yelled back at him.

The second figure quickly told the first to shut up. Then there was silence for a time before the second figure said, "That you, Bobby?"

"Who's that? DiLorenzo?"

"Yeah. Me and Toolie."

"Who just tried to spit on me?"

There was silence again for several seconds before DiLorenzo said, "I think that was an accident." And Toolie said, "Yeah, that was a mistake, Bobby."

"I oughtta come up there and kick your ass."

Bobby could see the two figures exchange looks. He could see them glance around as though they actually thought there might be an escape route down.

"Hey, Bobby," DiLorenzo said, "Toolie told you it was a mistake. He's been drinking, you know? I mean, what do you think we're doin' up here, anyhow?"

"You guys both been drinking?"

"Yeah." DiLorenzo's voice was hesitant, as though he were willing to make the admission and just as willing to retract it.

"Okay," Bobby said. "You tell Toolie I'll spit on him sometime." He started to walk away and then he stopped. "You guys shouldn't go screwing around too much up there. You fall, you're gonna get yourselves killed."

There was a short laugh from DiLorenzo. "We'll be all right. I'm hanging on and Toolie's promised that if he falls he'll land on his head."

"See you guys."

"See ya, Bobby," DiLorenzo said, and Toolie, sounding as though he had just won a door prize, shouted out the same thing.

There were no more parking lots after the A&P. Bobby cut over to the sidewalk and followed the Artery up past the cobbler's and the television repair shop and the auto parts store where Butchie Keane and Brady had been caught breaking in last winter. All they had wanted was an alternator for an old junkbox of a car that someone had given Brady, and that was all they had taken. But the one they took was the wrong size and they had gotten caught breaking in a second time, trying to exchange the one they had for the one they wanted.

Beyond the auto parts store was the Villa Roma bar, and then a dry cleaner run by a family of Iranians who always kept a pair of crossed American flags in the window, and then the florist. After the florist the houses started. The small yellow clapboard where Mongoloid Eddie lived with his parents. The series of identical five-room brick units with the starved hedges and the bare spots in the middle of their uniformly sized lawns. Then there was the green-shuttered, three-bedroom Powers house, with its swing set and bicycles and wagons and other signs of eight adolescent children. The only light in the Powers house came from a color TV in the living room, and the set was turned up loud enough so that Bobby could hear every word of dialogue as he passed.

Bobby turned on Church Street. There were no lights in any of the houses here. Maybe, if he didn't look up, there wouldn't be any lights in any houses on Water Street, either. He rounded the corner from Church to Water with his head down. He could keep lights from being on just by not looking. He could follow the cracks in the sidewalk all the way to the driveway, follow the driveway to the porch steps, mount the steps, open the door . . . all without looking. And Friday night would be over without the lights being on.

A hundred yards. A hydrant. A light pole. A driveway. A second driveway. A set of hedges. An oak tree. A third driveway. Fifty yards. The sidewalk buckled where it had been pushed up by the roots of a tree. You had to raise your eyes a little bit or you would lose perspec-

15

tive. He couldn't stop himself. He looked. The lights were on. The whole goddamn downstairs was lit.

Bobby came to a standstill at the end of his driveway. The Impala was there, parked as it always was on Friday night, blocking the steps. He stood behind it and waited, listening. It took more than a minute, but the sound came. A crash: the sound a tray makes when it is kicked over.

Bobby walked to the driver's side of the car and stared in. His mother's sunken eyes looked back at him. Next to her was his sister Rita, who glanced at him dully, as though he were a pedestrian on a street corner. Roxanne, the little one, was asleep in the back seat. She was in her pajamas and she had with her a stuffed animal that was nearly as big as she was. All four doors were locked, as he knew they would be.

Slowly, his mother rolled down the window. "I wounnent go in there now, Bobby. He's not ready yet."

"Ready" was a euphemism Patricia O'Berry often used. They all knew what it meant.

Bobby looked off toward the house. "He bad tonight, Ma?"

"Oh, just the use-yal. Your father had a tough week, this week." It was hard for Bobby to understand her, the way she was covering her mouth.

"Jesus—the usual, Ma. The usual means you gotta lock yourself in the car every time he gets his paycheck. . . . You think anybody else considers that usual, Ma?"

His mother shook her head. Her unkempt hair got tangled and retangled and she tried to smooth it out with the fingers of one hand. But the other hand she kept over her mouth. "He's not aw-ways like this, Bobby. You know that."

Something else fell inside the house and they both glanced up quickly, even though they could see nothing. When Bobby's eyes returned to the car they came in contact with Rita's.

"He hit Ma in the mouth," she said.

"Hush, Rita," Patricia O'Berry said, and she slapped at her daughter with the hand she had been using to hide her face.

It was not a slap that was meant to hurt, but Rita did not even attempt to get away from it. "He got mad because the stew was taking so long to cook," she told her brother. "Ma told him that's how long stew takes and he belted her."

Bobby thrust his hand through the window and pulled his mother's

16

chin toward him. Her upper lip was swollen and skinned as red as a piece of beef. "Aaagh," he said, and jerked back.

Rita, her voice almost monotone, said, "She told him she was only making it because it was his favorite and he said it tasted like shit, like all her food does. He knocked the whole pot on the floor and told Ma to lap it up. He pushed her down on the floor and told her to lap it up like a dog or he was gonna beat her head in."

"Bobby!" his mother screamed, but it was too late. He was already running for the house.

He was glad that he was not thinking; that he was reacting on instinct, anger and hatred. It got him through the door and into the house and if he had immediately seen his father it would have gotten him to the point of attack. But by the time he found him he was thinking again. That, Bobby would reflect later, was his mistake.

Jack O'Berry was standing in the middle of the kitchen, the familiar gold can of Miller in his hand. He was wearing a white sleeveless undershirt stretched over his gut, but still tucked into his gray work pants. He was shoeless, and his white socks were stained with everything that was on the floor: brown liquid and brown chunks of meat, gray onions and orange carrots. Near him, on the kitchen table, was an empty cardboard container that had once held a six-pack of beer. Another empty six-pack was on the floor next to the paper bag that his mother used to collect trash. Here and there were empty cans of beer, all of them bent in the middle where they had been hand-crushed. On top of the washing machine, which stood against the back wall of the kitchen, was the half box that his father had used to carry in the case of beer he had been drinking.

"Hey, look who's here," Jack O'Berry said. "My son the tough guy."

"You hit Ma."

The older man tilted forward at the waist, squinting his eyes. "What are you sniveling about, tough guy?"

"You hit Ma," Bobby shouted. "And I'm not sniveling."

Jack O'Berry stepped closer, his body still tilted, moving his feet in a crablike walk. "You are too sniveling, you little fairy. What are you crying about?" He reached his son and put a hand on Bobby's chest. Just the tips of his fingers rested there for a second, and then he shoved.

Bobby stumbled backward, thrusting his hand behind him to try to catch the wall before he banged into it. "You're not supposed to hit

17

her." He couldn't control his voice; he couldn't keep it from getting high. "You're not supposed to hit girls." It sounded funny to him, parroting something he had heard all his life, trying to make it apply to his mother. As his father looked mockingly at him, he shouted out one more word. "Ladies."

But it made no difference. Jack O'Berry advanced again. "Who's gonna make me stop?" he said, sneering. "You, you little fairy? Big-shot weight lifter. You gonna tell me what to do in my own house?"

Bobby was backed up as far as he could go. He was against the wall, his arms spread. If he had been only sniveling before, he was crying in earnest now. There was no hiding the tears that were rolling down his face. They made him ashamed. And that made him angry. "Don't ever hit my mother again."

There was a sparkle in Jack O'Berry's eye as he said, "Since when are you giving orders around here?" He had been pushing with only one hand because he still held the Miller in the other, but now he raised the can of beer and splashed it in his son's face. Not much came out, but it was enough.

Bobby's hands shot out, both of them, palms forward. They hit his father high on the chest and Jack O'Berry went over backward, landing in the midst of the beef stew. Without making any effort to stand, he spun around and threw himself at his son's knees.

Bobby felt something sharp rip into the heavy cloth of his pants, and then the sharpness spread, becoming a wedge of pain, and Bobby realized his father was biting him. Grabbing for anything he could, he got hold of his father's ear and pulled until his father's jaws were forced open. The moment he was able to wrench his leg away, Bobby ran.

He stopped when he reached the living room only because he could think of no other place to go. For an instant he prayed that his father would not follow. He even opened his mouth to yell that he was sorry, to beg for forgiveness . . . but then his father was lurching through the doorway, his clothes spattered with food, his face twisted demonically; and slowly Bobby put up his hands in a fighter's posture.

His father came on, taunting him. "Little baby starts to cry, huh?" Almost casually he slipped an open hand inside Bobby's guard and cuffed him in the face. "Big weight lifter, huh? Tough guy, impresses all the girls with his muscles."

"Stop it, Dad." The tears flowed faster as Bobby backed up.

"Can't even take a forty-year-old man. All these big fights I been hearing about. You must be beating up a bunch of girls."

18

"You should talk, you bastard," Bobby screamed. "Gettin' your kicks beating up Ma all the time. You fairy. You fucking queer."

Bobby swung. He tried to catch his father on the point of his chin, but he hit him further up, on the mouth. Jack O'Berry's head snapped to the right as though he had been jerked by a chain. His whole body pitched to the side, and then, almost in slow motion, he straightened up again.

Bobby saw the punch coming and he dodged it easily. As his father's arm went shooting past his ear, Bobby pivoted just enough to grab his father in a headlock. He began uppercutting him, making contact any-place he could. There was a sudden joy at the realization that he was beating this man, this opponent. The knowledge that he could beat him at will was something he was as certain about as his ability to walk or talk, think or hear. Then, perversely, the joy disappeared as quickly as it had come, replaced with a feeling of almost crushing disappointment.

Bobby's punching hand faltered and when it did his father surged, twisting and bucking and wrenching himself around until Bobby could only hold the headlock by using two arms, gripping his wrist with his opposite hand and squeezing for all he was worth. It was some moments before Bobby realized his father was not the only one he was fighting. It wasn't his father who was clinging to his back, pulling at his hair, trying to tear his arms away.

"Let go of him, Bobby. You let go of him. Leave him a-"—and, ex-hausted with effort, his mother screamed the last syllable into his ear— "-lone."

Bobby whirled, wrenching his father around with him. His mother was hovering there, her face a mask of horror. Behind her was Rita, awestruck, as though she were seeing a magic show. Bobby cinched his grip tighter while his father's fingers clawed at him.

"It's all right, Ma," he yelled. "I got him now." Seeing his mother, her lip swollen, her eyes buried like two seeds in a mass of wrinkles, sent a new charge of adrenaline through him. "I'm gonna kill the bas-tard," he screamed, and lurched for the nearest wall. He was, he knew, going to bang his father's head into that wall until he was unconscious.

His mother knew it, too, and she was there first. "No, Bobby, no." She raised both her fists in the air and brought them straight down. They hit on Bobby's forehead, stunning him far more than anything his father had done. She hit him again, this time on his shoulders, and Bobby slowly released his grip on his father. Jack O'Berry sank to his knees, gagging and clutching at his neck.

19

Patricia O'Berry stopped hitting her son. She looked at him as if he were an intruder, a captured trespasser, and then she knelt down and took her husband's head in her hands and tried to hold it upright.

"Ma . . ."

"Get out," she said, not looking at him.

"Ma . . ."

Growling like an animal, Jack O'Berry started to move off his knees. "Kill me, will you? I'll bust your goddamn head open—"

But his wife was all over him. "No, Jack, no. Just let him go. It'll be all right. He dinn't mean it. He's just a boy. He dinn't know what he was doing."

Bobby waited only long enough to make sure of what he was seeing. He looked to the hallway that led to the front door. Rita was all that stood between him and the relative sanity of the night. His eyes met his sister's, and she stepped out of the way.

He ran through the door and down the steps. As he passed the car, just because he felt like it, he beat on the back window and yelled for Roxanne to wake up.

CHAPTER THREE

He ran down Water Street to Washington and turned right. If he followed Washington all the way up, he would come to the Center. He could get on the T there and ride it into Boston. The T still operated at this time of night. It went all day, twenty-four hours a day. His hand went to his pocket and felt nothing. He couldn't ride the T; he had no money.

If only he hadn't thrown those bills at the Greek. It hadn't been much more than he owed, but it had been enough. Anything was better than nothing.

He was growing cold. He didn't remember being cold before, but he was now. Where did she expect him to go in the middle of the night with no money and no clothes? The bitch, the goddamn old bitch, what did she want from him? He had only tried to help her. And he had nailed him. He had kicked his ass. His fucking ass.

Tears of injustice were in Bobby's eyes as he passed the doctor's house and the beauty parlor, crossed Thomas Street and Thomas Circle. He kept his head down and wiped at his eyes whenever no cars were going by. As always, it made him feel mad to cry, and he wanted to strike out at something. In front of the milk store at the corner of Barker Road he kicked over the trash. He tried to push over the mailbox, but it was bolted to the cement; so he kicked in the *Christian Science Monitor* display rack instead. A porch light came on in one of the houses across the street and Bobby ran. Running made him feel better and he ran until he was exhausted. He ran until he reached Warring Road.

If he turned right on Warring he could follow it through the marshes until it came out at the Bowl-A-Rama. Butchie was supposed to get let off there and Butchie might have some money he could borrow. If he had twelve bucks Bobby would have enough for the Old Boston Motel. Butchie would have something. He was sure of it.

From Washington to the Bowl-A-Rama was about a mile and a half. The buildings ended a hundred and fifty yards from where Bobby turned the corner. Then the wetlands began and the only other structure along the road was a radio tower. Still, there were streetlights every hundred yards, a legacy of Gino's cherry Mustang.

There were crickets in the marshes and their relentless callings made Bobby feel very much alone. A car came up behind him and he stuck out his thumb, but the driver only hit his high beams and increased his speed. As the car roared around the next bend, Bobby could see the backs of a male driver and a female sitting as close to him as she could get. He was thinking how very much he would like to be that driver, whoever he was, whatever he looked like, when another car came from the opposite direction. It was a red Coronet and the moment he saw it Bobby began waving.

He ran into the middle of the road, swirling his arms over his head until the Coronet slid hard into a skid that ended within five feet of where he was standing. Then Bobby stopped waving because Butchie was not driving. He was not even in the car.

Barbara Cochrane rolled down her window and put a lit cigarette in her mouth to talk. "What's goin' on?" she said.

Bobby walked over to her window and looked into the back seat, half hoping Butchie was lying there playing some sort of joke on him. "I thought Butch might be with you."

"That creep," Barbara said. "I threw him out. What are you doing out here, anyway?"

"You take me back to where Butch is?"

"I told you, I threw him out. That's the one place I'm not going back, is to look for him."

"How about taking me to the T, then?"

Barbara took her cigarette out of her mouth for the first time and squinted at him. "You in some kind of trouble, Bobby?"

Bobby hardened his eyes. "Me? Why should I be in trouble? I'm never in trouble."

"Your folks kick you out or something?"

Bobby shrugged and looked off in the direction from which she had come.

22

"Okay," she sighed. "C'mon in. I might even know a place you can go, if you need one."

He got in the car because nobody else came down the road to give him a better offer. The first thing she did was hold out her cigarette pack, and after he shook his head the next thing she did was turn up the radio. "This place I'm thinking of," she said, finally putting the car in gear, "is kind of a secret place."

"Right at this moment I'm not too choosy."

"It's not exactly inside, but it's not outside, either. Thing is, though, I don't think anybody else knows about it."

"Sounds better and better all the time."

"What I'm telling you is that it's sort of my secret place."

"My lips are sealed."

Barbara looked over at him. She looked long enough that she made Bobby nervous. "Hey," he said, putting his hand lightly on the wheel, "you mind watching where you're going? A friend of mine once got killed here."

"I knew Gino," she said, and she looked back at the road.

The place to which Barbara Cochrane took Bobby O'Berry was a three-story green wood-frame home. The backyard dropped down Loomis Hill and the only visible evidence of a neighbor was a roof on a house on the street below. The front yard held a For Sale sign.

Barbara cut her lights to go up the driveway, which twisted around behind the house and ended at the doors to an attached two-car garage. She stopped once the car was in front of the garage and she pointed.

"You can't get in the house because it's all locked up, but underneath that porch there there's like a room where the people who lived here used to keep their lawn mower and stuff. It's a dirt floor, but it'll be good as long as it doesn't get too cold at night."

In the darkness, Bobby could only make out the shape of what she was talking about. Because of the way the house was built into the hillside, the floor of the screen porch at the rear of the house was about five feet off the ground and was supported by cement posts. In between the posts was latticework that could effectively keep anyone but the most determined from seeing in.

23

Barbara mistook Bobby's silence. "It's perfectly safe," she said. "I've been here a few times on my own. When I wanted to be all by myself."

"Hey, I don't care whether it's safe or not."

"The only thing you gotta worry about is if the real estate guy comes around to show it to somebody. That only happens during the day, though. So all you gotta do is not leave your stuff out."

"I don't got any stuff."

"I got a beach blanket in the trunk. You can use that, if you want. Oh, and here." She turned on the overhead light and began searching around in her pocketbook.

The pocketbook was huge. To Bobby's eyes it looked like a small duffel bag with a shoulder strap attached to it. On the very top he saw something tan and netlike, and when Barbara's hand moved it he realized it was a pair of panty hose. He looked at her legs and saw they were bare.

"I know it's in here somewhere. Ah, there it is." She came up with a tube of Crest and a toothbrush, held together with a rubber band.

"Jesus," Bobby said, accepting the gift. "What are you doing with all that stuff in there?"

"Oh," Barbara said in a way that Bobby thought was surprisingly cool, "you never know when it might come in handy." She reached across him and got a flashlight from the glove compartment. "C'mon."

Barbara led him to a gate in the latticework, pulled it open and shined the light inside. "What do you think?"

The dirt was hard-packed. There were a few rakes, a few garden utensils, a plastic trash barrel, and a row of partially filled cans of paint. "I hope there are no rats," Bobby said.

He was expecting her to reassure him, but she only said, "I hadn't thought of that."

Bobby asked her how she knew about the place and Barbara waved her hand vaguely and said something about a friend of hers showing it to her at one time. "But," she said, "he's not around anymore, so you don't have to worry about him."

She had the light shining at their feet, close enough that Bobby could see her thick and rounded shins. He looked away and said only, "Well, I guess this'll do." He tried not to sound hopeless.

"If you really don't like it, we got a toolshed out the back of our house. You'd be okay there as long as you don't wake up my brothers."

The thought of Terry and Billy Cochrane finding him in the family toolshed had even less appeal than the possibility of rats. Bobby said no thanks. He said the place was looking better and better by the minute.

Bobby hung out at the usual spots on Saturday. Nobody came looking for him and he didn't talk with anyone about not being at home. At noon he let Mullaney buy him a Quarter Pounder after reminding the redhead that he had bought him something the week before. Still, not having any money made Bobby feel constantly hungry. That night he went over to Paul Lynch's and ate snacks while the others played cards. He kept saying he didn't want to play, but he watched the others until after midnight. Then he left by himself and hitchhiked back up Loomis Hill.

When he got to the house there was a Styrofoam cooler waiting for him. Taped to the cooler was a note that read, "Hope the rats don't get this first!" Inside were two sandwiches, a box of cereal, a bowl, a spoon, a quart of milk, an orange and two cans of beer.

On Sunday he was awake by six o'clock. By seven-thirty he was bored and by eight he was thumbing to the beach at Nantasket. It took him some time to get the right combination of rides, but he was on the beach by midmorning, dressed in dungarees and his black T-shirt, the same clothes he had been wearing since Friday night. He knew the area where the guys would gather if they came down and he waited there, sprawled against the seawall, trying to capture as much shade as he could.

At eleven, Linehan and Mullaney showed up. They had a football and Bobby threw it around with them, lunging into the surf for low passes until his jeans were stiff and wet and loaded with sand. He told everyone he had left his bathing suit in the car of someone who had given him a lift.

By noon Carelli was there and so were Julie Sabatini and his brother Dom. The Sabatinis had a ghetto blaster and they turned it up loud enough to discourage most everyone who came to the beach from putting down a blanket within thirty feet. Brady and Lynch arrived eventually, and with them was Butchie Keane, who told everyone he had gotten laid Friday night and then took immense amounts of abuse when Brady announced that it was Babs Cochrane who had done the dirty deed. While all this was going on, Bobby made no mention to anyone of his contact with Barbara.

Tony DiLorenzo came walking along the beach with a skinny girl

25

named Mary, who wore a white two-piece and had a hairline that ran down from her navel. DiLorenzo stopped when he saw the gathering and began telling jokes. Most of them were addressed to Bobby. "Hey, Bobby, you hear the one about the Polish gangster, got told to blow up this guy's car? . . . Burned his lips on the exhaust pipe."

Linehan said he had heard that one, but it was about an Italian gangster. Brady said that wouldn't be funny, because all gangsters are Italian.

DiLorenzo said, "Hey, Bobby, there were these two girls, see, and one of them says, 'Oh, no, my boyfriend's coming to see me this weekend.' The other one says, 'So what's wrong with that?' And the first one goes, 'He'll probably bring me flowers and then expect me to spend the whole time lying on my back with my clothes off and my legs in the air.' And the other one goes, 'Whatsamatter? Don't you have a vase?' "

The girl, Mary, said, "Oh, Tony, you're disgusting," and slapped him on the arm. She turned and walked away and that made everyone laugh harder as Tony chased after her.

At three in the afternoon Bobby was bored and wishing he had somewhere else to go. He was gazing along the sands with that thought in mind when he spotted his sister in red shorts and a halter top. She saw him, too, and she came directly to him.

"I took the bus," she said. "I been walking up and down looking for you all afternoon."

She and Bobby walked to the end of the beach and sat down on the rocks at the water's edge. "Daddy feels real bad about what happened," she told him.

Bobby snatched a handful of stones and casually heaved them into the ocean one at a time. "He always feels bad the day after because he's got a hangover."

"Yeah, but it's like he doesn't even remember what started it. He just knows you and him were punching each other."

"He never punched me. Not one that landed."

Rita did not look impressed. She picked up a stone of her own and rather absently flipped it into the water. "It's Ma you gotta think about anyway, Bobby. She's been worried sick and I don't think she's been to sleep since you left."

"It's Ma I was thinking about when I went after the old man. Then she turns around and kicks me out. Tells me not to come back."

"Oh, Bobby. She never told you not to come back and you know it. She just wanted you out so that you and Daddy wouldn't kill each other. You know how Daddy gets. What was she supposed to do?"

"She could have kicked him out."

"Yeah, sure. Then he'd come back and really kill her."

"He won't if I beat the shit out of him."

"Oh, Bobby, big deal. Then what's Ma supposed to do? How are we supposed to live? How's she gonna get any money? Ma's never even had a job and all she knows how to do is raise a family."

"She could get work. She could go to Woolworth's or someplace like that. They're always looking for help. They'd hire Ma."

"Sometimes you're so dumb, Bobby, you really make me mad. You think you can solve all Ma's problems for her in one night and then in a couple of weeks you graduate from high school and take off. That's all so easy for you, but what's she gonna do with me and Roxie? In case you don't know it, you don't just run a house and everything for three people on what she could make in a five-and-ten."

"She could get the old man to pay her support. They got ways of making him do that."

"Who's they, Bobby? Lawyers? How you think she's gonna pay for a lawyer?"

Bobby threw every throwable stone within his reach before he spoke again. "She never should have married him in the first place," he said.

Rita was two years younger than her brother. They were close enough in age that they didn't know how to look at each other and almost never made eye contact when they spoke. If someone had had the courage to ask Bobby how his sister was built, he would not have been able to answer in any meaningful way. If asked what color her eyes were, he would have been able to guess but he would not have been positive. Now, when she stood up and moved in front of him so that he had to look at her, he found himself surprised her complexion wasn't better.

"So maybe you're right," she said. "So maybe if she had it to do all over again she wouldn't. But she's been with him nineteen years and she's gotten old and she doesn't know what else to do. No matter how bad it is, being married's all she's got. It doesn't do her any good for you to come along and make it worse."

"I was trying to make it better—"

"What, you think you fight with a guy like Daddy, he's going to change overnight?" Rita took both his hands in hers. "You want to make her life better, you try to make it as easy as possible. Not hard, like you're doing."

Bobby pulled his hands away and looked to see if anyone had seen them touching.

27

Rita straightened up. "You gotta come home, Bobby. If not for Ma's sake, do it for yourself. You only got a little bit of school left and if you don't go you're not going to graduate."

"They're not going to hold me back. They know I wouldn't show up again next year."

Rita pushed her fingers into the top of her shorts and thought about that. "What would you do instead?"

"Alls I know is I'm outta here. As soon as I can save enough money to get me a motorcycle, I'm gone."

"Where?" There was no enthusiasm in his sister's words.

"Everywhere, Rita. I'm gonna work my way across country and if I see someplace I like I'll just stop there. If it's a good place, maybe I'll even settle down. Then I could send for you and Ma and Roxie." He cocked his head and studied her reaction. "If I did that, found some good place, I mean, would you come?"

"Cripes, Bobby, you don't even know what place you're talking about."

"Maybe it'll be in Kansas. I bet you'd really like Kansas, I've always had this thing for Kansas ever since I saw it in *Superboy* comics. Smallville, that would be nice, someplace like that."

"You think there's a real place Smallville, Bobby?"

"No," he said. "But I think it's based on a real place. I think there gotta be places like that out there. Or Colorado—how about Colorado? The mountains and all. Wouldn't that be great?"

Rita suddenly turned her back to her brother and looked along the entire length of the beach. It was a hot day for June and a lot of people had come out to the ocean. Between the crashing of the waves and the shrieks of children, the air seemed filled with violent sounds. "Yeah . . . well, I'll go right home and pack my stuff, Bobby," she said, but because her back was turned, most of her words were blown away. All Bobby could tell was that it sounded as if she was about to cry.

Barbara came again on Sunday night. Her mother had made a ham for dinner and one of her brothers hadn't been home to eat it, so there was an extra twenty-five pounds or so of meat. She brought something else with her, too. She brought a hammock.

Without too much difficulty they were able to string it under the porch, and when Bobby lay in it his butt cleared the dirt by several inches.

"Maybe I could get a radio," Barbara said. "Would you like that, a radio?"

And Bobby said yeah. He thought a radio would be real good.

He met Rita in the alley behind the central library on Monday morning. She had a grocery bag that she had filled with two short-sleeved shirts, a long-sleeved shirt, a pair of black cotton pants, some socks and underwear, and some toiletries. When he admitted he was broke, she gave him her lunch money. He told her she could sell all of his tapes if any of her girlfriends were interested. She said she would ask around.

Bobby changed in the alley while Rita stood guard for him. Then he took the bag of clothes to school and hid it in his locker.

He saw Barbara only once during the day. Going from metal shop to English, he passed her in the hallway. She was walking with a girl named Gloria, who was long-legged and short-chinned and had supposedly once given a hand job to some guy Carelli knew. Barbara was carrying her books in both arms, cradled to her chest, and her face lit up when she saw Bobby. But Bobby was walking with Brady and Brady was making pig noises which could have been directed at either Gloria or Barbara, so Bobby only jerked his head up and down as a means of saying hello.

He was sorry about that later. He had not gone to Linehan's house after school to work out as he usually did on Monday afternoons, because he was afraid his mother might call there looking for him. He started to hang around with Paul Lynch, but when Lynch wanted to go to the Bowl-A-Rama to shoot some pool, Bobby thought of the fifty cents he had remaining in his pocket and begged off. Then, having nothing else to do, he hiked up to the house on Loomis Hill and spent the last part of the afternoon eating the ham that had been sitting in the Styrofoam cooler all day.

He was bored again by six, and began hoping that Barbara would return. He told himself it was because he wanted the radio and because she might bring some new food.

She wasn't there by eight and Bobby was sure it was because he had snubbed her. He wished now that he had reacted differently when he saw her. What would have been the harm of saying "Hi, Barbara"? What did he care what Brady thought? Brady was nuts anyway.

Without Barbara, there wasn't a thing for him to do but lie in the

29

hammock and think. He tried to imagine all the places he was going to go to when he got his motorcycle. He had a picture in his mind of waking up on a cold morning with fog coming off a nearby lake. He saw himself making coffee over a breakfast fire and then climbing onto the seat for a day's ride. He thought of all the things he would see: bright red Georgia clay, Kentucky bluegrass, the mighty Mississip. He thought of the things he'd like to see. The Indianapolis 500 had just been run, and he had the idea that the motor speedway was one place he shouldn't miss. In Texas there would be cowboys. In Arizona, Indians. He had imagined himself as far as Las Vegas, when he heard a car start up the driveway.

It was dark now and Bobby was unable to see. He lay as still as he could and waited, knowing that if it was anyone other than Barbara he was going to be caught. Headlights appeared and Bobby was sure it couldn't be her. The car stopped, the lights went out, and footsteps sounded on the gravel. They came closer, then stopped altogether. A flashlight was turned on and it shined directly through the latticework.

"Bobby?"

"Yuh," he said, masking his relief at the sound of Barbara's voice.

She opened the gate and came in, bent over. "Jees, Bobby, you're sitting here in the dark."

"It's all right," he told her. "I was just thinking of going out."

"Oh," she said. He couldn't see her face, but she sounded disappointed.

A moment passed. "You want to sit down?" Bobby said.

She moved the beam of the flashlight, sweeping it around the floor. "I got white pants on," she said.

From what Bobby could see of her, she appeared to have on bib-type overalls. "You could probably sit on this with me," he said, surprising himself with the offer.

Barbara turned the light to the hammock. She went over to it slowly and sat down gingerly, but as soon as her weight was off her feet the hammock dropped and they both scraped bottom. Giggling with embarrassment, she made a move to get up.

"No, don't," Bobby said. "I mean, what difference does it make?"

She giggled again and shut off the light. "I got you some more stuff," she said. "The radio, and a towel. Some canned peaches. I figured they wouldn't spoil."

Bobby had to put his arm somewhere. It was too awkward sitting with both hands in his lap. And she was sitting forward. She didn't care

30

if his arm was behind her. "Hey," he said as he stretched and yawned, "why are you doing all this for me?"

"I don't know," she said. "I guess I like to help people out." She took no note of his arm. She just leaned closer to him because it was more comfortable sitting that way.

He started to tell her that he didn't need any help. But then he didn't bother. With just them sitting there in the dark, that, too, didn't seem to make any difference. So he said instead, "You're the only one knows I'm here."

"I know," she said. "That makes me sort of special, doesn't it?"

Barbara Cochrane, in her white overalls and her white blouse, felt very special sitting alone in the dark with Bobby O'Berry. She was trying to keep her heartbeat under control. She was trying to keep her giggles from exploding into all-out nervous laughter.

"Bobby," she said quietly. "I haven't had a cigarette since this morning."

"Good. That shit's bad for you."

"I know you don't like it." After a moment, she added, "I didn't want the smell to be on my breath."

Bobby turned his head. She was very close to him, somehow closer than he had realized. Her face was turned up to his. And she did smell good. Raising his hand slowly, he touched her cheek with the backs of two of his fingers. The skin he touched was softer and smoother than anything he had ever felt in his life. His fingers slipped over it, came back and did it again.

"Oh, Bobby," she whispered, her voice almost no louder than her breath, "I'll do anything for you."

He hesitated for just an instant, his mind flying away to wonder what Julie or the other guys would say if they could see him. But they couldn't see him. They didn't even know where he was. Only she could see him, Babs Cochrane, the girl from detention, the friend of the hand job queen; Butchie Keane's date, who drank beer out of a bottle and stripped off her panty hose when she went parking. She was here and Julie and the other guys weren't.

He touched his mouth to hers. It felt of lip gloss and tasted not of cigarettes, but of something that seemed vaguely like asparagus. He pushed down and her lips, incredibly soft, gave way beneath his.

He found himself being guided around in a quarter circle, his head held in both her hands, his body lowered onto hers. He could feel her breasts through the heavy cloth of her bib, feel the expanse of her bra,

31

and he grew excited, pushing down between her legs until she gave one long, slow rotation of her hips that left him unmistakably erect. Her mouth spread into a smile and their teeth touched, but Bobby was only concerned with getting her bib unbuttoned, her shirt open.

He was reaching behind her, groping for the way to undo her bra, when she whispered that the snap was in front. His hands flew back, found it between the hard lower rims of her cups and let the snap go. It was like opening a bottle of champagne. The bra fell away in two pieces and her enormous breasts broke across her chest, flopping to either side, trailing after the ends of the bra.

Bobby's hand went from one to the other, his kiss became feverish, his body movement rough and powerful. Gradually Barbara pulled up her legs, lifting them so that she was resting only on her back and her hips, holding them in the air so that they were bent at the knees; and Bobby, when he realized what she was doing, gave one more hard thrust and came in his pants.

CHAPTER FOUR

By Wednesday most everyone knew he was out of the house. His mother had called Julie and Carelli and Mullaney. Butchie had been by, looking for him. She told each of them that she was scared out of her mind. She wanted to know where he was and if he was all right. She wanted him to come home. She wanted them to pass the message along.

At first Bobby wouldn't tell anyone where he was staying. But Julie kept the pressure on and by Wednesday afternoon Bobby gave in and brought him back to the house on Loomis Hill.

"Jees, this is great," gushed Julie from his seat on the wooden box that Barbara had added as a furnishing the day before. "This is almost like having your own apartment. Get some broads up here . . ." He gestured to the hammock and made little bucking motions with his body. "Whumpetta, whumpetta. You tried that yet?"

Bobby shook his head and changed the subject. "If I want to wash up, there's running water at the faucet on the side of the house. I think they leave it on in case anyone who comes here looking to buy the place wants to take a piss or something."

"Boy, you can live like a king here for nothing." Julie surveyed the place once more. He tapped the beer Bobby handed him from the cooler. It was one of the two that Barbara had brought on Sunday night and Bobby, seated on the hammock, was opening the other one.

"The only thing is, though," Julie said, scowling at the beer, "you gotta figure out some way to get some ice. This warm shit will kill you."

It was still light and they were still under the porch talking when Barbara arrived. Bobby had assumed she would be coming after dark, as she had the night before and the night before that. Julie, he had thought, would be long gone by then. But there she was, opening the lattice gate and holding it back with her leg because her arms were filled with food and the laundry she had done for Bobby.

Julie sat frozen on the box. Bobby, still on the hammock, said nothing; Barbara, left to make some move of her own, let the gate swing shut and walked in as if she were returning to her own place and Julie was not even there.

"I got all your things clean," she said. "Where do you want me to put them?"

Julie's jaw dropped open. He looked at Bobby uncertainly, as though expecting him to say that Babs Cochrane worked for a catering service that made deliveries to people who lived underneath porches.

"This is my friend Julie," Bobby told her; and Barbara said, "Hi."

"Holy shit," said Julie.

She was wearing a brand-new pink sweatshirt that did nothing for her, but she had put on makeup and carefully brushed her hair and it was obvious to Julie that this was not a casual visit.

"Barbra helped me find this place," Bobby said.

An awkward silence fell over the three of them until, finally, Julie got up from the box. "Well," he said, "I guess I gotta get going."

Neither Bobby nor Barbara made any effort to stop him.

Julie told Linehan, Linehan told Brady, and Brady told everyone who cared to know. Rita heard the story at noon. One of her girlfriends told her at lunch that her brother Bobby was living with Babs Cochrane in an old abandoned house on top of Loomis Hill. She immediately went looking for her brother to see if the story was true, but Julie told her he hadn't come to school that day. Julie would not, however, tell her exactly where the house was.

Rita fretted all afternoon about what to do, and then she told her mother that Julie knew where Bobby was. Patricia O'Berry had gone all through school with Julie's mother's sister and so by evening she, too, knew the house Bobby was using. Then she fretted.

Barbara got up from the hammock and put on her panties. They were yellow and they had the word "Thursday" on them in brown script, just above where the legband bit into her thigh. The top of the panties was almost obscured by the roll of her belly, so that they looked even smaller than they were.

Bobby stayed where he was, lying in the hammock with his arms behind his head, staring at the floorboards above him. She looked down at him and misread the look on his face.

"What you gotta do, Bobby, once you're in there, is think about something else. Count to a hundred or remember baseball games. That's what my brother Terry tells me he does. But don't worry about it. It just takes practice, that's all."

She bent down and nibbled at his chest. She decided she liked doing that and crawled back into the hammock, draping an arm and a leg across his body and cuddling into him with one foot still on the ground.

They had almost drifted into sleep when the car pulled into the driveway and stopped. The lights and engine stayed on as two doors opened. They could hear two sets of footsteps on the gravel. Then there was a third set of footsteps and then a fourth. A young girl's voice whined and an older girl told her to shut up. A man called out Bobby's name.

"Oh, my God, it's my family," Bobby said, and he and Barbara tried to leap from the hammock at the same time. Hands and feet, arms and legs, were caught in the loose webbing. The hammock ripped and Bobby crawled out. He made a grab for his pants and was still pulling them up when the lattice gate opened and his father poked his head inside. His father took in the scene at once. He drew his head back from the doorway and said, "Patricia, kids, don't come in here," and then he looked in again.

"Jesus, God," Patricia cried. "Is he all right?"

"He's all right," Jack said. "It's nothing. Just stay back for a minute."

But Patricia pushed her way to the gate anyway. She saw Barbara with her back to her, naked from the waist up, still getting dressed. She saw Bobby pulling his shirt over his head. She saw and eventually she comprehended what she was seeing. Then she returned to the car and told her kids to get in with her.

There was no way Barbara could retreat gracefully unless Jack O'Berry got out of the doorway and moved his car from behind hers. He made no attempt to do either, but just stood where he was, watching the two get dressed. Finally, without a word being spoken, Barbara walked to the gate. Bobby's father waited until she was only a few feet from

35

him before he stepped out of the way. He watched her walk to her car and get in. He waited until she had shut her door and started her engine and then he turned back to Bobby.

"Kind of fat, isn't she, son?"

"Ma's going to have to back down the driveway so she can get out," Bobby said.

His father nodded and did nothing. "You know," he said, "this was your mother's idea, us all coming here like this. And now you've gone and disappointed her again. If it was up to me, you could rot in hell for all I care. Any kid hits his old man when he ain't looking ain't worth shit in my book."

"You were looking. You were coming after me."

"Yeah? Well, we'll see how much you're looking next time I come after you. Because this ain't the end of this between you and me. I ain't never lost a fight yet and I'm not about to start losing 'em to some snot-nosed kid. Especially my own kid. But for right now, your mother wants you home and I said I'd talk to you. That's all I said I'd do. Whether you come home or not don't make no difference to me. My deal with your mother is I just gotta tell you you can come home and promise you I won't do nothin' if you do."

"What about Ma? Will you promise not to hit her anymore if I come home?"

"Hey," his father said angrily, "didn't I just tell what the deal was? I don't gotta make no more promises. You want to stay here in the dirt, sleep in a volleyball net with fatty out there, that's your business. You want to come home, sleep in nice clean sheets, get your mother to cook you dinner, you can do it. That's all I'm saying."

Jack O'Berry looked back over his shoulder and wiped his mouth. "But as for that other thing, I'll tell you this. That was a mistake. I wished it hadn't happened. Your mother's a good woman and I'd pop any sonofabitch myself who laid a hand on her. All I can say is it's different when two people are married. You'll find that out for yourself someday. Women have their ways and men have theirs, and sometimes women are a lot more in control of things than you think."

"Are you saying Ma wanted to get hit? Is that it, Dad?"

"Look, you . . . look. I'd had a tough week at work. I come home, I'd had a few cans of fruit juice, and your mother starts giving me some lip. A man can't take that. He's gotta run his own house like a castle. You ever hear that expression? That's what it means. A woman's gotta know her place, and that's not giving a man a bunch of shit after he's had a hard week. I put up with all the shit I'm gonna take at the plant, and I'm not about to put up with any more from you or her or anyone else. Got that straight?" He hitched his pants. "Alls I'm saying is, men are men and women are women, and women got their own way of handling things. Comes the right time, a man will do anything a woman asks. That's nature. That's how God evened things out."

Jack O'Berry was not one who liked to talk around a point. He threw one more quick glance over his shoulder. "Fact is, your mother's cut me off. I don't get back in the saddle till me and you's had this talk."

The bluntness of his father's message stunned Bobby. Without being able to articulate why, he felt betrayed. He had an image of his mother sitting in the car with a locked treasure in her lap. He thought of his father kneeling at her feet, begging to be parceled out a little piece of the treasure. In the instant of his vision his mother's face was mournful as she reached into her treasure box and came out with a little cube of gold, which she placed on his father's tongue. A chill went up Bobby's spine. "Are you going to hit her anymore or not, Dad?" he said.

Jack O'Berry's jaw bulged. "I'm gonna run my house my own way without your advice is what I'm gonna do." He paused, got hold of himself. "But I'm telling you right now, I made a mistake. All right?"

"You're not much of a father, are you, Dad?"

The words came out before Bobby had a chance to think about them. Curiously, they did not make Jack O'Berry mad. "What do you know about it?" he said, squinting one eye. "You think you got it tough, you shoulda seen my old man. What I remember about him, I remember he used to clam into a handkerchief. He'd work six days a week, ten hours a day, down the shipyard, and on Sundays he used to stand around hawking up stuff from his throat and clamming into that handkerchief. You think he wasn't much of a father? You told him that, he would have squeezed your head between his thumb and his forefinger until it popped. But we woulda never dreamed of telling him that, because he was what us kids had. And me, I'm what you got, so you better make the best of it."

Out in the driveway, slumped miserably behind her steering wheel, Barbara Cochrane watched the lattice door open and a figure step out. It was Bobby and in his arms he was holding all his clothes, the dirty ones and the ones she had laundered for him. His father came out behind him and the two of them walked past her without saying a word.

In her rearview mirror, Barbara watched Bobby get into the back seat of his father's car with his two sisters. She could see Mr. O'Berry staring at the back of her head. And then she saw him shrug. She averted her eyes, not wanting to see anything else. A moment later she heard the sound of a car door slam and then the Impala was backed slowly down the drive.

CHAPTER FIVE

She caught up with him in the hallway. He heard her footsteps slapping up behind him and he felt as if the skin were shrinking right off his face and leaving him with nothing but a skull with which to confront her.

"Hi," she said, and he said the same word back, speaking without changing his pace, without really looking at her.

"Everything okay at home?"

"Sure. Everything's fine."

"You and your father doing okay?"

"Yeah."

They walked on. He came to a stairway and started up it. She went with him, her feet hitting heavily on the steps in an effort to match his stride.

"I guess that means you're not coming back, huh?"

"I don't know. You can't tell what might happen."

They turned on the landing. There was some jostling with the kids coming down, but Bobby made no effort to slow his pace. She was running when she caught him again.

"I've been up there a couple of times, just to see if you might be there. I figured you might want to talk or something."

"I been pretty busy."

"Yeah. I asked Tommy Mullaney."

Bobby grabbed the handrail and stopped suddenly. "You did what?"

People were bumping into her from behind and Barbara had to move out of the way. "I just asked him about you, that's all." Looking distressed, she said, "He already knew about us, Bobby."

"Knew what?"

"Knew we been seeing each other. Your friend Julie must have told him."

Bobby's grip on the handrail tightened. Somebody scraped against him in passing and Bobby shoved the person with his forearm. "We weren't seeing each other, Barbra. You helped me out when I was in trouble and that was it. We weren't going out or anything like that."

"Does that mean we're not going to see each other anymore?"

Bobby didn't answer. He threw her a searing look and ran the rest of the way up the stairs.

The graduation ceremony was on a Saturday in the football stadium. Bobby sat on a folding chair in the middle of a field along with 523 other seniors in mortarboards and black gowns while a man who was vice-president of a razor blade company gave an address in which he urged that the graduates spend the first twenty-five years of their lives getting education, the next twenty-five making money, and the last twenty-five giving their money away. Bobby walked up and got his diploma and returned to his seat without incident. His mother took his picture with a Polaroid, but the range was too far and it didn't come out.

At the parents' reception afterward in the gymnasium, Bobby's father complained about the cookies and stuffed them into his pockets nonetheless. It was a warm day, but Bobby's mother never took off her eggshell-colored coat because she felt it to be both more fancy and more appropriate than the dress she was wearing. Bobby made it a point not to hang around with either one of them.

Later, at a cookout celebration at the Sabatinis', Patricia O'Berry stayed in the kitchen with the other mothers. From time to time she would glance out the window at her husband, who was powering down beers in the backyard. The other men were calling her husband Jackie and trying to talk him into eating his beer glass, something he had apparently been known to do in the past. Bobby, who was watching for that sort of thing, caught a look of concern pass between Mr. and Mrs. Sabatini, and cut out with Brady and Lynch the first chance he had.

The old man got him a job at the plant. Five o'clock in the morning until noon, Monday through Friday, loading trucks at the shipping dock. He liked the lifting, he liked the money, he hated the hours.

40

Every night the guys would be hanging out, going down the beach, going into Boston. They had found a bar in the Combat Zone that would serve them and they liked going in there. For two weeks he tried keeping up with them, but he found himself dragging and he began going home earlier and earlier. Ten o'clock was the cutoff point. If he was going home any earlier than that he might as well not be going out at all.

He was, of course, still living with the family. Since the night of the fight there had been no further incidents. His father continued to drink, and he still had his Friday night binges, but he hadn't hit anyone and no one had had to sleep in the car.

Bobby would have been well on his way to accumulating the $2,500 he figured he needed for a half-decent motorcycle if it had not been for two things. The day he got his first paycheck the old man told him he had to start paying rent; and from the first of July on, he was going down the Cape every Friday afternoon and not returning until Sunday night. In between Friday and Sunday night he was spending every cent he had.

Brady, Lynch and Butchie Keane had gone in on a cottage in Falmouth and the weekends were nonstop party time. He met a girl there over the Fourth and when he didn't find her the next weekend he met another girl. From that point on, Bobby was on the prowl, sometimes successfully, sometimes not—but always looking. With so many new girls in his life, with the knowledge that they were out there, everywhere, he never gave a thought to Barbara Cochrane. Except once.

In late August she telephoned him at home. She said she wanted to tell him goodbye, that she was moving to Arizona to stay with her oldest brother for a while. Bobby said goodbye and hung up the phone quickly without asking why she was going.

Labor Day weekend was depressing. Everything on the Cape was closing up, the parties were quiet and sparsely attended. Carelli was getting ready to go off to UMass. Mullaney was going in the Air Force. Linehan had gone up to Maine to get in the pipefitters' union. Butchie Keane and Paul Lynch were working down at the shipyard at $9.25 an hour and Brady claimed he was going to junior college, although he hadn't done anything about enrolling yet.

For the first time in his life, Bobby was facing a fall without any plans. He still was two thousand dollars short of what he needed for his

41

motorcycle and he was beginning to think that maybe he should buy a car instead.

On the last night of the three-day weekend, Bobby and Julie, the only ones who were still at the cottage, sat on a raft that had been towed to the edge of the pond in preparation for winter storage. They shared a bottle of Tanqueray and discussed the advantages of a car over a bike, the Marines over the Navy, living in Portshead versus Kansas or Colorado or California.

"All things considered," Julie concluded, "there isn't noplace else I'd rather live."

"Well, I'm glad I grew up there," Bobby admitted, "but I keep thinking: there must be something else out there. You see these movies, and these people are doing all kinds of stuff: hang gliding and wind surfing and climbing mountains and hunting elephants. Don't you ever get the feeling you'd just like to do everything there is to do in the world?"

Julie thought about it for a minute. He drank while he thought. When he put the bottle down he said, "Not really. I never wanted to go see a circus."

The conversation sapped Bobby. He killed the bottle and never got drunk. He just felt miserable.

He was still feeling miserable on Tuesday when he took his late morning break at the plant. He was sitting alone at the end of the loading dock eating a Snickers bar and thinking how this was the first day that he was working at something other than a vacation job. From far off he heard his name mentioned and he looked up to see the dock foreman directing someone his way.

The man coming toward him got larger with every step. He was well over six feet and easily two hundred and fifty pounds. He wore his short-sleeved shirt loose and outside his pants, and he wore jogging shoes. Bobby knew instinctively who he was and at the very same moment, without any hint other than the look on the man's face, he knew why he had come.

The man crashed to a squat in front of Bobby. His breathing was tight, as if he was making an effort to control himself, but he was smiling as though he was about to do something he liked.

Balancing on his toes, he stared into Bobby's face and almost casually balled one ringed hand and smashed it into the open palm of the other.

"You Bobby O'Berry?"

Bobby nodded. He was holding the Snickers bar in front of his face, not chewing what he had in his mouth.

The open palm that had been wrapped around the big man's fist cleaved the air so suddenly that Bobby did not immediately recognize it was being offered as a handshake. Bobby held out his own right hand and found himself jerked off the seat of his pants and into a squatting position of his own.

"Terry Cochrane," the man said, "and I understand you're friends with my sister."

Bobby, unable to get his hand free, said, "Barbra?"

The giant smiled. "I understand you been real friendly with her."

Another voice, coming from off to the side, said, "Too friendly," and Bobby looked around to see a big, balding head resting on the edge of the dock. What was most amazing about what he saw was the fact that the edge of the dock stood exactly six feet off the ground. "I'm Billy," the head said, the face smiling as if it knew Bobby was going to hate what he heard next, "and I'm Terry's big brother."

Bobby tried tearing his hand away and Terry wrenched his grip tighter. "Ooh, he's a strong one, Billy. We can use a big strong boy like him."

Bobby wasn't going to cry out, but he did give a quick glance down the dock to see if anyone was watching. The foreman was there, hands on his hips, looking in their direction. Bobby intensified his struggle. "What is this?" he said, managing to snap his arm free. But almost immediately Terry had him by the front of the shirt, just below the neck. He bunched the thin cloth and lifted Bobby upright. In the distance, Bobby saw the foreman signal wildly to someone else.

"You've broken our little sister's heart by never calling her," Terry said, his voice a hum in Bobby's ear.

"And you've broken ours by busting her cherry," Billy intoned sweetly.

"She's not . . . ?" Bobby didn't want them misunderstanding the fear that he knew was in his eyes and so he said the word: "pregnant?"

"Oh, yes she is," Billy said. He seemed uncommonly cheery about the whole thing.

"And you did it to her," said Terry.

Once again Bobby looked down the dock. Two people were standing with the foreman now, but no one was doing anything other than looking at him. It seemed incredible that they would just stand there and

43

watch him get manhandled. And then Bobby heard the whir of an approaching forklift and he understood what was happening.

Staring into Terry's eyes, he said, "Bullshit. She's fucked half the guys in the high school."

The crack that exploded in Bobby's ear seemed to come a full second after the sting of Terry's slap. "You better not be calling your future wife a whore, Bobby, or I'll beat you like a drum."

Bobby tried to wrestle his way out of the bigger man's grip, but Terry caught him, thrust one massive forearm under his chin, and drove him back into the wall against which he had been sitting a few minutes before.

"Me and Billy are just here to give you the good news," Terry said. "We knew you'd want to have an opportunity to share in the excitement as soon as possible."

Bobby tried to kick him. Terry drew Bobby out from the wall and slammed him up against it again. He didn't have time to do anything more because at that moment the forklift came onto the dock.

What he should have done, Jack told everyone later, was drive the machine right into the bastard. What he did instead was try to leap on Terry Cochrane as the forklift went past. It was a move that might have looked good on television, but it didn't play well on the loading dock. Terry caught him in the air with one arm and swept him into the wall next to his son.

Howling, screaming angrily, Jack made an effort to scramble back to his feet. He made it halfway before Billy Cochrane shouted for him to freeze. The significance of that word didn't seem to sink in immediately. Jack turned in the direction from which it had come and even took one crouched step forward. Then he saw Billy's arm extending across the dock, and at the end of the arm he saw Billy's coal-black semiautomatic pistol.

"You lookin' to get hurt, pally," Billy said, "interferin' in other folks' business."

Afraid of what any one of these three men might do, Bobby spoke up loudly. "This is my father."

A smile came over Terry's face. He grabbed Jack O'Berry's hand and pumped it. "Congratulations, sir," he said. "I understand you're going to be a grandpa."

* * *

44

"Me," Jack O'Berry said, pounding the dinner table until the glasses and silverware jumped. "Some fat punk pulls a gun on me. At my work. He's gonna shoot Jack O'Berry, all because of lover boy here, knocks up his sister. Jesus, is the whole family fat or what, Bobby? You couldn't pick a skinny broad with skinny little brothers? You should have seen 'em, Trish. Two of 'em. As big as goddamn mountains."

Bobby was silent. Except for his father, everyone at the table was silent. The food lay on their plates growing colder and harder and stickier.

"Well," Jack said, finishing off his beer, "you done what you done and now you gotta do the right thing. You're no different from anyone else gets caught in these situations, you know. Your mother and me wasn't exactly planning on getting married when you came along—"

"Jack . . ."

"—but we did it and it's worked out okay. You just become a man a little sooner than you were expectin', that's all."

"Jack . . ."

"Ah, for Chrissake, Trish. If the boy hasn't figured it out by now it's only because he's too dumb to look at a calendar. Besides, if he's old enough to get married, he's old enough to know he ain't the first one this has happened to."

"He's also not the only one at the table, Jack."

With something akin to surprise, Jack looked at the two girls. Rita's head was down, Roxanne's eyes were fixed on her mother. "Well," Jack said, a little less forcefully than before, "alls I'm saying is that sometimes these things that you don't expect work out just as good as anything else."

Patricia O'Berry began gathering the plates in front of her, scraping everybody's uneaten meal on top of her own. Without returning anyone's look, she said, "I'm sure Barbara's a very nice girl and I'm sure she and Bobby will be very happy if they decide to get married."

"If?" Jack shouted. "What do you mean 'if'? If he gets her preganant, he gets her married. That's the way things work around here. That's the way it worked for me and that's the way it'll work for him. You don't leave no bastard child running around with no last name. Suppose I'd done that to him? How would he like that, huh? Then he'd be Bobby Nobody."

Jack was glaring around the table, daring anybody to dispute him. No one did. No one even looked at him.

45

With nothing left within her reach to scrape, Patricia concentrated on lining up the dirty dishes so that the edges were perfectly straight. "Tell me about her, Bobby," she said in measured words. "What's she like?"

But before Bobby could answer, his father, just as if he were the one being addressed, said, "She's a fat shit."

Bobby was on his feet, his eyes narrowed, his fists clenched. "So are you," he said, and then he turned and stomped from the room.

"Hey, you," his father called out as he shoved his chair back across the floor. But Bobby didn't stop. Not even when he heard all three females scream. Without thinking about it, he could distinguish the message of each voice: his mother's was panic, Rita's was anger, and Roxanne's was fear. And over them all, his father was bellowing as if he were the one who had been made to suffer some severe and grievous insult.

CHAPTER SIX

Friday night. Bobby felt as if he had been sleepwalking for three days. He had not heard again from the Cochrane brothers, but he knew they hadn't forgotten about him. He had neither seen nor spoken to Barbara, but he was putting that off on an hour-by-hour basis. Every hour he did not have to confront her was one more hour in which he could enjoy life. Except he wasn't enjoying it. Not one single minute.

Other people weren't enjoying it much, either. He had walked into the kitchen early that morning and found his mother crying. She was sitting alone at the kitchen table with a half-drunk cup of tea and an ashtray full of cigarettes, and Bobby knew she had been up most of the night. He had tried to get her to tell him what was wrong, even though he knew, but she had only cried harder and said she didn't feel well.

He had yet to tell any of his friends, and because they didn't know, they had said and done things that made the situation seem even worse. Brady had tried to fix him up with a date for the drive-in. Bobby made up an excuse, said he couldn't go, and Brady had given the date to Butchie Keane. The resentment Bobby then felt toward Butchie for taking his place was compounded by his growing conviction that Butchie was to blame for the whole situation with Barbara, and out of that resentment came the beginnings of Bobby's plan.

It was, he realized, a calculated risk telling Butchie. Of all the people he knew, Butchie was the least likely to keep a secret. But Bobby decided he had no choice.

On Saturday morning he found Butchie in front of his house, washing his father's car. Butchie had, it turned out, really enjoyed his date and he was going to see her again that night. This time without Brady.

"I got her in back, you know, Bob? And I'm tryin' to tell her how great love is. Two people who really care about each other, expressing their feelings through physical contact. Giving each other their most personal possession. And I'm in the middle of this whole line, you know, whisperin' it in her ear, and all of a sudden this stink comes over the car and I realize Brady's got the other one down on the front seat with his hand between her legs and makin' more noise than a popcorn machine. My date goes to me, 'I think we gotta go to the snack bar,' and the next thing I know I'm outta the car followin' her up to the stand."

Bobby had a smile on his face. He didn't even know what Butchie was saying. "I gotta talk to you, Butch."

Looking surprised, Butchie said, "So talk."

Bobby got him to stop washing the car. The two of them leaned against the fender, their arms folded. "You remember that time I saw you down the Bowl-A-Rama with Barbra Cochrane?"

Butchie smirked. "Babs Cochrane. Fuckin' A, I remember." He flexed his arms out as if he were trying to encircle a tree and he flexed his knees up and down. "Oom-pah, oom-pah," he said.

"Yeah, well." Bobby shifted his eyes. "You screwed her that night I saw you with her, didn't you?"

"Let's put it this way—I didn't go home unhappy."

"Yeah, but I mean, like, you actually screwed her, didn't you?"

"I cannot tell a lie. Everybody's screwed Babs. Hell, I heard you were screwing her for a while." The last word tailed off. A different look came over Butchie's face. "Holy shit," he said. "Don't tell me she's . . . ?"

"Just tell me if you screwed her or not."

"What do you want to know for?"

"Just tell me, Butchie."

"And I said, what do you want to know for?"

Bobby looked off toward the Keane house. He looked up and down the street. "Her brothers are trying to blame me, man."

"Holy crap." Concern flowed into Butchie's eyes. "What are you gonna do, man?"

"I was hoping you'd help me out."

"You need some money?" There was an eagerness in Butchie's voice, a hoping that money was what Bobby was seeking.

"All I need, Butchie, is for you to say you got her about the same time I did. That's all. Then they can't prove it was either one of us."

"You mean she's gonna have the kid?"

"That's what I hear," Bobby said glumly.

Butchie appeared to be thinking. "And it's yours?"

"How do I know if it's mine? It might be yours."

Butchie looked the other way. He moved his folded arms up higher, tucking his hands into his armpits. He worked his lips a few times and then spit into the street. "No way it was mine. I never did get in her."

Bobby thought of the panty hose he had seen in Barbara's pocketbook. He remembered Butchie's big talk afterward, his talk just a few minutes earlier. "You fucking liar," he said.

Butchie pushed away from the fender. "Hey, don't fuck with me, Bobby. I never fuckin' touched her. We fooled around some, but I never got anywhere. She got pissed at me because I ripped her stockings and I got pissed at her because she wasn't puttin' out. That's all there was to it. She took me back to the bowling alley and I didn't even say goodbye to her."

"You told everybody you got her."

"That was just talk. Guys bullshit all the time. Whatsamatter? Haven't you ever bullshitted before?"

Bobby was off the fender now, advancing on Butch, making him retreat. "I'm in trouble, Butch," he said. "They're trying to get me to marry her."

Butchie stopped backing up. "Well, I'm sure as shit not going to marry her," he said.

"Nobody's asking you to. But if I can just get you and a couple of the other guys to say they got her, too, there's no way they can pin it on me."

Bobby knew, just looking at him, that Butchie was going to say no. He watched Butchie's mouth, and after a moment it took everything he had to keep from swinging at it.

Butchie's eyes flicked from Bobby's face to his right hand and back again. His body was tensed, ready to move in any direction if the need should arise. "No way, Bobby," he said. "No way I'm gonna tell the Cochrane brothers I was fuckin' their sister. Those guys are killers, in case you don't know it, man. They got one of them, Tim, he did so many things for the Mafia he had to leave the state, for Chrissake, go to Arizona or somewhere like that. I'm not about to start messin' with those guys."

Desperate, Bobby said, "You told everybody you got her. I'll get everybody who heard you—"

49

"I was bullshittin', man. There's no way you can prove I did anything."

Taking a step backward, Butchie went from the street to his driveway. He hesitated before taking another step. Then he turned and began walking rapidly toward the rear of his house. This time Bobby didn't follow him. He just called out, "Thanks a lot, Butch. I'll remember this." And when Butchie didn't respond he punctuated his call. "Asshole."

Bobby telephoned Brady and Brady said he'd go along with Bobby's plan, but only if everybody else did. The problem with Brady, however, was that nobody was likely to believe him. He had that look about him, that inherently unbelievable look. Besides, Brady wasn't altogether sure which one Babs Cochrane was. "Is she the one who gives the hand jobs?" he asked.

Brady sent him to Lynch and Lynch said no. He had already heard from Butchie and was primed with his answer. He had to live in Portshead, he said, and he wasn't about to spend the rest of his life having everybody think Babs Cochrane's kid might be his.

Mullaney, too, said no. He did it by putting his big brother on the phone. Mullaney's brother sold appliances for Sears Roebuck. He said, "Tommy feels terrible about this. He'd like to help you because you're his friend. But he's supposed to go in the Air Force next Thursday and something like this could keep him out. A real friend wouldn't ask him to do what you're asking, Bobby."

By nightfall Bobby had talked to everyone except Julie Sabatini, and he still had nothing but Brady's conditional promise. Julie had been out on the ocean all day fishing with his brothers and he had been spared Butchie's warning call. When he met Bobby at the Greek's his face was ridiculously sunburned and yet locked into an enormous smile. Under his arm was a brand-new metal-flake helmet.

"Hey," Bobby said, guiding him into the booth that had been occupied by the former Mrs. Gallagher on the night she had passed out. "There's something I gotta talk to you about."

"Me, too," Julie said, proudly displaying the motorcycle helmet by placing it in the center of the table.

Bobby, who until that moment had been sure he could count on Julie above everyone else, suddenly felt his intensity drain out of him. "What's this?" he said, tapping the helmet.

"C'mon and see," Julie told him, picking up the helmet and starting for the door.

Bobby followed him outside, followed him to the far corner of the Greek's lot, where there was a light over a billboard that advertised the benefits of heating your home with gas, and where the only vehicle parked was a freshly washed Honda 750.

"That's Carelli's bike," Bobby said.

Julie put on the helmet and straddled the seat. "Not no more. His mother just sold it to me."

Staring at the bike, Bobby felt as though his heart had just dislodged and dropped into the pit of his stomach. "I didn't even know it was for sale," he said.

"I didn't, either. But I said once to him, 'If you ever want to sell it, you know, just give me a call.' So yesterday he calls me up from UMass, just out of the blue, and asks me do I want to buy it. 'Sure,' I says. 'How come?' and he says he can't use the bike up there until he's about a senior and he needs the money because he's gonna join a fraternity. Two thousand bucks is all he wants, so I bought it. Pretty neat, huh?"

"Where did you get two thousand bucks?" Bobby asked softly.

"My old man. That's what we were talking about on the boat today. He gave me a loan for it and I went right to Mrs. Carelli's and picked up the bike this s'afternoon."

"What are you going to do with it when you go in the service?"

"Ah." Julie got off the bike and removed the helmet. "That's the other part of it. You see, this guy whose boat we were on was a friend of my father's and he said he needed to hire a guy as a deckhand. So my father's loaning me the money on condition I take this job, starting Monday."

"You mean all this happened at once?"

"I know. It's something, isn't it?"

"And you're just not going to go in the service?"

Julie shrugged his shoulders and flexed the earflaps on his helmet. "I don't know. That's what I still want to do, but now I got this responsibility. Before, you know, I could just say what it is I wanted to do, but now I sorta gotta do this other thing for a while. But who knows? Six months, a year from now, I can still go in. I might even like being a fisherman, might want to do that for a while. I got all kinds of things I can do."

Bobby was silent, his eyes still on the bike. He had spent the last two hours rehearsing how he was going to bring up the subject of Barbara's pregnancy, and now nothing that he had practiced seemed to be relevant. When Julie finally got around to asking him what he wanted to talk about, he said simply, "You ever think of getting married?"

Julie hooted. "Yeah, right. Who to? Maybe that Swedish exchange student who was here last year. Yah, yah, I tink I coodt do dat."

Julie was so busy mugging he almost did not hear Bobby say, "I'm gonna have to get married."

Then he realized Bobby was serious. "Who to?" he asked, and when Bobby told him he said, "Oh, my God."

"Her brothers have already paid me one visit and I've gotta make up my mind pretty quick about what I'm gonna do."

"What do your parents say?"

"The old man says I gotta do the right thing. It's what he did, he says. It's the price of being a man, he tells me. Big fuckin' deal."

Julie looked genuinely scared and it made Bobby feel strangely gratified to see it. He said, "All my so-called friends, there's not one of them willing to help a guy out when he really gets in a jam. I think of some of the things I did for those guys and I wished I'd never done them. Remember the time Lynch was getting beat up behind the Burger King by those guys from Dorchester? I took on both those guys for him while he's lying on the ground hiding his head."

"What have you been trying to get 'em to do?" Julie asked warily.

"I figure, if I could get a bunch of other guys to say they stuck her, too, there's no way the Cochrane brothers can say I'm the one who's the father. But so far only Brady says he'll go along with it."

"I wouldn't trust Brady."

"Neither would I." Bobby looked out of the corner of his eyes. "How about you, Julie? You want to bail out like everybody else?"

"Shit, no," Julie said, his face as long and straight as his honor. But he waited, without volunteering.

"You'll say you slept with her?"

"If anybody asks, sure."

"How about going in court and saying it? Will you do that?"

Julie swallowed hard. "Is anybody else gonna?"

"Brady. He said he might."

Julie nodded. He wasn't looking at Bobby any longer. "Jesus, my old man's gonna kill me," he said. "Isn't there anything else we can do?"

And Bobby, who had been waiting for such an opening, who had pushed Julie into a hole and had been waiting for him to crawl out, burst into a shout. "All right, forget it, Julie. Forget I asked. I don't need you. I don't need anyfuckin'body."

His last chance, he figured, lay with Barbara herself. He had no idea where she lived and only found her address because there was a Terrence and a William Cochrane both listed at the same number in the phone book. On Sunday night he took a bus to within half a mile of their house and then walked the rest of the way. He had the semiformulated idea that it would have been unbecoming to have been seen disembarking from a bus on the corner of the street where the Cochranes lived.

The house, once he had found it, shocked him. It had a stone exterior partially covered with lush ivy growth, and a front yard that was at least a hundred feet deep. A pebble driveway ran to a barnlike garage that was set apart from the house, and the yard was rimmed by woods. A small, gabled porch covered his head as he stood on the front step and waited for someone to answer the doorbell.

The someone turned out to be a very normal-sized white-haired woman wearing an attractive print dress with a patent-leather belt at her waist. She looked at the anxious face of the young man standing in front of her and said only one thing: "I'll get Barbara."

Bobby waited on the step, not entering the house even though the door had been left open, and after a few minutes Barbara appeared. She came alone, wearing a sweatshirt hanging loose over a pair of baggy white slacks. She was barefoot, but her skin glistened as though it had just been scrubbed, and her hair was neatly brushed. She leaned against the doorjamb and they talked without her ever going outside or Bobby ever stepping in.

It had to be his, she said. He was the only one she had slept with during that time. Oh, she had heard that Butchie was saying he had done it with her, but boys always talked like that and, besides, what could she do about it?

Another reason she knew it was his was because she remembered exactly when it happened. It was the second night they tried it, the first night he had stayed inside her. She had known as soon as she had gotten out of the hammock, and she had gone home and washed everything out, but it hadn't done any good. After that she figured it didn't make any difference.

53

It was too late to do anything about it now. She was more than three months along, and she had already told her mother. She wouldn't have done that if she had thought Bobby cared anything about her, but after what he said that day on the stairway and after he was just going to let her go off to Arizona, she knew she was on her own. It was her mother who had told her brothers and they had gone to him on their own. It hadn't been her idea.

Now all she cared about was having a healthy baby. She'd like it to have a name so that it didn't have to grow up with everyone knowing it was born out of wedlock, but she was prepared to raise it by herself if necessary.

Bobby told her he was trying to get things straight in his mind and he would let her know as soon as he figured out what to do. She told him she understood why he was scared. He said he wasn't scared at all.

It was starting to rain when Bobby left the Cochrane house. It wasn't raining hard enough to soak him, but Bobby could see big raindrops hitting the ground in front of him and he could feel them hitting his head and his shoulders.

The air felt good. It was heavy and quiet and it darkened all the colors around him. Bobby tried to be very conscious of his enjoyment of it, telling himself that this was something he could remember, reminding himself that he could have moments like this whether he was married or not. Whether he was a father or not.

A car rolled up beside him and slowed down to match his pace. Bobby glanced at it and saw that it was a gray Continental and that the smiling face behind the wheel belonged to Billy Cochrane. He stopped and so did the Continental. The passenger window rolled down by itself.

"Get in, Bobby. I'll give you a lift home."

Bobby looked off down the street. Billy laughed and leaned across the seat to open the door. He did it with such assurance that Bobby got in, even though he would have preferred to walk.

"You like this car?" Billy said, pressing the gas.

"It's all right."

"You knew how much it cost, you wouldn't just say that. The reason I'm telling you"—Billy saw a traffic light turn yellow and he sped up to catch it before it turned red—"is because right about now you might be kind of wondering if it's all just bad stuff, you getting married to my sister and all." The light turned red, but Billy was almost there and so he went through it anyhow. "I'm here to tell you it's not all bad."

Bobby looked out the window and didn't say anything. He had never been in a Continental before, at least not a new Continental, and he was impressed with how quiet it was. Billy had some wordless music playing very softly on the radio and it created an atmosphere that made Bobby think of the waiting room at a doctor's office.

"When me and my brothers started out we weren't much different from you, Bobby. But we got into a good business, see, painting lines in parking lots. You probably seen our work all the time and don't even know it. This whole part of the state, any parking lot you see has our lines in it. Business is so good, you know, me and Terry don't ever have to do any of the painting ourselves. We just make sure we get the business."

"You own the company?" Bobby was not sure why he asked the question; it was almost as if Billy had willed him to ask it.

Billy chuckled. "In a manner of speaking. Actually, we own part of it and this corporation we work for owns part of it. It gets sort of complicated, but the point is that this is the part of the corporation's business that me and Terry run ourselves. That's one point; the other point is that there's going to be a job there waiting for you, if you're interested."

"What? Painting lines?"

The smile disappeared from Billy's face. He concentrated on a couple of traffic maneuvers before answering. "Hey, you think you can get ten bucks an hour working someplace else, go right ahead. But I know that's not what you're making where you are now. What I'm saying is, you marry my sister and we'll start you out right. You choose, you don't want to do nothin', you'll still make four hundred bucks a week just because we want to make sure Barbara and the kid do okay. On the other hand, you work hard, you keep your mouth shut, there's no telling how much money you can earn working with us. You want, you can get a car like this one someday. You see the house we bought my mother? And we got another one down in Osterville, too. You should see that. We got a little condo in Boston, right on the water, high-security building, nights we want to stay in there. You followin' what I'm saying?"

Bobby nodded, "I'm followin'."

"Well, look a little happier about it, then. Not every kid gets these opportunities. In fact, you might just find that taking advantage of my sister's the best thing that ever happened to you."

"I can get out up here."

It was raining hard when Billy pulled the Continental slowly to the curb. He looked around. "What do you want to get out here for?"

Bobby opened the door. "I got things to do."

Billy caught him by the arm. "If you think I don't know where you live, you're wrong, kid. I wanted to tell you that. I wanted to tell you the good stuff first, so you don't think I'm just threatening you."

The rain blew in the car and Bobby drew the door closed because his arm was getting soaked. He waited for Billy to continue.

"I know what you been doing, trying to get your buddies to say that they might be responsible for Barbara's condition. We put the word out. First guy who says he did it to her is gonna get his fingers broke. Next guy, his arm. And it goes on from there. You follow me now?"

Bobby didn't have to say anything. The acknowledgment was there in the look that passed between them.

Billy released his grip on Bobby's arm. He spoke gently. "And about your father, Bobby—we know his reputation. We don't take chances with guys like him. We also don't always do our fightin' with our hands, see? We join these two families, it might be very beneficial to your old man. But you decide not to do the right thing here, don't look to your old man for protection unless you want to see him get hurt."

Billy Cochrane patted Bobby on the shoulder. It was a way of telling him he could go.

CHAPTER SEVEN

It was set for the first Saturday in November. Barbara would be more than four months along, but given her natural size, she would not be showing *that* much. She would wear off-white. Not a formal wedding gown, but a very nice, very special, satin-bodice dress with skirts that fell to the floor. Bobby would wear a suit. If he could get one in time.

Two weeks before the wedding he went to Sears and was surprised that he could not find anything to fit him. If a jacket hung right on his shoulders, it dropped like a tablecloth along his ribs. At one point, thinking he could do no better, he took a suit into the dressing room and tried on the pants. The waist was at least six inches too big and he felt like a clown. He returned to the floor holding the pants up with his hand by bunching all the material just above the zipper and looking around for a salesman. The only one there was a kid whom he recognized from high school and Bobby wasn't about to ask him any questions. Instead, he put the suit back on a hanger and went home.

Barbara kept asking him for his invitation list and he kept putting her off. Her plans changed. She originally had talked about renting the Knights of Columbus Hall, then the Neighborhood Club. Finally she asked if Bobby wanted to have the reception at her house and he said he didn't care. It was the most positive response she had gotten from him and it gave her an idea of how small he wanted the wedding to be.

He told her Julie Sabatini would be his best man and she asked his sister Rita to be her maid of honor. Rita refused. She said she didn't want to be in the wedding party. When Mrs. O'Berry found out what her daughter had done she made her telephone Barbara and apologize. She made her ask if she could be maid of honor after all, and Barbara agreed.

Barbara pushed again for the invitation list and Bobby gave her Linehan's name and told her she could reach him in Maine by calling his parents. She said that he had to have more than just two friends at the wedding, so he told her to invite Brady, even though he was sure he would not come. He had not spoken to Butchie Keane or Paul Lynch or Loogie Carelli since he had gone to them seeking their help, and he wasn't about to invite any of them at this point. With Mullaney gone, he could think of no one else. At the last minute he gave her DiLorenzo's name. He said if she really wanted to she could invite DiTullio along with him, but personally, he couldn't care less about DiTullio.

"I don't care" was positive. "I couldn't care less" was negative. She left DiTullio off the list.

On the first day of November Bobby confessed to Julie about his problems in getting a suit. Julie had a brainstorm. They went down to Mr. Dan's and rented Bobby a tuxedo. The jacket was red and black paisley. But it was muted. Julie told him it looked sharp.

Bobby quit work at the loading dock on Wednesday. He gave no notice, he just told the foreman he wouldn't be back. The foreman started to chew him out until Bobby said he had to get married and then the foreman stopped hollering. He asked if Bobby wasn't going to need some work after the wedding and Bobby said no, he was getting a job painting lines in the street.

That night he went into the Greek's at about ten o'clock. He was hoping Julie might be in there, but he wasn't. Thinking that he might wait fifteen or twenty minutes, Bobby sat down by himself in a booth and unrolled the Marvel comic book he had been carrying in his back pocket. He had read it before, but he remembered it as being a good one and he was willing to read it again. Except he didn't. Holding the magazine out in front of him, he listened instead to the conversation going on between the two women in the booth behind him.

One of them he recognized as a pizza maker down at the Leaning Tower. The other was Fran, the waitress at the Mai Tai. Fran was still wearing the black skirt and white blouse that served as the Mai Tai's uniform and she was occasionally taking drags from a cigarette she held up in the air.

"And then I got this pain in my stomach," she said.

"My Joe had the same thing," said the pizza lady.

"So I went to Dr. McCreary."

"I kept trying to get Joe to go."

"And he says, 'Fran, well, we know you're not pregnant.' "

Both women sputtered with laughter and when they stopped, Fran said, " 'But what you got, I think, is an ulcer. All the worrying, the running around you do.' "

"Same thing with Joe. His is so bad sometimes he's gotta burp somethin' awful."

"So he gives me this stuff to drink, tastes like cat's pee. He tells me I gotta give up drinking, smoking, running around worrying about things all the time. I felt like saying, 'Hey, Doc, you ever have five kids and a husband works nights?' I mean, what's he know about real life? He probably plays golf, for God sakes. The day I got enough time to walk around a golf course is probably the day they bury me.' "

"Well, you got most of your kids outta the house now, don'tcha?"

"What, are you kidding me?" Bobby could hear the ashtray rattle as Fran ground out her cigarette. "They're more trouble when they're gone than when they were home. The oldest one, Jane? She's the one run off with the bum. They go live down Hull in a trailer. 'Don't call it a trailer, Ma, it's a mobile home.' I go there, I sit on the can, I got just enough room to close the door. I gotta stick my nose out the window, otherwise I got the sink about two inches from my eye. She's got two babies now, you know. So I goes to her, I goes, 'Why don't you get your husband to get a job, move you and the kids into a real house?' She goes, 'He's not my husband, Ma.' I go, 'As long as you're living together and he's the father of your two kids, I consider you Mr. and Mrs. Eddie King.' She says 'We don't want to be married. We want to be free.' Right? You know what I'm saying? I look at her, up to her keester in wash while her boyfriend, or whatever she wants to call him, is sprawled out on the couch watching *Bowling for Dollars*, and I think, 'Free, hah.' "

There was a clucking of sympathy from the pizza lady. "Jane's what now, twenty-three?"

"Twenty-three going on forty-five. Honest to God, I don't know what it is with kids these days. I mean, back when we were their age we didn't know any better. We thought that's all you were s'posed to do was get out of school, get married, have kids of your own. But there are so many more opportunities now. I'll tell you, I wish to God I had it to do over again."

"Aw, but you got a family, Fran. Your youngest, how old's she now?"

"Debbie's fourteen. She just started up the high school."

"No."

"Oh, yes." Fran laughed.

"Jees, the high school. I was thinking she was still just a little kid. I remember her when she was just this high."

"Hey, Margaret, I remember when we were just that high. And now look at us."

"You ain't so bad, Fran."

"Yeah, right."

Bobby heard the scratch of a match. He smelled the acrid odor of a freshly lit cigarette. Through the seatback they shared he could almost feel Fran draw smoke into her lungs.

She spoke again. "I'm not so bad compared to being dead." Suddenly she laughed again. "But who knows? Maybe someday my ship will still come in."

Bobby got up from the booth and fled.

His mother had a black kerchief that she wore on her head whenever she went to church. Sometimes it would sit on the closet shelf for months without ever being used. Other times they would find it sticking out of her pocketbook or her coat pocket and they would know where she had been.

It was lying on the kitchen table when Bobby finally got out of bed on Thursday morning. Patricia O'Berry came in from the back pantry and saw him staring at it.

"I been to the priest," she said.

Bobby nodded and got orange juice out of the refrigerator. He stood at the refrigerator door, drinking it straight from the pitcher. His mother, who usually would tell him not to do that, said only, "You want some eggs?"

Bobby told her he didn't. What he said was "Nah."

"English muffin?"

"I can do it, Ma."

"It's no trouble. Just sit down at the table. I'll have it for you in no time."

Bobby watched her scurry from one end of the kitchen to the other. He saw that he was going to get the eggs anyway, that she had already forgotten he had said "Nah."

She stood at the stove with her back to him. "Father Donahue says we must learn to accept the things we cannot change. He said to tell you that God has a purpose in everything He does, even though you might not always be able to see that purpose yourself."

"Do you ever think, Ma," Bobby interrupted, "that if you had it all to do over again you'd do it differently?"

She didn't answer for a long time. Her fork was clacking against the frying pan. It hit, scraped, and whirred through the air as fast as a lawn mower blade. And then it stopped. She stood very still for a long time and Bobby knew she was crying. He thought about going to her, putting his arm around her, but he knew that if he did he would start crying himself. It was better this way, better to pretend he didn't know why she was standing so still and so silent.

The smell of burning egg rose from the stove and she reached out and shut off the gas. "There's three hundred dollars hidden in the cookbook you kids gave me one Christmas," she said. "I was saving it just in case I ever had to . . . I'd like for you to take it."

"Ma, I can't do that."

"Go on, Bobby. It will make me feel good. It will be almost the same as if I used it myself."

CHAPTER EIGHT

Barbara told the manager they were on their honeymoon. He didn't seem impressed. He was a tall, thin man with short gray hair and a scruffy beard. He wore a blue plaid shirt and green woolen pants and he seemed far more interested in the television show he had going in the room adjacent to the office than he did in the young couple he was registering.

"You get your pick of cabins," he said, squinting at the line in the registration book where Bobby had written Mr. and Mrs. Robert O'Berry.

"You got a honeymoon cabin?" Barbara asked. "We made reservations."

"They're all honeymoon cabins," the manager said, "this time of year."

"You got one right by the water?" It was the first time Bobby had spoken up since they walked into the office.

"Number nine," the manager said, handing over a key that was attached by a lanyard to a major piece of wood. As soon as he let go of the key he went back to his television show and Barbara and Bobby were left to find their own way to their cabin.

Getting back into Barbara's Coronet, they followed a rutted, unlighted path that felt soft beneath their tires and smelled strongly of pine needles. They passed two or three detached cabins without being able to see the numbers on any of them. Once Bobby turned into a driveway and shined the high beams on a door, but it was only number 4. They counted from there, driving along the edge of the lake until they reached number 9, off by itself at the very end of the road.

The cabin was musty and had about it the feeling that it had not been opened in some time. There was dust on the mirror attached to the dresser and there was a spider's web in the corner behind the wood-burning stove. The walls were pine paneled, with large, smooth boards containing large, smooth knots.

The bed was against the back wall, flanked on one side by the entrance to a tiny bathroom and on the other by a closet. When Bobby touched the bed it sagged. He grunted and slung Barbara's suitcase on top of it.

"Oh, Bobby," Barbara said, spreading her arms, "isn't it romantic?"

Bobby looked around skeptically and said nothing. He looked back at Barbara and saw that she was frowning at the door.

"You know, Bobby, you really should have carried me across the threshold."

"I can't."

Barbara's eyes flashed, but only for a moment. Since the moment he had shown up on her doorstep, she had never once shown him anger or sadness or doubt, and she was determined not to do it on her wedding night. "I won't always be this big," she said. "It's just while I'm pregnant." She smoothed down her skirt so that it covered the plumpness of her knees. It was a blue and white checked skirt with a matching vest and she had bought it specially for the occasion. Somebody at the wedding had called it her trousseau and that was the way she thought of it as she ran her hands along the cloth. "Besides, I'm not exactly a whale or anything, you know." She looked at her husband for confirmation.

Bobby said, "You want to go swimming?"

"Bobby," she cried, "this is our honeymoon night." Then, catching herself, she turned a quarter turn and slipped one leg out in front of the other. "Aren't you interested in anything else?"

Bobby looked at the leg and looked out the front door. He could have been weighing the merits of each and Barbara did not give him a chance to decide against her. "Besides," she said, kicking the door shut, "it's too cold to go swimming." She bent over the suitcase on the bed and popped it open. Then suddenly she shut it again and straightened up. "You go out and get the rest of the bags and when you come back I'll have a nice surprise for you."

Bobby dutifully left the cabin and Barbara, waiting until he was gone, drew what she wanted from the suitcase and ran into the bathroom. It was ten minutes before she was ready to come out.

"Bobby, are you ready?"

"Ready for what?"

63

The answer did not come right away. When it did come it was spoken in a voice slightly brittle with sweetness. "Ready for me, silly."

Bobby looked down at the three suitcases he had thrown on the bed. Barbara's were red and as big as trunks. His was brown and battered and had a sprung lock.

"Are you in bed yet, honey?" Barbara called.

"Give me a minute," he said.

"Do you have the champagne my brother Terry gave us?"

Still standing, still looking down at the suitcases, he said, "I can't find it."

"It's in one of the small bags that I brought in. Look over by the door."

Bobby found the small bag. It had two straps and it reminded him of something people would bring to the beach. There was a bottle of French champagne in the bag. There was also a portable radio and cassette recorder with a handle, half a dozen cassette tapes, and a clear-topped pink box with what looked to be a set of hair curlers inside.

"You find it, Bobby?"

"Give me a minute, I said."

He got out the bottle and opened it with a loud pop that sent the cork zooming into the rafters. The champagne came bubbling out right behind the cork and Bobby quickly covered the end of the bottle with his mouth. When it stopped bubbling he placed the bottle on the floor next to the head of the bed, piled the suitcases in the corner, stripped off his clothes and got in between the sheets. "Okay," he said. "I'm ready."

"Did you shut off all the lights?"

"Jesus," he said, but he got out of bed and flicked off the two switches that had been on.

"I'll leave the one on in here."

"Well, c'mon if you're coming." Bobby lay flat again and folded his hands across his stomach.

The latch to the bathroom door was lifted and the door opened. "Da, da," Barbara said, emerging with one arm extended straight above her head and bent only at the wrist. She was wearing a black negligee that was in three pieces. A top piece fit like a short-sleeved jacket that tied at her neck, so gauzy as to be see-through. Beneath it there was a thin-strapped fringe top that covered only to her waist, and through it Bobby could make out the lines of her heavy breasts. The bottom piece was a pair of satin-rimmed panties with a filigree pattern in the crotch.

"Da-da-da-tidah-di-di-di," Barbara sang softly, kicking one leg out, drawing it back and kicking it out again. Moving in rhythm, she spun a half circle so that her back was to her husband and then, looking coyly over her shoulder, she played with the ties of the jacket, pulling first one and then the other until at last it slipped from her shoulders. She let it drop to the floor and turned to face Bobby full front again.

With her hands on her hips, her pelvis moving in and out, she shifted her voice into the drum portion of the music she was singing. "Boom-badata-boom-badata-boom-boom-boom," and as she was singing, she crossed her arms and lifted her fringe top over her head so that now when she danced her breasts swung back and forth and the folds of her stomach slid up and down.

Back she went to the "Da-da-da-tidah-di-di-di," as she hooked her thumbs into the band of her panties and eased them down, first while facing him, then while facing away. She got them only as far as her thighs, and then she quickly stepped out of them and collapsed laughingly on top of him, covering his face with kisses and reaching down beneath the covers to touch him. And then she stopped.

Even with the dimness afforded by the bathroom light, he could make out the disappointment on her face when she said, "Oh, Bobby, you're not even hard."

"Maybe," she said, "we should try doing it outside." She looked up at her husband to see if he appreciated her humor, but his eyes were closed and the only look on his face was one of concentration. She looked down again and her hand began moving faster. She threw back the sheets and tried a different motion, but she lost her grip and she lost him along with it. He rolled over onto his side so that his back was to her.

Throwing herself onto her own back with a particularly loud sigh, Barbara was silent for a minute. Then, because she was afraid that Bobby was falling asleep, she said, "We still got some more of that champagne."

She picked up the bottle and drank from the neck. "Jees," she said, gasping, "this stuff gets up your nose."

Bobby got out of bed and went into the bathroom. She could hear the water running into the sink for what seemed like a very long time.

"It's okay, you know," she said. "We got lots of time to practice."

The water shut off.

"I'm kind of tired tonight, anyway," she said.

The door opened and Bobby came out with two glasses which she had seen in plastic wrappers on the top of the toilet tank. He handed them to her and she noticed they were both completely dry. She filled each glass with champagne and returned one to Bobby.

"Here's a toast," she said, clinking glasses. "To a healthy baby and a long and happy life together."

Bobby said, "To a healthy baby," and then Barbara watched awestruck as he drained the entire glass in one gulp.

"All right," she said, and tried the same thing herself. She stopped when there was still an inch left in the glass and offered it to Bobby.

He drank what was there and then lay down next to her, not saying a word. Propped on one elbow, Barbara dragged her hand up and down his stomach. "You have such a magnificent body," she said."I know I really don't deserve you, but I'm going to get better. I promise." She traced his pectoral muscles, bent and kissed his nipples. "As soon as I get done having this baby I'm going to get in shape just like you. They have this club back in Portshead with Nautilus equipment that they let girls work out on. I saw it advertised and I'm going to join. I know how much you hate fat, Bobby, and I'm going to get rid of all of it." She kissed his sternum, kissed his belly. "I just never had anybody to get skinny for, that's all."

"Let's go swimming," he said.

Barbara sat up slowly. "I just don't seem to be able to get through to you. This is supposed to be our honeymoon night."

"That's right," Bobby said, getting out of bed. "So let's do something we'll remember the rest of our lives. We'll go skinny dipping."

"Bobby, no."

"Why not? There's no one else here. You could see that driving in."

"It's too cold."

"Well, I'm going. You can come if you want."

"At least put some clothes on to wear down there."

Bobby went into the bathroom and emerged again with a towel around his hips. Barbara, fumbling through one of her bags, came up with a robe and put it on. Complaining to herself, she followed Bobby out of the cabin, past her car, across the road and onto the beach.

She caught up with him at the water's edge. She was standing next to him as he dropped his towel. She saw his white skin caught in the flash of the cabin light. She saw him step away from her and splash into the water.

"Is it cold, Bobby?" she whispered.

"Jesus, it's freezing," he called back. And then he dove.

It was a calm lake, pitch dark at this time of night. In the daylight she would be able to see islands, maybe even see all the way to the other side. In the summer they operated a ferryboat that took tourists around on half-day cruises. There were homes and summer camps and cabins and campgrounds all along the rim. But right now there was only darkness.

She listened for Bobby to surface and heard the sound about thirty yards from shore. Already he was out of sight.

"Bobby."

"It's like ice, Barb."

She walked in up to her knees, pulling at her robe so that it wouldn't get wet. It didn't seem that cold to her.

She heard his arm hit the water. One stroke. Two. He dove again.

"It's not that bad, Bobby," she called.

There was no answer.

She strained her ears. Had he come up again since that last dive? She couldn't remember. "Bobby, you're too far out. I can't see you."

There was a splash, but it was far away. It couldn't be him, she was sure of it. "Bobby?"

She waited, holding her breath in case she missed something. "Bobby?" She waited again.

"Bobby?" And this time she knew he wasn't going to answer and she threw herself into the water, screaming his name over and over again.

Chris Cage

CHAPTER ONE

Chris Cage looked across the paper-strewn expanse of his desk at the young couple and tried to keep his expression both sympathetic and expectant. His eyebrows were slightly raised; his startling blue eyes were wide and staring without being penetrating. I wish I could do better, his eyes were telling them, but there is nothing more I can do.

Chris's thin-lipped mouth was closed, but his jaw was loosely set; and the couple could see that he was not irrevocably committed to the course of action he was suggesting. If they really wanted to try a different approach, he was at their disposal. He just thought it would be a mistake, that's all.

The woman was crying. She was a big woman, big without being fat or awkward. Just big in the sense that she had big bones and stood close to six feet tall—although she would deny it if asked, and insist that she was only five nine. She had long, straight black hair, worn in the outdated fashion of folk singers, and eyes that were a deeper blue than Chris's. She used them to look at Chris in a way that was both seeking and expressing sympathy. She knew he had worked hard on this case and she did not want to let him down, but at the same time this settlement seemed so unfair.

Chris met her gaze, receiving it like a catcher squatting behind home plate: pulling it in, offering encouragement, lobbing it back to be burned in to him again. In actuality, Chris's expression revealed nothing of what was going on inside his head; which was fortunate because he was daydreaming, imagining how this woman would look with her clothes off, how she would look flat on her back, how she would look with her big blue eyes squeezed shut in ecstasy.

Chris had never been to bed with a woman of her size. He wondered if she would crush him with her long arms and legs, if she would tear the skin off his body with her fingers. He wondered if she would lie there like a huge mountain of flesh and let him crawl all over her.

The woman's husband moved and Chris's reverie came to an end. He turned a "perhaps you can help her cope with this" expression on Phil Porter and Phil responded by getting up from his chair, going behind his wife and gently massaging her shoulders. Phil had strong, capable hands, the kind you would expect a good high school athlete to have. Everything about Phil reminded Chris of a good high school athlete, the sort you would always want on your adult softball team. He would bat Phil fifth, just by the looks of him; maybe second or even third if he proved he could make contact. He would play in the outfield, most likely, since he probably had good speed. . . . Except the reason he was in Chris's office was that he had suffered a bimalleolar fracture. You break your ankle like that and you don't do too much running anywhere, fast or slow. All right, Chris would play him at first base.

Phil looked apologetic. It was a little thing, but Chris picked up on it immediately. Getting to his feet, he said, "Maybe I ought to leave you two alone for a while to talk this over. I'll be out in the hallway until you need me."

Phil stopped massaging and leaned down so that he could see his wife's face. "That okay with you, honey? You want to talk it over?"

Martha Porter nodded miserably. Her eyes closed. The blueness was gone. Showtime was over. Chris stepped outside and shut the door behind him.

He was leaning against the wall when John Gregory poked his perpetually worried-looking face out of his office. "Well?" Gregory said.

Chris shrugged.

Gregory looked up and down the hallway and then made a quick summoning motion with his arm. Chris walked into his office and Gregory eased the door closed.

"They gonna go for it?" Gregory whispered.

"They're talking it over now."

"We've got to have that money, you know."

"I know," Chris said with exaggerated patience.

But Gregory was speaking, he wasn't listening. "We don't have it by the fifteenth, we're not gonna be able to make payroll and you're not going to have what you need to start the Kinsey trial."

"I know, John."

"That case will put this one to shame if Dr. Branigan testifies, but he won't go on the stand unless he gets his two thousand bucks up front."

"For Chrissakes, John, I'm the one who's going to be trying the goddamn Kinsey case. Pushing me's not going to change the situation any."

Gregory's face flushed. He ran his hand through his thinning hair and glared at his junior partner.

"Look, John," Chris said, his tone more conciliatory. "We've been through this a hundred times already. What do you think I went to Burt Carpenter for? I held out until trial, Porter's case would be worth another twenty, twenty-five thousand, easy. But everybody says we can't afford to wait that long. We've got to have money now in order to put on Kinsey. The staff's got to get paid. You and Bill and I haven't gotten our draw in six weeks. So I go to Carpenter and I spend three days talking him into getting his client to come up with fifty. Then I get the Porters in here and I spend practically the whole afternoon telling them how wonderful fifty thousand bucks is for a few hours of intense pain, a couple of months of inconvenience, and a lifetime of restricted movement. They look at me like a dummy and tell me how the goddamn attorney who sent them to us told them they had a million-dollar case."

"Who's giving you the trouble, him or her?"

"Neither one's giving me trouble. They're both nice people; they just don't understand, that's all."

"You told them how difficult liability is?"

"I told them. But the goddamn referring attorney convinced them it was a lock. Go up to San Francisco. See Gregory, Bunton and Cage, he says. They'll get you a million bucks just like that."

"Who's the referring attorney?"

"Smiley White, case-chaser extraordinaire."

"I suppose we owe him a third."

"Third of our net, that's right."

"Shit."

Chris Cage raised his hands in a show of helplessness.

"We get our expenses back, we'll be lucky to clear ten thousand bucks." Gregory pretended to be musing, but they both knew he was really complaining.

"All I can tell you, John, is that if we get the Porters to sign the releases, Shirley can walk them over to Carpenter's office and Carpenter says he'll put the check in her hot little hand. If we don't give Smiley his share right away, we'll be almost twenty thousand bucks fatter by nightfall."

John Gregory's mood improved considerably. "So you think they'll go for it?"

"He's talking to her now, that's all I can say."

"It's his injury, isn't it?"

"She's on the complaint, too. Loss of consortium, nursing services. If it were up to him alone, he'd just as soon get his ass out of here. But she's the thinker in the family, so she's the one I've been working on. . . ."

Gregory went behind his desk and sat down. "I'm sorry, Chris. I know you're doing the best you can and it's not your fault things are the way they are."

Chris put his hands in his pockets and stared out through one of Gregory's windows at the single lane of traffic moving along the street. The words John Gregory had just spoken meant something different to him than they would have to anybody else. "Bill come in late today?"

Gregory, his hands covering his face, said, "About eleven. Face red, eyes red, breath stinking of Lavoris. Who the hell uses mouthwash at eleven o'clock in the morning, huh? He goes in his office, closes the door, I hear him start dictating. I swear to God, it's the same dictation I heard him doing yesterday."

"He's just got the machine going?"

"How the hell do I know? Maybe Rose Mary Woods came in and erased his tape during the night, so he has to do it all over again. I'm just afraid if I go in there and catch him asleep I'll wring his fat little neck."

Gregory might have said something more, but just then the intercom signaled and Shirley came over the loudspeaker asking for Chris. The Porters, she said, were ready to see him again.

Martha Porter twisted a lump of Kleenex into an unrecognizable knot. "We've decided to hold out," she said. She spoke the words proudly, as if she and her husband had just reconciled their marital difficulties and were prepared to live out the rest of their lives in connubial bliss.

"Okay," Chris said, picking up the telephone. "I'll just call the defense attorney and tell him the whole thing's off and we'll continue getting ready for trial." He tapped out a few numbers on the push-button plate and then stopped. Still holding the phone, he said, "You understand, of course, all that this means."

74

Martha nodded. Phil said, "What?"

Chris hung up the phone. "Well, we're sitting here like Caesar on the banks of the Rubicon. Once we cross over, we're committed. So far we've got, what, a couple of thousand bucks in expenses. From here on in we really start spending money, and that all comes out of your take in the end—assuming you get one. Once we start trial, anything can happen. We could get a bum jury—we could get stuck with a panel full of engineers, nurses and retired military people. Our expert witness could fall apart—I've seen that happen more than once. We could very well lose this case. We could win and get less than fifty. We could get forty or twenty or even sixteen five, which is all we really have in medicals and lost wages. Who knows? Maybe the jury will find you comparatively negligent; give you an award and take away a percentage of it. Or maybe we'll hit big, in which case the defense will be sure to appeal, hanging us up for another year at least. Then, too, the moment we start trial my fee goes up from one third to forty percent. So there are a lot of things to think about when you're comparing the possibilities of a trial with the sure thing of a settlement."

Martha had worked the Kleenex to the point where it was falling apart. She looked for someplace to put it. Chris leaned across his desk and held out his hand. She hesitated and then gave it to him, then watched as he did not throw it away. He put it in his pocket and she saw him do it.

"I don't know, Martie, maybe we shouldn't screw around," Phil said.

Martha's eyes were fixed on Chris. They were assessing him now, looking for cracks, blemishes, weak spots. Chris looked back at her with the open innocence of a choirboy. Whatever you want, Martha, his face said.

Once again she began to cry and Phil, very quickly, glanced at Chris for instructions. Chris pursed his lips and flicked his index finger toward the door.

"Why don't you let me speak to Martie for a minute, Phil?" he said, and Phil gratefully hobbled from the room.

Chris got out of his chair and fed Martha Porter a new Kleenex. He sat on a corner of the desk and dangled one foot in the air. "What you've got to understand, Martha, is that Phil isn't really hurt all that badly. I mean, a bimalleolar fracture is nothing to laugh at, but look at him now. He's young. He's strong. The only thing he can't do is play racquetball, and I'm not sure how much a jury's going to think that's worth."

75

"But he loved playing racquetball. It was the only thing that ever got him out of the house."

Chris laughed. She looked up, startled. Then she realized what she had said and laughed with him.

"I guess you're going to be stuck with him every night," Chris said. She nodded and patted away the last of her tears.

"Looks like you'll just have to find a way to get out yourself. Hell, maybe you can start playing racquetball."

"Oh, shit," she said ruefully. She blew her nose and laughed again, this time with embarrassment. "Let's just get this thing over with."

Chris leaned down from his desktop perch. "Tell you what," he said, squeezing her shoulder. "We'll call Phil back in here, get the releases signed, and then I'll take you both out and buy you a drink in celebration. Sound okay to you?"

"Thanks," she said. "I'd like that." She smiled at him and Chris squeezed her shoulder once more, letting his fingers dally a little longer this time, letting his eyes hold hers until she felt compelled to look down into the new ball of tissue she had rolled.

They talked about the 49ers as they sat in a booth in the main part of the glass-walled bar on the ground floor of the Transamerica Building. Phil knew the team best, but he didn't argue any of his opinions when they differed from Chris's. Martha offered a few insights of her own, and there was nothing wrong with any of them; they just did not ignite any follow-up comments from the two men. Chris looked at her with rapt attention when she started explaining why she thought the 'Niners could get away with the crew of linebackers they had, but he was not hearing her words so much as watching the way she talked. The concentration he was giving her kept him from immediately noticing the arrival of the short, handsome man in the gray suit, checked shirt and striped tie. It was Martha who glanced at him first.

Leigh Rossville stood there with a drink in his hand and smiled his smile of thirty-two perfect white teeth. He professed great interest in the state of Chris's physical and mental well-being, but Chris knew the real reason he was standing there oozing charm. So he introduced him to Martha, long, tall Martha with the deep blue eyes; and then, to be polite, he introduced him to husband Phil, he with the outfielder's legs and the first baseman's ankle.

Leigh squeezed into the booth next to Chris. He would just finish his drink and then he had to go. One of the neighbors was having a barbecue and he had to get home for that. It was in honor of Roarke Robinson, who had just bought a house up the street.

Phil Porter sat up straight. "Not *the* Roarke Robinson? Not the baseball player?"

Leigh smiled bashfully. The Bay Area newspapers had recently been filled with the story of how the Oakland A's had purchased the contract of the aging Yankee slugger, and Chris waited for Leigh to explain to the Porters how it was that Robinson happened to be moving to his street.

But Leigh didn't explain. He simply sat there beaming at the lovely Mrs. Porter until Chris felt compelled to intercede.

"Leigh's with the firm of Rossville, Dailey, Cheshire and Cooper," Chris said, and waited again before adding, "Leigh's father is Leigh Rossville senior. . . . He handled the negotiations for the A's."

"Jesus," Phil gushed, his face brightening for the first time that day. "Did you get involved?"

"Well," Leigh said, modestly lowering his eyes, "tangentially."

Chris had seen this routine before. He stared at Leigh just long enough to let him know that he knew what was going on and then he said, "Part of the deal was that the A's had to buy Robinson a house, and since he's been living in New York for the past fifteen years he didn't know where to look. Leigh's job was to find him one. So he got up one morning, walked three doors up the street to the first For Sale sign he saw, agreed to the asking price, turned around, and went back to bed. Then he billed the A's for a week's worth of looking."

"It was a tough assignment, but somebody had to do it." Leigh grinned at Martha over the top of his glass, and when she smiled back he winked at her. Chris caught the movement and his stomach seized for an instant at the prospect that things could suddenly get very uncomfortable around the table unless his none-too-subtle friend was steered off in a new direction.

"Tell me," he said, "how have the toney denizens of Tranton Park taken the news that you're personally responsible for bringing one of our third world brethren into their midst?"

"Hey," Leigh said, tearing his eyes away from Martha and missing entirely the tongue-in-cheek inflection in Chris's voice. "You'd think it was Prince Charles who's moving in, for God's sake, the way everyone's acting. The only one who pretends he's not excited is John Clarke Lane, and he tells me he doesn't know who Roarke Robinson is. I tell him, 'He's only one of the best hitters in all of baseball,' and John Clarke looks at me like: baseball? Is that something they do on the moon? So then I say to him, 'The A's are only going to pay him eight hundred thou per, for three years,' and John Clarke sniffs, you know the way he does, and says, 'Well, as long as he can afford to live here, I don't care what color he is.' And I had to laugh, you know, because I'd never mentioned the fact that Roarke Robinson is black."

"Jesus," Phil said. "Roarke Robinson."

Leigh nodded gravely and turned his attention once again to Phil's wife. Quickly Chris asked him who was putting on the barbecue.

"Jay and Janice Butler, but it was everybody's idea. The women are all playing guessing games about his wife, the men are all trying to figure out how they're supposed to act. Blinky Gould says, 'Suppose he doesn't want to come? Suppose he doesn't like to meet the public?' Do you believe it? I said to him, 'Blinky, if there's one thing a baseball player with a high school education and eight hundred thousand bucks in his pocket wants to meet, it's an investment counselor.' So that calms him down. So then Gary Martel calls me up. He says, 'Leigh, what about the fact that there won't be any other minorities at the barbecue—you think that he'll notice that?' I say, 'Gary, I think he'll notice that right off the bat.' Gary says, 'Well, listen, there's this guy in my office who's black. Maybe we should invite him.' It takes me about an hour to get him talked out of that idea and then—listen to what he says next—he says, 'All right, if we're not going to do anything special because he's black, then we've got to make sure we do nothing that looks special. No watermelon. No ribs.' " Leigh slapped the table. "Can't you just picture it? All of us standing around with Velveeta sandwiches and glasses of milk, trying desperately not to make ethnic references. 'Golly, Mr. Robinson, I sure do think you'll find it keen around here.' "

The monologue brought faint smiles to the faces of Chris and Martha and a look of wistful longing to Phil Porter. Obviously disappointed that nobody had laughed harder, Leigh finished his drink and made a move to get up.

Chris nudged him with his elbow and motioned with his head. "I've got to talk with you for a second about something before you go," he said.

The two men excused themselves and slipped out of the booth. It was

78

Friday night crowded in the bar and they had to push their way all across the room before they found space to talk.

"Hey," Chris said, "what do you think?"

"Oh, God, I'm in love. Who are these people? Where did you find this woman and what's she doing with that goofball? Please tell me he's her brother or her chauffeur or her bodyguard or something like that."

"He's her husband and he's my client and he's really a pretty good guy if you give him a chance."

"Good. You take the guy, I'll take the wife."

"How about taking all of us? To the barbecue, I mean."

Leigh looked back across the room, his head bobbing around as he searched for the booth where the Porters were sitting. "Gee, I can't do that."

Chris slipped his hand inside Leigh's elbow. "Why the hell not? The kid wants to meet Robinson, for crying out loud. We bring him, we bring her."

"Lots of good that's going to do me. My wife's going to be there. Hello Cath, goodbye Martha."

Chris jostled him good-naturedly. "Ah, you don't want her. She's an Amazon, for Chrissake. She stands up, she's probably got four inches on you."

Leigh started to tell him he had a few inches for her, and then a look of enlightenment spread slowly across his face. Chris saw it and responded with a great show of shock.

"Hey, c'mon, Leigh. She's a client, remember?"

"Oh, that's right. Canon of Ethics number one-two-three bullshit: No diddling clients."

Chris dropped his voice into a tone of compelling seriousness. "Look, these are nice people and I feel a little sorry for them. They just accepted a settlement with asshole Carpenter, and neither one of them's very happy about it. They agreed, of course, but I think they feel I pressured them into it and I don't want them going away saying bad things about me. So I'm asking you, that's all. A personal favor."

Leigh stroked his chin and looked at his wristwatch. "I don't know, Chris, it's not my party."

"Leigh, a party's a party. Nobody's gonna care if two or three more people show up, and I'll take full responsibility for them. I'll make sure neither one pisses in the bushes and I promise not to make fun of your Jaguar the next three times it breaks down."

Leigh hesitated.

Chris's hand went from Leigh's near elbow to his far shoulder. "Ah, it's only a cookout," he whispered. "There'll be enough food for everybody."

"Ah, what the hell," said Leigh, just as Chris had always known he would.

Jay Butler was a dentist. His wife, Janice, was a dentist's wife who always made reservations in the name of Dr. and Mrs. Butler and who occasionally referred to her husband as "the doctor," as in "When the doctor and I first got married . . ." Janice Butler looked as though she had once been very attractive and now bleached her hair, rubbed avocados on her face and wore expensive clothes to make up for the facts that she had turned gray, developed wrinkles and put on a good deal of weight around her hips. She liked to speak of her cheerleader's legs and her cheerleading days. She liked to give the impression that she had been relatively wild as a kid, but nobody believed her.

Jay and Janice had one child, Arthur. He had been known as a fairly good athlete until he was about sixteen, and then he had undergone a rather dramatic personality change. He had become much less competitive, much quieter, and much happier. He began to sing to himself, to giggle at odd moments, and to smile at everyone. He also began to forget things; but Jay and Janice felt he had become such a nice kid that they sucked up their pride as his grades fell from Stanford to USC to Cal State to junior college application level. At that point, somewhere around the D's of Arthur's senior year, they bravely announced to their friends that Arthur was simply going to have to make it in life on the basis of his personality. "He's just such a delight to be around," Janice said. And in truth he was easy to be around. As he served drinks at his parents' party he was blissfully polite to all his parents' friends and never once got mad when anyone asked about his earring or his spiked hairdo.

It was Arthur who greeted Leigh and his entourage as they stepped through the gate at the end of the driveway and entered the backyard. "Hi," he said. "How are ya? . . . Would you like a drink? . . . I'm doing good. . . . That's nice. . . ." And then he turned and drifted away and the four perplexed newcomers were left holding unknown and unordered concoctions in their suddenly sweaty hands.

80

From where he stood, just inside the gate, Chris could see the Martels, the Lindsays, the Goulds, the Butlers, the Hartrys, and a dozen other people whom he didn't recognize. Most were dressed nicely casual, but holding court at one end of the cement patio was a silver-haired, silver-mustached man in a bow tie and a pin-striped suit. Chris knew this pillar of civility to be the redoubtable John Clarke Lane, senior partner in a law firm even bigger than that founded by Leigh's father, scourge to plaintiffs' attorneys throughout California.

Chris was still staring at him when Janice Butler came up to them, effusing all the graciousness that she associated with hostessing. "How nice to see you, Leigh. And you've brought your friend Chris. Hello, Chris, I haven't seen you since tennis. And who might these people be?"

Leigh tried to introduce the Porters, but he forgot Phil's name and an awkward moment occurred when he sort of waved his hand at him. "Phil," said Chris. "Phil and Martha Porter. Friends of mine."

"How nice," said Janice. Then, turning to Leigh, she pressed his striped tie flat against his checked shirt. "And how unusual you look, Leigh. Dressed yourself, did you?" Before he could respond, Janice spun halfway around and said, "Have any of you seen my son Arthur? I saw him coming out with a round of drinks for the Hartrys and the Goulds and I don't have the faintest idea what he did with them."

Suddenly she was gone, and a moment later Leigh, his eyes fixed on his tie, mumbled something to himself and wandered off before anyone could catch the gist of what he was saying.

Chris, caught unexpectedly by Leigh's sudden departure, surveyed the clumps of guests. "So," he said, "I guess Roarke isn't here yet."

"Maybe," Phil said, holding his untouched drink in both hands, "Martie and I really ought to go. We have a lot of stuff we have to do this weekend and, ah, it's gonna take us a long time to get home."

"Nonsense," Chris said. He took all three of their drinks and put them down in the grass. "Let's go over here and pour ourselves something we recognize. I'm as anxious to meet Roarke Robinson as you are and if you leave me I'm not going to have anybody to talk to."

They ended up getting beers, Moosehead beers, out of a trash can filled with bottles embedded in shaved ice. They drank Moosehead and ate deviled eggs and picked at the fruit salad.

"This sure is a big house," said Phil.

"It's a beautiful house." His wife's voice was filled with admiration.

Chris stared at the back of the house, trying to imagine it as the Porters saw it. He remembered when it was being built. He remembered when the whole neighborhood was being built and each house was designed to be unique in character on nearly identical half-acre lots. The one the Butlers owned was California-Georgian in motif and it had always reminded Chris of a Monopoly piece plunked down in the middle of a square.

"What do you think a place like this costs?" Phil said; and after a moment he answered himself. "Half a million, easy."

Martha glanced uncertainly at Chris. "You don't live around here, do you?"

Chris laughed. "I live in a condo in the city."

Martha nodded and waited for more. But Chris was swallowing beer and then studying the label on his bottle.

"Alone?" she said. Then, as though afraid he hadn't heard, she said, louder, "Do you live alone?"

"Yeah," said Chris, smiling.

Martha responded with a small laugh and then cut her eyes quickly to her husband. Seeing that he was not paying attention, she still sought to explain herself. "It used to be you just asked someone if they were married. Nowadays, with people living together and everything, you kind of phrase it different. First you say, 'Are you living with anyone?' and then you ask if they're married."

"And if they say no you ask if they ever have been."

Martha nodded, an impish grin stretching the corners of her mouth. "So how about you, Chris, you ever been married?"

"No."

"Any children?"

Chris burst out laughing so suddenly that Phil, his face smiling in good-natured bewilderment, was brought back into the conversational pattern. "Jesus, Phil," Chris said, "I think your wife has just blazed a new inroad into California etiquette."

Phil turned his smile questioningly on Martha, but she only gave him the briefest of glances and continued talking directly to Chris. "Well, you know, that's not such a social stigma anymore, either, is it? Not in swinging San Francisco, I mean."

"Oh, hell, I don't know that San Francisco's so different from anyplace else. I used to think so, but I'm not sure anymore."

"I've heard that if you're a guy in San Francisco you're either gay, married or lucky."

Chris chuckled and looked at the ground. "Yeah, I've heard that myself."

"So which are you?"

Martha was smiling, Phil was smiling, Chris was smiling. And they were all different smiles. "None of the above," Chris said. "I'm just a guy who spends his days working and his nights wondering where the days go."

"That doesn't sound healthy," Martha said, her voice suddenly sympathetic.

"It's not. Neither physically nor mentally." Chris's beer was gone. He put the bottle aside and drew another out of the ice. He took the top off and started to drink out of the bottle. Then he stopped and handed it to Phil. Now Phil held a bottle in each hand as Chris drew out another for himself.

"The weird thing is, I don't even know how it got this way." He smiled. "It wasn't part of the plan when I started out, believe me."

The three of them drank in silence for a few moments. Phil had gone back to inspecting the rest of the partygoers and his face had assumed a puzzled expression. "These people," he said. "I mean, like, is this the crowd you normally hang out with?"

Chris felt genuinely surprised that someone would ask him that. "Not really," he said. "I'm a friend of Leigh's and that's about the extent of my connection." He shrugged, feeling something more needed to be said, if only to keep the conversation from dying again. "To tell you the truth, I'm not even sure this crowd hangs around with each other. From what I can see, about the only thing most of these people have in common is that they can afford to live here. Like this guy, the bald one with the plaid sport coat and the video camera on his shoulder. His name's Blinky Gould and he's about the nicest man you'd ever want to meet. Makes around two million dollars a year—but he's also the sort of guy who learned to ride a bicycle when he was about sixteen. If we were still in school, people would be tying his shoes together and he'd be falling on his face. Still, here he is, beautiful house, cute little wife . . ."

Chris gestured toward the other end of the yard. "Then there's the guy over there, the one with the bow tie. See him? He's a defense attorney who actually refers to himself by both his first and middle names. I usually try to avoid talking to him at all costs, but sooner or later somebody who thinks that lawyers are absolutely rabid to speak with each other will push us together and I'll be stuck listening to his

83

acid-tongued diatribe against ambulance-chasers, the decline of the work ethic, and the Communistic threat being imposed on us by lily-livered Democrats and the left-wing news media."

Phil nodded, marking John Clarke Lane as the embodiment of everything Chris had just said. "Which one is his wife?"

Chris glanced around. "I doubt she's here. Rumor has it there's something wrong with her. Some sort of emotional problem. Leigh and Cathy Rossville have lived next door to the Lanes for several years and, if I'm not mistaken, they've never even met her."

Phil's question might have been prompted by a group of people standing just a few feet away. Chris recognized the auburn mane of Aurora Weissock as she stood with her back to him. Next to her was a diminutive lady with short, very dark hair, a single dimple, and round eyeglasses that seemed far too big for her pretty little face. It was Marietta Gould, and Chris tried to get her to notice him so that he could wave to her, perhaps get her to come over to meet the Porters. But Marietta's attention was on someone else.

Chris leaned in her direction and saw that she was listening to Gary Martel, a coarse-looking, swarthy man with something of a barrel-shaped physique. "And this John Irving," Gary was saying, "have you read him?"

"Yes," said Marietta softly.

Aurora's eyes were roaming. "John who?" she said.

"Irving. He wrote a book called *Garp. The Gospel According to Garp.*"

"*World,*" corrected Marietta.

"Oh," said Aurora. "The one with Robin Williams."

"I'm talking about the book. You feeling good about yourself, Aurora? Feeling pretty good about life? Read this thing. It'll turn your stomach."

"I liked it," Marietta said sweetly.

Gary Martel regarded her as if he had just seen her hatch an egg. "What I want to know," he said, choosing his words deliberately, "is what kind of mind the man must have to write the things he writes. I mean, how can he even think those things in the first place? Never mind put them down on a piece of paper for other people to have to look at. He's got to be some sort of deviate." He issued his final sentence as though it were a proclamation; as though any further argument would be grounds for a scream, a gob of spit, a punch in the face. Marietta, who clearly wanted none of those things, simply smiled. Aurora, her teeth nibbling the edge of her plastic glass, tucked one arm around her rib cage and casually slipped away from the conversation.

Chris was just about to speak to Marietta when a pair of hands suddenly slipped around his waist and he was pulled into an embrace from behind. He knew right away whose hands they were and he turned and kissed Cathy Rossville on the cheek. She laughed and held her face against Chris's chest for a moment. When Chris introduced the Porters she gave them each a warm handshake and welcomed them as though she meant it. They practically leaped at her in gratitude.

Of all the people at the party, Cathy was dressed the most informally. Her sandy hair fell in natural, almost tangled waves that cascaded well past her shoulders; she had on no discernible makeup, and she was wearing an open-neck shirt that stretched tight across her bosom and then slanted radically into the slim waist of her faded jeans. The jeans were Levi's and they were as tight as a Danskin leotard across her hips and down her legs.

"So, you guys here to meet Roarke?" she said.

Chris nodded. "He's still coming, isn't he?"

"Hah. Wouldn't that be hysterical?"

Before Cathy could finish laughing, another voice cut in. Janice Butler, who had returned to the refreshment table to make sure everything was in its assigned position, said, "That would be a real joke, Cathy, after everything I've gone through."

"Oh, c'mon now, Janice, lighten up. Roarke's just another person like everybody else."

Janice patted one of the cakes into place. It apparently had slipped off the direct center of its plate. "Oh, what do I care about an old baseball player anyway? It's his wife I'm interested in. What did you say her name was?"

"Ann." Cathy said the word as if she knew it was a hard one to pronounce and that was why Janice must have forgotten.

"Ann," Janice repeated. "And Leigh said they have two kids in their early teens, is that right?"

"A boy twelve and a girl sixteen."

"Well, they must have gotten married awfully early, if he's only thirty-eight. My guess is she's somebody he knew from home. Wherever that is."

"Leigh said he grew up in South Carolina."

"Wherever that is," Janice Butler repeated. Staring worriedly at her watch, she walked away.

85

Cathy Rossville glanced at Chris with a half-suppressed smirk on her face. Chris looked at the grass between his feet and Cathy's eyes slipped past him to the Porters. Both she and Martha suddenly burst into laughter.

Reaching across Chris and touching Martha on the arm, Cathy said, "Isn't she a howl? She's sure Ann Robinson's going to turn out to be this little old Aunt Jemima that Roarke's been dragging around with him from city to city."

"Speaking of little old ladies," Chris said, "has your husband found you yet?"

Cathy's eyes narrowed as she struggled to put the two halves of Chris's sentence together. "Oh," she said, "you mean about the tie?"

"He didn't go home to change, did he?"

"Never let it be said that Leigh Rossville is immune to public opinion."

"Even when expressed by Janice Butler?"

"That, my dear, is how we come to know what public opinion is."

There was a flutter at the gate and everyone turned to see what was causing it. Jay Butler literally ran across the lawn, wiping his hands on a towel. He pushed his way through a small knot of people and a moment later emerged with an escort hold on two handsome people. The man was a rich brown color, with a strong, prominent forehead, large eyes and a tapered jawline. He was smiling and happily shaking every hand that was thrust in front of him. On his arm, looking strangely removed from the whole process, was the erstwhile Aunt Jemima. Ann Robinson was nearly as tall as Martha Porter. She had shimmering yellow hair, pale skin and eyes as blue as a summer sky. She virtually radiated beauty.

In the center of the backyard Janice Butler valiantly maintained her composure and accepted Ann Robinson's hand as if it were a bouquet of flowers. She stepped away after the briefest exchange of greetings and June Hartry took her place. Then Marietta Gould stepped in. Then Gary Martel and his imported wife, Eva. Circling the pack of bodies was Blinky Gould with his video camera, trying to get everybody to smile and generally acting as if he were taking a series of snapshots.

Chris turned to Phil, who was on his tiptoes, straining to catch a glimpse. "Go on over there and introduce yourself," he urged him. "Robinson's never met any of these people before. He doesn't know who lives here and who doesn't."

Just then the gate opened and Leigh Rossville, wearing a black sport shirt with the insignia of a polo player on it, came striding into the yard. Chris whispered in Cathy's ear and she immediately took Phil's hand and said, "C'mon. I'll get Leigh to introduce you." She pulled him away before he had a chance to decline.

Martha waited. "Thank you for doing that," she said after they were out of earshot. "You've really been very nice." She put her bottle down on a table and held her hands in front of her, fingers intertwined. "I'm sorry about this afternoon. All the crying and everything. And I just want you to know that Phil and I really are grateful for all you've done. I even know that everything you told us was true. . . . It's just that we were counting on so much more."

"That's all right," Chris said. "The defense was counting on so much less."

Martha looked around at the Butlers' house and the houses on either side of them, the Martels' colonial and the Hartrys' mock Tudor. "You see what we've had to go through to end up with a few thousand dollars and it makes you wonder who can afford all this. What they must have done to get here, I mean."

Chris thought about what she had said for a moment. "Well, my friend Leigh was born the son of a rich and successful lawyer. There was never much question but that he would be a rich and successful lawyer himself. Some of these other people, though, they're a different story. Guys like John Clarke Lane have sacrificed all their lives so that they could make the world a better place for insurance companies. My premium, right or wrong; that's the motto John Clarke has instilled in all his clients. And Dr. Butler, here. Ever since he was a little boy, all he wanted to do was stick his fingers in people's mouths and jerk their teeth out. It was either go to jail or dental school for this strange predilection, and his guidance counselor wisely directed him to dental school. His has been a course of singular commitment, and this house—why, this is just a place to while away the hours between extractions."

Martha Porter had been listening seriously at first. Now she cocked her head. "Why do I keep getting the feeling you're not just the workaholic attorney you make yourself out to be?"

Chris turned so that they were standing directly in front of each other. His eyes roamed back and forth across her face, taking in every nuance of her expression. "C'mon," he said. "Let me show you the house."

Slowly she swiveled her head toward the crowd of people standing

87

around the Robinsons. She could easily have said no. She could even have accepted the invitation as it ostensibly was issued. But when she looked back at Chris, when she met his gaze and nodded her head, both of them knew she was not just accepting a guided tour, and Chris's heart slipped into racing gear.

They walked around the food tables and across the patio. They went up four or five stairs and entered a back door. "This way," Chris said, and directed her to a staircase that led to the second floor. From there he guided her into the first dark room they came across.

Initially they were very conscious of the time. Martha had let him undress her in the middle of the floor, reaching down and holding him through the cloth of his pants while he unbuttoned her blouse, slid his hands across her skin, pushed up her bra.

She had stood with her head thrown back, her hands on her hips, her black hair dropping straight toward the floor as Chris had buried his face in the thin, silky material of her underwear. She had moved her legs apart. He had held her buttocks in his hands and she had pushed herself into him. And they had forgotten all about time.

The underwear had come down and Chris had stayed on his knees. He thought of her as a goddess, standing there in the center of the room, her back arched, her breasts thrust up in the air, her leather boots the only article of clothing she was still wearing. Six feet tall and powerfully built. He tried to tilt his head back so that he could see her, so that he could remember her in just this position.

"Oh," she said. "Oh, my God." She grabbed the back of his head and pulled him close, thrusting herself forward so that Chris had to tighten his hold on her in order to keep them both from falling over. "Oh, I've wanted you ever since I first saw you," she gasped.

The tendons in her thighs stood out in isolated ridges as her legs bent forward, and Chris sank deeper beneath her. He shifted his own legs, moving them out in front of him until he was lying flat on his back and she was kneeling above him, balancing on her knees and the toes of her boots. She reached her hand between her legs and guided him to her, lifting his head off the floor, holding him up. And that was the position they were in when the door opened and the light from the upstairs hallway came streaming into the room.

It all happened in an instant. Martha went as still as a photograph.

Chris, impossibly trapped, tried to spin to see who was there. A figure stood briefly framed by the light and then the door was pulled shut.

"Oh, shit," Martha said, the words rolling slowly out of her mouth. Then urgency overtook her and she began grabbing her clothes as quickly as she could, stabbing around in the darkness for her underwear, her bra, her slacks, her blouse.

Chris, who had to do nothing but tuck in his shirt, pull up his tie, put on his suit jacket, was following her about the room. "Was it him?" he whispered.

"It was a woman," she said. "Goddamnit, how do I get myself into these messes?"

"What woman?" he said. "Could you see who it was?"

"She was just a shadow. An outline. And she was only there for a second. Jesus Christ, what am I going to do now?"

"Look." Chris took her by the shoulders. She tried to wrench free and he gripped her tighter, wanting to calm her down, wanting to calm himself down. "You think whoever it was is going to go running downstairs and tell your husband? You think she's going to shout it out to everyone?"

They were both silent, listening. Somehow they had not noticed before that the noise of the party filtered into the room. They heard Jay Butler call to his son Arthur. They heard him call a second time. They heard Blinky Gould yelling at everybody to wave into the camera. They heard a very loud, deep and resonant laugh, a sound so foreign they both knew it had come from Roarke Robinson.

"I can't go out there again," Martha said.

Chris sighed. He moved behind her, lifted her hair and kissed her gently on the neck. It was meant to be a soothing kiss, it was meant to show her everything was going to be all right after all. When she did not move away from the kiss he pressed into her and again she made no effort to get away.

"Don't worry," Chris said as he moved his hips ever so softly against her. He had things under control again, he was sure.

He was wrong. Martha suddenly jerked herself away from him. "My God," she gasped.

Chris, startled, reached out to pull her back, but she would have none of it. She was staring at him with such incredulity that he began to feel extremely foolish standing there in front of her.

"You're right," he said, dropping his hands to his sides. He wanted to apologize, but he was uncertain as to what he should say, how far he should go. "I wasn't thinking," he said. "I was . . . well, for a second I just lost my head."

Martha Porter said nothing and Chris, because his eyes were on the floor, could no longer tell how she was regarding him. And then he felt her hand touch his cheek. The smooth skin of her palm ran down the length of his jaw. Encouraged, he looked up at the exact moment she drew back her hand and softly cuffed him.

Before he could react she was gone. The door opened and closed behind her and Chris was left standing alone in the darkness of the room.

"Damn," he said aloud.

From down in the backyard came the sound of the same deep resonant voice he and Martha had heard laughing a short time before. "What?" it shouted. "No ribs? How can you have a barbecue without no ribs?"

CHAPTER TWO

The victory, for some reason, just made him feel sadder; although Chris would not have used the word "sad" to describe the way he felt. Depressed, he would have said; or perhaps, given the company and the moment, bummed out. Leigh, though, appeared to be oblivious of his mood.

"Beer," sneered Leigh, addressing the plastic cup in Chris's hand. "One should only drink beer while playing softball. The most proletarian of drinks for the most proletarian of sports."

Chris looked into his cup protectively, and then he slowly raised his eyes until they focused on the top of his friend's head. "Has it come to this? I'm being lectured on my drinking habits by a man with a propeller on his hat?"

Leigh swept the blue and gold beanie from his head and held it out as if it were the skull of Yorick. Gazing at it admiringly, he said, " 'Tis a great day for the University of California, laddie, and you should be wearing the colors your ownself."

They were standing in the middle of Berkeley's Faculty Club, amid what seemed to be a thousand or more Bear Backers and their friends, acquaintances and assorted hangers-on, all reveling in the momentary glory of their team's unexpected and pronounced victory over the vastly superior forces from that noted football factory down south. The annual Cal-USC game had been played to a sellout crowd; the November air was clear and warm; and Leigh and Chris had been drinking since the Fiji cocktail party at eleven-thirty that morning. And only Leigh was happy.

He was trying to replace his hat. "Now," he said, as he stumbled from one foot to the other, "it's time for your quiz. If beer is the proper drink for the proletarian sports, what, pray tell, is the proper drink for football?"

Chris squinted at him, unsure if he wanted to bother responding. "Beer," he said after a moment.

Leigh, planting his beanie as securely as if it were a flagpole, made a noise that sounded like an aggravating, obnoxious buzzer. "Wrong. Football, being the mainstay of institutions such as this one, ipso facto requires an educated tongue." He thrust out his own tongue, then he hoisted his plastic cup into the air, sloshing some of its contents on the tweeded sleeve of an aging blond whose angered look would have cut him dead if only he had been paying attention. "Bourbon is the drink of football," he cried. "Or Scotch, if you're so inclined. Surely you remember that from our cherished undergraduate days."

"I only remember drinking beer."

"That," said Leigh with a twinkle in his eye, "is because you're confusing the after-game fraternity parties, where drinking beer was de rigueur, with the during-game activity of swigging from a flask."

"It seems to me that we used to smoke pot at the games."

Leigh glanced extravagantly around the main room in which they were standing. He actually bent his knees and swept his upper body in a semicircle. "Now you're dating yourself, my ancient companion. You want some of these young lovelies who might be casting covetous eyes our way to think that at one time we might have been antiestablishment, semi-hip members of the counterculture of the sixties? You must never do that, Chris. You must never let on that we are anything but upwardly mobile urban professionals who want only to purchase things for ourselves and those who sleep with us."

Leigh was beaming at someone over Chris's shoulder and Chris turned disinterestedly to see who it was. What he saw was a willowy brunette in her early twenties who seemed distinctly out of place among the alumni and who was doing her absolute best to stare right through the two of them.

"I think she likes you, Leigh," Chris muttered. "I can tell by the way she refuses to acknowledge you exist."

"Ah, there's your problem," Leigh answered, taking his eyes off the young woman only when her date returned to slip a drink into her hand. "You're too easily daunted."

"Maybe," said Chris, shrugging. "Maybe that explains why the Kinsey jury voted against me. They recognized right away that I was a man who drank the wrong things, didn't project the right image, was easily daunted. . . ."

Leigh, who had begun a new scan of the room, slowly slid his eyes back to Chris. "Hey, I draw on the old man's half a century of season tickets, don't even offer one to my wife, drag you out so you can sit on the fifty-yard line for the game of the year, and all you want to do is use the opportunity to turn morose on me."

"It was only the most unbelievable jury verdict of all times," Chris insisted. "That's no reason to turn morose, is it? I mean, nine to three that a motorist who crosses over a white line, smashes into an oncoming motorcycle and leaves the poor fucking motorcyclist a paraplegic is not guilty of negligence. It seems to me, I get hit by a jury verdict like that, I'm entitled to feel any damn way I please."

The look of mock annoyance Leigh had been showing disappeared. He tried to move Chris out of the stream of people who were pushing and shoving around them. He tried to get him to a spot where they could speak without shouting for all the world to hear. "C'mon, buddy," he said quietly. "You can't go on blaming yourself for that. It wasn't your fault."

"Whose fault was it, then?" Chris snapped, not caring to speak quietly. "The thing we were fighting over was damages. I mean, the guy was driving a car belonging to a company that had a million dollars' worth of insurance. The only question in anybody's mind was how much of it Kinsey was going to get. My doctors say he needs the whole million for his past and future medicals. Their doctor says he only needs a couple of hundred thousand. The jury says he doesn't get a bloody cent." He pulled away from Leigh, expanding the gap between them. "Jesus Christ, you tell me not to be morose now. . . . You should have seen me earlier this week when I was sitting at home by myself, wondering if I shouldn't just stick my head in the oven."

Leigh, alarmed because people were beginning to turn around to see who could possibly be saying such things amid all the frivolity and high jinks, inclined his head until he was speaking directly into Chris's ear. "You figured out yet if you've got any grounds for appeal, new trial, anything like that?"

The thought brought a new note into Chris's voice. "Oh, do I have grounds," he said. "My investigator has interviewed the whole jury and we're convinced we've got one of them cold on misconduct. . . . Of course, you're asking me and what do I know? I was convinced this same juror never should have been allowed to sit in the first place, but the judge wouldn't let me challenge him."

"Well, then," Leigh said encouragingly, "maybe you've got the judge on legal error."

"As far as I'm concerned, I do. The question is whether his ego will allow him to admit it and grant me a new trial, or whether I have to take him up on appeal."

Leigh peered intently into Chris's face for a few seconds and then lapsed into a show of great relief that the problem had been solved. He slapped Chris on the back just hard enough to cause him to slop his beer down the front of his sweater and told him not to worry.

And now that Chris was good and drunk, he was feeling better about himself. Or perhaps now that he was feeling better about himself, he was good and drunk. He couldn't remember exactly when he had submitted to being drunk, but that was inconsequential compared with some of the other things he couldn't remember—such as how he had gotten into this strange room.

What he could see, given the current limitations of his vision, was that he was sitting in a leather armchair in someone's once well-appointed office. Leigh was seated someplace directly in front of him, behind what appeared to be a desk, and Leigh was bent at both the waist and the neck. He was performing some sort of fine and intricate maneuver that obviously required a great deal of concentration as well as hand-eye coordination. Chris gave up watching him and let his head loll back. Leigh had talked him into coming in here, that was it. Leigh had a present for him. A special treat.

"I swear to God," Leigh was saying, "I don't know what to make of him."

"Hunh," said Chris.

"Or her, for that matter."

Chris grunted in sympathy. He didn't know what to make of them, either.

Now Leigh lifted his face, positioning it within Chris's range of clarity. "I mean," he explained, "if you were to take all the women in the world and divide them into categories, attractive and unattractive, Janice Butler would be in the attractive category. Wouldn't you say?"

Aha, thought Chris, that's who we're talking about.

"And if you took the attractive women," Leigh went on, "and di-

94

vided them into good-looking and pleasant, Janice would be considered good-looking."

"Sure." That seemed safe enough.

"There on in, though, you gotta start considering. And personally, I don't think she'd make too many more cuts. You know what I mean?"

Chris pondered the idea of Janice Butler. "Personally," he declared, after giving her all the thought of which he felt capable, "I wouldn't fuck her with your dick."

"Then what's Roarke Robinson want to fuck her for?" Leigh demanded.

Startled, Chris snapped forward in his chair. Roarke Robinson? How had he gotten into the conversation?

"That wife he's got is the most beautiful woman on the whole planet," Leigh cooed. "Beautiful and nice and good and kind. I think she's wonderful."

"No shit," Chris said.

"You know how it all got started?"

Chris blinked at him. How what had got started?

"That very first barbecue we had for him, remember? You were there. You brought those clients of yours, remember?"

Oooh, Martha Porter. Long, tall Martha with the deep blue eyes. He had meant to call Martha.

"Everyone in the subdivision was there, just about goose bumps to meet the guy, and he shows up late. Right away he starts complaining about the food. Were you there for that?"

"That," said Chris, his voice sounding curiously grave, "was about the time I left."

"Yeah? Well, you should have stuck around. The guy gets absolutely blotto on the liquor and starts telling bawdy baseball stories." Leigh got busy again with whatever it was he was doing. "How come you left?"

"One of my clients got sick."

"The stories, some of them were pretty funny, but they cleared about half the women out in no time. And then he starts putting the moves on Marietta. I mean, his own wife's right there, sipping martinis or something and looking like she's at a wedding, and Robinson's slipping his arm around Marietta, whispering all these things in her ear."

"What's Blinky doing? Videotaping it?"

Leigh Rossville slowly drew back his head. "Oh, you're cold, you are," he said, and then feigned shock while Chris sputtered in delight at his own warped sense of humor.

95

"You want to hear the rest of this story, Chris, or you want to keep telling yourself jokes?"

"Hey, Leigh," Chris gasped, getting himself under control again, "I think I heard all this before."

"Except now I'm getting to the new part, the part I only just found out about from Cath. Apparently what happened was, a couple of days after the barbecue a bunch of the women were out at the kids' soccer game: Marietta, June, Janice, Aurora Weissock. It seems they're all talking about this guy and how nobody ever met anyone like him before. And Aurora, who's kind of kinky anyhow, starts telling them how she once brought this black guy home to meet her parents. Her folks were real Johnson-Humphrey-type liberals. You know the kind I mean? Anyhow, this guy teaches with Aurora at some high school—this is before she married Arnie, obviously—and her parents are, like, delighted that she's got this nice young black friend. The guy talks sports with her father, compliments her mother on what a nice house she keeps, the whole bit. Does all the right things. And the whole time he's sitting there charming the pants off Aurora's folks, his sperm's dripping down Aurora's leg because the two of them have been screwing each other all afternoon on the floor of the science lab. The only reason she brought him home was to goof on her parents."

Chris leaned in closer so that he could get a good look at Leigh's face. "I don't get it," he said.

"Gettin' it isn't the reason for telling the story," Leigh told him. "The thing is, after Aurora tells the girls this, everybody starts asking her all about black guys. Is it true what they say about them, that sort of thing."

"Who? Who's asking this?"

"Marietta, June and Janice."

"Wait a minute. Sweet little Marietta Gould? June 'I only live for tennis' Hartry? Nasty old Janice Butler?"

"I couldn't believe it, either. But Cath, when I say that to her, tells me, 'Hey, they're all grown women. They're all college educated. They all read *People* magazine.'"

Chris's mind clouded over before he could think of something to say about Cathy's remarks. Leigh, in any event, was not waiting for a response. He was carrying on more of a monologue than a conversation.

"Suddenly this becomes the hot topic in Tranton Park. I get these images of the women sitting around discussing the length of guys' schlongs and so forth—and Cath tells me the most interested one of all is Janice Butler." Leigh paused for effect. "Now comes the kicker. You ready for this?"

Chris gripped the arms of his chair to show that he was.

"The other day Cath goes to aerobics with Janice and afterwards they're sitting around having a Perrier or whatever it is they drink, and suddenly Janice isn't asking about black guys anymore—she's telling."

It took a second for Chris to comprehend the triumphant note in Leigh's voice. "Aha," he said. "So that's why you figure Janice has been having an affair with Robinson."

Leigh shrugged modestly.

"Janice say she's been with Robinson?"

"Who else would she have been with, Idi Amin?"

Chris nodded slowly. "Good evidence, Leigh. You'd make a hell of a trial lawyer."

"Why, it's as plain as black and white." Leigh thought he had made a joke.

Chris didn't. "Never assume anything is as it seems. That's the first lesson in being a litigator."

"I'm not being a litigator. I'm being a person. As a person, I know what I know."

"And as a litigator, I know what you don't know."

"Well," said Leigh, picking up the object on which he had been working for so long, "you can argue all you want, but you can't change reality."

"Ah"—Chris smiled—"but that's just the point. Litigation is the one area in this life where you can change reality. If you don't believe me, just ask Mr. Kinsey."

"Not Kinsey again. I thought we'd gotten you over that."

"In litigation you have what actually happened, then you have what the witnesses say happened, and then you have what the jury decides happened. Now you tell me, counselor, which one's reality?"

"Reality," answered Leigh as he presented a small makeup mirror with four neatly spaced and nicely molded lines of white powder on it, "is in the nose of the beholder."

CHAPTER THREE

John Gregory stared at the piece of paper that Chris had handed him. He studied the letterhead and the signature. He turned the paper over. He searched for the giveaway that would tell him this was all a joke. Finally he dropped the paper on his desk and slumped back in his chair.

"You've got to apologize to him, Chris. Whatever it is that happened, you really pissed him off and now you've got to apologize."

"All I did, John, was we were picking the jury, we've each got six challenges, I use four, the defense uses four. I pass. Defense uses five. I pass again. Defense uses six. Last juror comes up and he's a goddamn cop, for Chrissake. Tom Kinsey's a paraplegic because the defendant's car slams into his motorcycle and here comes a goddamn cop to sit on his jury. Of course I ding him, or try to, anyway. All of a sudden Gifford's great gray eyebrows go up and he says, 'Sorry, Mr. Cage, you've already used your six opportunities. You've passed on this jury.' I ask for a recess. I argue till I'm blue in the face. I tell him I never passed on the jury with this guy in it—and the old man just smiles at me like I'm some kind of idiot who's never tried a case before.

"For the next three weeks the evidence goes in and everything goes my way. I win all the motions, I win all the arguments on jury instructions. The jury goes out. Six hours later they come back in with a nine to three defense verdict. I'm so stunned I can't even talk to them. Two days after that I get a phone call from one of my three jurors telling me how they get in the jury room and the cop takes over all the deliberations. He had worked on a case just like this once, he says, and then he proceeds to regale them with all kinds of facts and figures about motorcycles and motorcycle riders, none of which has anything to do with the evidence. I get affidavits from six jurors that he does this—my three and three who voted against me. Of course, none of the three who voted against me will admit to being influenced by this Nazi, but they all claim he brought in outside evidence.

"I file my motion for new trial on two grounds: legal error in allowing this cop to sit in the first place; and juror misconduct. I've got the judge cold on the law, but I've only got an argument on the misconduct because the defense has three jurors plus the cop himself denying he brought in any matters not in evidence. So what does Giff do? He finds juror misconduct and never mentions legal error. Now the defense takes him up on appeal for the ruling on misconduct and I've got no choice but to cross-appeal on the legal error just in case they win. So now you want me to apologize. What am I going to apologize for, John?"

Gregory covered his face with both hands. "Find something, anything. You let him stick us with this thing and we might as well just go out of business." Suddenly he sat upright and grabbed the letter that had come from Judge Gifford. "You had anybody research this case he cited? *Yarbrough* v. *Superior Court*, 150 Cal. App. 3d 388. It say what he says it says?"

"Anybody? What do you mean, anybody? I got me and I got Shirley. I had to let my clerk go when we lost *Kinsey*."

Gregory flung the paper across his desk. It caught a draft and wafted to the floor. "Look, Chris, you're the one who's gotten yourself into this mess. A court order appointing you to defend an indigent prisoner in a civil suit for wrongful death—who ever heard of such a thing? Indigent, you know what that means? He doesn't have any money. Prisoner, you get that? He's already been convicted of the goddamn crime and now the victim's family has brought a lawsuit against him to try to recover compensation. How you going to defend him if the guy's already been found guilty? The test in a criminal case, in case you've forgotten, is guilt beyond a reasonable doubt. There's nothing left to argue."

"So fine. So what difference does it make? If the guy's in prison and he can't afford a lawyer, what's he care if the other side gets a million-dollar judgment against him? He's not going to be able to pay it no matter what it is."

"And he's not going to be able to pay you, either," Gregory shouted.

Josie, the receptionist, came over the intercom. In a singsong voice she said, "Mr. Gregory, I just wanted to remind you that Mr. and Mrs. Hoffman are still waiting out here in reception." She was telling them to quiet down, that their yelling was scaring off the prospective clients.

John Gregory looked momentarily chagrined. "Chris," he said, his voice barely audible, "I don't have to tell you how devastating this is. Not only does this letter mean that you're going to have to provide free legal services, but the way I read it, we're expected to pay the costs of defending him. Depending on what this case involves, that could be ten, twenty, fifty thousand bucks. If you don't obtain experts, transcripts, investigations, our unwanted client, whoever he is, can sue us for malpractice. We're sunk any way you look at it. Whatever you did to Gifford, whether it was justified or not, he's paid us back plenty."

Chris Cage took a deep breath and fixed his eyes on a point where the walls and ceiling came together. "Funny thing is," he said, "up until the Kinsey case I always thought old Giff was a pretty fair guy. Mean, short-tempered old bastard, yes, but fair, I always thought."

Roarke Robinson had an unusual way of playing tennis. When serving, he would toss the ball up, crank his racket in a herky-jerky motion, and then smash downward. The ball would leave his racket with blinding speed and as often as not would hit the top of the net, exploding off the tape with the crack of a gunshot. His second serve would inevitably be as hard and as fast as his first, but he almost never double faulted. If his opponent was lucky enough to return the serve, he would find Roarke racing to the net, able to cover enormous amounts of ground by thrusting out his racket as if it were a rowing oar. There were never any long volleys with Roarke Robinson.

They played single-set matches. Roarke disposed of Gary Martel 6–0 and he got off to a surprise lead with Mark Hartry. But it was Mark's court and once Mark started playing ten feet behind the baseline and dinking the ball over Roarke's head, the tide turned. Mark finished by taking five straight games. As Roarke watched his last shot fly out of bounds, he turned to the spectators and let out an unearthly roar. He sank to his knees, his hands clutching the end of his racket, and dropped his head into his arms.

Everyone watched in silence while he held his pose and then Aurora Weissock sprang from her chair and yelled, "Mixed doubles. I'll take Roarkie," and she ran onto the court, her auburn hair streaming, her smooth thighs jiggling. She bent over Roarke and helped him to his feet.

Roarke rose like a battered warrior, and when he was standing tall and steady, a huge smile spread across his face. "Ooo-eee, he kicked my ass," he shouted.

The women tittered. The men smiled. Roarke slipped an arm around Aurora's shoulders and limped to the side of the court.

"Not me, baby," he said. "I'm gonna go for some of that hard liquor and let some of these other folks get out there and make fools of theyselves." Spying his wife, he said, "C'mon, Annie, get out there and show your stuff."

Ann Robinson, cool, slender and silent, put down her drink and walked out on Mark Hartry's side of the court. Arnie Weissock chugged out next to Aurora, who tried not to show her disappointment.

Roarke approached the table where Chris Cage was sitting with the Butler family and the Rossvilles. The perspiration stood out on his brow, it beaded at the ends of his hair. If he had shaken his head it would have flown off and made him look like an actor in an Orange Crush commercial. Chris, who had missed meeting him at the Butlers' party, waited now for someone to introduce him, but no one did.

"Oh, Roarkie," Janice said, her voice high and soft, her tone mocking, "you were wonderful."

Chris and Leigh exchanged glances, but nobody else seemed to notice. Roarke grabbed a chair and pulled it in between Jay and Arthur. He looked around from face to face. The last face he looked at was Arthur's, and Arthur grinned merrily at him.

"What's wrong with you, dude?" Roarke said, slapping Arthur on the arm with the back of his hand. "Why aren't you out there playing tennis? You don't even have no tennis clothes on."

Jay Butler leaped in with a good hearty laugh. "Arthur's not much of a tennis player. Baseball was always his game, wasn't it, Arthur?"

Arthur grinned some more.

Roarke looked him up and down as if he couldn't believe it.

"Made high school varsity as a sophomore, didn't you, son? Was in Pony League, made American Legion."

Roarke peered closer. "So what happened to you, you so good?"

Jay said, "Nothing happened. I think he'd still be a good ballplayer if a few of his coaches had only had a little more patience with him."

Chris assumed Jay Butler was talking about the need for coaches to be a little more understanding of Arthur's unusual appearance, but Roarke Robinson interpreted him differently. He leaned back coolly and surveyed the spike-haired youth. "Oh, you need some tips, do you? Okay, I got some tips."

Roarke thrust himself forward again until he was only inches away from Arthur. "The first thing you gotta learn to do is develop a stone face. Got that? No matter what people yell, you don't hear it. You hear your own mother yelling from the stands, you ignore her. You hit a home run, the crowd asks you to come out, you come out for one second, touch your hat—act like it's a pain in the ass. Okay, try it."

Arthur kept right on grinning.

Roarke waited a few seconds, until it was obvious Arthur was not going to change his expression. Then he said, "That's good, boy, you're getting close. Now second thing you gotta learn, that how to chew. Best thing to chew these days is sunflower seeds. You want to be like a old-time ballplayer, you chew tobacco. But sunflower seeds, they don't put that big bulge in your cheek, and that's good because someday you take that tobacco out, your cheek gonna fall down like a old lady's tit." Roarke's eyes flew around the table until they came to rest on Janet Butler's drink. Sticking his fingers into her cup, he pulled out a small ice cube. "Here, boy," he said, "practice on this," and he pushed the ice cube into Arthur's mouth.

Roarke sat back in his chair and folded his arms. He surveyed Arthur Butler's mastication with satisfaction. "That's it, I think you got that part down. Best chewer I ever seen was Reggie Jackson. He split them sunflower seeds with his teeth, suck in the meat, spit out the shells. Awesome sight to behold. Sometimes you bat after him, you get up there and the batter's box be knee deep in shells. Sometimes he get a three and two count, maybe foul off a couple of balls, he run outta seeds and have to call time out. Go back to the dugout, get some more."

Suddenly Roarke seized his tennis racket as if it were a baseball bat and got to his feet with the frame resting on his shoulder. "Okay, nex-test thing you're up at bat." He spread his legs and took a few half swings with the racket. He leaned forward and tapped the end of the racket on an imaginary plate. He stared out at an imaginary pitcher. He took a few more practice swings. "And what you gotta learn here," he demonstrated, "is how to hustle your balls." With his hand on the crotch of his shorts, Roarke Robinson moved his genitals first one way and then the other. "You never can tell when the camera's gonna be focusing in on you, so you gotta be prepared to do it all the time. Go left, go right. Okay, Artie, baby, let's see you get up and do it now."

He grabbed Arthur by the arm and pulled him to his feet. He moved him into position and propped the racket in his hand. Then, like a movie director, he ran around to the other side of the table and began hollering instructions. "Okay, Artie, get that grin off your mug. Stone face, stone face, baby. That's the other thing. Baseball players always say everything twice. Atta boy. Atta boy. Take those cuts. Now spit. That's good, that's good. Plenty of time now, plenty of time. Hustle those balls. You gotta be quick, but you gotta get a good handful. C'mon now, he ain't gonna make that pitch yet. Hustle. Left, right, back the other way. You got it."

Chris and the others sat with stunned smiles on their faces as Arthur soared happily through his pantomime, responding to each of Roarke's cues. The frieze the group formed ended only when there was a shout from the tennis court. Everybody glanced in that direction just as Arnie Weissock sailed his racket into the net. His wife, Aurora, was pulling at her hair with both hands. They were arguing, Arnie was walking off, and already Mark and Ann were looking for new challengers.

Janice Butler suddenly bolted to her feet. "C'mon, Doc," she said. "It's our turn." She threw one quick glance toward Roarke and ran toward the court.

Jay, smiling bewilderedly, picked up his racket and followed her. Off to the side, Roarke returned to a standing position. He addressed Leigh and Cathy and Chris with an exaggerated shrug and then he motioned to Arthur, who still stood with Roarke's racket on his shoulder, and said, "C'mon, Artie, let me buy you a drink."

Only after everyone was gone did Chris and the Rossvilles look at each other. "Holy shit," Leigh said.

"What?" Cathy asked.

"That guy is weird," Chris said.

Leigh watched Roarke disappear into the house, then he turned and watched Janice Butler, her lower lip clenched between her teeth, determinedly smacking warm-up balls over the net. "Can you believe Janice Butler letting somebody get away with that? With her son? In front of her?"

Chris said, "Hey, did you see the way she looked at him just now?"

Leigh shook his head. "What do you think she sees in him, anyhow?"

Cathy dropped her forearm on the table loud enough to make both men look at her. "Are you kidding me? What do you think she sees in him?"

"That's what I just asked." A look of surprise crossed Leigh's face. "Oh, c'mon, Cath. I know the guy's been the subject of a lot of talk lately, but he's hardly worth messing up your whole life for, is he?" He waited for her to assure him that he was right.

But Cathy, her voice suddenly sharp, said, "So what makes you think Janice is messing up her life? Maybe she just wants to try something that's a little bit different. It doesn't mean anything; isn't that what you men always say?"

"Hey, Cath, you're talking about things guys say when they're sitting around bullshitting. It's not as though anybody's out there actually doing anything." He looked at Chris for support and Chris nodded gravely. Encouraged, Leigh went on. "Here's Janice, she's been married about twenty years, got herself a nice secure little nest, home, family, everything she could possibly want, and you're saying it's all right for her to wig out over the first guy who comes along who's a little bit different?"

"He's not just a little different," Chris interjected. "He's a lot different."

"Not to mention rich and famous and good-looking," said Cathy.

Leigh promptly changed whatever he had been about to say. "You think he's good-looking?" he asked.

"Of course I do," she said. "Everybody does."

"Well, Jesus, we've certainly come a long way from the days when you were telling me how loud and crude you thought he was."

Cathy didn't look at her husband. Her eyes were fixed on the tennis court; except they weren't watching the action, they weren't going back and forth from one side to the other. "Maybe that's part of what makes him interesting."

"Janice's own husband is interesting."

"Her husband's a dolt."

Leigh carefully turned his eyes to Chris, and Chris said, "I have to agree with her there, buddy."

Leigh forced a smile to his lips. Talking to Cathy, but still looking at Chris, he said. "I know what you like about him. You like what Aurora was saying about the guy she was with. Well, let me tell you, babe, you can't stereotype people that way, either."

Shoving herself angrily to her feet, Cathy said, "Now you're the one who's being crude, Leigh."

She started to walk away, but Leigh brought her back with his next comments. "Crude is the way he's always pawing everybody else's wife.

Crude is the way he fractures the English language whenever he speaks."

Cathy pushed her knuckles down on the tabletop and leaned toward her husband. "How do you know?" she said. "You ever really talk to him? You ever find out how smart he really is? You ever think he might just be putting one over on whitey?"

"Oh, whitey, is it?" Leigh laughed cynically. "All of a sudden, I'm whitey? And who are you—Miss Chocolate Milk?"

Cathy shook her head. "That's dumb, Leigh. Even Chris isn't laughing."

"I'm smiling," Chris volunteered.

"And as for all the pawing, as you call it, well, maybe even that's better than being ignored all the time. Maybe, just maybe, Janice enjoys being appreciated by a man instead of taken for granted."

The moment grew awkward. Chris's presence, at least in his own mind, became magnified. He tried to look away, he tried to look as though he were tremendously interested in the action on the court, as though he were not conscious of every detail of the domestic exchange being played out next to him.

Leigh had slumped back in his chair, but the rapidity with which he spoke belied the casualness of his repose. "That's great, Cath," he was saying, "but what does she think it's going to get her? Nobody in his right mind would want her when he had Ann Robinson."

"To do what?" Cathy fired back at him. "To model clothes? You really want a challenge, try having a conversation with Ann Robinson sometime. See if you can come away without suffering brain damage."

Chris continued to stare at the court, where Ann stood at the backline, one hand on the handle of her racket and one hand on its neck. She swayed slightly, but she didn't move as Mark Hartry ran in front of her to take a shot and then raced back into his own half of the court to keep the volley going.

"Ball hog," muttered Leigh.

"Now look at Janice," Cathy said. "Just because you don't like her doesn't mean other men don't find her attractive. Look at her legs."

"Her cheerleader's legs," Leigh said.

"I never liked cheerleaders," Chris said.

They watched as Janice approached one of Mark's shots. Suddenly she pivoted and rammed her return down the alley that Ann Robinson was supposed to be guarding. Ann turned slowly, but just the way she was supposed to, and stuck out her backhand. The ball hit her strings and caromed high in the air. It seemed to hang up there for a long time, but when it fell it fell on Ann's own side of the net. Janice thrust her fist skyward.

Cathy clapped. She cupped her hands to her mouth and yelled, "Yea, Janice." Then she turned to the two men at the table and said, "Standing around looking pretty only gets you so far in this life."

Chris put his hand to his brow and peered out from beneath it. "Boy, I'll take a woman who can kick ass at tennis anytime."

"That should be the name of a country western song," said Leigh. " 'I Got Me A Tennis Playin' Woman.' "

"Can't get a bowler, get a tennis player, I always say."

Cathy said they were both hopeless, and stomped away.

CHAPTER FOUR

John Gregory's concern was apparent. It stretched his features, made his long face seem even longer. His elbow was propped on the arm of his swivel chair and his chin was resting in a pocket that was formed by the fingers of his hand. The man he was looking at was moon-faced and gray-haired. There were broken capillaries in his cheeks and his eyes were red. He was breathing rather heavily for someone who was only sitting on a couch. Each time he breathed out, the roll of fat around his stomach shimmied.

The moon-faced man was looking at Chris Cage, who was leaning forward in his chair, gesturing to make his points. Chris's tie was loose, his collar was open. Chris was working.

"The guy's name is Doheny, Bill, and he's as nice a guy as you'd ever want to meet. In fact, that's why he's in the trouble he's in. He's a male nurse, R.N., and he was doing home care for this poor bastard who was suffering from amylotrophic lateral sclerosis, ALS. Lou Gehrig's disease, they call it.

"This patient's muscles had literally wasted away to nothing. He couldn't move, he couldn't breathe without assistance, he couldn't feed himself. They cut a hole in his throat and attached him to a ventilator which breathed for him and after that he couldn't talk anymore. The only thing the guy had left was his mind, and that was intact. The guy was thirty-nine years old, the same age as Doheny, and Doheny says the guy asked him, begged him, to disconnect him from the ventilator.

"The patient, his name was Johnson, had a wife and two kids and he was a partner in a small real estate brokerage at the time he was stricken. The way the partnership was set up, he continued getting his share for as long as he was disabled, but there was no right of survivor-

107

ship. He dies, the partnership ends, the wife and kids don't get any part of it. Johnson tells our boy Doheny that that's the only reason his wife won't pull the plug on him. By this time Doheny knows the wife's no good anyhow, out playing around while her husband's wasting away, and he believes Johnson. So one day the wife's out, the kids are at school, Doheny's reading Johnson's lips and Johnson's pleading with him to let him die with some dignity. . . . Doheny disconnects him.

"The part Doheny gets screwed up comes after Johnson dies. He reconnects him. His plan was to wait awhile, then call the ambulance, have him declared DOA at the hospital. Except the wife comes home unexpectedly and sees her husband is still blue from oxygen starvation. Doheny tells her it must have just happened, just that minute. Tells her his lungs must have gotten clogged, that's what usually happens to these guys with ALS. Tells her to call the ambulance while he tries to do CPR.

"The wife gets suspicious. She insists on having an autopsy done. Johnson's lungs were clear. No unusual amounts of secretion, no pneumonia. The guy's dead from oxygen starvation and Doheny's stuck trying to explain how this could have happened when he's got a machine breathing for him and there are not one but two different alarms that go off when there's a disconnect. He finally tells the whole truth, admits mercy killing. The goddamn DA over in Alameda tries him for murder. Jury doesn't know what to do and convicts him of voluntary manslaughter. Judge doesn't seem to know what to do, either. Gives him three years in minimum security. Got the picture, Bill?"

The moon-faced man sighed. He glanced uncertainly at John Gregory and then looked back at Chris. "Mama's suing Doheny for wrongful death, claiming damages for all the partnership earnings she and the kids would have gotten if Johnson had lived?"

"Right."

Bill nodded, dragged his hand across his lips. "Nurse Doheny will be out of prison in another year or so. If he hasn't been defrocked or disbarred or whatever it is they do to nurses, he'll be in a position to make a half-decent income again. Mama wants part of it."

"You got it, Bill. Everything Doheny had he spent on his criminal-defense lawyer. He's a penniless man with the potential for earning some money when he gets out, and the Honorable Roger Gifford has appointed us to defend him in the lawsuit."

Bill Bunton asked for the letter of appointment and took his time reading it. "This says you've been appointed, Chris."

Chris Cage and John Gregory forced themselves not to look at each other. Their silence, the way they kept their eyes fixed on their partner, eloquently summarized the situation for Mr. Bunton.

"I gotta lot of stuff of my own to do," he said.

"Bill," John Gregory said softly, "I was kind of thinking this might be a good refresher course for you. You really haven't been in a trial for several years now—"

"That's because all my cases settle."

"Settle?" John Gregory's voice rose far beyond the level he meant to use. "When was the last time you settled a case?"

Bill Bunton looked down at the letter in his hands. Chris looked at the floor. John Gregory got to his feet, hoisted his pants by grabbing at the waistband, and then, energy expended, sat down abruptly.

"Bill, we're teetering on the edge of bankruptcy here. It cost us thirty-five thousand dollars to lose the Kinsey case. Chris has got the McCarthy medical malpractice case going to trial in two weeks. I'm up to my neck with four cases set in four different courts. That means we've got to count on you, Bill. I mean, I wouldn't ask you to do this if there were anybody else . . . but there just isn't."

"There's nobody else, Bill," Chris chimed in. There was concern in his expression, anguish in his voice. He wanted Bill to know that he hated himself for having to make this imposition. And when Bill looked back at him, holding his gaze far, far longer than he needed to, Chris almost did hate himself. Almost.

The holiday, as far as Chris was concerned, could not have come at a worse time. The idea that he was supposed to spend all Thursday sitting around his mother's house in Sunnyvale seemed crazy when he looked at all the things he had to do. Even with Bill Bunton taking over the Doheny matter, he still had to prepare the transcript for the court of appeal in the Kinsey case. He still had expert depositions to take on Monday, Tuesday and Wednesday in the malpractice case against nasty old Dr. McCarthy. He had a thousand things he needed to do, and taking time out for Thanksgiving was not one of them.

Besides, Chris knew exactly what the situation was going to be like. The morning's exchange of greetings, the hugs and kisses, the hustle and bustle of preparing the meal and setting the table, would carry them through until they sat down to eat. Then his sister Jenna would start with a story about her work as a bookkeeper at Stockton's finest hotel. It would remind his mother of an incident where some sales-person had been rude to her and they would hear in detail every excruciating aspect of that encounter. That would prompt his sister Stephanie to complain about the prices in various stores of kids' clothes, kids' toys, kids' foods.

Round and round they would go: Jenna with her tales of no interest to anyone, his mother with her accounts of daily skirmishes, Stephanie with her laments about a world whose mysteries she took for granted. Then suddenly the meal would be over and his mother and two sisters would be hauling the dishes off to the kitchen, clamorously insisting they didn't need any help, leaving him to stare across the dining room at the dismal sight of his two brothers-in-law.

Ricky, who no doubt would be wearing a T-shirt of some sort, would smile nervously and drink his coffee with the spoon still stuck in the cup. Ralph would sit glumly, never addressing Chris, almost never looking at him. Chris would ask about Ralph's kids, the ones he had by a former marriage, before his tubes were tied; the ones who were living with their mother in a schoolbus on some hidden tract in Humboldt County. Or perhaps they would discuss Ricky and Steph's kids, the ones who would have already bolted from the table to throw themselves in front of the television set. Maybe they would talk about Ricky's job with the telephone company, or Ralph's job at the meat-packing plant, but they would never mention Chris's job. They would never, for that matter, bring up anything Chris had been doing. When the subjects of climbing poles and hauling animal carcasses had been exhausted, the conversation would wind down to virtually nothing, just three men sitting in silence while three women yakked away in the adjoining room.

At such times, Chris would long for the chores of the kitchen. If he went in to help, he would be pushed back out again with cries that there wasn't enough room for him. "Go talk men-talk," they would say, never seeming to realize the sentence of servitude they were imposing on him.

It was with these thoughts in mind that Chris set out in search of a liquor store on Thanksgiving morning. Today he would break the silent dictate that had governed his mother's house ever since his father had died and he would bring as his contribution to the meal a little conversational stimulant. He would tell his mother that Julia Child recommended it: a little white wine with turkey, a little red with cranberry sauce, a little cream sherry with dessert. He would explain that it wouldn't be like real drinking.

Off 19th Avenue he found a corner shop with a Middle Eastern proprietor, a counter tray full of baklava, a selection of soups and soaps, canned meats and vegetables, a freezer full of Popsicles, a glass-doored refrigerator full of cold drinks, and a wall full of wines and liquor. Chris agonized over his choice. There was no Fumé Blanc, no Cabernet, and almost nothing from any winery whose products he would serve in his own home.

The proprietor began to grow concerned at the length of time Chris was taking. He stopped watching the Macy's parade on the tiny television he had behind the counter and began devoting his attention exclusively to Chris.

What difference did it make? Chris asked himself. His mother wasn't going to drink anyway . . . and his brothers-in-law were likely to drink absolutely anything. This whole venture was merely an experiment, an attempt to loosen things up, to see if putting a little something in their bellies would get the Ricky and Ralph show into gear. Maybe it would get them talking about fishing. He had heard Ricky and Ralph do that once when he was out of the room. Or maybe they could talk about cars, the merits of four-wheel-drive vehicles, turbos, fuel injection, metal-flake paint jobs. He would ask them questions, and the wine would relieve them of the suspicion that he was trying to trick them. Ricky and Ralph would answer in whole sentences, they would become eloquent discoursers on the things they knew best. They would talk to him about . . . kids. Kids say the darndest things, don't they, Ralph? They sure do the darnedest things, don't they, Ricky? Tell me about some of the darned things your kids do.

Panicked with the thought of his own impending conviviality, Chris bought two bottles of Almaden chablis and one bottle of Christian Brothers Private Reserve. He would present the brandy to his brothers-in-law after dinner; then he would sit back and watch them search the label in vain for the name of the fruit that would tell what flavor it was.

He took 19th Avenue to 280. Near the airport he crossed over from 280 to 101 and then he took 101 south to the Sunnyvale exit that was closest to his mother's house. Leaving the highway, he drove through eight sets of traffic lights, past three one-story shopping centers, four convenience stores, fifteen fast-food franchise restaurants and one six-screen movie theater complex.

On reaching his mother's neighborhood, he drove past streets named

111

Emerson, Longfellow, Thoreau and Frost before he finally reached Poe Court, a cul-de-sac serving seven different modified ranch-style homes. He squeezed his BMW into the tail end of his mother's driveway and left it sticking out into the street because there was no room for him to do anything else. Gathering his resolve along with his bag of wine and brandy, he marched up to his mother's door.

"Hello, everybody," he called out as he stepped inside.

From the living room directly in front of him came the sound of the television turned up louder than it needed to be. It was being watched by his sister Stephanie's two boys, who glanced at him disinterestedly. "Hey," said one of them. "Hi," said the other. Neither so much as changed his slouch.

Chris's mother appeared from the kitchen, busily wiping her hands on her apron. Her hair had been done for the occasion and the dress she was wearing seemed to be new, but the expression Chris saw on her strong, well-tanned face was something he had seen many times before.

"What's wrong?" he said.

"I'm so glad you're here," she told him, and pushed him backward, gesturing in the direction of what she liked to call his room.

Without saying anything more, Chris turned and led the way. They entered a small room that was dominated by a maple bed and a matching bureau. Chris's high school graduation picture stood on a bedside table and his bachelor of arts degree hung from one wall, but other than that the room was anonymous. The picture and the degree were things his mother had when she had moved into the house. He had brought nothing to her since then and she had found nothing else that was sufficiently personal.

She closed the door and mother and son stood face to face. There had been no kiss. Something obviously had occurred which was too urgent to allow time for that. Chris shifted the bag of bottles from one arm to the other, but his mother did not seem to notice.

"Ralph has left Jenna," she said.

Chris smiled. A look of startled anger came over his mother's face and Chris sucked in the corners of his mouth.

"Don't you feel anything for her?" his mother snapped.

Chris's first reaction was to snap back, but he fought it off. He made his voice ring with reason. "I'm sorry, Mom, I really am. But for God's sake, the guy was fifteen years older than her and had the personality of a warthog. There wasn't one of us who ever understood what she saw in him—you included."

His mother's head tilted so that her chin was pointed fiercely at him. "She's in love with him, that's all any of us needs to understand."

"Well, that wasn't the way you thought when she first brought him home, was it? Ralph was the last person on earth you wanted her to marry, as I recall."

"That was then and this is now. You don't go around saying I told you so to someone who's been hurt like your sister has. But if you don't want to take any responsibility in this matter, if you want to blame it all on Jenna or me or anybody else, that's up to you. Just go along life's merry way, just as you've always done. As long as it doesn't affect you, what difference does it make what happens to anybody else?"

Chris silently put his hand on his mother's arm, but she pulled her arm away and, unfortunately, pulled loose his tongue along with it. "Hey," he demanded, "what are you talking about? I'm not her father, you know."

"Maybe if you'd been a little more like one after Daddy died this wouldn't have happened. She wouldn't have gone running off with a man so much older than her."

"Mom, you're talking about a couple of adults. There was never anything I could have done about her and Ralph."

"And there's nothing you can do now, either, I suppose."

"If she's hurt or upset, I'm concerned, sure. I'm only trying to tell you—you know, here we are, behind closed doors and everything—that maybe this is the best thing that could have happened to her. . . . Hey, Mom, where are you going? For God's sake, why don't you stand here and talk to me?"

But his mother already had the door open. She was already striding away. "I should have known better than to count on you," she was yelling back. "You want to give your little speeches in court, that's fine, but you don't talk that way to me in my house."

It was with a good deal of timidity that Chris retraced his steps to the living room. He was still wearing his raincoat, still carrying his bag of wine and brandy, when he came once again upon the two boys watching television.

"Where are your folks, kids?" he asked.

Jason, the older one, looked up. "Dad's out in the garage fixin' up some wiring for Grandma. My mom's helping Aunt Jenna get over her cryin'."

"Oh," said Chris. "What are you watching?"

"Nothing," said Jason.

113

"I don't know," said Joshua.

"Oh," said Chris again. Feeling rather shell-shocked, he put the wine bag down on the floor, laid his raincoat over a chair, and walked back down the hallway to what his mother called "the girls' room."

He tapped softly on the door. "Jenna?" he said.

He could hear voices. He could hear some sniffling and some feet shuffling. He could hear bedsprings contracting and expanding. "Jenna?" he said again.

It was Stephanie who answered. "Jenna doesn't really feel like talking right now, Chris. She says she'll see you at dinner."

"Hey, Jenna," he said, beating harder on the door. "This is silly. If you've got a problem, I want to help."

He heard the shrill, muffled sound of Jenna screaming into a pillow and the rising, authoritative voice of Stephanie saying, "I don't think she wants to talk to any men right now."

Chris slammed his shoulder into the door and then he let his head slump into one of the panels. "I'm not just a man, Jenna. I'm your brother. If you've got a problem, than I've got a problem."

"Great," Jenna screamed. "We'll be divorced thirty-three-year-old women together."

"There are a hell of a lot of worse things, Jen. Heck, look at me." His tone turned light, invitingly jocular. "I'm nearly five years older than you and I can't get married even once."

"Your biological clock isn't ticking like mine is," she shouted back.

"That never seemed to bother you before. I mean, the guy was fixed, wasn't he?"

Jenna's answer came out in a burst of sobs. "He said he was going to get it reversed. . . . And don't call him a 'guy.' He was my husband."

Chris waited, his head still against the door. He wondered how he had gotten himself into this situation, how he could get himself out. His sister was crying and he wanted her to stop, but at this stage of their lives he knew so little about Jenna that he virtually had to rack his brain for something to say. "You want me to go have a talk with Ralph?" he asked finally. "Would that do any good?"

Jenna screamed. He took it to mean no.

He could hear Stephanie trying to calm her down just before she called out, "I don't think you're going to be able to find him."

"Maybe you better tell me what happened, Steph."

Stephanie hesitated. "He went back to his first wife."

"The one in the bus?"

"Yes goddamnit," cried Jenna. "Don't make me feel worse."

Stephanie said, "Ralph's ex-wife's new husband got caught growing marijuana. The whole farm they were living on got raided and burned, so she brought the kids down to stay with Ralph and Jenna. Then her husband couldn't make bail and she had no place to go back to, so Ralph said she could park the bus in their yard and stay there for a while. . . ."

Chris had to ask what happened next.

"Jenna came home early from work yesterday and everybody was gone. They had all taken off together."

"They didn't stick you with the bus, did they, Jen?"

Jenna spoke. "Very funny, Crisco." It was a childhood taunt, one he had not heard in twenty years, and Chris thought it gave him a clue as to how to respond when Jenna said, "That's what they used to get away from fat old ugly me."

Affecting an air of weariness, Chris said, "Jenna, you're not fat, you're not old . . . but Jesus, you are ugly. I don't know how we're ever going to get another man to look at you."

Jenna shrieked and Chris had to start banging on the door again. "Jenna, that was a joke. Like you calling me Crisco. I was trying to make you laugh. Jenna . . ." Without breaking contact with the door, Chris, let his body slide slowly to the floor. "Try to put this thing into perspective, Jen. No matter what happens, you've still got Steph and Mom and me. What do you expect—something goes wrong in your life, we're going to think any the less of you for it?"

Jenna's response was quick. "You don't think about me one way or the other, Chris, and you know it. So don't try to pretend any different."

"That's not true, Jenna."

"It is," she screamed.

Chris's position, his back wedged between the door and the doorjamb, his knees drawn up, had become a slump. He tried to picture what his two sisters looked like behind that closed door. Jenna, too big, too squarely framed for most people to notice how pretty she was. Stephanie, the cute one, who had always been so slender and shapely, who had never wanted to do anything more than get married and have babies. When was the last time he had seen them? Last Christmas? Eleven months ago? No, Steph and her kids had been at his mother's house when he had dropped by one day in the summer on his way back from court in San Jose. How had so much time gotten away from them?

115

It wasn't as though he had been trying to avoid them. God, he loved his sisters. He'd always loved them. Everyone was just so busy, that was all.

The sound of footsteps made him look up. Ricky turned the corner into the hallway and stopped. Chris knew it was Ricky because that was who it had to be, but otherwise Chris was not sure he would have recognized him. Ricky's hair was slicked back in a most unnatural manner. He was wearing a blue, short-sleeved, double-pocketed wash-and-wear shirt that was tucked into a pair of brand-new blue jeans with bell-shaped cuffs. Only the dab of mayonnaise at the corner of his mouth stood out as a reminder of the way Chris was used to seeing him look.

Ricky's eyes went from Chris to the closed door behind Chris's back. "Your mother told me to tell you the turkey's ready," he said. Then, cupping his hand to his mouth and inadvertently wiping it clean of mayonnaise, he shouted at the closed door, "Hey, you guys. Turkey's ready."

Getting no answer, Ricky shrugged. He smiled wanly at Chris and turned on his heel. He had not said hello. He had not asked why his brother-in-law lay crumpled on the floor in the corner of his mother's back hallway with his eyes glazed and his mouth hanging open. Ricky was never one to inquire about the secret ways of lawyers.

CHAPTER FIVE

"So what did he say, the old drunk?" Leigh was trying to catch the waitress's attention. He was interested in carrying on the conversation, but not single-mindedly devoted to it.

"Mr. Bunton said," Chris told him, "that he would take a look at the file."

"First thing a defense lawyer's supposed to do is go right after the plaintiffs. Depose 'em, grill 'em, let 'em know they're not in for a fun time. Hit them with a thousand form interrogatories."

"We don't have form interrogatories."

"Whoops, can't be a defense firm, then."

"We don't want to be a defense firm, Leigh. That's just the point. Everything we do is on a contingency basis, and as long as we stick to that arrangement we're okay. If we have a good case we can usually be assured of getting paid somewhere along the line and we can plan accordingly. But now that this crazy judge has ordered us to defend this indigent, we're stuck with a situation in which we have to bill on an hourly basis without any expectation of ever collecting a damn thing."

But now Leigh wasn't listening at all. He had his arm around the waitress and was purring in her ear. "My demented friend over here and I are drinking bourbon tonight and our glasses are empty. Big M, small t. If you ever want to see our smiling faces around here again, you will fill them, pronto."

"In that case," the waitress said, "expect your drinks around midnight."

Leigh telegraphed a swipe at her ass and she laughed and swatted his hand away. "I'll tell your wife," she joked.

"You'll have to find her first," Leigh said, and all three of them laughed as though this were really a clever remark.

The waitress was not all that much to look at, but she wore her skirt short and her blouse open to a point of interest and she kept up a light-hearted exchange throughout twenty-four dollars' worth of drinks. Chris tried to make a grab for the bill, but Leigh insisted on putting it on his credit card. "We talked business, didn't we?" he said; and Chris, who couldn't remember talking any business, said they must have.

"Now," Leigh announced, writing the waitress a six-dollar tip, "it is time for us to go to Diamond Lil's."

Chris glanced at his watch. "It's almost eight o'clock, Leigh. Won't Cathy be expecting you?"

Leigh made a mess of ripping his receipt from the rest of the credit card voucher. Two or three pages of the voucher got torn, his fingers got caught in the carbon paper. "Cathy," he said, "is living in a world without time. Her evening is measured in terms of preprogrammed entertainment. It's Friday night, you say? In that case I know exactly what she's doing. She's gone to the video store and rented a couple of movies and she's curled up on the couch in front of the VCR watching some old Jimmy Stewart flick." He did a passable imitation of Jimmy Stewart: "Walll, walll, walll . . . As I was shtelling Maaartha . . ."

The waitress came by and apparently thought Leigh was having trouble talking. She asked him if he was going to be able to make it home okay. He put on a hangdog look and said he didn't think so. He asked if it would be all right if he stayed at her place for the night. There was a moment's hesitation before the waitress realized he was kidding. "Anytime," she said, and danced away.

Leigh and Chris walked outside. Chris plunged his hands into his trouser pockets and followed his friend in the direction of the Embarcadero Center, a four-block interconnected high-rise complex of offices, restaurants, shops, stores and bars, including Diamond Lil's.

"Every weekend it's the same thing," Leigh was saying. "I come home Friday night, have a couple of drinks, watch the movie and fall asleep in my chair. Saturday night we go out to dinner or get together with the Hartrys or somebody. Sunday night we watch *60 Minutes* and do bills. Tonight I just want to have some fun."

Chris said, "Fine. You stay out and have fun. I'll go home and crawl up on the couch with Cathy," and they both laughed.

During most of the year Diamond Lil's set up rock bands on its patio on Friday evenings, but this was December and everyone was crowded

118

indoors. Leigh and Chris found themselves pushed up against a wall, talking to two young secretaries and trying desperately to convince them that they were widget salesmen from Detroit. One of the secretaries said she had heard of widgets, but didn't know what they were. The other said she knew. She said they had something to do with automobiles. Chris and Leigh wrote them off as airheads and spent a good deal of time and drink-money trying to prove that thesis.

"Is this my car?"

"This is your car."

"Jees." Leigh bent close and looked at the paint. He looked in the window. He stepped back and stared at it in awe. "It got big, didn't it?"

Indeed, the Jaguar did look big in the light of the streetlamp.

"How am I gonna get this big old car out of this little tiny sparking pace?"

Chris surveyed the scene. He made a thoughtful study of it and then he reached his conclusion. "You go back, boom, and you hit this car. Then you go forward, boom, and you hit that car. Before you know it the space will be big enough. Promise. I've seen it done before."

Leigh stared at the two cars on either side of his and contemplated Chris's suggestion. A dim gleam of recognition came into his eye. He held out his hand vertically, fusing his fingers together. "Boom," he said, moving it to the left. "Boom," he said again, moving it to the right.

It took Leigh more than a few seconds to get his key into the door lock, and by the time he got into his seat and leaned across to open the door for Chris another half minute had passed. "Home, James," he said.

The engine turned on. The Jaguar surged forward, made hard contact with the bumper in front of it, and both men were flung against the dashboard. "Holy shit," said Leigh, as though there were something wrong with his car.

He was more careful about putting it in reverse, keeping his foot hard on the brake and draping his arm across the back of Chris's seat so he could turn his head and look directly through the rear window. Slowly he backed up until he hit against the car behind. Slowly he spun the wheel until it was as far to the left as he could get it. Then he put the car into drive and guided it out onto the street. "Ha, ha," he said. "That was easy enough."

Chris lost a little bit of traveling time. One moment he knew where they were and where they were going, the next moment he realized they were on the approach to the Bay Bridge. "Hey, what are we doing?" he demanded.

In a low, guttural accent, Leigh said, "I goin' the Holiday Inn."

It was a line from an almost forgotten anecdote Chris had once told about a taxi ride he had been on in St. Louis. It was an "in" joke, the sort of thing that was funny now only because Leigh remembered that it had once happened to Chris. It made Chris laugh while he hollered in protest and shouted nonsensical directions.

Leigh blew right past the final turnoff and Chris knew they were headed for home, Leigh's home.

"Hey, c'mon, man. How am I going to get back to the city?"

"I'll drive you. We'll get a drink and I'll drive you."

"Cathy's going to kill us."

"We'll get Cathy to come with us."

They made it across the opening span of the bridge and it was not until they entered the tunnel at Treasure Island that Leigh really began to lose control. He swerved across one lane, hunkered closer to the wheel, and a moment later drifted into another. Chris, who had put on his seat belt, was now gripping it with both hands. He felt, suddenly, almost sober. He felt more than a little terrified.

"Jesus Christ, Leigh, do you know what you're doing?"

"It's the lighting," Leigh said, waving one hand. "It's making my eyes go shut."

Panic raced through Chris. He thrust his head around, looking for someplace they could stop. There was none. He pressed the electric buttons and took down both the front windows. He hit the radio and turned it up painfully loud. "Hang in there, Leigh," he shouted. "Just hang in there until we get across the bridge."

"Yeah," Leigh shouted back. With his chin close to the top of the wheel, his two hands gripping it on either side, he might have been a fighter pilot zeroing in on his target.

"How we doing now?" screamed Chris.

"I'm driving the car," Leigh screamed back.

"Not what, how?"

"How what?"

"Never mind. Just slow the fuck down."

Seconds later, Leigh's foot came off the accelerator. The speedometer reading fell, but Leigh didn't seem to be watching and Chris couldn't see the numbers from where he sat.

"Not that slow, Leigh," he begged.

The Jag picked up again. They were proceeding over the cantilevered section now, heading downward toward the East Bay shore.

"Get to the right, Leigh."

Inexorably, the Jag changed lanes. Its right wheels hit the bumps of the lane dividers and rode them for fully a quarter of a mile. "Keep going, Leigh, keep going," Chris urged as, almost by centrifugal force, they managed to make it into the right-hand lane. They came into the runoff at the end of the bridge, a wide open area.

"Pull over here, Leigh. You dumb bastard."

The problem with driving the Jaguar, Chris discovered, was that it was almost too comfortable. It was almost like not driving at all. The steering was power and all he had to do was keep the lightest pressure on the accelerator. Once the windows were up, there was virtually no noise except what came from the radio. Leigh certainly wasn't making any. He was slumped against the door, dead to the world.

He was still that way when Chris turned into his driveway. Chris shut off the engine and walked around to the passenger's side. He opened the door and Leigh fell into his arms. Chris managed to get the smaller man to his feet, but he could not get him to stay upright. It was as though all Leigh's weight was in the lower half of his body; his torso kept folding over, wanting to drop like a plumb line to the ground.

An outside light was suddenly snapped on and Cathy Rossville came running out in a white bathrobe. "Oh, wonderful," she said, and draped one of Leigh's arms over her shoulders.

Her husband's eyes rolled open. A leering smile spread across his lips. "Hi, babe. Wanna screw?"

"Not tonight, dearie," she said and, sharing the load with Chris, half dragged, half carried Leigh across the lawn to the house.

"Upstairs?" Chris asked.

"Like fun," Cathy said. She pointed to a guest room just off the front hall. "In there."

They slung Leigh onto a twin bed made up with a brown and cream comforter. Leigh landed in a face-down sprawl and they had to take his feet and pull his body around so that his head was up by the pillow. While Chris removed his shoes and socks, Cathy wrenched him out of his suit coat. She struggled with his tie for a few seconds and then gave up and moved down to his pants. When she was done Leigh was lying still, with nothing on but his white shirt, his silk Cable Car Clothiers

121

tie, and his monogrammed Wilkes Bashford boxer shorts. He had begun
to snore.

With Leigh's suit draped over her arm, Cathy led the way out of the
room. "You want some coffee?" she said to Chris as she shut the door
firmly behind him. "You look like you need it."

They had instant. Cathy offered to make some drip, but Chris said he
drank the instant all the time, it didn't make any difference to him.

She opened a few cabinet doors and came out with a bag of Pep-
peridge Farm cookies, which she dumped on a plate and put in front of
him. "Okay," she said, sitting down across the table from him. "Where
did you go?"

"We started off at Tappers."

"Tappers closes at eight." She smiled.

Chris shrugged. "Then we went to Diamond Lil's. We ended up on
Union Street."

"Any luck?"

"Yeah, we got drunk."

Cathy bit into a cookie. The crumbs broke off on her lip and she
flicked them away with her tongue. Chris, in a slow-witted way, thought
it a surprisingly sensuous thing to do.

She said, "Uh-huh, I can see that. I can also see it's two o'clock in the
morning and I can't believe a couple of stud horses like you guys did
nothing but drink for eight hours. C'mon, Chris, you can tell me. What
did you do? I won't get mad."

"I don't know, Cath," he answered, meaning it. "I don't even remember the names of the places we went."

Cathy's expression turned conspiratorial and she gave an exaggerated
nod of her head. "Right. Listen, Chris, you think after ten years of
marriage I'm going to get pissed at him because he spends a night out
with the boys chasing women?"

Chris had to admit she didn't look pissed. Sitting there in her white
robe with her hair slightly tousled from sleep, she looked athletic and
firm and voluptuous. She looked sultry and warm. She looked happy
and interested. But she did not look pissed. He drank his coffee silently
and suffered manfully while too much of the hot liquid burned its way
down his throat.

She leaned forward, her arm on the table. "That's how he and I met,
you know. On a Friday night at Duckworth's. Leigh was just graduating
from law school and still getting divorced from Linda. I was working in
a dive shop at the time and giving scuba lessons. He spent the whole

night asking me questions like he wanted to know all about diving, and I, like a fool, didn't realize he'd been diving all his life and was just putting me on."

"He used to be good at that. He was the best put-on artist in our entire fraternity."

A spark of recognition appeared in Cathy's face. "I forget sometimes," she said, "that you go that far back with him. Back to the Linda days."

"We were all at Cal together. He and Linda and I. Huh, I'm the one who introduced them, for God's sake. I was going out with her first."

Cathy tilted her head back, the better to scrutinize him. "So how come she didn't stay with you?" she said after a while.

Chris shrugged. Or at least he thought he did. But the way Cathy kept looking at him made him wonder if the motion had actually made it from his mind to his shoulders. "I don't know," he said. "Leigh was more her type, I guess. He was more charming."

"Leigh? Charming?"

"He can be, you know," Chris insisted. "When he's not being obnoxious."

"It's a fine line sometimes, isn't it?" And then Cathy smiled, and when she smiled her eyes danced. "Of course, you usually forgive him for being obnoxious because you figure he's doing it on purpose."

Chris had always like her eyes. He liked the brilliant green color. He like the shape and the way they sparkled and never seemed to get hard, not even when she was angry. As he thought about it, he could not remember any time when her eyes had ever appeared to him to be anything but friendly and inviting.

"Leigh also had a car," he said suddenly. "An Austin-Healey. And his own apartment. Those things helped back then."

"And what did you have?" she asked mischievously.

"Me? I had a friend with a car and an apartment."

"Ooh, the memory hurts, I see."

Chris's eyes opened as wide as they were going to get at this late hour. "Does it sound that way? It wasn't supposed to. It was supposed to be funny."

But Cathy was not laughing and Chris hastened to explain himself. "Look, back in those days I was just a valley kid who got good college board scores and went to Cal because it was the best place my mother could afford to send me. I somehow ended up joining this fraternity where the poorest guy's allowance was probably more than my mom's

123

take-home pay. Of course, I don't manage to realize this until I'm half-way through pledging and then I try to drop out. Leigh was the one who saved me, so to speak. He was a year ahead of me and was sort of the house legend. Mr. Suave and Sophisticated. He's the one who was always throwing the parties at his family's ski cabin up at Tahoe, or who was always dashing off to his parents' condo in Hawaii for the long weekends. And he was the one who shows up in my dorm room and tried to talk me into coming back to the house.

"He thinks, you know, the reason I dropped out was because I couldn't stand the hazing. When I finally told him the truth he acts like it's the dumbest thing he ever heard of. 'Don't worry about it,' he says. 'Hasn't anyone told you about the house scholarship?' Jesus Christ, Cathy, I was in that house for three years before I discovered he'd been paying the dues himself. Didn't he ever tell you about that?"

Cathy slowly shook her head from side to side.

"The only reason I ever did find out was because the clown finally graduated and when I showed up the next year the house treasurer presents me with a bill. I try to tell him I'm on the house scholarship and he looks at me like I'm absolutely nuts."

"Nobody ever said Leigh couldn't be generous . . ."

"Well, it's things like that that are far more important than whether he beats you out of some girl you don't particularly care about in the first place."

"It's a carryover, you see from the fact that he himself has always had everything he ever wanted."

Chris looked at his coffee mug and saw that it was nearly empty. He was able to tip the mug up on its edge without its spilling. "You know, Cathy, I get the feeling things aren't going so well between you guys at the moment."

"Oh, it's not that," she said quickly, but she looked away when she said it. When she looked back she was wearing a dazzling smile, a Miss America smile.

"You want to tell me about it?"

"Oh, it's nothing. Really." The smile faded a bit. "I think Leigh's just tired of being married, that's all." She twisted her shoulders a little as if to say that she could accept that sort of thing.

"Bullshit," said Chris. "If ever a guy liked being married, it's Leigh Rossville. Or haven't you noticed that between you and Linda, he's been married practically all his adult life? If he suddenly starts thinking living by himself's so hot, he should try going to the laundromat sometime. Or cooking alone. Tell him to try that, see how much fun it is. The fact is, you just don't do it."

Cathy poked the cookies around on the plate as though she were trying to make up her mind whether to have another. "If it's so great, how come you've never gotten married, Chris?"

The question startled him. Indeed, the whole conversation was startling him. But he tried to approach it seriously, objectively. "I suppose," he said, "it's because I've reached an age where I understand the concept of agreeing to spend the rest of my life with somebody." He smiled slightly. "And frankly, the idea scares me to death. I mean, back in my twenties, my early twenties, I thought of getting married as just the next logical step in a relationship—a step I never got to with anybody, and I suppose if I tried hard enough I could blame that on Leigh, too. But now, you know, the years have passed and I know what I can do on my own, even if it is just going to a laundromat or eating dinner at Burger King, and . . . well, I'm comfortable with it."

He started to say something more, but Cathy cut him off. "What do you mean, you suppose you could blame that on Leigh, too?"

"Oh." Chris waved one hand. Then he tucked both hands under his arms and sat back in his chair. "That year Leigh got out of college he spent bumming around Europe and he made it seem so utterly fantastic that it was all I could think about doing. Except, by the time I'm ready to join him, his father's already talked him into coming back and going to law school, so now he gets all enthused about that. He tells me his father's got pull, which of course he does, and he can get us both in. 'It'll be a gas,' he keeps telling me. 'Three more years of school, fooling around, no responsibilities.' So the next thing I know, there I am, studying to be a lawyer and discovering that Leigh's the only one who can spend all his time fooling around because he's already got a position secured with his father's firm. Me, I've got to bust my ass night and day just to learn the difference between a tort and a ton of shit."

Cathy giggled and Chris, smiling harder, pushed on with his monologue. "Then," he said, "while I'm in the midst of having all this fun, Leigh comes back to the apartment one night and announces that he and Linda are getting married. Hey, okay, great, now I'm left to do the whole law school trip, which I hadn't even planned on doing, by myself."

"This has all the makings of a wonderful relationship, Chris. So far, he's stolen your girl, transformed your life, and abandoned you on the road to legal heaven."

Chris stopped smiling. "But it wasn't really like that. I mean, I learned early on that you had to accept Leigh for what he is. The very things that make him the most fun are the things that most drive you crazy. He's a great idea man. He's always up for anything, anytime, anywhere. And look at the things he's gotten me into. What, I'm sitting here complaining because he got me into law school and made me become a lawyer?"

Cathy's eyes were focused far away, someplace the other side of Chris's shoulder. It took a while for her to speak. "When I first met Leigh I thought he was the most exciting guy I had ever known."

"And now," Chris said softly, "you don't?"

Cathy sighed. "I guess you can't expect to maintain that intensity over so many years."

"Well, he was working overtime when he first met you."

She focused on Chris again. "What does that mean?"

"He thought you were special the first time he ever saw you."

Cathy waited to see if this was the start of a joke. "How do you know that?" she said cautiously.

"He told me."

"Back then?"

Chris nodded.

She thought about it. "What else did he tell you?"

Chris covered the rim of his coffee mug and idly rocked the mug back and forth. He was trying to keep his lips still, but he couldn't do anything about the light in his eyes.

"C'mon," Cathy said, reaching across and shaking his arm. "What else did he say about me back then?"

Chris's lips got away from him. "He said you were the best piece of ass he ever had."

"Oh." Cathy's reaction was late, as if she didn't know quite how to respond. "Better than Linda?"

"Jesus, anybody's better than Linda. Using your hand's better than Linda." Chris looked around the kitchen. "Fucking the garbage disposal's better than Linda."

Cathy didn't laugh. The crudity was wasted.

"You know?" Cathy said after a while. "From experience, I mean."

Chris nodded. "Once or twice," he said softly.

"Was this before or after she and Leigh got married?"

Chris didn't answer. He was rocking his coffee mug again.

"I'm sorry. Or course you wouldn't do anything like that. Not with a married woman."

There was mockery in her words, enough to make Chris glance up again.

"You especially wouldn't do anything to a married client, would you, Chris?" She sat back in her chair, triumphantly pleased with the look of shocked recognition that was slowly spreading over Chris's face.

"So you were the one who opened the door on us at Roarke Robinson's welcoming party," he said.

"Lucky me. Other people pay good money for performances like that."

Chris felt his face flush. He touched his cheek with his fingers. "I'm embarrassed."

"Don't be. I was the one who was embarrassed at the time. Later on, of course, I had other thoughts, but at the time I couldn't think of anything to do except run."

"What other thoughts?"

There was no answer, only a cock of the head as if to say that she could not possibly tell him that.

"Ooh, you're nasty."

Cathy smiled playfully. She spread her hands. "Like I said, I was embarrassed at the time."

"Did you tell anybody else?"

"Are you kidding? Oh, I did tell Leigh, but I made him promise not to let on. There, now I've confessed to you and you have to confess to me. Did you do it with Linda while she and Leigh were married?"

"No. I did it with Linda in my fraternity room while listening to a Mamas and Papas album."

Cathy looked disappointed. "Then you can't really say if she's good or not. You haven't been with her in at least fifteen years."

"Linda Rossville, the last time I saw her, which wasn't that long ago, would not have been good for anybody."

Cathy studied him. "Linda's awfully pretty."

"She's got a fat ass."

"That's a handicap of age, Chris. It happens to the best of us."

"It doesn't have to. Look at you."

"You don't think my ass is fat?" There was a certain element of enthusiasm to the way she asked the question. She knew it and tried to correct it. "Not fat, I mean, but big?"

"You've got a great ass."

Cathy grinned. "Well, thanks." A few moments later she added, "I didn't think you ever noticed."

Chris felt himself blush. He was ninety percent sure he wanted to say the things he was saying. He was ten percent sure he didn't. "I'd have to be blind not to."

Cathy leaned her elbow on the table and rested her cheek against her hand. She didn't appear to be the least bit uncomfortable about the discussion. "Whenever people compliment me on my body I always assume they're talking about my tits."

Chris let his gaze drop to the lapels of her robe, to the deep, narrow line he could see between the tops of her breasts. "You got something to talk about, Cathy."

"They're not what everybody thinks."

Chris laughed. "Why? They're not real?"

Cathy looked off in the direction of the room where Leigh was sleeping. She listened for a few seconds and then she slid her chair around the table, closer to Chris. She opened her bathrobe just enough to make it loose. Taking Chris's hand by the wrist, she guided it inside.

Gently cupping the end of her breast, Chris whispered, "They're real, all right."

Cathy leaned further forward. There was almost a note of distress in her voice as she said, "Can't you feel? There's no nipple. They're inverted."

Chris's fingers moved. For one instant they were no longer sensuous, they were clinical and probing, and then they spread wide and slipped around the orb. Cathy's green eyes watched him uncertainly and then, very slowly, they slipped shut.

Like a pair of trained dancers, they rose to their feet together. Chris undid the belt of her robe and let it drop to the floor. He put his hands against the bare skin of her waist and pulled her closer to him. She turned her head just enough so that he could bring his lips to hers, and she turned her body just enough to free the paths of his hands.

Chris Cage had one of those moments when he woke up. He was alone in a strange room with strange light coming through the window. He started and made it halfway to a sitting position before the pounding in his head brought him to a stop. He had been drinking. That was why his head was pounding like this. A new thought came to him, a thought important enough to make him rip off the bedcovers. He was naked and his penis lay shriveled and exhausted on its side.

He looked at the pillow next to him. She had been there, Leigh's wife. She had been there when he had fallen asleep. He patted the mattress, felt where she had lain, looked for some sign to confirm what he knew. There was only his clothes, thrown haphazardly on the room's only chair.

He got up and went to the door. Opening it, he saw he was on the second floor of the Rossville house. From down below he could hear the sound of a blender whirring in the kitchen. A whirring blender. He looked at the carpet-covered stairs and vaguely remembered coming up them with Cathy. He touched himself and his fingers came away sticky. He knew what had happened. He knew everything that had happened.

Chris went back to the chair and got dressed. His white shirt was wrinkled to the point of being ridiculous, but he put it on anyway. He put on all the clothes that he had worn the day before, everything but the tie, and that went into his coat pocket. On his way downstairs he stopped in the bathroom, washed his face, combed his hair, gargled with tap water. He stared into the mirror above the sink, thinking he must be seeing himself as others saw him: square-shouldered, red-eyed, dying youth. Ladies and gentlemen of the jury, the paragon of decency who stands before you today grovels on the edges of human depravity by night. Heed my words and not my deeds. Look at my suit and not at me.

He went down to the kitchen. Leigh was sitting at the table with the brown and cream comforter wrapped around his shoulders. The comforter covered the back of his chair and spread onto the floor. He was holding a mug of steaming coffee by the handle, but he wasn't drinking from it.

Beyond Leigh, at the other end of the kitchen, Cathy was pouring orange juice from the blender into three glasses. "Good morning, Chris," she said. "You look about as chipper as your partner in crime over here." She was wearing the same bathrobe she had worn the night before. It rose as she lifted her pouring arm and the cloth clung to her buttocks . . . just as he himself had done.

Silently, Chris sat down. His eyes passed from Cathy to Leigh, who for the first time looked directly back at him, Leigh shook his head, his face a mask of disbelief.

Leigh's mouth opened, but no words came out. Only a noise. "Awwwhhh."

129

"Translated," said Cathy, delivering the juice to the table, "that means Leigh isn't feeling very well. How about you? Do you need some Alka-Seltzer or an aspirin or anything?"

Chris nodded, too apprehensive to speak out loud.

"What," Leigh suddenly said, "did you do to me last night?"

He was looking directly at Chris, but Chris couldn't answer. Behind him Cathy banged a cupboard door. Chris jumped. Leigh smiled painfully.

"Dragging me all over town. Making me drink all kinds of foul spirits. I think it's a bloody miracle we even made it home."

Cathy slid the aspirin onto the table. "You can thank Chris for that," she said. "He's the one who drove."

"I'll surely do that," Leigh told her, "as soon as I'm feeling better."

"I don't remember much myself," Chris said, but he was mumbling and it was possible nobody else heard him.

Owen Carr

CHAPTER ONE

What Owen was good at, plain and simple, was surviving. The realization had come to him slowly, over the course of many years, but now it was reinforced with every funeral he attended, every retirement announcement he received. Indeed, hardly a day went by when he was not served with some reminder as to how few people were left from when he first started out. It made no difference whether they had been investigators, cops, lawyers, judges, clerks or criminals. It made no difference how rich or glamorous or successful they once had been. When they were gone, they were gone.

But Owen Carr was not gone, and the pride he took in this fact was reflected in the words painted across his office door and emblazoned on his business cards: "Never A Day Off Since 1949." With this motto, he had taken a situation that might have been bitter, lonely and unhappy and created of it a world of achievement and accomplishment in which he was uniquely and supremely master.

Whether the words were one hundred percent accurate was not so important as was the fact that they were indisputable. If Owen had not actually worked every day for over thirty-five years, he had, at least, been available to work every one of those days. There was no one alive who could say that Owen Carr had not been willing to work a Sunday or a Christmas, a Thanksgiving or a Fourth of July. Indeed, many of his best calls were made on Sundays and holidays, when families were most likely to be together or in touch with one another.

And sometimes his best calls came in on such days, like the call from Newhauser, the diener down at the morgue, which caught him even before he had got the Mr. Coffee machine working. It was a Sunday in early March, and on winter Sundays Owen did not generally arrive in

133

his office until eleven o'clock. His best referral sources tended to know that, and so the ringing of the telephone at five past eleven was a matter of some importance to him. It was important enough that he preferred to lose count of the spoonfuls of coffee he was dropping into the paper filter rather than take the chance that the caller might hang up.

"Owen," whispered Newhauser, "I got one I thought I might run by you."

"How old?" was all Owen said.

Newhauser hesitated, perhaps turning away from the phone. "Oh, I'd say about nineteen."

Owen sighed. "The body, Dale, not the person. How long's it been dead?"

Newhauser was a slimy sort. He oozed slime over the telephone wires. "Yeah, heh, heh, I musta misunderstood you there. Thing is, it just came in, Owen. First time I eyeballed it I thought of you. That one's got Owen written all over it, I said to myself. I'd say, by the looks of him, he musta gotten it during the night. You interested?

"Give me the details and I'll tell you."

Newhauser was quick off the mark on that one. "Oh, no. The details are what I got to sell. If you want them now, you gotta pay for 'em. Otherwise, you can wait till it comes out in the papers."

"Nineteen-year-old boy, huh? No ID?"

Newhauser laughed softly into the phone. "Nice-looking kid. White. Big. Real good build."

Owen grunted.

"Usual arrangement, Owen?"

"What am I going to get, Dale? I could track down the boy's mother and father and then hit them for the costs spent trying to find them, but how much would that be? People aren't so good about paying when you tell them their boy's been killed, you know. They tend to act like the messenger did it. . . . By the way, he was killed, wasn't he?"

"That's the angle, Owen. That's what's going to make you buy this case."

Owen thought about it. "What are his teeth like?"

"Good teeth. Got 'em all."

"What you're supposed to be looking for is someone who might have a trust. Person dies before the trust vests, the money goes to somebody else. Those people pay."

"That's not why you're going to like this one, Owen."

134

The certainty with which Newhauser spoke rankled Owen. He did not like being so easily diagnosed by anyone and he punished Newhauser by making him wait a long time for the answer they both knew was coming. "All right," he said at last. "Usual arrangement."

Newhauser's laugh slithered across the line again. "You're on." He paused, demonstrating the Newhauser technique of dramatic effect. "They found the kid in the bushes off Skyline Boulevard, where the Angels used to dump people back when they were into that sort of thing. Blond hair, blue eyes, no clue to his identity except, like I said, the teeth make me think it's not biker business."

"How are the hands?"

"Nothing special. He's not a workman, that's for sure. He's got callous pads, but that could be from lifting weights—which this boy looks like he's done."

"Drugs?"

"I don't know. Autopsy will show that. But it doesn't have that look to it. The kid's young, he's got the muscles, and he comes in with no shirt on. Blue jeans, socks and boots, but no shirt."

"Labels?"

"One. On the underpants. Says Filene's, irregular."

"What's Filene's?"

"Hey, maybe it's a fancy boutique. Maybe it's your clue. Except it doesn't look it. It looks like a stock label, like a J. C. Penney's label. You know what I'm talking about?"

"Not particularly."

"Yeah, well, you'll see. You want to come down, take his picture?"

"Oh, definitely."

"That's good, Owen, because I saved the best till last."

"The way the boy died, you mean."

"With an arrow of some sort, Owen. In the throat. You see why I thought of you now? Who shoots people with arrows? Hunters, that's who. People who might be willing to pay for their mistakes."

Owen's lack of enthusiasm was not lost on Newhauser. "You still coming down, Owen?" he asked.

It took Owen a few moments to say that he was.

And Newhauser, put on guard, said, "Make sure you bring the twenty-five bucks. Cash."

* * *

135

Late in the afternoon, Owen Carr sat in the Oakland Public Library, one block from the courthouse, three blocks from his office, seven blocks from his rooming house. He had before him a huge loose-leaf binder from Value Line, a stock reporting service, and he was reading through the descriptions of corporate retailers. He was not even at it long enough to take off his raincoat. There it was, Filene's, a member of the Federated Department Stores chain, with stores exclusively in the Boston area. Owen smiled inwardly. He had been living alone too long to do it any other way.

"No," said Philpott, "I got no unclaimed vehicles with any New England plates all this month except this stripped Corvette from New York."

"New York's not in New England," he was reminded.

Philpott glanced up angrily. He did not enjoy being corrected on something he had no desire to know in the first place. "Yeah?" he said, pushing himself away from the computer terminal and smoothing out the wrinkles in his Oakland Police Department shirt. "Well, in that case I got nothing."

But Philpott took the key to the locker at the Greyhound station anyway. The fact that he had not been able to give Owen the information he wanted did not make him any the less thirsty.

Richmond had nothing unclaimed. Neither did Emeryville. Berkeley had a 1972 Volkswagen bug with Rhode Island plates and a UC student parking permit on its bumper, but a check of the university registration records revealed that it belonged to a young man named Kim Hollister, who turned out to be alive and well and living in a woodshed in somebody's garden. He was wearing a red sheet when Owen found him and he was surprised to learn that his car had been impounded. But he did not really care. He wasn't into material things anymore. And besides, his name wasn't Kim anymore. It was Swami.

Owen nodded and looked around the woodshed. He saw an electric typewriter in its case, apparently left over from the days when Kim Hollister had been into material things. He asked if he could have it. He used the name Swami when he made the request.

Swami gave Owen the typewriter. Owen said, "A thousand blessings on your house," and left while Swami was still deliberating on what he was going to use for a new table support.

He could have gone south to Hayward or San Leandro, but he chose to try across the Bay in San Francisco. Owen knew nobody to tap in the San Francisco Police Department, but a few phone calls got him to the garage of the private company that had the contract for towing vehicles.

The kid on duty at the garage wanted to know which car was his. Owen said he was looking for Alexander Hamilton's car and gave the kid a picture of Hamilton on a ten-dollar bill. The kid stared at the picture for a long time and Owen wandered off to look for what he was looking for. In fifteen minutes he found it three different times, and Mr. Hamilton's picture was still valuable enough to get him a rundown on all three.

A brown Karmann Ghia with Maine plates had been taken from the Marina Green after it had collected ten days' worth of parking tickets. It had been sitting in the garage for a week now and it looked like nobody was going to claim it. Owen wrote down the information out of caution more than enthusiasm. The victim didn't look like the Karmann Ghia type—and where would he have been all the time between the first ticket and the date of his death?

A white LTD with Massachusetts plates had just come in that day, but that was even less likely a vehicle for the dead boy to be driving. Besides, it had been towed from a bus zone in the Financial District. Given the fact that it was Monday, the LTD conceivably could have been sitting in the bus zone since Saturday, but it was unlikely. Still, he wrote down that information as well.

But it was the third vehicle that primarily interested Owen Carr. It was not an automobile at all, but a motorcycle, and it, too, had Massachusetts plates. It had been taken in on Sunday night after a complaint call from a Union Street area singles bar known as McGuppers. Owen thought he would start there. It seemed more promising than Hayward or San Leandro.

He timed his entry for five o'clock. Late enough to be open, early enough to avoid the Union Street regulars. He was ready for McGuppers, but it was not quite ready for him.

The muscular, mustachioed bartender with the tight green shirt stopped pouring ice from bucket to beer chest and straightened up suspiciously. He gave Owen the same look he would have given the Department of Health. "Can I help you?" he demanded.

Owen showed no hurry. He climbed onto one of the stools and sat there with his hands folded on the bar. "Vodka twist," he said.

The bartender showed no care in getting it for him. He splashed the liquor and threw in the precut lemon peel and then he plunked the drink in front of Owen as it if were a challenge. "Two fifty," he said.

Owen's hands stayed folded. He smiled at the bartender. "I wonder if I might see your manager."

"He's not here."

"What's your position?" He smiled again. "If you don't mind."

"Assistant manager."

"I'm a private investigator," Owen said. His right index finger moved, his thumb came up from the hollow formed by his folded hands, and a business card snapped to the surface.

The bartender's head rocked back a little in surprise. He stared at the card without touching it. "No shit," he said.

Owen spread his hands and the card fell to the bar. The bartender read it, reading upside down. Owen brought his hands together again, scooping up the card. He twisted his hands one way and then the other, as if he were packing a snowball. He opened his hands once more, palms up. The card was gone and a twenty-dollar bill was in its place. "For the drink," he said.

The bartender's face softened. "Aww-right," he crooned. He picked the bill out of Owen's hands and inspected it to make sure it was real. Seeing that it was, he turned to look over his shoulder and Owen knew he was going to call one of his co-workers to come see the old man do magic tricks. Owen didn't want that. He had just exhausted his repertoire.

"I'd like to ask you a question," he said quickly.

"Sure," said the bartender, turning back.

"A motorcycle was towed from this area yesterday after somebody from here called up to complain about it."

The bartender knew right away what he was talking about. "Hey, it had been sitting there in the loading zone since sometime Saturday night. It was there when I closed the place. It was there when I opened yesterday afternoon. By last night I figured it was abandoned, you

---

138

know? Nobody who cares about his bike is going to leave it that long. Not in a loading zone."

"Any idea who it belonged to?"

"Didn't belong to anybody I know." The bartender touched his mustache. "Had out-of-state plates, didn't it?"

Owen Carr used the traditional method of producing a photograph. He took it out of the inner pocket of his suit jacket and laid it down facing the bartender. "You ever see this boy before?"

The bartender bent his head at the neck. Then he bent down closer and leaned his hands on his knees. "That boy looks dead," he said.

"You remember him? Couple of inches over six feet, real blond hair? Might have been some sort of athlete."

The bartender straightened up and looked around the bar again. "Hey, Goose," he called. "Come here a minute, will ya?"

A bearded man waddled over. He, too, seemed wary of Owen, but he nodded and smiled half a greeting.

"You know this guy?" the first bartender said, thrusting the picture at him.

Goose looked at the picture. He had to lean his head to one side to do it, and when he looked up at Owen he kept his head at that same angle. "I don't know him," he said. "But I think I seen him before. You his grandfather?"

The first bartender slapped Goose lightly on the shoulder. He glanced quickly at Owen as if to tell him not to pay any attention. "This guy's an investigator," he said, pointing with his thumb. "He's looking for this other guy."

Goose tilted his head back where it belonged. "He was in here one night last week. Wednesday, I think, or it might have been Thursday. The reason I remember is, I thought he was going to be trouble when he first came in. Just the way he looked, just the way he looked around the place, I mean. Sort of squinty-eyed, like he's looking to see if anybody might want to mess with him."

Owen nodded sympathetically. "Could it have been Saturday when he was here?"

"No, it definitely wasn't Saturday," Goose said. "I would have noticed the guy if he came in again. Night he was here he stood at the bar for a long time."

"You see him talk to anybody while he was here?"

"Just some guy in a business suit. I remember that, too, 'cause, see, this guy's wearing a white T-shirt and some kind of windbreaker and the guy he spends all the time talking to has got like the three-piece suit and silk tie. The guy in the suit is doing all the buyin', but it wasn't like they were fags or anything. It was more like they were doing business. You know what I mean?"

"Not really," Owen said.

Goose shrugged. "Yeah, well, at one point the young guy asked me for a pen and paper so he could write down directions."

Owen tried not to jump at the information. He didn't want to panic Goose and cause him to forget. Taking his first, last, and only sip of vodka, he said, "You know where to?"

Goose shook his head. Then he snapped his fingers. "Wait a minute. After the guy in the suit left, the young guy asked me something funny. He asked if I knew Tranton Park. You know, that place over in the East Bay."

Owen put his glass back on the bar. "What did you tell him?"

Goose said, "I told him sure, I knew where it was. Then he asked me, and this was the funny thing, he asked me if that was a place where rich people live. I said it's gotta be. That's where Roarke Robinson just bought a house, isn't it?"

"The kid say anything after that?"

"He left."

Owen got to his feet. "Then so, Goose, will I. One last question, though. Can you tell me anything about the man in the suit: what he looked like, how big he was . . . ?"

Goose said, "Hey, I was pretty busy. I didn't pay that much attention to him." He looked at the other bartender, the assistant manager. "He was just a guy in a suit, that's all."

Owen pointed one yellowing finger at the twenty-dollar bill the assistant manager was still holding. The man quickly rang it into the cash register and put Owen's change on the bar. Owen smiled and left him a nice tip.

He only took the big bills.

CHAPTER TWO

Owen knew Tranton. He had known it when it had been a hilly little appendage to his own city of Oakland. He had known it when people had to be truly affluent to live there, when all the homes had at least ten rooms and all the yards were measured in acres. In those days people from Oakland only went to Tranton to cook, or wash floors, or mow lawns, or take care of children.

But Tranton had changed, just like every other place within commuting distance of San Francisco. The doctors discovered it; so did the lawyers; so did the lieutenants of industry—the people of the City who wanted a little country living or who wanted a nice home and a Bay view but couldn't afford Pacific Heights. The estates were broken up and sold off in parcels. The houses that were built were smaller, less formidable but still expensive structures that gave up grandeur and gave off the California experience.

The people from Oakland didn't go there to cook anymore; Trantonites were gourmet cooks, both the men and the women; they took cooking classes and got recipes out of specialty magazines. The people from Oakland didn't go there to take care of children so much anymore, either; Trantonites used au pairs circulated from Scandinavia or France or England. But people from Oakland did still go to Tranton to wash floors and mow lawns; the town hadn't changed that much.

The area known as Tranton Park, from what Owen recalled, had been something of an audacious experiment. It had sprung, full blown, from the lands of a long-dead shipping magnate. A street designed like a hangman's noose had been put in and the houses had all gone up at once, each designed in a different style by a different architect. The price tags had started at three hundred and fifty thousand dollars for the flatland homes and they had risen as the road rose. It went up a small hill and then around in a loop that gradually eased back down to intersect with itself.

"Climb to the top," the original advertising had urged, "and project yourself in a custom home worthy of your individual and professional achievement." And climb to the top people did. For several weeks, spurred on by newspaper and television accounts of this uniquely pricey tract development, people had come from all over the Bay Area just to drive by and say, "Can you imagine paying that much for this place?"

The question had been appropriate enough when nobody lived there, when Tranton Park had seemed nothing more than the preposterous folly of some deluded developer; but then the houses started to be picked off, individual owners started moving in, and gawking quickly ceased to be such sport. A few of the gawkers even started making inquiries as to how they could go about projecting themselves into a custom home worthy of their own individual and professional achievements—if not in Tranton Park, then surely in someplace like Tranton Park.

Owen Carr had not been one of those people. He had, in fact, never been to Tranton Park until the morning after he spoke with the bartenders at McGuppers. On his first pass around the street known as Tranton Park Lane he did nothing more than take in the contrasting styles. There were single-levels, splits, two-stories. Some cascaded, some towered, some rambled. Some even hunkered. All looked expensive. All looked out of place sharing the neighborhood.

He made a second pass and noted which houses had fences and where they had them; he noted which houses appeared to have kids; and he noted the makes of the cars he could see in the driveways and garages. He counted nine Mercedeses, three of them wagons, the rest either silver or some shade of blue. He counted four BMWs, two Volvos, a Peugeot, and a Porsche. The only American car on the street was his own Dodge Dart.

When he had seen all that he could see, he drove back to a 7-Eleven store he had noticed near the entrance to Tranton Park Lane and went in to talk with the kid behind the counter. The kid was about six feet eight and wore a Thin Lizzie T-shirt. Owen showed him the picture of the dead boy.

"He doesn't look like he comes from around here," the kid said, pulling at his chin.

142

"Could you have seen him at any time last weekend? Did he come in and ask for directions, anything like that?"

"Cheesch," said the kid, pushing his hair around. "How do you expect me to remember back then?"

Owen agreed that it was difficult. He tried another approach. He asked about motorcycles, whether there had been anybody who had ridden by on one over the weekend. The kid stretched and couldn't remember that, either.

"Tell me, you know anybody in Tranton Park who owns a motorcycle?" It was unlikely, but Owen thought maybe that was what the dead boy and the man in the suit had been talking about in McGuppers.

The 7-Eleven kid couldn't help. "Beats me, mister. I don't have any idea what goes on in Tranton Park." Then, taking time to make a few long scratches on his very long arms, he said, "I'm from Oakland myself. I just come here to work."

Owen nodded. "You and me both," he said.

They both peered off in the direction of Tranton Park as though it were a very foreign place indeed.

The motorcycle was confusing Owen. The kid had Boston underwear. The motorcycle had Massachusetts plates. The kid was in McGuppers on Wednesday or Thursday night. The motorcycle was there on Saturday night. The kid was killed on Saturday night. Dumped on a ridge in the East Bay. And sometime after the kid left McGuppers he was supposed to go to a neighborhood in the East Bay. If the kid owned the motorcycle, wouldn't he have ridden it to the East Bay? If the kid owned the motorcycle, what was it doing outside McGuppers when the kid wasn't inside? If the kid owned the motorcycle.

Owen sat down at his desk and spun through his Rolodex. He was looking for the name of an investigator in Massachusetts. He had met one once, at an investigator's seminar in Coronado. A fat, red-faced Irishman who had formerly been a Massachusetts state trooper. A "statie," he called himself. Owen came across the name Gleason and believed it to be the same man, since he could think of no one else from that part of the country whose name would be in the Rolodex.

Gleason, as it turned out, remembered Owen quite well. "Old guy?" he said when Owen got him on the telephone line. "Never a day off since nineteen twenty-nine?"

"Forty-nine."

143

"How you doin', you old buzzard?"

Owen sucked in his breath and muttered that he was doing very well, thank you. "I've got a case I'm investigating," he said. "It may lead back to where you are."

"This isn't one of those missing-heir things you were always working on, is it?"

"A young man was murdered. I'm trying to find out who he is."

Gleason smacked his lips as though he were weighing the possibilities. "I thought what you did was you researched probate files and got lists of estates where people hadn't claimed their inheritances. I thought you went around trying to find those people."

"I do that sometimes, too," Owen said. "This is something different."

"Branching out, huh? That's good thinkin', Owen. Now you don't have to wait around till an estate gets filed. You start right away with the body. See if he's got an estate. Beat everybody else to it." Gleason paused. He wheezed into the phone. "Kind of a long shot, isn't it?"

"I'm following a hunch. I think it may lead to something."

"What about the police? They following the same hunch?"

"No contact with them. If they're on to what I'm on to, they're way behind."

The noise that came over the phone was so prolonged it could not have been a wheeze. It had to be a sigh. "You're not getting paid for this, are you, Owen?"

"Not yet,"

"I won't go splitzies or anything with you, Owen, if that's what you're asking. Not on a chaser like this. I'll do you a favor because I'm guessing you probably need it, but I can't afford this spec stuff."

"Just a favor, that's all I need," Owen agreed.

"Okay," Gleason said cautiously. "Shoot."

Owen give him the license plate number and description of the motorcycle and asked him to trace it. Gleason, sounding relieved, said that would be easy enough and he'd call back as soon as he had it. Owen told him to call collect if he liked. Gleason said no problem. Owen didn't argue. Gleason had, after all, made him beg for the favor.

CHAPTER THREE

Meals were something that Owen Carr merely tolerated. His appreciation for food had been severely damaged by his years in Europe during the war, and it had been destroyed entirely by the practices of the young English wife he had brought home with him. Hilary's idea of cooking was to fry everything. Her knowledge of spices was limited to salt and pepper. Her concept of varying meals was nonexistent.

But when she was gone and Owen was suddenly left on his own, he had found himself neither knowledgeable of nor interested in the ways of the kitchen. The oven in the little house he and Hilary had shared grew moldy with disuse. The refrigerator, which to Hilary had been America's greatest wonder, was disabled by a freezer which became so filled with ice that he had difficulty in closing its door.

Eventually he solved these problems by moving out of the house and into an apartment that had no kitchen at all. He set up a hot plate to solve his cravings for coffee during the day and tea at night, he bought a tiny little icebox to keep his milk and his soda in, and he was satisfied. Breakfasts were skipped, lunches were sandwiches, and dinners were either taken around the corner at Nigel's Café or at a series of bland Cantonese restaurants scattered throughout Oakland's Chinatown. The difference in his evening eating spots was not that great. Nigel himself was from Hong Kong.

It was to Nigel's that Owen went on the night following his first series of interviews with the people of Tranton Park. Although he had the choice of nearly any table he wanted, Owen went directly to a corner booth. He had things to do and he did not want to have to listen to Nigel harass whatever immigrants he happened to have working for him at that particular time. The immigrants came and went. The food

145

stayed the same, as constant as Nigel's fat, sour-faced wife, who lived in abject silence on a stool in front of the cash register.

Once seated, Owen spread across his tabletop five questionnaires, one each for June Hartry, Janice Butler, Eva Martel, Polly Lindsay and Aurora Weissock. Of the five women, most of his time had been spent with June Hartry, who had answered her door wearing clothes that said she was pregnant and an expression that said she was not at all happy to find an old man standing on her front step.

Owen turned to her questionnaire first, but before he could begin reviewing his notes, Nigel started making clicking noises at him from his post behind the counter. Owen flashed him three fingers and Nigel, knowing exactly what it meant, turned and barked maniacally at some poor refugee in the kitchen. "Chi, chi, chi," he said, or something to that effect.

June Hartry had looked closely at his brown suit, his gold shirt, his brown tie with the gold doodads. She had stared at the yellowish raincoat and then had glanced up at the sky to confirm that there was not a sign of rain.

Owen had shown her his clipboard, his notebook, his pen. He had told her he was doing a survey of the area, trying to find out what services were most needed in and around Tranton Park. She had answered quickly: "A locked gate and an armed security guard."

Owen had started to write that down and then he stopped and slowly lowered his clipboard to his side. "I'm sorry," he said. "I'm just trying to do a job."

June Hartry, who had been all set to say something more, began blowing air across her upper lip and pushing her hair back from her eyes. Instead of looking angry, she suddenly looked as if she wanted to cry. "Forgive me," she said. "I'm . . ." and she pointed to her stomach and waved her hand in a show of helplessness.

Owen had smiled benignly at what he took to be a bulge beneath the man's dress shirt which she wore outside the waistband of her baggy jeans. "A little one," he said. "How wonderful."

She had softened then, leaning back against the doorframe and returning his smile sufferingly. "Look," she said, "will this take long? I really don't feel that I can stand up for more than a few minutes."

"We could sit down out here," Owen said. She considered it for a second and then invited him into the house.

146

They had paused briefly at the entrance to the living room and then she had led him straight back to the kitchen, where they took seats in a breakfast nook. Mrs. Hartry apologized for the dirty dishes and open packages of food that were still out on the counters, but Owen barely looked around. Without even taking off his coat, he simply poised himself to write.

"Everything seems to be getting away from me," she said plaintively. She glanced at the counters almost as though she was willing to get up and take care of them at that very moment. "I don't know why. It's not as though I haven't been pregnant before."

Making her face into a picture of resolved bravery, she said, "But our other kids are nine and eleven. I feel like they're practically grown up and here I am, starting all over again."

Owen inclined sympathetically and was rewarded when a slight, unexpected, not altogether merry giggle escaped from Mrs. Hartry's lips. "I blame it on the Butlers' hot tub," she said.

Owen cocked his head curiously, just enough to show he was interested without being prying. She asked him if he had interviewed the Butlers yet and he said no.

"He's a dentist and she . . . well, let's put it this way: You're not going to be able to get the opinion of the neighborhood unless Janice has something to say about it." Covering her mouth with her fingertips, she said, "I hope that came out right. I don't mean to sound catty or anything, it's just that . . . let's put it this way: Janice likes to give her opinions on things. Anyhow, they're our really good friends and Janice had a hot tub put in a few months back—an early Christmas present for Jay, she called it—and of course we had to try it out." She rolled her eyes and then tossed her hand ruefully as though she was sure Owen understood the words left unspoken.

But Owen merely sat as he had before, listening politely, showing no signs of judgment whatsoever. If there was one thing Owen had learned over the years, it was how to listen.

"I don't know why I'm telling you all this," Mrs. Hartry said suddenly. "I think I'm having a hormonal rush or something. I should really read one of those books they've got out now. Of course, I read them all the first time I was pregnant. I read everything in sight then. But they understand so much more and they've written about it so much more just in the years since Garret—he's my nine-year-old—was born." She laughed in embarrassment. "Would you believe I have a master's in child psych? That's why all of this is so funny. I've never

147

done anything with it, but now that the kids are at an age where I can leave them at home during the day, I was really hoping to do something in the field. I was going to take a refresher course, try to get a job as a counselor, maybe. Isn't it strange, the way you're willing to do for others what you're not even willing to do for yourself?"

Owen nodded.

Mrs. Hartry nodded back. They moved their heads in harmony.

"Somehow I just can't bring myself to go out and buy these books that talk about the stresses on expectant mothers. . . . I don't know. Maybe the truth is I'm really not interested in psychology anymore. Maybe it was just something I was interested in when I was younger and thought everything was explainable."

Owen chewed his pen thoughtfully. Then, looking at her over the top of his glasses, he asked, "What would you like to do instead?"

June Hartry shifted her position. She groaned a little when she did so. She had been sitting on the tail of her spine and now she moved to her right hip, clasping her hands down by her side for balance. "I think what I'd really like is to get involved in a small business of my own, like Cathy Rossville. She's another one of the women in the neighborhood. She has a little travel agency down in the village. Has one or two people working for her . . . goes in when she wants to . . ."

Owen, hunched over his clipboard, said, "Sounds like this project I'm doing might be right up your alley. Any particular business you were thinking of getting into?"

"Oh, Janice and I talked about a bunch of different things, but that was just talk. What she'd really like to do is get into real estate, something like what Marietta Gould does. Those people make a killing. I know, believe me."

She suddenly leaned forward, her elbows on the table, her arms crossed in front of her. "There's this house up the street that Marietta sold, and from what I understand, her commission on that one place alone ran about twelve or fifteen thousand dollars. Can you imagine? And like Janice says, Marietta didn't have to do anything. She had the listing and Leigh Rossville, that's Cathy's husband, more or less arranged the purchase so that Marietta got to represent both the buyer and the seller and not have to split the fee with anyone. The brokers get about half the commission, don't they? I think so. Anyhow, Janice is just green with envy about the whole thing. She figures if sweet little Marietta can do it, she can do it, too."

Mrs. Hartry shrugged. She and the old man exchanged glances of the kind that only pass between friends. "What's your name?" she asked him.

Owen told her.

"Well, Owen Carr, what is it you're here to ask me?"

Owen put down his pen for the first time since he had come in. "I don't know," he said, leaning against the back of the bench on which he was sitting. "Maybe I'm wasting my time in this neighborhood. It sounds as if everybody's so busy I'm not going to be able to get all the information I need."

"Oh, nonsense. I'm home today. Janice will be home if she's not at aerobics. Ann Robinson's probably home; God knows where else she'd be. You might find Marietta and I'm sure I saw Aurora Weissock drive up the street a little while ago."

"You seem to know just about everybody in Tranton Park."

"Well, there are—what?—about thirty-six houses and we all belong to the home owners' association, so I at least know the names of everyone, although that's all some of the people are is just names and faces."

"It would help me very much, ma'am—"

"Hartry. June Hartry." She held out her hand, her fingers rigid and pointed, and Owen, rising in his seat, shook it formally.

"Yes," he said. "Well, it would help me very much if you could more or less let me know who might be where and when would be the best time for me to try to reach them."

Mrs. Hartry commandeered Owen's notepad and sketched a hangman's noose on it. Starting on the left outside of the loop, she drew a box and put an X in it. We're here," she said. "Next door, right here, is the Butlers'. See, I'll put a little circle in their backyard for their infamous hot tub. Next to them are the Martels. He calls himself an account executive, but he's really just a stockbroker—although, from what I can see, he makes a fortune. Next to them are the Lindsays. They're nice people, but they're an older couple so we don't see too much of them. He owns some sort of plumbing supply store."

She moved her pen to the inside of the noose. "Okay, right across the street from us are the Lanes, John Clarke and his wife, Mary Elizabeth. I wouldn't bother with them, though. He'll be at work and she won't answer the door."

"Eh? Why's that?"

"She's just weird, that's all. She almost never comes out of the house. I see her looking through the windows or doors sometimes, but that's about it. She's not exactly your friendly type." She drew another square

149

next to that which marked the Lanes' house. "Over here are the Ross-villes. They might be away. I haven't seen them in a couple of days. Up around the corner are the Goulds—that's Marietta I was telling you about. Her husband's name is Bert, but everybody calls him Blinky. There's another couple next to them I don't know very well. It's some Armenian name. He used to be chairman of the board of some big corporation, but they're retired now. Next to them are the Weissocks—no, the Robinsons. You've heard of him—Roarke Robinson, the famous baseball player? And next to them are the Weissocks. You'll like them. He's an optician and Aurora has a mail order flower business."

June Hartry went back to the outside of the noose and ticked off a few more names. She was pretty much able to put everyone in place as long as she stayed on the hill where the loop was located, but it was clear that she was losing interest in the task. When she got to the road leading up to the loop she stared uncertainly. There were some Iranians among the flatlanders, she said, but she wasn't sure who belonged where. She scribbled in some lines on both sides of the road to show that she was not going to do any more and then irritably pushed the notepad back across the table.

She looked at Owen as though he had just made her very tired. "Anything else?" she said.

Caught somewhat by surprise at the suddenness of her mood swing, Owen turned too quickly to his questionnaire. Pointing to the top of his list, he said, "I'd like to know what magazines you and your husband subscribe to."

The question made June Hartry stiffen. "Did you come here to sell magazine subscriptions?" she asked.

Owen glanced back at the list of questions. He made a mental note to bury that one further down the list. Sheepishly, he shook his head. "I'm just supposed to find out what interests people in the area have and this is what's known as the scientific method of doing that." He gestured at the list. "Instead of coming right out and asking what you need, we try to establish a profile so we can tell you what you need."

It was clear from her narrowed eyes, her hardened jaw, her clenched fist, that June Hartry was now regretting ever letting him into her house. But Owen was returning her gaze with such equanimity that once again her anger abated. He could see her slide, almost wearily, back into her seat again. Slowly, she opened her hand and flicked out her fingers. *"Sports Illustrated* and *U.S. News & World Report,"* she said finally. "Those two and a bunch of computer magazines my husband gets."

The tomato sizzling rice soup was gone. The ball of potato had solidified and the pork chop was hacked to the bone. Nigel's Number 3, "American Special," was history and Owen was sipping at his tea and studying the map Mrs. Hartry had drawn for him.

No one had been at the Robinsons' or the Goulds' or the Rossvilles'. A man had come to the door of "the Armenians," but he would not answer any questions. "No solicitors," he had said, and slammed the door. Finally, no one had answered his knock at the Lanes', but Owen was sure someone had been home, because he had seen a drape moving and because after a while he could feel somebody standing there, just on the other side of the door.

Of the five women whose statements he had taken, no one knew anyone who was interested in motorcycles. No one was interested in hunting and no one thought opening a hunting store of any sort anyplace in Tranton would be welcomed by anyone. "Hunting?" Aurora Weissock had said. "You mean, like killing animals?"

Indeed, the interests of those to whom he had spoken had been remarkably uniform. "Tennis," said Mrs. Hartry, Mrs. Butler, Mrs. Weissock. "Sailing," said Mrs. Martel, meaning that was what her husband was interested in. "Golf," said Mrs. Lindsay, meaning the same thing. "Golf and fishing." Everyone claimed an interest in baseball, or at least in the A's, or at least in the career of Roarke Robinson, who apparently had just gone off to spring training in Arizona. Everyone thought youth soccer was a good thing and should be encouraged. "It's so much safer than football," offered Mrs. Lindsay; and Mrs. Martel, who was obviously foreign born, said she liked it better than football because they didn't make the boys wear those things on their heads that make them look like race car drivers.

Owen had wanted to know what they thought about weight lifting. Mrs. Butler, who, like Mrs. Weissock, Mrs. Martel and Mrs. Lindsay, had been interviewed in her doorway, had been the only one to show any curiosity whatsoever. She had looked into the weight room of the athletic club to which she belonged and she had seen women in there. She had thought she might like to try it herself, but she didn't need to have a club built near Tranton Park just so she could do that. And no, her husband wouldn't be interested in weight lifting. He was a jogger.

Owen was in the midst of preparing a list of names and professions for the people in Tranton Park when Nigel came by to clear away his plates. Owen asked him if he had a San Francisco yellow page directory and a moment later a dog-eared copy was thrown in front of him.

If the dead youth had met a man from Tranton Park wearing a suit in a San Francisco bar, then Owen was willing to assume that such a man would be someone who worked in his suit in San Francisco. That let out Mr. Lindsay, the plumbing supply store owner. It probably let out the retired Armenian. It would have been one more reason to let out Roarke Robinson, if any were needed. Of the rest, the City directory showed no opticians named Weissock and no stockbrokers named Martel. There was, however, an investment counselor named Bert Gould, a lawyer named John Clarke Lane, and two lawyers named Lee Rossville, both of whom spelled their names L-e-i-g-h. Any one of them could wear a suit.

There was nowhere in the yellow pages to look for a computer software marketing manager named Mark Hartry, and with the other names Mrs. Hartry had given him, Owen also had no luck. Except there, listed under dentists, was the name Jay Butler, with an office on the fifth floor of a Sutter Street medical building.

Owen felt a small tingling of excitement. Of all the people with whom he had spoken, it had been Mrs. Butler who had interested him most. There had, for example, been that blast of rock-and-roll music that had come from inside her house while they had talked. She had made a face and explained that it was only her son Arthur. "The teenager," she explained. "He just bought himself a new stereo." Owen had looked at her uncertainly, and she had said, "How these kids manage it, I don't know." And then she had glanced at her watch—a golden oval without any numbers—and had seen that she had already given Owen too much of her time.

She had begun closing the door in his face, telling him that Arthur must be done with his schoolwork now and that he'd be wanting a snack soon. "I've got to run," she said, and the door had latched shut, leaving Owen to wonder what kind of boy it was who was old enough to buy his own stereo and yet still needed his mom to fix him an afternoon treat.

There were, Owen thought as he finished his tea and reviewed his notes of the Butler conversation one last time, a multitude of things about that family which bore further investigation. But what he needed to know first, before he tried to make something out of the hot tub, the teenager with the new stereo, or the keenness on physical fitness, was whether a dentist who worked in San Francisco would wear a suit.

Dentists wore white coats in their offices. What did they wear to and from the office? This was a matter that Owen had never considered before. Not once since 1949.

Resolving to notice things like that more often, Owen gathered up his papers and trekked down the aisle to the cash register to pay off the effervescent Mrs. Nigel.

CHAPTER FOUR

Owen took the call from Gleason in his office on Wednesday morning. It came in on Gleason's dime, a favor on top of a favor.

"I found your bike for you," Gleason said. He paused, a natural actor, building suspense. "But you ain't gonna like it much."

"Shoot," said Owen. It was an expression he remembered Gleason using in their first conversation.

"It was reported stolen back last October from a beach just south of here called Nantasket. Not unusual. Things get stolen down there all the time. What's unusual is it turns up in San Francisco." He pronounced the name by accenting the "Fran." He said, "Usually they just file off the numbers and paint 'em different. Either that or chop 'em up for parts."

"You got the owner's address?" Owen wanted to know.

Gleason snorted. He could spot a sense of humor a continent away. "You're not gonna chase this baby that far, are you?"

"Did you manage to get it?" Owen insisted.

"Hey," Gleason said, his tone suddenly indignant. "I managed. It belonged to a kid. Julius Sabatini, age nineteen. Lives at 74 Quarry Street, Portshead. It's a shipyard town about halfway between here and Nantasket."

"I've got a picture I'd like to show him, Dan."

"So show him. Next time you're in town."

Owen was silent. He listened to Gleason wheeze.

"Oh, Christ," Gleason said at last. "I get forty-five bucks an hour, you know."

"Whether I collect or not?"

"Ah, shit." The wheeze became a sniffle, a nasal inhale; and Owen pictured fat Gleason rubbing the end of his nose back and forth with his thumb and forefinger.

"Awright, Owen. If you don't get anything outta this, just put it on the ledger. It'll save me from going to confession one of these days."

"I'll send the picture today."

"I'll get down that neck of the woods sooner or later."

By telephoning Dr. Butler's office and pleading, unsuccessfully, for the last appointment of the day, Owen was able to ascertain that Dr. Butler would be leaving at four-thirty. Since Owen did not know what Dr. Butler looked like, he camped in his hallway at four-fifteen, leaning against a gray marble wall and studying a *Wall Street Journal* which he had neatly folded into quarters. It was Owen's belief that nobody ever bothered a man reading a *Wall Street Journal*, although he was less confident of the paper's charms in the afternoon than in the morning, when the stock market was still open.

By four-forty-five the only man with a proprietary air who had emerged from Dr. Butler's office had been wearing a grimace, a leather jacket, a gold chain, and no suit. It was, Owen realized, a less than satisfactory way of making a decision about Dr. Butler's sartorial tendencies. What he needed was confirmation.

"We're closed," the fat, Hispanic-looking girl behind the sliding window announced when he walked into the office.

"Can you tell me," Owen asked politely, "if Dr. Butler ever wears a suit to work?"

The fat girl had one hand in the air ready to slide the window shut. "What's this, a gag?"

"No, I'm very serious. I'd like to know if Dr. Butler ever wears a suit to work."

"Why, you got one to sell?"

"Not exactly."

"A *suit* suit?"

"Yes, exactly."

"Criminies, I dunno. I never really thought about it before." Her dark eyes narrowed. "You know, I think he used to do stuff like that, wear sport coats and stuff, but he's sort of changed lately."

"In what way has he changed?"

The fat girl waved her hand. "You know, he's just changed. Wears his hair different. Yeah, now that I think about it, he's really started

155

dressing different in the past couple of months. He's got the chains, the unbuttoned shirt now. He never used to wear stuff like that before. Course, none of that stuff's helped his mood any lately."

"He's been in a bad mood, has he?"

This time the fat girl flattened her hand and used it as if she were fanning her face. Part of what she was telling Owen was done by tilting her jaw down and away from him, looking at him balefully out of her closest eye. Suddenly she stopped her little act. "Say, what is it you want, anyhow?"

"Root canal."

The hand went to the window again and started to slide it closed. "Come back tomorrow."

"Well, I'm not going to have it done if the doctor's in a bad mood," Owen said, and left with a flourish of his raincoat.

Gould, Lane, Rossville; possibly Hartry. Any one of them could wear a suit. But after meeting Blinky Gould, Owen Carr was willing to make a new assumption about the man who had been seen talking to the dead boy in McGuppers. He was willing to assume that even Goose the bartender would have remembered a man who looked like Blinky.

Blinky, or Bert, as his wife called him, was about six feet four, as skinny as a thermometer, and completely bald except for a caterpillar of hair that ran from the back of one ear to the back of the other. When his wife called him to come participate in the survey Owen was conducting, he came thumping down the stairs of their split-level with his big feet flopping as though he were wearing snowshoes.

The Goulds, for some reason, seemed almost delighted to have Owen step into their house and ask them questions about the services they wanted or needed in the area. But then again, the Goulds were, to Owen's eye, a most unusual couple. They had recently returned from two weeks on Maui and both of them were still quite tanned. Blinky obviously was growing a beard, and gold stubble was neatly sculptured across his face and under his chin. Marietta, who was at least a decade younger than her husband, was also growing some hair. She was wearing a thin green tank top, quite inappropriate for a cold March day, and she seemed to accept every possible opportunity to lift her arms and reveal to Owen the little black bushes blossoming under each.

Owen was immediately taken with her, something that almost never happened in his experience with women of any age. But Marietta was petite, and lively without being bold or loud. Her skin would have been dark even without the tan; her brown hair was cut in an informal shag; and her eyes, which were nearly the color of her hair, looked at him with an intensity of interest that Owen found extremely flattering. The only thing that bothered him was the tank top. It was too tight and too sheer to be worn without a bra, even by somebody with Mrs. Gould's boyish figure. And she obviously had on nothing underneath it, because Owen could see the outlines of her tiny breasts, he could see her nipples pointed straight at him, and it embarrassed him.

Owen found himself concentrating heavily on the questionnaire he had attached to his clipboard. He was standing in the middle of a foyer and Blinky Gould was seated on the stairs that led up to a raised living room. His wife leaned against the railing of the stairs, sometimes with her back, sometimes by propping herself at arm's length. They appeared so open, so ingenuous in their responses, that Owen had no problem presenting the question he had been afraid to put to any of the other people in Tranton Park.

"In terms of entertainment," he said, reading directly from his questionnaire, "what do you like to do on weekend nights?"

"Oh," said Marietta, "get together with friends, go out to dinner, go to a movie. The usual."

"Well, last Saturday night, for example, what did you do?"

The couple looked at each other. Marietta touched her fingers to her lips. "What did we do?" she said. "Oh, of course, we got home from Maui that evening and we just unpacked and watched a little TV."

"We wanted to go over the Butlers' and take a hot tub, remember?" Blinky volunteered. "To unwind after the plane trip. But they weren't answering their phone."

"Perhaps they weren't home," Owen said casually.

"Well, their cars were there and their lights were on when we drove by. That's why we thought about it. But we let the phone ring a couple of times and nothing happened, so . . ."

"There wasn't a party or anything like that going on, was there?" Owen smiled, as if he couldn't have cared less what the answer was, as if he were doing nothing more than making small talk while he searched for his next question.

"Gosh, I don't think so," said Blinky. He looked a little worried at the prospect that perhaps there had been a party and they hadn't been

157

invited. "The only thing I can think of is that a few people might have gone over the Robinsons' house to say goodbye because Roarke was going down to spring training on Sunday."

"That's another thing we're going to be doing for entertainment," Marietta said. "We're buying some tickets for the A's." She grinned happily at her husband. "I can't wait until they start. I've never been to a professional game before."

"It's kind of funny you should ask that question about entertainment now," Blinky Gould said. "You see, Marietta and I have just made some decisions to change certain things about our lives and that's one of them." He looked at Marietta to see if it would be all right for him to say more, and Marietta beamed her approval.

"You see, we went off to Hawaii and everything was just so relaxed there and it was the first time we'd had in years to sort of sit down and assess things, like where we're going and what we're going to do." Blinky was speaking directly to his wife. He was reaffirming whatever agreement they had made and Owen was merely a witness to their vows.

As Owen watched Marietta look at her husband, he realized what it was that intensified her gaze. She was wearing contact lenses and she was not wearing them well. They made her stare longer than most people did. They made her squint. Owen felt a slight pang of disappointment and then quickly drove the feeling from himself. He was here to work, not to have fantasies about young women.

"Hawaii can be very enlightening," he said.

Blinky nodded vigorously. "We went there with that idea in mind. I mean, things around here had gotten so out of hand, it seemed, we just wanted to go someplace and get a different perspective. We decided even before we left that we were going to try some new things, get as far away as we could from what we've been doing. For me, just going to Hawaii was new. I'd never been there before. Truth is, I wasn't much of a swimmer. So that was one thing I promised myself, that I'd at least give it a try."

"By the time we left, Bert had practically turned into a fish." Marietta laughed. "I couldn't get him out of the water."

"Well, we had borrowed some equipment from our neighbors. Masks and snorkels and flippers. Actually, we didn't really borrow. We let them use our video camera and they let us use their skin-diving stuff. It was Marietta's idea. I didn't think it was anything I wanted to try, but I did and I loved it. You don't have to be a good swimmer just to float around on top of the water, you know. And that's all you really need to do when you go snorkeling. Last couple of days we were there, we went to this place called Black Rock and I swam way out to the point and, I'll tell you, I've never seen anything like it in my life. Fish you wouldn't believe were out there. And they were everywhere."

"Bert liked it so much he wants to take up scuba diving now."

"That's right," Blinky said enthusiastically. "Cathy Rossville, she's our neighbor who lent us the equipment, used to be a diving instructor and I'm going to see if she can't give us lessons. Maybe use the Martels' pool."

"Or the Weissocks', even."

Owen felt like a spectator. The Goulds talked ostensibly to him, but almost as though he were not even present. Whatever mid-life crisis they were experiencing was turning out to be the best break he had had since catching June Hartry in the midst of her hormonal rushes, and he sought to push it for all it was worth.

"Say," he said, tapping his clipboard with his pen and chewing his lip thoughtfully. "When you said things were getting out of hand around here, did you mean the building development that's going on or anything like that?"

Blinky was quick to respond. "Oh, no. I just meant in our lives personally. I mean, so many things have been happening lately, so many things that we didn't care anything about but found ourselves caught up in—and one day we just said to ourselves, 'Hey, this isn't right. Here we are, accomplishing everything we ever wanted to accomplish, and we're still not happy.' And we said to ourselves, 'Why is that?' " Blinky examined Owen to see if he was making sense. He got back a look of befuddlement.

This seemed to disturb Blinky. He quite clearly wanted to be able to communicate. "Look, let me give you an example," he said. "Marietta is a real estate agent. It's not something she works at seven days a week, but she has her listings and she generally meets her quotas. A few months back she was very fortunate in that she was able to get both the buying and selling commission on a house up the street here." He looked at his wife to be sure that it was all right to say she had been fortunate. When she nodded he went on. "Admittedly, Marietta didn't have to do a whole lot of work on this sale, but she was delighted and she expected her friends would be delighted, too. Instead, she's gotten so much grief from everyone about the money she made that she feels

159

as though she has to apologize instead of just being able to enjoy it."

"It wasn't everyone, Bert. It was really just one person."

"But she wasn't alone, sweetie. You know how it is around here. She starts something and everybody else follows. We even wondered at one point if we weren't becoming just like that ourselves, remember? Adopting her values and everything?" Blinky turned his attention back to Owen. "What kind of a game are we playing? we asked ourselves. Here we have everything we could possibly hope for in life and we spend all our time worrying about what everybody else in the neighborhood is thinking and saying and doing—"

"Instead of just enjoying what we have," added Marietta.

"That's right." Blinky nodded earnestly. It's all so simple, his expression seemed to be saying to Owen. It was simple for us and it can be simple for you, too.

Owen, his feet growing tired from standing on the hard foyer floor of the multi-hundred-thousand-dollar abode of these practitioners of the simple life, smiled noncommittally. Blinky, meanwhile, went into a paroxysm of eye closures.

"We all have so much to be grateful for," he said insistently. "Take this woman we were talking about earlier. I mean, she apparently came from a very nice home life. She was Miss Everything in high school—"

"A cheerleader," said Marietta.

Blinky nodded. "A cheerleader. Went to a good college, married a professional man who makes a good enough income so that she never has to worry about bills or anything like that. What else, sweetie?"

"A son."

"Well, he seems to be the source of some problems, but he's a very nice boy and I'm not sure everything is quite his fault. Anyway, the point is that she's attractive, smart and has all these things going for her, and all she seems to want to do is tear other people down."

"Or get whatever it is they have away from them."

Blinky's head shot up. "Now, wait, we don't know that she's really been doing that," he cautioned, and once more Owen found himself out of the conversation.

"Oh, Bert, it's so obvious to everyone. Besides, she all but admitted it to Cathy a few weeks back."

"Still," Blinky said firmly, "we don't need to cast aspersions. We can use the example of your commission instead." He turned to look at Owen. "After going around telling everyone what a crime it was for

Marietta to get what she got, this woman's decided to go out and get a real estate license of her own."

"It's as though she's never satisfied with what she has," Marietta said sadly.

"She never can be, because she's not satisfied with who she is," her husband explained.

Now it was Marietta's turn. "And we've decided that's the problem with so many people these days, ourselves included. So we've agreed to stop trying to be someone we're not. Instead, we're going to try to enjoy who we are, without apologies or excuses." She gazed at her husband fondly. "Bert's already joined a men's support group."

Blinky blushed. He looked at his feet. "We've reached an age where we realize, you know, that we're not going to be here forever. Marietta's a little different, but I've wasted a lot of years being uncomfortable with myself. I look back now and I see that I'm not really going to get another chance at those years. What I've got is this year and next year and the years to come."

Marietta drew herself close to the banister, hooking her arm around it. "What it involves, we think, is just adopting a more positive approach toward life."

Owen seized the moment and twisted it into the shape he wanted. "And this other woman you've been talking about, you think she essentially has a negative approach toward life?"

Blinky Gould's face opened up. His eyes drew wide with sincerity. "We think so," he said.

Owen nodded. He dropped his clipboard to his side and pushed his free hand into the pocket of his raincoat, wishing vaguely that he had been trained as a Jehovah's Witness so that he could know better how to go door to door engaging in discussions about the meaning of existence with people who didn't even know his name. "But," he said, "isn't it possible that you and your friend are striving for the exact same thing? To get the absolute most out of every minute of life?"

Blinky and his wife gaped at him. They clearly were not prepared to believe that their newfound enlightenment and their neighbor's negativity could be waters from the same well.

"But she's willing to hurt other people," Marietta protested. She looked at her husband and her husband, after a moment, dipped his head. Permission granted. The point had to be made. "Even her own family."

"Not to mention other people's families," said Blinky.

Outwardly Owen shrugged. Inwardly his heart was starting to move a little faster. There were enough clues now that he was willing to hazard a guess on the true subject of what was upsetting Marietta Gould. "I don't know much about these things, of course, but I wonder about them sometimes, just like you. Suppose a person is happily married, but bored. Couldn't that person be displaying a positive approach to life, just the way you've described it, if he or she, say, got involved in an affair for its own sake? Couldn't that person be involved in the affair just because she wanted to seize the moment and experience what life has to offer?"

The real answer to the real question Owen was asking was imprinted on the Goulds' faces. It was confirmed when Marietta licked her lips and said, "Hey, do you live around here?"

Owen shook his head as if he did not understand why she would ask that.

"You wouldn't know who it is Bert and I are talking about, by any chance?"

"I just know a little bit about human nature," he said. "And the more I know, the less I understand. I find that sometimes you just can't tell what will possess people to act the way they do." Encouraged by the Goulds' reaction to his first guess, Owen tried another. "Example. These days, if you can believe what you read, there seems to be quite a movement afoot for older women to have affairs with younger men. The housewife reads about the movie stars doing it, maybe she thinks she'd like to try it, too. Doesn't necessarily mean she's going to be hurting anybody."

"Unless her husband finds out," Blinky said. He wrinkled his forehead.

"Ah." Owen smiled. He took his free hand out of his pocket and held it up in surrender. "The husband finds out, he gets hurt. Yes, I agree. Maybe the errant wife gets hurt. Maybe even the other man."

"And the other man's wife," Marietta chimed in.

Owen kept the smile on his face. "If the other man has a wife," he said.

"Oh, he has a wife, all right." Marietta glanced knowingly at her husband, who grimaced at the lacquered stair between his feet.

Blinky Gould, it was clear, wanted no further part in the discussion. Marietta quickly discerned that and the whole atmosphere changed palpably. Owen was no longer a sounding board for their gestating philosophies; he was a stranger in their house posing embarrassing questions about real people. The opportunity to ask how they could have known that the other man had a wife was lost and the interview wound down to nothing.

A few moments later, Owen Carr stepped outside, feeling a little more enlightened and a little more confused than when he had stepped in.

CHAPTER FIVE

Gleason considered himself fortunate to have caught Owen in his office on a Saturday morning. Owen did not disabuse him of that notion. He did not tell Gleason that he always worked on Saturdays, that he had been in the office since eight o'clock, or that he was surrounded by stacks of papers, notes and questionnaires in preparation for his third assault on Tranton Park.

Gleason, in all likelihood, did not care anyhow. He was cackling like a mad actress.

"Owen, me boy," he said, "I have been to see one Julius Sabatini, age nineteen, of Portshead, Massachusetts, and I am here to make my report." He cleared his throat, needlessly ensuring Owen's attention. "Mr. Sabatini stands about five foot seven, has a rich head of curly hair that tumbles down his forehead, the eyes of a Parisian waif, the ears of a Grecian urn, and the nose of a South American toucan. He works as a deckhand on a fishing boat, which is where I caught up with him, and he purports to have no knowledge whatsoever as to the disappearance of his motorcycle. He drove it down Nantasket, he says; he parked it with all the other motorcycles, he says; he went to the amusement park and walked around, he says; he came out and it was gone, he says. He called his father and his father came and picked him up. They reported it to the police, they drove around the area looking for it, and that was it. Insurance company apparently treated it as routine and paid blue book."

Owen waited until it was clear that Gleason was done before he commented. "An excellent report, to be sure, Dan, but I don't quite understand your excitement."

"Because, Owen, then, after he was done reading me the script, I showed him the picture which Federal Express was kind enough to deliver to my office the day before last." The cackle came again.

"And?" Owen said.

"And he shit."

"What do you mean?"

"I mean just that. He shit right in his pants. It was beautiful, Owen. You should have seen it. Starts off, the kid's sort of a punk, you know. Not a wise guy or anything, but the hanging mouth, the hostile attitude, the suspicious eyes, and I got him out there on the dock with his friends on the boat near enough to see him but not near enough to be part of what's going on. 'Yeah,' he says, he had a bike was stolen. 'Nah,' he says, he never got the bike back, never heard a thing about it again . . . doesn't know who did it. And I'm real sympathetic, you know? Real susceptible. 'Oh, poor guy. Gee, that's terrible. Nice bike like that. And you hadn't had it very long? Just a couple of weeks? Bought it from a friend. Oh, that's too bad. Say, you wouldn't know this kid, would you?' and I whips out the picture.

"Now, we ain't dealing with no Henry Kissinger here, Owen. Young Julius stares at the picture and all the color drains from his face. It's as though his eyes have magnets, he can't take them off it. He says, 'He looks dead.' I says, 'That's right.' And poof, the kid shits."

Owen waited. Gleason wheezed. "Then what happened, Dan?" Owen said.

"That was pretty much it. The kid shits. He says he's got to get away, he's got to get to the head, and he takes off back to the boat before I can say another word to him. I wait around on the dock for a while and then this big old fisherman comes up to me with a grappling hook in his hands, tells me it's time I left."

Owen, his voice the epitome of politeness but containing not a trace of discernible feeling, said, "So you did."

There was a delay in Gleason's response. "Hey, Owen, I'm only marking this down on the ledger, right? Owen Carr, two hours, ninety dollars on account. You're not paying me prizefighter's wages, are you?"

"No, no, absolutely you did the right thing, Dan. Still and all, it's pretty exciting, isn't it? What you learned, I mean. Julius knows the dead boy and when you show him the picture after questioning him about his lost motorcycle he didn't say, 'That creep, I should have known it was him,' or anything like that."

Gleason understood what Owen was telling him. "You want me to do something more, is that it?"

165

"I did have something else in mind."

"Take my word for it, it's not worth it. If the boy you're after comes from Portshead and he's a friend of Julius's, I can tell you one thing right now: he ain't rich. He ain't rich and his parents ain't rich." Gleason emphasized his point with a booming laugh.

"That's okay, Dan. I'm working on something on the other side and I'm beginning to feel good about it. What I need is the boy's identity."

"C'mon, Owen," snapped Gleason, his laugh over, "enough's enough. Look, I think it's wonderful you're still out there trying to earn a buck and everything, and I hope to Christ I still have the energy to do it when I'm your age and all, but I can't waste my time doin' all this stuff you're asking just because I feel sorry for you, you know."

Owen bit down hard, but the silence that ensued was so fragile that even the slightest word from Gleason was enough to set him off.

"Owen?"

"You don't have to feel sorry for me, Mr. Gleason," Owen hissed. "I am good at what I do and the mere fact that I'm still here doing it after all these years is all the proof you need. And don't you think for one minute that you know who I am or what I'm like or that you have one hope in a thousand of doing what I'm doing when you are my age. I work the trade the way it used to be worked, without computers, without gadgets, without fancy trappings and without anyone giving me orders. I find cases, I invest in them, and I keep what I earn. Do you understand what that means? That means if I don't invest wisely I starve. And I can assure you, Mr. Gleason, I am very well fed."

"Well," said Gleason, "if that's so, then I guess there's no need for me to do any more charity work, is there?"

"Nobody asked you to do charity work. I work contingency and if I get paid, you'll get paid."

"That's great, Owen. I appreciate you're looking out for me. Not only do I get some undetermined percentage of a case I know nothing about, but I get to pay my own expenses along the way."

"You want expenses? Fine. At this very moment I'm putting a check for fifty dollars in the mail."

"Fifty dollars," Gleason sneered. "That's one bet at the dog track, which it sounds to me like I'd be a heck of a lot better off doin'."

This time Owen did not respond.

Gleason, breathing heavily, said, "You got anything more to tell me about what you're workin' on, Owen? What it is you feel so good about

166

that I should keep runnin' back and forth to Portshead for? Because if not, I think we can call things quits."

Owen said, "If you find out who this dead boy is, then it might help me find out who killed him. It's as simple as that."

"Owen, that's police work. There's no money in police work."

"You ever heard of a civil suit for wrongful death?"

"Suits are brought by lawyers. We're not lawyers."

"Suits are brought by heirs."

Gleason let the words sink in. When he spoke again there was a little bit of awe in his voice. "You're talking blackmail, aren't you, Owen?"

"I'm talking compensation for loss of care, comfort and society. I'm talking fifty, a hundred, five hundred thousand dollars, whatever we can get for the heirs that will keep them from going to a lawyer."

"What heirs?" Gleason asked after a long moment.

"That's what I need to find out."

It was when Gleason grunted that Owen knew he had him. "Just take the picture to the high school where Julius Sabatini went, Dan," he said. "Find one of the guidance counselors or somebody in the principal's office. Show it to anyone you can. That's all you have to do—just get me the boy's name and his address."

"And for that I get what?"

"For that we become partners. You'll get a quarter of any fee I get."

"Yeah, right. Well, in the meantime, send the fifty bucks, will ya?"

"It's in the mail."

"Sure it is, Owen. And I'm not going to have my head examined, either."

It was close to eleven o'clock when Owen called on the Rossville house, but the unshaven, grumpy man who answered the doorbell was still in his bathrobe. The man had enough color in his cheeks, enough peeling red skin on the end of his nose, to enable Owen to surmise that he had been in some hot, sunny place.

"You've been away," Owen said, by way of greeting.

The bathrobed man leaned forward a little bit, trying to figure out why Owen was being so familiar with him.

"This is the first time I've caught you at home all week," Owen said. "Hawaii?"

"Mexico."

"Ah. Puerto Vallarta?"

"Cozumel."

"You don't say. Nice time?"

"Yeah." End of discussion on that point.

Owen explained that he was conducting a neighborhood survey, try-ing to find out which services were most needed or wanted in the area. He had, by this time, hit twenty-six houses in Tranton Park, but he told Mr. Rossville he had made contact with just about everybody but him.

Rossville grunted. He rubbed his eyes, which, Owen noted, were quite red around the rims. He said he didn't think they wanted any ser-vices.

Owen murmured sympathetically. He said the survey was designed to tell them the services they wanted. Rossville slumped against the door-jamb and Owen seized on that as a sign of resignation. He quickly read his first question.

"Where do you do your food shopping?"

"Safeway in Tranton village."

"Do you find it convenient?"

"I guess. My wife goes there mostly."

"Where do you do your liquor shopping?"

"Village Liquors." Then, anticipating, he added, "It's convenient enough and we probably wouldn't change, because we like the wine se-lection."

"You drink other liquors, though, don't you?"

"Sure."

Owen made a meaningless mark on his questionnaire. "Heh, heh, haven't found anybody in the neighborhood who doesn't."

"Marietta Gould. Mr. and Mrs. Artinian."

"Oh, yes, of course, the Armenian couple. Older, retired, I remember now. Let me see now, what television shows do you watch on a regular basis?"

"Rumpole of the Bailey."

Owen looked up. "Rum Pole?"

"PBS. It's a series about a British barrister and it's hardly ever on."

"I see. So what do you watch when it isn't on?"

"Movies."

"Television movies?"

"Sometimes. Or we rent them. Videocassettes."

"A video rental store is one of the things I'm supposed to ask about. Can you tell me where you presently rent videotaped movies?"

168

"Village Videos."

"And is that convenient?"

Rossville shrugged. He was looking out to the street, occasionally rubbing his eyes or his nose or his mouth. "We go to the Safeway there, Village Liquors, Village Videos. I've got to pass by them on the way home from work. . . . My wife's business is there—"

"How about on weekends?"

"My wife's still there."

"What do you do for entertainment on weekends?"

Rossville straightened up and arched his back in a stretching motion. "Oh, I don't know. Different things all the time."

"Well," Owen said. He put his pen in his mouth while he stared at the pages on his clipboard. "What did you do last Saturday night? For example."

Rossville stopped stretching. "We were home," he said. "We spent a quiet evening at home celebrating my wife's birthday."

Owen's pen went to the questionnaire again. "Oh, you had a party?"

"No. Just her and me." Rossville's teeth flashed in a brief smile. "No one else."

Owen smiled, too. He said, "Ah." He asked what vehicles the Rossvilles owned.

"An XJ6 and a Beemer."

"A what?"

"A Jag and a BMW."

"Any motorcycles?"

The smile Rossville had resumed with his explanation of the vehicle names slid off his face. "No," he said.

Owen nodded, wrote something down. "Any interest in them?"

"No."

"Funny," Owen said. "They seem to be a pretty unusual commodity in Tranton Park."

There was no answer from Rossville. That was fair enough, thought Owen. There had been no question. Except that Rossville seemed poised to say something. Owen waited. Nothing came.

"Any interest in hunting, Mr. Rossville?"

"No."

"Own any hunting or sport weapons? Rifles, pistols . . . bows and arrows . . . crossbows?"

"No."

The next series of questions that Owen had prepared began by asking

169

what the interviewee did for physical fitness and ended by asking if the interviewee would be interested in a club that provided weight-lifting facilities. But the only question Owen actually asked went like this: "You interested in weight lifting, Mr. Rossville?"

Rossville reacted suddenly. He jerked his right arm out of the sleeve of his bathrobe and cocked it in a flexed position. "Yeah," he said, and turned his most devilish grin on Owen Carr. "Doesn't it look it?"

Owen stared at a perfectly normal-appearing bicep. After a moment he acknowledged the joke by laughing softly. Rossville, pushing his arm back into the sleeve and belting his robe tight again, laughed with him.

"Not saying I couldn't use it, mind you. It's just one more thing I haven't gotten around to yet. Any more questions? Because if not, I'd kind of like to get back inside to my cup of coffee."

"No. No more questions at this time."

"Okay. So long, then." But Leigh Rossville made no immediate move to go back within the house.

Owen thanked him, but he, too, made no move to leave.

"Goodbye."

"Goodbye, Mr. Rossville."

And Rossville, who had not given his name to Owen, looked just a tad uneasy as he turned his back and let the door close behind him. Or so it seemed to Owen.

He had covered everyone around the loop now except the Lanes and the Robinsons. He needed only to hit them in order to be finished with the first phase of his investigation. But he had tried the Lanes' house that morning before the Rossvilles'. For the third time he had thought someone was home, and for the third time no one had answered the door. Surely, Owen thought, even if Mrs. Lane was a recluse, her husband the lawyer had to be around sometime. He decided to try the Robinsons again, and then go back to the Lanes' house once more.

It was no more than a few hundred yards from the Rossvilles' to the Robinsons', but Owen chose to drive. There was nothing to be gained by letting those he had already interviewed see him still tramping through the neighborhood on his door-to-door calls.

A dusty-brown boy with dusty-blond curls and startlingly hazel eyes was standing in the Robinsons' driveway when Owen pulled up in front of the house. He had his hands in his pockets and he wasn't doing anything at all except watching Owen. He watched Owen get out of his car and he watched Owen walk directly up to him.

"Whatcha doing?" Owen asked him.

"Waiting."

"Whatcha waiting for?"

"Nothing."

"That's good," Owen said. "You won't have long now." He looked toward the house. "Your folks home?"

"My mom is. My dad's down at spring training."

"What's he, in the Marines or something?"

"You never heard of my dad? Roarke Robinson?"

"Oh, for heaven's sakes. Roarke Robinson, the famous baseball player? He's your dad? Why, you lucky boy."

"Yeah."

"Is your name Roarke, too?"

"Nah. My name's Roy. Roy Campanella Robinson. You musta heard of him."

"Who?"

"Roy Campanella, the guy I'm named after. Haven't you ever heard of him?"

"I guess so. Never met him myself. I would, however, like to meet your mother, if that's okay."

Roy Robinson gave a quick shrug. He said, "Sure," and led Owen up the steps to the front door. He opened the door and kept right on walking, and Owen, not being told otherwise, followed after him. As they proceeded down a hall, Owen heard a woman's voice, soft and light and vacant, say, "But you don't understand. I am dumb."

"Nonsense," said a very soothing male voice. "I wouldn't be sitting here talking to you—"

And then Roy and Owen entered the room where the two speakers were conversing and the conversation stopped. The room was a huge tile and oak kitchen that dropped down a few steps to a sun porch that was both separated from and part of the kitchen itself. Two horizontal rows of windows ran along the back wall, providing an open view of green lawn and a patch of trees beyond. Off to the right, as Owen entered the kitchen, was an oblong breakfast table being shared by a man and a woman who were staring at him incredulously.

The woman was wearing a full-length white and pink bathrobe. Her blond hair hung straight and uncombed and her outstretched hand was

171

gripping the handle of a coffee cup. Seated on the chair next to her, but turned so that he was sideways to the table and so that he could cross his right ankle over his left knee, was a silver-haired man with a silver mustache. The man was wearing expensive-looking loafers with brass buckles on them, pressed brown slacks, a yellow crewneck sweater, and a brown pin-striped shirt with a starched collar that he kept outside the neck of the sweater.

"Roy . . . ?" the woman said, and the boy answered, "This man wants to talk to you, Mom."

Owen looked embarrassed. "I'm sorry," he said. He glanced back at the front door and held his hand out toward it. "I just asked if I could speak with you."

The woman, still retaining the position she had been in when she first saw Owen, asked what he wanted. Owen told her about the survey. He gestured with his clipboard. He apologized some more.

The woman looked to her companion, who thrust his arms across his chest and said, "Say, who the devil are you?"

"My name is Owen Carr."

"Who do you work for?" the man demanded.

"I was just hired to do this survey." Once again he waved the clipboard.

"Who hired you?" the man insisted. "What's the name of the company? What makes you think a survey needs to be done? This area isn't even zoned for business."

Owen looked down at his feet. "I'm just trying to do my job," he said.

But the silver-haired man was not as easily moved by these words as Mrs. Hartry had been. Speaking sharply, he said, "And I want to know what your job is. I understand you or somebody who fits your description has been coming around all week asking questions of everybody in the neighborhood and I want to know why. Now, you either show me your credentials or I'm calling the police."

Owen said, "I'm sorry, what is your name, sir?"

"My name," the man said, not unlike someone calling the thunder down from the heavens, "is John Clarke Lane and I happen to be an attorney."

Owen put on his glasses and scrutinized the paper attached to his clipboard. He wrinkled his nose. "I must have made a mistake," he said. "I have down here that Mr. and Mrs. Lane live at number one twenty-four. I thought the Robinsons lived in this house."

John Clarke Lane sucked in his breath as though he had been

172

pricked with a needle. "The Robinsons damn well do live in this house and I happen to be visiting them."

"Oh," said Owen, glancing around innocently. "Is Mr. Robinson here? It's him I really came to see."

Mrs. Robinson turned her back on Owen. She was staring at the wall on the other side of the table. Lawyer Lane sputtered. From his spot in the middle of the floor, young Roy looked wide-eyed from one adult to another as he tried to figure out what was going on.

"You're too clever by half, Mr. Carr," Lane said at last. He got to his feet and reached out his hand for Owen's clipboard. "I'd like to see what you have there."

Owen pulled the clipboard away. He removed a single piece of paper from it and gave the paper to Lane, who scanned it quickly.

"This is just a bunch of questions somebody typed up," Lane said. "There's no identification anywhere on it. Where did you get this?"

Owen took back the paper and looked it over as if he were being asked to verify its authenticity. "Wrote these up myself," he said.

"Why?" Lane said ferociously.

"Wanted to learn a little bit about the people who live around here."

The answer did not please Lane, who was obviously used to being in charge when he asked questions. "What concern is it of yours?" he demanded.

Owen fumbled in his pockets until he came up with his business card. He showed it as if it were a pass, and Lane angrily snatched it from his hand.

" 'Owen Carr, Private Investigations, Never A Day Off Since 1949,' " Lane read jeeringly.

Mrs. Robinson looked curiously over his shoulder. Her son said, "Wow," and let out enough air to fill a small balloon.

"Mr. Carr," Lane said, drawing himself into his best posture, "I'm going to see that you're charged with fraud, misrepresentation, trespassing, and gaining access to people's homes under false pretenses—"

"Gee, that last charge is a new one on me."

"I hope you have plenty of insurance, Mr. Carr, because you're going to need it."

Owen scratched the top of his head, which, even in his stoop-shouldered stance, was considerably above that of the ramrod-straight Mr. Lane. "Think you'll be able to come up with a lot of damages, do you?"

"Fraud can lead to punitive damages," Lane decreed.

Owen nodded. His clear eyes did not show the least bit of concern

173

about Lane's threats. "I don't think you'll be able to prove that I ever said one thing to any of these people that wasn't true. I have been conducting a survey and I have been trying to find out what services are needed in the area."

Lane raised his curled index finger and thrust it out at Owen, stopping just short of his chest. "Assault?" Owen asked softly, raising one eyebrow.

Lane withdrew his finger, snapping it back into the palm of his hand and holding his fist up in front of his own shoulder. "I insist that you tell us why you've been doing what you've been doing," he said.

Owen barely reacted. He merely flicked his eyes toward young Roy and then flicked them back to his mother.

"Out, Roy," Mrs. Robinson ordered, and the boy howled in protest. "Out," she said again.

"Oh, Mom." Roy Robinson stomped his foot and threw his head back with a pained expression on his face, but he did as he was told.

When the front door had shut, Owen handed Lane one of the pictures he had taken of the dead youth in the Alameda County morgue. "Recognize him?"

Lane studied the picture closely. "No," he said, and passed it to Ann Robinson, who saw what it was and looked away quickly.

"Mrs. Robinson?"

"No," she said.

"We have reason to believe he was in this neighborhood just before he was found dead last Saturday night in the Oakland hills."

"What? Hey now . . ." Lane stopped sputtering just long enough to take another look at the picture. "You can't really believe . . . this is a neighborhood of professional people. What was he—shot in the throat with something?"

"An arrow, maybe. Or a crossbow. Know anybody around here who uses either one of those weapons?"

"No," said Lane, and Ann Robinson shook her head.

Owen touched the picture, which was still in Lane's hand. He touched it very gently, just to draw Lane's attention back to it. "This young man was a weight lifter, we believe. He came from Boston, or just outside of it. He rode a motorcycle and he was seen in a San Francisco singles bar receiving directions to Tranton Park from a well-dressed man. If we can discover who he came to see we might be able to find out why he died."

Lane's jaw tightened. "So you're willing to disturb the lives of everyone in the community while you pursue some harebrained lead that may or may not provide you with a clue." Disgustedly he snapped his tongue against his front teeth.

Owen was unmoved. "Did either one of you notice anything unusual around here Saturday night? Was there a party this boy could have been invited to? Could there have been a break-in at anybody's house? Could he have been baby-sitting? Can you think of any reason why he would have been in Tranton Park?"

Mrs. Robinson's eyes glazed with the effort of thinking back. But John Clarke Lane held out his hand to quiet her in case she was going to say anything. It seemed to be a practiced maneuver on his part.

"We don't have to answer any of your questions," Lane said. "You're asking them without any legal authority whatsoever. In fact, everything you have done so far has been without legal authority, either explicit or implicit, and I think I'll report you to the state licensing authorities, whoever they happen to be."

Owen took back the picture. "Keep the card," he said. "While you and your neighbors are discussing me, one of you might come up with something you think I ought to hear." He turned to the woman seated at the breakfast table and touched his index finger to his forehead. "Mrs. Robinson."

The boy was waiting for him outside, as Owen knew he would be.

"That man in there." Owen pointed back to the house with his thumb. "Is he a friend of your father's?"

Roy Campanella Robinson screwed up one side of his face while he tried to remember. "Mr. Lane?" he said. "I don't think so. Not really."

"Gee," said Owen, "you better not tell him he was over here visiting, then."

CHAPTER SIX

Owen stood at his cornermost window on Sunday morning and stared out through the rain. Sunday mornings he inevitably had the building to himself. Rainy Sunday mornings he had the universe to himself.

He loved rainy Sunday mornings. He loved gazing at the empty streets and deserted buildings and knowing that he was the only pocket of life in the whole area. If an occasional car or bus passed by on the street below, that was all right, too; the sounds of water spattering from its tires or its softly whirring engine would only enhance the solitariness he felt as he stood secure in his own little pocket of light and warmth.

The scene outside his window had changed greatly over the years. The superb view of Lake Merritt he had once had was now a superb view of the immense circular parking garage that the county had built on the lot directly across the street. He now sat in shadows for much of the day, and at night he walked out into an artificial wind tunnel; but he accepted it all without complaint.

The building, more than anything else, was Owen's home. He had moved in at a time when the rent had seemed exorbitant and the location ideal. His fellow tenants had been established law firms, accounting firms, architectural firms, insurance firms and reinsurance firms. He had been acutely aware of the prestige of the address and had felt himself in need of keeping pace. He had put curtains on the windows, a carpet on the floor, and he had lined his walls with framed letters of commendation which he had received from officials of the Southern Pacific railway.

But the last of those letters was dated 1963 and both Owen and the building had remained in operation since then. The curtains had come down, the carpet had grown frayed, and the lawyers, accountants, architects and insurers had moved on to the huge glass and steel structures that now lined the shores of the lake. Entire floors of Owen's building had been given over to jewelry wholesalers, telephone answering services, mysterious import-export businesses, and even a barber college. Only Owen had remained constant, his mere longevity giving him a certain eminence in the landlord's eye, which allowed him to talk his way out of a series of general rent increases. Even now, as the building was beginning to evidence some attraction as a base for one- and two-man law firms whose clientele were causing everyone to keep doors locked during business hours, Owen was able to maintain his two corner rooms on the third floor for less than a thousand dollars a month.

This amount Owen paid gladly, and always within ten days of its due date. The outward condition of the premises was of no great concern to him since he no longer had any walk-in business, and the location was as perfect as ever. If he heard others moaning in the hallways or the bathrooms or the elevators about the electricity going out or the plumbing leaking or the heat failing, Owen remained silent. He had learned long ago that you exploit shortcomings; you don't let them defeat you.

He was reminding himself of this thought, this creed, when the ringing of the telephone broke his Sunday morning vigil at the window. He put down his mug of coffee and glanced at his watch. It was eleven-fifteen and the same stirring of excitement he had felt the week before came to him. Then he picked up the receiver and he was disappointed.

"Heh, heh, how's it goin', Owen?" Newhauser chanted.

It occurred to Owen that he hated Newhauser. But the feeling manifested itself only in the slight hesitation that took place before he responded to the greeting.

"This is getting to be quite a regular habit, Dale. Got another possible for me or are you just checking on the last one?"

"Owen," Newhauser protested, "I'm just trying to see if I can't be of any further help."

"With what?"

Newhauser smothered him with condescending little chuckles. When he was done he said, "How about the autopsy report?"

Owen's reply was immediate. "How much?"

Hurt crept into Newhauser's voice. "Aw, c'mon, Owen, this is a business arrangement we got goin' here. What's good for you should be good for me."

177

"I don't know, Dale," Owen said. "I don't see much possibility for this dead kid. I think I'm going to chuck it in."

"Twenty-five."

"I got another case I'm going to work on instead."

There was silence on the other end.

"Thanks anyhow, Dale. Call me if you get something else."

"Fifteen."

Owen told him to read what he had.

Newhauser said, "Beginning with the first page, all right?" Then, in a halting, monotonous voice that reflected a surprising command of medical terms, he read: " 'Anatomic Diagnosis: One. Traumatic laceration of neck with destruction of carotid artery, jugular vein and vagus nerve, right. Two. Exsanguinatory hemorrhage secondary to above. Cause of death: laceration of right carotid artery and jugular vein.' " He stopped there to explain. "That means he got cut in the neck."

Owen said he understood.

"Okay, next page. 'The body is that of a well-developed, well-nourished Caucasian male appearing about nineteen years of age, measuring seventy-four inches and weighing one hundred ninety-eight pounds.' " Newhauser suddenly laughed. "I feel like a boxing announcer, Owen. 'And in this corner, weighing one hundred and ninety-eight pounds—' "

"Just read on, Dale."

"Okay, Owen. Just trying to have a little fun because some of this is heavy going, you know. 'General Description' is the next heading. Then it says, 'When first viewed, the body is clothed in heavily bloodstained Levi blue jean pants, white Jockey-type underwear with a Filene's irregular label, dark socks and ankle-high laced boots. The body is cold. Rigor mortis is generalized and marked. There is a through and through wound in the right neck with anterior circular wound four centimeters lateral to the midline at a level of the upper border of the larynx. It measures one point one by zero point seven centimeters. The edges are inverted, with rather sharp, clean borders, free of grease, dirt and other foreign material. There is extensive hemorrhage from these wounds, which will be described below, and obvious hemorrhagic and ecchymotic muscle is visible in the depths.

" 'The eyes are blue, pupils equal and about zero point five centimeters in diameter. Nose has an old fracture deformity. Oral mucosa and tongue are free of traumatic lesion. Teeth are in good repair and intact. There is no lesion of the face, neck, torso anteriorly or pos-

178

teriorly save the described neck lesion. Extremities show no injury. Hands show no bruising or injury but are calloused, the nails irregular but not broken. No needle marks or scar tracks can be found in any of the usual locations.' "

Newhauser paused and took a breath. "Next is 'Internal Examination.' Here goes. 'The neck wound reveals a tract connecting the apparent entrance wound anteriorly and the apparent exit wound posteriorly measuring almost one point five centimeters in diameter in the tissues. It passes through the subcutaneous tissues and through the sternocleidomastoideus muscle to destroy both the common carotid artery and internal carotid artery, the jugular vein and vagus nerves. It passes posteriorly just lateral to the spine at about the third cervical level to exit from the back of the neck through the trapezius muscle, subcutaneous tissues and skin. Careful search for foreign bodies such as dirt, organic or vegetable material, grease and metallic fragments of a projectile reveal none that can be found.

" 'Upon opening the body with the usual Y-shaped incision, all cavities are free of fluid and gas and serous surfaces are smooth and glistening.'

"Hmmm." Newhauser paused. Owen could hear a page turning. "Okay. Now we're into all the nuts and bolts. You want to hear the rest of this stuff?"

"Read the headings," Owen said. "I'll let you know."

" 'Cardiovascular System.' Heart weighs three hundred fifty grams. No big deal there . . . 'Myocardium, mahogany brown . . .' All right, here: 'The vessels of the right neck are divided at the level of the bifurcation of the common carotid to destroy all immediate regional structures.' That's about it there.

"Under lungs, it says . . . let's see . . . right weighs four hundred ten grams, left three sixty . . . 'The neck organs reveal an intact larynx, normal vocal cords and larynx and no lesion of the thyroid except for some hemorrhage into the surrounding tissue on the right.'

"Then he's got 'Gastrointestinal Tract' . . . nothing there. 'Pancreas' . . . nothing. 'Spleen . . . liver . . . adrenals . . . kidneys' says, 'slight lobulation but the capsules strip with ease, leaving otherwise smooth, glistening surfaces . . .' "

"Keep going, Dale."

"Don't like that one, huh? Well, all right. Next is 'Head. Skull is not fractured and there is no hemorrhage in the galea or about the dura.' "

Newhauser began reading quickly, more to himself than out loud, slurring his words indistinguishably until he said, "Hey, 'section of the cerebellum, brain stem and pons reveals no noteworthy abnormality.' That's good to know. I'm always afraid one day one of the docs around here will cut somebody open and find he's an extraterrestrial or something like that.

"Okay. Last page. 'Provisional Diagnosis. One. Traumatic laceration of neck with severance of the right common carotid artery, right internal carotid artery, jugular vein and vagus nerve. Two. Exsanguinating hemorrhage secondary to laceration of the above vessels.' Pretty much the same as when they started out, huh, Owen?"

Owen ignored the question. "Any microscopic study? Any toxicologic report?"

"Micros. 'Soft tissues of neck.' It says, 'Hemorrhagic fatty, muscle, areolar, vascular and nerve tissue show no abnormality save for the hemorrhage. No foreign material can be identified.' Heart, liver, kidney, brain, nothing there. And the tox study? Why, it's attached. 'Blood. Ethyl alcohol zero point zero two gram percent.' That's like less than a glass of wine, Owen. 'No other volatiles seen. No evidence of narcotics, barbiturates, amphetamines or other common drugs.' Nothing in the urine, either. That's it."

Owen took his time before he asked the next question. As much as he disliked Newhauser, he knew that the man's long experience assisting the autopsy surgeons and doing the odd jobs around the morgue sometimes made his opinion every bit as valuable as that of the doctors for whom he worked.

"What do you make of it, Dale?"

And Newhauser, given the forum to pass as an expert, dramatically took his time in answering. "Shot in the neck by an unknown weapon. Goes in one side, comes out the other. Funny thing, though. No foreign material left behind. No grease, dirt or powder markings. Can't be a bullet, we figured that out before. But now it doesn't look like anything organic, either. The holes, they're not big enough to come from anything larger than an arrow, it would seem. But if it's an arrow, how did it get pulled out? And where's the feathers, the splinters, the stuff they coat the shaft with? Nope, doesn't make sense. I'd say what you got here's a real puzzler, Owen."

Owen thanked him, put the phone back in its cradle while Newhauser was still howling for his fifteen bucks, and resumed his staring. In the time he had been on the line, the rain had intensified to the point where it was now hitting the window hard enough to form rivulets that

180

were sliding across the glass. Owen focused on the water and saw nothing beyond the slithering shapes it made.

An arrow. No evidence of wood, no evidence of feathers. A steel-shafted, featherless arrow. A spear. But a very narrow spear. Could one throw such a spear? And if one could, could one throw it hard enough to go all the way through the neck of this particular victim, big and fit as he was? Owen walked around his office hefting various objects as if he were going to hurl them across the room. A javelin, perhaps? Too big. Besides, who, of all the people he had met, would be likely to own a javelin? Or a spear, for that matter?

Owen sat himself down on his couch, one hand flung over the armrest, and continued to stare at the window. Once again he went over the clues to the dead youth's appearance in Tranton Park. A man in a suit in a San Francisco bar. Based on the interviews he had done so far, that could only be Lane or Rossville, maybe Hartry. Possibly Butler. A man in a suit in a San Francisco bar, without any features a bartender could remember a few days later. He had already determined that a bartender should have been able to remember Blinky Gould. Wouldn't he also have remembered John Clarke Lane, with his silver hair, his silver mustache and his silver airs? Rossville and maybe Hartry. Possibly Butler.

Hartry's wife is pregnant and Butler's wife is having an affair. What could either of those facts have to do with anything other than Dr. Butler's bad mood? Mrs. Butler's partner in the affair seemed to be well known to the Goulds. Maybe Mrs. Butler was having an affair with Mr. Hartry. "Oh, he has a wife, all right," Marietta Gould had said. The object of Mrs. Butler's affections has more than just a wife; he has a wife, all right. A wife who is pregnant is a wife, all right. But regardless, why would either a pregnant wife or an affair cause a man in a suit to send the dead boy to Tranton Park?

Owen sank lower in the couch. Butler doesn't wear a suit and Hartry is an unknown quantity. So, too, are another ten men in another ten Tranton Park houses that haven't been approached yet. But Leigh Rossville wears a suit. And he works in San Francisco. And, once shaven and dressed, he could fit in very well at a bar like McGuppers. And Leigh Rossville had been at home in Tranton Park on the Saturday night the boy died. A quiet evening at home. His wife's birthday. And he was home the following Saturday morning. Yesterday. But in between he was away. Mexico. Cozumel. Short trip.

181

CHAPTER SEVEN

There were three desks, three desktop computers, one Telex machine, one Xerox machine, two racks of brochures, one poster of the azure Aegean as seen from a whitewashed Greek villa, and one poster of Hawaii with the ideal couple strolling hand on arm down an ideally deserted beach. Each desk had a nameplate and two desks had people sitting at them, but the old man in the beat-up tennis shoes, the ancient tennis shorts and the spotted white V-necked tennis sweater with the red and blue stripe across its waist headed straight for the desk with the nameplate that said Cathy Rossville.

The woman at the desk was on the phone. Her head was tilted so that she could hold the receiver between her ear and her shoulder while she tapped something out on the keyboard of the computer. She seemed agitated. Her green eyes stared unhappily at the screen of the computer as though she were dealing with a disciplinary problem.

"Well, I'm sorry, ma'am, that's the only thing they seem to have available. . . . I can try, but I don't think it's going to do you any good. . . . Fine, fine, I'll do it. It'll take a few minutes. Listen, hold on for just a second, will you please? Thank you."

She punched the hold button on the phone and glanced up at the tennis player. "Yes?" She barked first, smiled later.

"I wanted to talk to you about a vacation spot," the tennis player said.

"I'll be a little while," the woman said. "Maybe Doug can help you."

The tennis player swung his hips as though he were going to look for Doug, but he only turned partway. "I like your tan," he said. "I'll wait for you."

The woman glanced hurriedly at her arm. She regarded it as though something were stuck to it, and then she looked away and held up her index finger as a sign that the man should wait.

The tennis player took the vinyl and chrome seat next to the woman's desk and eavesdropped while the woman put her phone customer on two different airline wait lists and then patiently explained to the customer what she had done. Five minutes passed before she was able to tend to the tennis player.

"Sorry," she said.

"No problem," the tennis player told her. "I'm just looking for a getaway week for a couple of active, not quite senior citizens who like the sun and the water. I'm looking at you, young lady, and thinking I bet you've just been to the place I want to go."

The woman smiled. She had a nice smile in that it showed a good set of teeth and made her eyes crinkle, but it wasn't genuine. The tennis player noted that when she stopped smiling not all the crinkles left the corners of her eyes, and he realized that she was probably a few years older than he had first thought. The tumbly hairstyle and the firmness of her body tone had fooled him.

"Mexico," she said.

"Puerto Vallarta?" he asked.

"Cozumel."

"You don't say?" The tennis player sounded impressed. "I've heard of it, but I know nothing about it."

"It's a beautiful place. Here, let me get you some material on it." She got up from behind her desk and moved to the brochure rack. The tennis player saw that she was wearing designer jeans tight enough to have been ironed onto her legs. She caught him looking and misinterpreted his attention.

That made the tennis player blush. "Sorry," he said.

If she heard him she did not acknowledge it. She came back to the desk and spread four or five brightly colored pamphlets in front of him. "This place is very nice. They have tennis courts," she said.

"Is that what you did? Did you go there to play tennis?"

"Not exactly."

"No. Mexico is too hot for tennis. Now that I think of it, Mexico may be too hot for anything. What is there for us to do in Cozumel besides drink and lie in the sun?"

"Do you like to snorkel?"

"Is it good there?"

"Some of the best in the world."

183

"Is that what you did?"

"Well, sort of. My husband and I like to scuba dive. That's really why we go there." For no obvious reason, the woman's lips began to quiver.

The man said, "And you had been there before? Scuba diving in Cozumel, I mean. Or was this the first time for you?"

"No. We've been there several times." The woman's voice had dropped to just above a whisper. She reached out, her fingers splayed, and pushed the brochures. For a long minute nothing more was said. Then she smiled her biggest and least warm smile yet. "You want to take these home?" she said. "Let me know later if you're interested?"

The tennis player gathered up the brochures in his slightly yellowish hands. He said he would do just that.

Owen seated himself at a familiar table in a corner of The Chinese Pancake House. The waiter brought him tea and a menu. The waiter said, "Good ee-yung, Mistah Cah-suh," and then stood straight and tall with his pencil hand and his notepad hand clasped at about the height of his bowtie.

Owen studied the daily dinner specials and went with number four: a cup of eggdrop soup, a spring roll and cashew chicken. The waiter made a single slash on his notepad and said that was a very good choice. He did not mention the fact that it was the same choice Owen made at least once a week, and Owen did not mention the fact that some of the spots on the oilcloth table cover were ones that he himself had probably left.

Owen searched his raincoat pockets for something with which to write. He took out a pen and then slid his arms from the coat and let the coat drape over the back of his chair. Using his paper napkin, he began to jot down figures: $40.00 to Newhauser, $7.89 for a bottle of Scotch, $10.00 to a parking lot attendant, $5.00 for a drink and tip at McGuppers, $2.00 for bridge tolls, $12.00 to the Salvation Army for his tennis outfit and sneakers. Gas, phone calls, miscellaneous materials—that had to amount to another twenty or twenty-five bucks. Add in the fifty he had promised Gleason and it all came to substantially more than he had initially budgeted for the case. He was reminded, as he often was, about the last time he had allowed investigation expenses to get away from him—when after six weeks of fruitless searching for a missing girl he had watched the $25,000 reward the girl's parents were offering be paid to some Houston psychic who dreamed the child had been eaten by a dog.

But this time there was no phantom dog and no crackpot psychic to compete for the business. This time there was an honest-to-God body and nobody but Owen to try to figure out what would possess such a smart young couple as the Rossvilles to take a sudden scuba-diving trip shortly after they had loaned away their masks and snorkels and fins.

He could, he decided, afford to budget a little more.

CHAPTER EIGHT

Gleason got hold of him late Monday afternoon. He was chortling with happiness. "I've identified your boy," he said, "and guess what?"

"I give up."

Owen's lack of competitive spirit did not seem to faze Mr. Gleason. He chortled some more. Then he gave him the answer. "He's dead."

Gleason's humor seemed entirely inappropriate to Owen, who pursed his lips and made a little sticking noise before speaking again. "I know he's dead, Dan. I saw his body. I took pictures. I sent one to you."

"I mean he's already dead."

Owen was silent. Gleason hung on, luxuriating in his surprise, wanting Owen to ask what he meant. And finally Owen asked.

"Robert Michael O'Berry, born nineteen years and one month ago. Graduated high school last June," Gleason said. "Business course, straight C average, no school activities whatsoever. Home address, 21 Water Street. Father's a forklift driver. . . . Ready for the big surprise now? School records show he died last November. I said that couldn't be. Little girl behind the counter shows me the file, it's stamped deceased. She knows, she tells me. She remembers the guy, remembers everybody talking about it when he died. So I go above and beyond the call of duty, Owen, because my curiosity's piqued, and I figured you woulda done the same."

Gleason waited for a sign of gratitude. Owen waited for the payoff.

"So I goes to the *Portshead Sentinel,* the local paper, and I check the November obits. There it is, not just a notice but half a news column. 'Missing, Presumed Drowned, Lake Winnipesaukee, New Hampshire, Robert Michael "Bobby" O'Berry, eighteen, of 21 Water Street, Portshead.' And get this, Owen, this is the part you're gonna love: It was his wedding night."

It was as though Gleason's voice had just soared off a springboard and was now suspended in the air, unable to come down until Owen gave the word. This time Gleason got what he wanted.

Owen expressed gratitude, amazement, overwhelming shock. He did it all with one heavily exhaled syllable: "No!"

Now that he felt he had Owen excited, Gleason quickly became blasé. "It's what the paper says. Survived by a wife, the former Barbara Cochrane of Portshead. You know what I figure, Owen? I figure a boy eighteen, just out of high school, he doesn't get married unless he has to. Not in this day and age. You follow me? He knocks up the girl, he has to get married, he doesn't want to get married, so he does it and he splits. Goes out for a swim on his wedding night and never comes back." Gleason made a spattering noise with his mouth. "As if anybody in his right mind would go swimmin' in New Hampshire in November. At night, of all times. Not even the fuckin' L Street Brownies would do that."

The image of L Street Brownies meant nothing to Owen, who said, "You think that kid Sabatini was in on it? You think he had his motorcycle hidden somewhere so this boy could swim to it?"

"That's what I'm thinkin', Owen. I'm thinkin' that's why little Julie shits when I show him the picture. I'm thinkin' little Julie helps his buddy do his getaway, reports his bike stolen, and then sits back fat, dumb and happy while old Bobby goes off to live the high life in California."

"Of course, you don't know for sure if they're buddies."

"I can find out damn fast."

"Push it, will you, Dan?"

As always, Gleason pretended that Owen's request was a major imposition, but this time his protest was almost perfunctory.

The phone rang again just as Owen was locking the office for the evening. It was already dark outside, but there was no particular reason for him to want to go home. He went back and answered it. "Owen Carr."

A woman's voice whispered hoarsely, "I know who you are and I've got what you want."

Surprised, Owen could think of no immediate response.

187

"I know about the motorcycle in Tranton Park," the voice continued.

Tumblers clicked in Owen's mind. Calculations were made, discarded, and made all over again in barely a second's time. "Mrs. Lane?"

There was a slight hesitation on the other end of the line, and then the whisper disappeared, replaced by a cool, professional tone of the type one uses in dealing with unwanted salesmen. "My husband told me all about you."

"Nothing but good things, I hope."

"He says you're a crazy old man and somebody should lock you up."

Owen was not quite sure how to react. He was almost grateful when Mrs. Lane suddenly laughed mirthlessly. "It's all right," she said. "He thinks I'm crazy, too."

"Sounds like we crazy people ought to stick together."

It was the wrong thing to say. "I'm not crazy," she snapped.

This time he responded correctly. "Neither am I."

"I want you to do something for me."

"What sort of something?"

"Does it make a difference? Do you really care? If you want to know what I know, you'll do what I want, won't you?"

"Well, I won't jump off a bridge or set fire to anybody's house."

"Very funny. I want you to watch someone for me."

"Watch someone do what?"

"Do whatever he does."

"Your husband?"

"I'll pay you."

"I think we should get together and talk about it, Mrs. Lane."

She took a deep breath. "Will you come here?"

"Anytime, day or night."

"Never a day off, isn't that what you claim? Not since nineteen fifty-nine."

"Forty-nine."

"Do you think I care whether it's fifty-nine or forty-nine?"

"I hadn't really thought about it."

"Well, I don't. Come to my house tomorrow morning. Will you do that?"

"What time?"

"John leaves for work at eight-thirty on the dot. Day in and day out."

"I'll come at eight-forty-five, then."

"No. That's about the time Mark Hartry leaves. And Leigh, old Leigh goes anytime he seems to feel like it. If he goes at all. Come at nine-thirty. If he's going he'll be gone by then, but it will still be too early for busybody Butler to come out of her house."

"You don't want anyone to see me."

"My, how perceptive you are."

"I'll wear a disguise."

"Yes," she said sibilantly. "Change your raincoat."

The inside of the house turned out to be immaculate. There was not a mark on the floors, a picture out of line, a spot of dust on the furniture. It was a silent house in which the ticking of a mantel clock could be heard distinctly.

He had used the brass door knocker just as he had always done, but this time she had pulled the door open immediately. She had glowered at him, dressed as he was in a pair of tan workman's coveralls with a matching baseball-style cap pulled down far enough to rest on the tops of his ears, but she had let him in the house.

She had looked at the seat of his coveralls to make sure it was clean and then she had shown him into her living room and allowed him to sit on her white sofa. She herself had taken an armchair, one with a raised pattern of blue birds interconnected across a white background.

Mary Elizabeth Lane was as fastidious about her own appearance as she was about that of her home. She was wearing a gray wool skirt with a cantaloupe-colored silk blouse that was buttoned to the neck and fastened with a cameo brooch. Her gray-black hair was cut short, her eyebrows were perfectly trimmed and she appeared to have applied a touch of makeup to what Owen assumed were permanent bags under each of her obsidian-like eyes.

She sat on the very edge of her chair, carefully placed one knee over the other, and covered the topmost knee with both her hands. Her nails were buffed and manicured, her stockinged legs smooth and slender, without so much as a single vein in evidence. Owen guessed her to be about fifty.

"You have a lovely house," he said.

She didn't answer.

He had his cap in his hands. He spun it while he glanced around. Then he put it on the floor, leaned back into the cushions of the couch and waited.

"Let me see the picture you have," she said.

Owen disassembled from the comfortable position he had just assumed. He took the picture out of an inside pocket, leaned forward and handed it to her.

She studied the dead face of Bobby O'Berry as if it were a mathematical formula or a combination to a lock. "You want to know about a motorcycle," she said.

Owen nodded. "A Honda 750. Massachusetts plates. Red and white tank."

"I didn't see the colors or the plates." She kept her eyes down, still on the picture.

"But you did see the motorcycle. And you saw this young man on it."

"I saw a motorcycle. Honda-shmonda. It was big and it made a lot of noise. I looked outside and I saw it."

"Was this boy riding it?"

"Which time?"

"Saturday night. A week ago Saturday night."

"And I said which time?" she demanded, thrusting the picture back toward him.

"Did you see this young man in Tranton Park at any time a week ago Saturday night?"

"I saw a motorcycle pass by my house. I couldn't tell who was riding it, but I saw whose driveway it turned into. Later on I saw the motorcycle again and this time I was sure who was driving it."

Owen held up the picture and raised his eyebrows.

"No," she said.

A buzzer could have gone off. A voice could have come over a loudspeaker moaning condolences about his incorrect guess. A pretty girl could have come into the room and led him away, to be replaced by the next contestant. But until then Owen was prepared to sit.

"My husband says the boy was killed and you think someone in Tranton Park did it."

"I don't know that that's the case, Mrs. Lane. I just think he was in Tranton Park shortly before he was killed. I want to know why he was here, what he was doing here." Owen spread his hands to show how simple his requests were.

"It could have been a number of things."

"Like what?"

"Like any one of the things that have been going on since that mixed couple moved in."

"Mexican?"

"Mixed couple, I said. You know who I'm talking about, the Negro and his pretty young wife and their little mulatto children."

"Ah, Roarke Robinson."

"Ah, Roarke Robinson," she mimicked. "As though that makes all the difference in the world."

"You don't believe in intermarriage."

"It's not a question of believing, Mr. ...."

Owen knew that she knew his name, but he accommodated her anyway. "Carr."

"... Carr. There's nothing to believe in. It's not a theory or a religion. It's just a matter of there being one set of rules for some people and another set for everybody else. Suddenly these people move in and everybody finds their ways of doing things not only socially acceptable but infinitely desirable." She turned her head slightly so that she was no longer looking at Owen. "It's as if everyone in the community has decided that if the Robinsons can get away with it, they can, too."

"Get away with what, Mrs. Lane?"

"Why, anything they please. Isn't that obvious? You're the one who has been going around from one to the other. You tell me, have you ever seen anything like it? And it's all since the Robinsons moved in. I mean, things may have been God-awful around here before, but nothing like what it has been the past few months. People cavorting around naked, running from bed to bed, having all-night traffic parading in and out of their houses."

"Cavorting around naked?" Owen was not sure he had heard right, but Mrs. Lane took his question as a challenge.

"They think I can't see them, but I can," she said indignantly. "Anybody can who's in our guest bedroom. You can't help it. You see right over the Butlers' fence, right into their backyard where they have this outdoor bath set up, this hot tub. They even have lights arranged so they can see each other at night. The later the better, they seem to think, because they're out there at all hours. There isn't one of them who hasn't been there at one time or another: the Martels, the Goulds, the Weissocks, the Hartrys, the Rossvilles. And of course she has *him* over there every chance she gets."

"She?" said Owen. "Him?"

"Mis-ter Robinson," she said, dragging out the title as though she had to get over a hurdle between the two syllables. "Mrs. Butler entertains

---

191

him when nobody else is around. I've even seen them get in that hot tub together during the day, and it was plenty obvious what they were doing in there. It was enough to make you sick."

"Maybe you shouldn't watch," suggested Owen sympathetically.

"How can you help it when they're practically flaunting it in your face? There's not a thing in this world you can do to keep any of those people out there from acting any way they please. The world's their oyster—didn't you know that, Mr. Carr? Why, they've invented computers in their garages, they've designed a whole new line of commodes or installed a chain of eyeglass stores in shopping malls. They've even learned to hit a ball with a piece of wood. Why should they respect tradition or custom or morals?"

Mrs. Lane turned her head again and gazed into a distant corner of the room. "It's like I told John when he insisted on moving here: You can't just plunk down a bunch of expensive homes on a hillside and expect them to be filled up with anything more than people who've recently made a lot of money. A community has to have some sort of roots to give it stability."

"Like a tree," suggested Owen.

Mrs. Lane ignored him. "People should move in with the idea that they're going to fit in, not take over the way this Robinson has done. And he's been able to do it simply because the neighborhood had no character. Everyone around here was just waiting for someone to come along and tell them how to act. John tried, God knows, but we're talking about people who have no breeding. Except for this Rossville next door, I don't think there's one of them who was ever in a social situation that didn't involve hot dogs and hamburgers. 'C'mon over and have a barbecue,' they're always saying, as if that's the very height of human existence." Her eyes moved to the bay window that was behind Owen.

Owen turned to see if there was anything particular that she was looking at and then he turned back to her. "Am I correct in assuming that you don't get out much these days, Mrs. Lane?"

"There's no reason to. There's nothing I want out there."

"Shopping? Do you ever get out to do that?"

"Sometimes. I go with my husband."

"Do you have any children, any relatives you ever go visit?"

"Children?" She looked again at Owen. "Our daughter died in an automobile accident when we were living in Atherton." Her eyes fixed on Owen's as if he should have known better than to bring up such a subject.

192

"I'm very sorry, Mrs. Lane," he said, and he looked sorry. But Mrs. Lane's glare was relentless until he said, "I had a wife who died very suddenly. I know something about what happens to you when you lose someone. It makes the whole concept of existence change, doesn't it? In my case I was left wondering what I was supposed to do now that there was no one left to go home to anymore." He shrugged. "I chose not to go home at all. You, you've chosen not to go out. But I don't think the way we feel is really that different. We were both trying to put the whole thing, life and death, into some perspective. Survivors do that, you know. But it's awful hard if they don't know why the person died."

Owen showed his photograph of Bobby O'Berry. "The family of this boy here are entitled to know that, just as you and I were. You must be aware of what's going through their minds since you've experienced it yourself."

"My daughter," Mrs. Lane said stiffly, "was nothing like that boy."

Owen looked at the picture. "Did you know him?"

She shook her head. "I don't have to know him. I can imagine what he was like."

"Why is that, Mrs. Lane?"

She grimaced in disgust and averted her eyes as if she could not bear to look at Owen anymore. Long moments passed in silence.

"Mrs. Lane, you asked me to come here for a purpose. You wanted me to do something and you promised to tell me something. I think it's time you explained yourself."

Her words came out in a rush. "Where did you run into my husband?"

Owen answered slowly. "At the Robinsons' house."

"Inside?"

"Yes," he said, his voice barely audible.

She nodded and concentrated on whatever was outside the window. "He told me he met you on the sidewalk. That he saw you going from door to door and that he demanded to know who you were and what you wanted."

"He sort of did—" said Owen, but she was screaming at him before he finished his sentence.

"Don't patronize me, Mr. Carr. Don't you dare. He was inside her house while her husband was away. He was doing just like all the rest of the people around here, wasn't he?"

Owen said, "Is that something you wanted me to investi—" But she cut him off again.

193

"He knows all about Roarke Robinson and Mrs. Butler because I told him. He waited and the first chance he had, he put on that silly little college boy's sweater and he went right up there to see if she wasn't just like her husband. I saw him before he went, standing in front of the mirror brushing his hair, and I knew he wasn't going out for any walk."

"Have you got everything you wanted from me, Mrs. Lane?"

She swung around in her chair so that Owen was looking directly at her shoulder and the side of her head. "Go," she said. "Get out of here."

"I think now it's only fair that you tell me who you saw riding the motorcycle."

"Fair? What is fair, Mr. Carr? My own husband's not even fair. Do you know why he wanted to move here? To this white elephant of a house? It was just so he could do things like this. Some men, they get his age, they buy a sports car. My husband, he buys a sports house so he can run around and play tennis with the computer man or chase after the baseball player's wife. You know what his plan for me was? Get me out of the Atherton house with all the memories of Emily, move me someplace where I'd be forced to see other people. Wasn't that nice? Get me into a situation where I'd be mingling with all the other little wives, maybe sitting around a swimming pool watching their children push each other into the water. Well, I won't have it. I won't have it and I won't have you, either, Mr. Carr. Now get out."

But Owen continued to sit where he was. "Are the rules different for you, too, Mrs. Lane?"

Still without looking at him, she said, "What rules? There are no rules anymore, didn't you hear what I just said?"

"I think there are rules in this house." Owen's eyes swept the living room, going from one neatly placed object to the next. "There's order here and you can't have order without rules. I think you look outside, Mrs. Lane, and you see disorder everywhere and it bothers you. You wonder how anybody can survive or why anybody would want to with everything being so uncertain. In here, where you have control, you know what's going to happen next because you know what's supposed to happen next. Out there, where there is no control, anything can happen." His eyes completed the circuit and came back to rest on her. "The problem for you at this moment, Mrs. Lane, is that I'm from out there."

Alarm slowly spread across the woman's face. "What is that supposed to mean?"

"It means that as long as we play by your rules, I tell you something, you tell me something, and I get up and leave. That's what I thought we were doing. If you don't want to play by rules, then you have no idea what I'm going to do next." And Owen continued to sit, just as he had been sitting for several minutes.

Mrs. Lane put her hand on the arm of her chair and pushed against it until her elbow locked straight. Her mouth opened and her breathing sounds became audible.

"Tell me about the motorcycle, Mrs. Lane."

"I heard it going up the street and I looked out and saw it. I was down here, looking through the window behind you, and I could see that it was going very slowly, as though it were searching for an address. I was afraid it was coming here, but then it went past and turned into the neighbors'." She pointed.

Owen followed her finger. "The Rossvilles'?"

She nodded.

"And later, when you saw the motorcycle again . . . ?

"It was very late. One or two o'clock, at least. I couldn't sleep and I was sitting on the lounge in my bedroom. I heard movement outside and I looked down. It was the motorcycle being pushed out the driveway, and this time, because I was looking down, I could see who was on it."

"Tell me."

"It was Leigh," she said. She read Owen's face and saw that he was satisfied. Her arm unlocked and she relaxed.

"Now get out of my house," she said.

CHAPTER NINE

Gleason picked him up at Logan Airport. Gleason, his face as red as a tomato, his belly swelling so much that his white shirt separated between his navel and the belt loops to his pants, was dressed as he had promised to be, in a blue blazer and a striped tie. He hadn't mentioned that the blue blazer would have dandruff on its shoulders or that the tie would only come halfway down his shirtfront, but Owen picked him out of the crowd in the arrival lounge anyway.

To Owen's surprise, Gleason drove a Cadillac as red as his face. It had leather reclining seats and push-button windows, a padded dash and thickly carpeted floors, and Gleason insisted on showing off most of its features before they could leave the parking lot.

"Automatic radio antenna," he said, demonstrating. "Turn the key on the driver's side and it unlocks every door in the car. Turn it again and it locks 'em all up. See that?"

Owen felt compelled to issue a stream of appreciative comments: "How nice" and "Isn't that amazing?" and "You don't say." Only when they both were safely belted in did he feel it appropriate to ask if Gleason ever used the Cadillac for surveillance.

"Nope," said Gleason with almost as much pride as he had shown in reciting the virtues of the car. "Don't do surveillance anymore. Do most of my work for attorneys now."

He stopped the car at a booth to pay the lot fees. He adjusted the tiltable steering wheel so that he did not have to move his hips, dragged a wad of bills out of his pants pocket, peeled off a single for the attendant, and asked for a receipt. Then he stuffed the bills back into his pocket, readjusted the steering wheel, and drove off with the air of a man who has everything but really doesn't like to brag about it.

"Attorneys, Owen," he said, "are the lifeblood of our industry. Line up a few witnesses, get some statements, secure some evidence, and get it into court when it's supposed to be there. I'm into videotaping depositions now. Piece of cake. Once you got the camera set up, you don't do a damn thing because all they want's a head and shoulders shot of the deponent anyhow. Lifeblood, Owen; forty-five bucks an hour no matter what I do. Of course, you got your way of doing things, like you said, and that's what we're here for, but I'm just trying to give you an idea what my operation is like so you can understand why I might a been a little skeptical at first about what you were proposing. See, I'm not used to going balls-out like this. I may not be getting rich, you know, but I got a couple of these small to midsize law firms sewn up and they come to me steady as rain. 'Danny do this and Danny do that.' And I say, 'Yes, sir, forty-five dollars. Right away, sir, forty-five dollars.' You ever work that side of the business, Owen?"

"Not yet."

A gleam came into Gleason's eye, a smile spread across his lips. Without looking, because they were approaching a tunnel and another tollbooth, he reached over and banged Owen good-naturedly on the bicep. "Not yet," he said. "Not yet."

Owen, who was clutching his valise in his lap, winced in silent pain.

The tunnel was old and narrow. The people drove it as if they had been projected out of a pinball chute, careening from lane to lane at speeds that Owen was convinced were unconscionably unsafe. Gleason, however, was casually leaning on his armrest, steering with one finger looped around the base of the steering wheel.

"The reason I'm telling you all this, Owen," he said, "is that I never done this kind of deal before and I'm kinda curious about it."

Owen, busy pressing his foot into the floorboards, said nothing.

Gleason looked over at him. "I gotta admit, now that you know who killed the kid and now that I found out who the kid is, it all looks brilliant." But there was concern in Gleason's manner. "I'm just wondering, though, if you ever done anything like this before."

"Sure," said Owen. Now that they were emerging from the tunnel he thought he could breathe easier. But Gleason, for no immediately perceivable reason, suddenly made a sharp right-hand turn into what looked like a little neighborhood street that ran in front of several Italian produce stores. In about a hundred yards he did a left turn that hooked them around in the opposite direction and a moment later they were shooting up a ramp to the expressway that was heading south of

Boston. Owen looked first over his inside shoulder and then over his outside shoulder before settling down again.

Meanwhile, Gleason was going through a struggle of his own. "Tell me, Owen—I mean, since we're sort of partners on this thing I hope you don't mind me asking, but I'd like to know how you came up with this kind of angle." He laughed in a self-deprecating manner. "Hell, I been in the business a few years myself and, frankly, nothing like this ever occurred to me."

"There's a lot of work out there, Dan. Sometimes it just takes a little creativity to find it, that's all."

"Yeah," said Gleason, pretending to be enlightened. "But, like, how did you get started doin' stuff like this? Is this something you did back in forty-nine or whenever?"

"I started out just after the war as a railroad detective with the Southern Pacific."

"Yeah? You like that?"

"It happened to be the first job that was offered to me. I was bright, eager, newly married, willing to do whatever anybody asked me. It made me a good employee."

Gleason nodded as though he understood. "Then why did you leave?"

"I had a boss named Clatterbuck and he took a shine to me. Showed me a few tricks, taught me a few skills, kept giving me better and better cases. I was there about four years when I had a personal tragedy come up and I guess you could say I wasn't coping well. Clatterbuck was right there to help me get through it, though. To get my mind off it, he said I ought to go out on my own. He'd keep me supplied with SP cases and I'd be so busy running my own shop I wouldn't have time to dwell on this thing that had happened. It was good advice. It worked. That was nineteen forty-nine."

"And this Clatterbuck, he keep his word? He keep feeding you cases?"

"Right up until the day he was arrested."

Gleason liked that. He did a slow take, just to make sure he was not being made the butt of some wry joke, and then he bellowed, "Arrested?"

Owen shrugged. "It seems somebody figured out that a man raising five kids on the salary paid the railroad's chief of detectives should not really be able to afford a vacation home at Lake Tahoe and a fishing boat on the Bay. The FBI got called in because of the interstate nature

198

of the railroad's business and by the time they convinced Clatterbuck to plead guilty to embezzlement, everyone associated with him had become *persona non grata* as far as the SP was concerned."

"No more referrals?"

Owen spit dryly.

"What did you do?"

"I increased the size of my ad in the yellow pages."

"Yeah? Did it work?"

"Sure. It attracted every ninny in town who wanted me to gather evidence for divorces. Couple of landlords wanted me to do skip traces. Neophyte criminal lawyers flocked to me for help in locating witnesses. 'He's a black guy,' they'd tell me. 'Dark skin, kinky hair, between twenty-five and forty, goes by the name of Willie.' "

Gleason shuddered in sympathy. "I stay away from the colored, myself. I have to go into Roxbury, someplace like that? I got me a kid who does it for me. An apprentice, you know? I pay him twelve fifty an hour, rewrite his reports and bill him out at my own rate. How'd you handle it?"

"It occurred to me," said Owen in a way that made it unclear whether he was responding to Gleason or ignoring him, "that no man who knows how to get someone to slip him a file or give him a name or an address or a piece of official information ever needs to sit around waiting for business to come to him."

They drove on in silence until Gleason said, "And you been developing your own business ever since."

"Ever since."

"And this kind of thing that we're going out on now, what I'm trying to get at is, you've had some success with it in the past, is that right?" There was hope in Gleason's face.

Owen drummed his fingers on his valise and looked out the window at the three-decker apartment buildings they were passing. "Dan," he said, "you told me we're going to see a teenage widow."

"That's right."

"You told me you suspect she's poor."

"She comes from Portshead, chances are she ain't rich, that's probably what I said. Poor, no, I wouldn't a said that."

"Your theory is she got married because she was going to have a baby."

"She got married in November; my guess is she's due about now."

"A poor young widow with a baby to feed is going to be interested in

199

the possibility of coming into some money, don't you think? Someone comes to her and says, 'Here, here's a way you can get some money at no cost and no risk to you,' why wouldn't she want to do it?"

"In other words, you think this is going to be an offer she can't refuse."

"Something like that."

Gleason burst into relieved laughter. After a moment he added, "Way to go, Owen. Some people get the Godfather, this poor girl's gonna get the Grandfather."

Gleason had obtained Barbara Cochrane O'Berry's address through his "source" at the high school. He seemed to have forgotten that he had already revealed to Owen that his "source" was simply one of the students who worked across the counter in the principal's office.

"Did you have much trouble?" Owen asked.

"I have my ways," Gleason told him with a meaningful side glance.

The Cochrane house turned out to be a surprise for both of them. Owen had expected a multifamily building, such as those he had seen along the expressway. What he got was a large, almost opulent stone home on a piece of property big enough to be called a mini-estate in California.

"Shit," said Gleason, stopping suddenly at the edge of the driveway and peering out between the top of his steering wheel and the top of his windshield. "This place must be worth nearly two hundred thousand bucks."

Shit, thought Owen, once he realized Gleason wasn't kidding; put it in the Bay Area and it would be worth six hundred thousand. Put it in Tranton Park and you could get three quarters of a million for it.

Gleason looked up and down the street. There were other large houses with trees and good-sized lawns, but none had the character that the Cochrane house had. "Maybe her old man's the local doctor," he said. "I hadn't thought of that possibility." He took his foot off the power brake so suddenly the Cadillac spat pebbles behind its rear tires as it surged forward.

A second surprise awaited them as they stood beneath the gabled overhang with Gleason's finger on the doorbell. The front door was wrenched open by a huge man, naked to the waist. The man had reddish hair that curled over his ears and flowed down his neck. His cheeks were unshaven and rough as sandpaper. His eyes were narrow and his nose seemed to be without a bridge. As he shifted into a slouch with one hand resting on the door handle, the layers of skin that padded his hips, his belly and his massive chest jostled up and down.

The man was not friendly. "Yeah?" he said.

Gleason, whose own fat gave him extraordinary size, looked like a whale pup next to the man at the door. He seemed to do a little dance that left him slightly behind Owen's shoulder when he said, "Um, heh, we're looking for a woman named Barbara O'Berry."

"Who?" the man said. Then he caught himself and changed the question. "Who's asking?"

Owen stepped forward and handed him his card. The man gripped it with the proximal joints of his fingers and stared at it. "California, huh?" He looked at Gleason and jabbed an index finger about the size of a hot dog at him. "Who are you?"

"Dan Gleason, a private investigator out of Boston." His card went across and the man stared at that for a while.

"What do you guys want with Barbara?"

Owen said, "I may have some news about her husband."

The man slowly raised his eyes. Say the secret word, win a hundred dollars. "Come in," he said, standing back to let them pass.

The two investigators stepped into a short hall and the door slammed behind them. They were directed into a broad living room. Their third surprise came then. A pink bassinet was in the center of the floor. A small pink blanket was thrown over the back of a couch. A box of infant's disposable diapers was sticking out from beneath a chair. "Wait here," the man said, as Owen and Gleason exchanged silent looks.

The man went through a swinging door in the far wall. For a few moments Owen and Gleason could hear him talking to someone. Then the door swung inward and an older woman poked her head into the room, only to withdraw it a moment later as the door swung shut.

A minute passed and then another. Owen and Gleason had time to study the room. It was a curious mixture of the formal (an unused fireplace with an antique mantel clock and a gold-leaf mirror behind the clock) and the informal (plain furniture, the baby items scattered about). They almost had the layout memorized before the man who had greeted them appeared again.

He had put on a plaid shirt, but he hadn't buttoned it, and he had brought a second man with him, a man barefooted and in a bathrobe. The second man's hair, what he had of it, was disheveled, and he had the look of a person who had been awakened before he was ready; but

201

what most struck the two visitors to the house was his size: he was even bigger than the first man.

The smaller of the two stepped forward. "We want to know what is it you want with our sister," he said. He passed his thumb between himself and his companion.

"Did you know her husband?" Owen said.

"She was only married to the guy one day." He stopped and looked back at his brother. "But yeah, we knew him."

Owen handed him the picture. "Is that him?"

Nearly six hundred pounds of Cochrane brothers huddled together. "Yeah, that's Bobby," said one. They spread apart again. The one in the bathrobe said, "You found his body finally, huh?"

"It was found in California," Owen told him.

The two brothers locked eyes. There was almost a palpable arc of thought that passed between them. How the hell did he float from Lake Winnipesaukee to California? Suddenly the big one grabbed the picture out of the less big one's hand.

"What's that hole in his throat?" he demanded. "That a bullet?"

"It's how he was killed. It may be from some sort of arrow—"

"Hunter, huh?" said the bigger one.

"Makes sense," said his brother. "They got hunters in New Hampshire in November. I think."

Owen, his mouth still poised from when he had been cut off, said, "It's my belief the wound came from an underwater spear gun."

"A spear gun?" said the smaller brother. "In Lake Winnipesaukee?"

"You think," said the bigger one, "Bobby went out for a swim, some asshole shot him with a spear gun? Hauled his ass all the way to California?"

"I think," Owen told them calmly, "that your brother-in-law swam away on purpose on his wedding night, that a friend of his had hidden some clothes, some money and a motorcycle somewhere around the lake, that he not only survived his swim but that he managed to make it all the way out to California, and that he was killed for real about two weeks ago."

There was silence in the Cochranes' big living room. It was a menacing sort of silence that was spared from erupting into violent noise only by Owen Carr's totally nonthreatening manner.

The brothers could have been a two-headed monster. They were standing together, their inside legs and shoulders touching, both of them holding the picture of a dead Bobby O'Berry. "Sonofabitch," one of them said, but the other was a little more practical. "You got any proof, old man?" he asked.

Owen gave a very slight lift to his hands. "I've got the body. It's in a morgue in Oakland. I've got the coroner's report, if you want to see that. It'll show that the person in that picture didn't die until a week ago last Saturday and the cause of death had nothing to do with a midnight swim."

The smaller brother, the redhead, his eyes on Owen, said, "You believe this, Billy?"

Billy said, "What is it you want, old man?"

"I think I know who killed him."

"And you want some kind of reward, is that it?"

Owen shook his head. "I want your sister to sue the killer."

"Sue him?" The redhead repeated the words as though they made no sense. He said them very slowly as though perhaps Owen had mispronounced them or perhaps he had misunderstood what Owen had said. Then, gathering momentum, he turned to his brother and barked the words as though they were the punch line to a joke. "Sue him!"

Big brother Billy said, "We got our own ways of takin' care of things like this. Who is this guy?"

"That's my information," Owen said.

An expression of incredulity came over Billy's face. He licked his lips. "Give him some money, Terry."

The smaller brother thought about it. "What for?" he said at last. "I don't give a good goddamn somebody snuffed Bobby or not. He cut out on Barb, he deserved it. He's lucky you and me didn't catch up with him, that's all I got to say."

Owen looked at the bassinet. The brothers Cochrane looked with him. "She had her baby, I see. Pink. Little girl? I assume it's Bobby's. Little girl will never get to know her father, never have him there to support her. And your sister, it might be okay now, the excitement of a newborn and so forth, all you people here to help her, but she's got at least twenty-one years to go, paying for the little girl's education . . . her clothes . . . her food. May be that your sister's very attractive, but we all know it's that much harder finding a new husband when you're bringing along somebody else's child. The other thing is, who's to say about Bobby? He was only eighteen when he took off. Youth can be impetuous. They do things that seem like a good idea at the time, change their minds later. He might have gotten to California, not liked it, come back. He might have heard about his little daughter and had a change

203

of heart. People do that, you know. It's one thing when the baby isn't there. Another thing when she is."

The brothers shrugged. In tandem.

"It's also possible that Bobby wouldn't have come back voluntarily. But he could still turn up. Not that easy just to disappear, what with computers and communications being the way they are these days. You find him alive, regardless of whether he's out in California or back here, he's still liable for support of his wife and child. Twenty-one years of child support alone, that's a pretty good chunk of money."

"I don't know," said Terry, his brow furrowing, "if Bobby would have been worth all that much."

"But you never will know," Owen said quickly, "because the man who killed him deprived everyone of the chance of finding out. He deprived Bobby of the chance of making something of himself. He deprived your sister of the chance of getting him back. He deprived your little niece of the chance of ever getting to experience her father."

This time both the brothers were silent, their faces clouded with thought.

"Under the law," Owen went on, "a widow and a child can sue for wrongful death of their husband and father. All you have to prove is that it is more likely than not that the defendant caused the death and then you're entitled to compensation for all the monetary damages you can prove resulted from the defendant's act. If you can establish that the defendant killed the decedent on purpose, you might get punitive damages. Teach him a lesson. Take every cent he has. In this case, that could be an awful lot of money."

Billy, the bigger one, elbowed his brother aside. "Don't they try people for murder in California anymore?"

"They do. When they have reason to. But I seem to be the only one who's made the connection in this case. Your brother-in-law's listed as a John Doe. His body was found by the side of the road in an area that motorcycle gangs and drug dealers have been known to use as a dumping ground. He apparently didn't have any fingerprints on file anywhere, and there's certainly been no hue and cry to find out who he is. I got in on the case early. I followed some clues, I had some luck, and nobody else seems to have picked up on what I've picked up on."

Terry flashed the picture. "You're the only one knows this is Bobby, huh?"

"You two, me, Dan here. We've shown the picture to a couple of others in order to trace your sister."

204

"But you're the only one official."

"I'm not official. But yes, I'm the only one investigating who knows the name of John Doe. You want, you can get him back without me. But I'm also the only one who knows the name of his killer."

"We could tell the cops. They could get it out of you."

"But you won't, because that won't do you or your sister any good. You see, what I thought she might like to do is attempt a settlement before we file suit. This man who killed Bobby, he seems to be in a fairly comfortable position: good house, good job, fancy cars, comes from a well-known family. He's not only not going to want to be convicted of murder, he's not going to want anybody to suspect what he's done. And right now, nobody does. But a civil suit gets filed, everybody will: his friends, the people he works with, the newspapers . . . the DA. On the other hand, he pays a little money for an out-of-court settlement, the whole thing is hush-hush. Our evidence, my evidence, never comes up again."

"That sounds illegal." Terry Cochrane did not seem to be shocked by the prospect; he seemed to want to be certain.

But Owen shook his head. "It's perfectly legal, as long as we go about it correctly. I'll fix you up with a lawyer in California. He presents the case in terms of a claim on behalf of his clients, your sister and her child. The man who shot Bobby will know what's going on. Unless he's completely innocent, which I doubt very sincerely, his only desire will be to see how little he can pay to make us go away quickly."

Billy and Terry Cochrane turned to each other and once again messages passed silently between them. "One thing," Billy said, looking over his shoulder at Owen. "Why did this guy kill Bobby?"

Owen met his gaze. "To be perfectly honest, that part I'm not sure about. I think I can find out, I've got some suspicions, but before I go any further in following up on them, I want some assurances as to whom I'm working for."

Terry suddenly had an idea. It made his eyes brighten. "What if we just rattle you? What if me and my brother just grab you and your chubby friend here and make you tell us everything you know?"

Owen shrugged. "You're still going to need someone to do the legwork. This case isn't handled just right, you'll find yourself in big trouble. And there's still, by the way, plenty more to do. I'm convinced I know who killed your brother-in-law and how, when and where he got killed, but that's all I'm convinced of. I don't yet know how he came to be shot with a spear gun. And that, of course, is crucial."

Terry looked glum. His brother looked even glummer. The four men stood in the open spaces of the living room, holding positions as revealing as those of the Burghers of Calais. And then, almost simultaneously, the brothers began to smile; and when they smiled, Gleason's mouth spread so fast a laugh escaped. Only Owen remained stolid.

Terry said, "I'll go get my sister," and Billy stepped forward and clapped Owen on the arm. He clapped him hard enough to leave a bruise that would remain there for weeks: a little memento from the Cochrane brothers of Portshead, Massachusetts.

Leigh Rossville

CHAPTER ONE

He was nervous and he was not doing a good job of hiding it. That was clear from the look that came over the face of the receptionist as he asked to see Chris. Why couldn't he remember her name? He knew her almost as well as he knew his own receptionist. He tried to grin at her while she told Chris he was there. He tried to wave goodbye to her after she told him to go on back. But he knew she thought he was acting strange.

Chris, too, gave him a funny look as he walked into his office and shut the door behind him. With a rather exaggerated effort, Chris pushed up his shirt sleeve and stared at his watch. "What," he said. "Sun gone over the yardarm already?"

Leigh chuckled. In his own ears it sounded as if he were saying, "Ha, ha," real loudly.

Chris leaned back in his chair. Leigh had forgotten how blue his eyes could be, how intensely they could focus.

"You got a problem, partner," Chris said, and gestured for him to take a seat.

Leigh realized he had been standing in front of Chris's desk with his thumbs hooked in his belt for what might have been an extraordinarily long time and he lowered himself quickly into the first chair he could reach. "So, how's it going?" he asked.

Chris said, "You want to tell me about it, whatever it is?"

Leigh said, "Tihh," and let his gaze slip toward the carpet in one corner of the room. He said "Tihh" again as he leaned his elbow on the arm of his chair and lowered his brow into the palm of his hand. What he wanted to do was scream or cry, get up and race around the room, tear things off the shelves and throw them to the floor.

"Everything all right with you and Cath?"

Leigh made a little sign with his mouth; a little affirmative extension of his fingers.

Chris put his hands behind his head. "You didn't get bounced out of your firm or anything like that, did you?" It was a line thrown out lightly, meant to make Leigh smile.

It did. Leigh said, "That's going to be the least of my problems."

Chris came forward in his chair, dropping his arms on his desk and folding his hands, signaling that his time and his attention were all Leigh's and that Leigh could take as long as he wanted.

"I'm being sued," Leigh told him.

"Malpractice?"

Leigh opened his suit jacket and took some folded papers out of his inside pocket. He hesitated when he had them in his hand. "Do you remember the time when we went late one night to Enrico's up on Broadway?"

Chris's teeth showed between his thin lips, more on one side than on the other. "That was a long time ago."

"But you didn't think there was anything weird about what we did that night."

"You mean with the chick who was there?"

"I don't even remember how we met her. I just remember we were real drunk and one of us wanted to sit out on the patio."

"She was with some other people and they had two empty seats at their table."

"Somehow she left those people and ended up with us, remember?"

"I remember."

"And the three of us, you, me and her, all ended up at her apartment at about four in the morning."

"We were both trying to get her at the same time and we couldn't do it."

"But we were all in bed together. . . ."

"There's no doubt about that."

"And, I mean, it was crazy, but it was fun, right?"

"What I recall about it, it was a hell of a time."

Leigh tossed the papers he had been holding onto the desk. The first page was a summons. The rest made up a complaint.

Chris scanned them and groaned when he saw the name at the end. "Oh, no. Not Reuben Wechsler."

"You know him?"

"I've just heard stories about him, that's all." Chris glanced up suddenly and there was both surprise and recognition in his eyes. "He was the one who sued the glue company down the Peninsula. Said the plant was ventilated so that the fumes went directly into the building next door, where some lady working as a secretary sat inhaling them all day. Claimed they made her a nymphomaniac."

Leigh wiped his mouth and did not laugh.

Chris said, "Jury awarded her three hundred and thirty-five thousand dollars. I thought everybody heard about that. For a while there, Wechsler was specializing in nympho law. Tried one against the City and County where he claimed that a lady who got hit by a bus turned into a nymph. Said after her close brush with death the lady realized how short and arbitrary life was and began boffing everything in sight. She didn't really like what she was doing, he argued. Cost her her marriage, her kids, her self-respect. Began spending a fortune on clothes designed to attract men and Wechsler wanted all those costs reimbursed as special damages. Jury didn't buy it. They not only said the City and County wasn't at fault for making her a nymph, they said it wasn't at fault for running her down. Rumor I heard was that he settled that case on appeal for his costs." Chris looked down at the papers in front of him. "What's he suing you for?"

"Murder."

Chris's head snapped back. Leigh wanted to say something more, but he could not get enough saliva in his mouth. His Adam's apple was running up and down his throat uncontrollably.

"You don't file a civil suit for murder, Leigh," and there was just enough lilt in Chris's voice to show that he was still hoping for some humorous explanation to this whole situation.

"Well, wrongful death, then. Whatever you want to call it. Wechsler's representing the family of a guy named Bobby O'Berry and he claims we killed him. Cathy and me."

Chris began furiously flipping through the pages of the complaint. "What is this, Leigh?" Now that he saw this was no joke he was angry. "Some kind of automobile accident? A boating accident? Why didn't you tell me about it before?"

"He says we shot Bobby O'Berry or stabbed him with an arrow, or bolt, or spear, or knife, or otherwise willfully and knowingly brought about his death by violent means. . . . Or words to that effect."

"This is crazy. Nuts. The guy's a lunatic. He should be locked up—"

"Chris—"

211

"No. This time he's gone too far. I'm going to report the sonofabitch to the state bar."

"Chris—"

"Hey, it's one thing to come up with interesting theories to try out some new cause of action against a corporation or a city or something. But to go so far as to charge a person with knowingly killing somebody—that's slander per se. Libel per se. This could ruin your career if word gets out—"

"Jesus Christ, will you listen to me, Chris? I did it. That's the thing. I did it."

Chris Cage stopped ranting. A calm settled over the office. "In that case," Chris said, "it's not just your career we've got to worry about."

Leigh knew Chris was waiting for an explanation. But every time he started to speak, the words got mushy in his mouth.

"First of all," Chris said, "let's remember that anything you tell me is coming to me in my capacity as a lawyer. That means the attorney-client privilege—"

"—applies. Yeah, I know, I know." Leigh felt a rush of annoyance. "But that's courtroom stuff, Chris. That's law and I need to talk about life. I'm in trouble and I need help."

"Look, it doesn't make any difference that I'm not the lawyer who's going to be representing you—that's all I'm trying to say. You're talking to me as an attorney and that makes everything you tell me protected. Okay?"

"Stop it," Leigh screamed so suddenly that it surprised even himself. As he fielded Chris's look of bewilderment, he also became aware that the typing had ceased in the adjoining rooms. He hunched forward so that he could whisper and his words could still get through. "Stop talking to me like I'm some client who just rolled in off the street. You've got to help me figure out what to do."

Chris, rebuked, held out his palm, welcoming whatever Leigh had to say.

Leigh turned to make sure the door was still shut. He repositioned himself in his chair. He drew a deep breath and he began. "It all sort of started out as a lark, Chris. . . . You remember my fortieth birthday?"

"January."

"Yeah."

"You celebrated alone with Cathy."

"Yeah, well, she had this special surprise lined up for that night and that's why . . . Look, maybe I better go back even further. Remember last fall when all the women were talking about Roarke Robinson and all that stuff? Janice Butler started carrying on that affair and everything? Shit, I don't even know if that's the right place to start." He began again.

"Look, we've been married how long? I don't know—eleven years almost. We lived together awhile before that, remember? Of course you remember." Leigh stopped, knowing he had to get control of his voice. "Anyhow, it's been a good marriage, Cathy and me, I mean, but it's been a long time and I guess you sort of get used to each other or something, start looking around for something different. Not like with me and Linda, where I just grew to the point where I couldn't stand her anymore, but just you get restless, start to think how you only pass through this life once and all that bullshit. You start doing other stuff after a while, start experimenting, sort of."

"Leigh, you've been experimenting ever since I've known you, whether you were married or not."

"I'm talking about at home."

"Oh."

"We've got this VCR that I got Cathy for Christmas one year. You know how she was always watching movies? That's one of the things I used to complain about. I come home on Friday and she's got the whole weekend planned watching movies on the goddamn VCR. So last fall I come home one Friday night after having a few, probably with you, and I flop down in the chair so I can fall asleep watching *The Philadelphia Story* or whatever it is she's got on, and she starts in feeding me pâté with truffles and she's got two whole bottles of wine on ice. Something's obviously going on, but I don't find out what until about midnight, when we're both plastered."

Leigh could feel his palms getting sweaty. He dragged them along his pant legs and then crossed them under his arms. He reminded himself that this was Chris to whom he was talking. His closest friend. "Turns out, she's got this 'special' movie she's borrowed from the Butlers, who got it from Roarke Robinson. You can guess what it was. Apparently, see, the Butlers were over the Robinsons' house one night and Roarke's got this whole shelf full of dirty movies, videotapes. At the time, you know, Jay Butler thinks Roarke's like this alien god. He lets Roarke talk him into taking one of the movies home. Roarke tells him to get Janice liquored up, put this thing on in the bedroom, and see what hap-

213

pens. Apparently it works, because Janice tells Cathy all about this outrageous thing she and Jay did and how Cathy should try it as a surprise on me.

"As I recall, the movie was *Debbie Does Dallas*, and it was really kind of fun. It wasn't like those movies we used to see at smokers in college. Not too much, anyway. We watched the whole thing and Cathy seemed to enjoy it as much as I did. So we have a good night, the two of us, maybe the best we've had in years, and the next week I go out and rent another one. *Debbie Does Dallas Two*, or something. Nobody knows about it, but it becomes a regular thing for us on Saturday nights after that. It got so I couldn't wait for them to roll around and sometimes Cathy would get all fixed up and we'd both get all excited and go at it right while the movie was going on. We'd do it on the floor, the couch, the bed, wherever we felt like it. It was sort of a private little joke between us, these nights we'd have.

"But seeing all that stuff, seeing all the things people can do to each other, seeing all the things they do do . . . jees, you know, it started us thinking, I suppose. And meanwhile, Janice Butler across the street has started carrying on this torrid affair with Roarke and she's all the time leaking these little juicy details to Cathy. . . . So here we are, watching all these beautiful women doing absolutely anything on the screen and hearing about all the adventures Janice is having and it starts seeming like we're the only ones out there not having this wild, uninhibited sex life.

"Yeah, I know what you're going to say, but if you think back to all the times you and I have chased girls together, there've been damn few that I actually caught. The fun of the chase is one thing, but I'd say the whole time I've been married to Cath I've probably had at most a dozen one-night stands. That's not much when you think about four or five thousand nights. Now, all of a sudden, I'm going into the supermarket and every woman I see in tight pants seems like this pulsating sex machine just waiting to screw my brains out. I know, it all sounds crazy, huh? But for a couple of months there I was sort of going around operating at peak libido all the time."

Leigh became aware that his left knee was bobbing up and down while he talked. He moved both hands to both knees and pressed down. "As for Cathy, well, she pretty much seems to be the same way. She and I are talking about things we never talked about before. Hell, we're doing things we've never done before. I mean, she was always pretty

214

good, but now all of a sudden she's like the world's best. She's like the queen of sex. There's nothing she can't or won't do."

Leigh saw what he thought was the beginning of a funny expression on Chris's face and, not wanting him to misunderstand, added quickly, "At home, I mean. She's not doing anything with anybody else, but there are times the two of us are getting downright raunchy with each other."

Chris nodded and it seemed to Leigh that there was almost a hint of relief on his face. It made Leigh laugh.

"And it was fun, Chris," he said. "That was the thing. I'm sleeping with this woman all these years to the point where it's sort of like going to the mailbox, and now suddenly I'm enjoying it like I never did before. All these years I been with this woman and now I'm thinking she's the sexiest thing on the planet. Nothing wrong with that, right? I mean, who were we hurting? We were just enjoying each other."

Leigh found himself with his mouth hanging open, the unwelcome residue of a laugh that had not been humorous to begin with. He licked his lips and wondered again why he could not get enough saliva into his mouth, why his mouth was so dry and his palms were so wet.

"Like I started to tell you," he went on, "my birthday was coming up and Cath kept telling me she had something *really* special planned for me. I figured it was going to be a surprise party or something, but nobody let on and so I didn't, either. I come home from work expecting everybody to jump out from behind the curtains or something, but there's only Cath, waiting at the door for me.

"She takes my coat. Undoes my tie. Gets me out of my suit. Then she leads me upstairs to the bathroom, where she's got a hot bubble bath all drawn for me and a bottle of Cordon Rouge waiting on the shelf at the head of the tub. . . . She leaves me there about half an hour, drinking champagne out of a long-stem glass, and when she comes back she's got this big, luxurious towel and a brand-new robe she's bought at Neiman-Marcus. . . . And the way she looked, Chris, oh, you wouldn't have believed it. I mean, as good as you've ever seen her look in the past, she was even better that night. This robe she had on was green silk and she had brushed her hair down over her shoulders. . . .

"She takes me to the sitting room we have off the bedroom, you know the one. She's got the speakers on and she's made a tape of, oh, you know, old Jackie Wilson songs, things like that. Soft primal-urge music. On the desk in the sitting room she's set up a mirror and the mirror has a little pyramid of cocaine in the middle of it. She's also got a silver ice bucket and another bottle of Cordon Rouge, so we open the bottle and we drink up the champagne and we toot up the powder and we listen to Jackie sing 'Your love keeps liftin' me higher,' and I get so goddamned high myself I feel like I can walk on the ceiling."

Leigh looked up and for a long time stared inquiringly at his friend. "Do you understand how I was, Chris? You ever been like that? I mean, just sailing? Soaring? Where you were flying so smoothly you didn't care what happened? Because I was just at that point when she got up and stepped out of her robe."

The intimacy of what Leigh was describing was limited by the intensity of his eye contact. Chris nodded slowly, carrying Leigh's head down with him and then bringing it back up again.

The silent affirmation made Leigh blink. He shifted his gaze to the corner of the room. He began telling the story again, no longer powering his thoughts across, but spinning them out, letting them flow. "She wouldn't let me touch her. She just sort of posed for me. Then she made me get up and turn around so that I was facing the wall. The lights went off, and still she made me stay like that. I could hear the bed creaking, and then one red bulb came on from a lamp in the corner, nowhere near the bed. I could hear the switch, I could see the reflection on the wall in front of me. 'You can turn around now,' she says, and I turn and there's Cathy, over on the far side of the room, over in front of the mirrored doors to the closets. She's nowhere near the bed, but I look over that way anyhow, and for a moment I don't understand anything, because there's the most gorgeous brunette I've ever seen lying there. That was Teddy. That was Cathy's birthday present to me."

Another time, another place, another reason for being together, and Leigh would have expected Chris to gasp at the story. Chris would have sung exclamations of wonder, demands for affirmation. His mouth would have hung slack, ready to spread into a full-face grin the moment Leigh let on that this was all made up, a fantasy they both could share. But now Chris only shook his head slowly, waiting for the bad part he knew was coming.

"I stood there like a dummy, Chris, gaping at her. This forty-year-old man with his pecker sticking out between his legs like some goddamn grinning pony. All of a sudden everybody starts laughing and the woman, Teddy, she holds back the covers. 'C'mon, get in,' she says, and I look and she's got tits that come straight out of *Playboy*, for Chris-

216

sake. I look over at Cathy and I say, 'What about you?' and Teddy says, 'C'mon, Cathy,' and the next thing I know, the three of us are in bed together.

"Can you imagine, Chris? I'm telling you, I could have died and gone to heaven. As far as I'm concerned, my wife's got the best ass in the world, but this other woman's tits were something unbelievable. You know how a lot of women sort of hang down or fall off the side? Well, this woman's breasts are nearly as big as Cath's, but they're sticking straight out, like they're on parade or something. I got one hand on them and one hand on Cathy and I'm rolling around like some twentieth-century Tom Jones. They could have pulled out a gun and shot me and I wouldn't have cared. Hell, I would have sucked on the barrel. As it was, me and Cath are down on this woman taking turns, and then we're up on her, and then they're both down on me. We were even getting into triangles. It was fun, Chris. It was the most fun thing I've ever done in my life."

The defiance that he was hearing in his own voice made Leigh stop. The emotions that were coming out of him were making his eyes cloud and he turned and looked into the corner again so that Chris wouldn't see. Chris turned with him. Two men, sitting silently, with their faces pointed at a juncture of baseboard and nylon carpeting.

"Doing it that one time like that actually seemed good for our marriage," Leigh said after a while. "I don't know if you could tell or anything, but I think we were getting a little bored or something with each other. Now we'd had this great . . . journey into depravity and come out of it unscathed and we began getting along better than we had in years. It was a little bond we shared. It almost put us into a we-can-do-anything frame of mind, if that makes any sense to you." He shrugged, not looking to see if it did.

"We went back to doing the movies after that, but now Cath's thirty-fifth was coming up and I wanted to do something really special for her, too. Something like she'd done for my birthday, only different. Something she'd remember all her life, that was sort of my motto. At this point, Jesus, it's like fate starts dealing everything into my hands.

"Blinky Gould comes over one day and tells me he and Marietta are going to go to Hawaii for a couple of weeks. They want to try snorkeling, skin diving, he calls it, and they want to borrow some of our equipment." Leigh hesitated, trying to decide how best to put what he had to say next in the proper perspective.

"You remember him at Roarke's welcoming party? Remember what

217

he was doing? He was videotaping. With a video camera. That's what gives me the idea. I figured that we were watching enough of these video movies; why not make one of our own? At thirty-five, Cath's at her peak, and at forty I'm certainly not going to be getting any better. Thirty years down the road we'll be able to haul out this film and look at it the way people do baby pictures." Leigh snickered harshly. "That's what comes of being forty, Chris. You start thinking about things like that. Like trying to preserve what you got because you realize you're getting worse instead of better. You're not quite there yet, but you'll see. What have you got, two more years?"

He didn't wait for an answer. "I was going to make our own video movie. Capture the moment for the rest of our lives. So I made a trade with Blinky. He takes our snorkeling equipment and leaves us with his camera. The only problem now was figuring out what I was supposed to do with the camera."

Nothing seemed to be staying in place. He adjusted his tie knot, ran his fingers through his hair, even snorted to dry up his nose. "I actually thought of you, Chris. What the hell, I think, you've seen Cath in hot tubs before. The frame of mind I'm in at that time, it actually makes sense to me to say, Well, you've seen her nude, there's only one step from that to seeing her make love. I mean, if anybody is going to see it, it might as well be our best friend, right?"

Chris cleared his throat and Leigh accepted that as an answer.

"Yeah, I admit it sounds crazy now. But the only reason I didn't do it back then was because, well, it was her birthday. Filming her with me, that's like giving myself a present, and what I really wanted to do was make it special for her. Sort of the ultimate escape from reality for just one night. That's when I decided a friend's not going to do it, I've got to get her a stranger, like she got me. See how this thing sort of escalates? The problem was, I didn't know how to go about getting somebody new. They got all kinds of services that will get you women, but I never heard of any straight services that will get you a straight man. I certainly wasn't going to try a newspaper ad. What I needed was someone who would be just like Teddy. Someone who would look good and be clean and disappear by morning. Never to be seen again."

Leigh closed his eyes. It was easier to speak that way.

"A week goes by and I don't do anything about it. By this time it had become obvious to me that the whole thing was a pipe dream and that it was never going to come off. Except that her birthday's on Saturday and by Thursday I've not only got no Teddy, I've got absolutely nothing for her at all. I go down to Union Street to get some leather pants, something, anything as long as it costs a lot of money, and I still don't get anything. The stores close and I'm trying to think of where to go to next, so I stop in at McGuppers for a drink. I'm standing there working on a beer, minding my own business, and all of a sudden the very guy I'm looking for walks in the door. . . .

"Actually, I saw him before he even came in. I'm staring out the window and this guy pulls up on a motorcycle, right in front of the place. Illegal spot, but he doesn't care, he's got Massachusetts plates. It's March. It's cold, it's rainy, but the guy's wearing a T-shirt and a thin jacket like he can't believe it's going to be so cold in San Francisco. Thing is, though, because that's all he's wearing I can see he's got this really good build. Big arms, big shoulders. That's one thing Cathy's always told me she likes on a man, big shoulders, and that's what starts me thinking. I mean, this is just a young kid, twenty, twenty-one or so, but he's good-looking, and so I make a little deal with myself that if he comes in I'll start talking to him, size him up, see if he's got a brain that's bigger than a pea."

Leigh sighed. He probed with his thumb in the corner of one eye. He sniffed his nose dry again. "Okay, he comes in. I watch him go to the bar and he's kind of moving his head around, checking out all the girls, staring down all the guys. He's like this for about two beers and then he gets comfortable. That's when I went up to him, started a conversation about his bike. Turns out he's just driven it across the country and when he tells me that I realize I've found my boy.

"We talk about bikes and traveling and New England and anything else I can think of while I'm buying him beers. Finally I ask him if he's interested in earning some money. Okay, the kid looks at me like I'm a fag, but then I ask him if he's got any experience with women. 'Yeah,' he says. 'Yeah.' Just like that. I tell him I've got this escort service where women will pay to have young men escort them to the opera and places so they won't have to go alone. I ask him if he's interested. 'Not in going to any fucking opera,' he says. I tell him my company provides other services as well."

Leigh stopped. He opened his eyes to make sure Chris was still with him. "Jesus, there are parts of this thing I can't believe even as I'm telling you, Chris. There I was, a hundred-and-sixty-buck-an-hour attorney, talking in circles to some boy biker. The kid sort of peers at me, says, 'These women, any of 'em good-looking?' So I told him about the one woman I had in mind for him. Really good-looking, I said. All he had to do was go to her house and do what comes naturally. You see the way I was screwing this thing up? I think I'm getting through to the kid, he gawks at me like I'm getting through, and I'm just assuming we've got a meeting of the minds.

"I tell him there's a hundred bucks in it for him, all he's got to do is enjoy himself. I give him the address and tell him when to be there." Leigh used a moment to wet his lips once more. "Okay, so I got that all arranged. Now my problem was how I was going to get him into the house and upstairs in front of the camera. Originally my plan was to have Cathy and me get in bed, and then I was going to slide out and have this kid take my place while I slipped into the closet where the camera would be set up. But I guess I lost my nerve, because in the end I just told Cathy what I had arranged."

Leigh smiled unhappily. "I waited until just about an hour before the kid was supposed to arrive, and then I sort of let her know that there was a surprise coming. I didn't know how she was going to take it, but by that time we were already into the champagne and the cocaine, just like we'd done on my birthday, and she . . . well, she went along with it . . . the, uh, the movie and everything."

Leigh was trying to adopt a matter-of-fact tone and he was having trouble with it. He thought it would help if he got up and moved around the room. He circled around until he was standing at the back of the chair in which he had just been sitting. Then, because it had helped before, he once again shut his eyes.

"Cathy met him at the door. She had on this green silk robe and she had . . . uh . . . she had some special underthings on. The kid, the kid shows up in blue jeans, some sort of boots. But he does have this tight knit shirt that looks good on him, so he's not totally inappropriate." Suddenly his eyes snapped open.

"Look, Chris, I know this probably all sounds unbelievable to you. It probably all sounds incredibly stupid, but it didn't seem stupid then, for some reason. It was just, well, daring. I mean, it had worked out okay the first time, the time with Teddy, I mean. I just sort of screwed everything up by getting this amateur involved. I didn't even see him when he first came to the house, of course. I was upstairs waiting in the closet like that guy in the old Kingston Trio song: 'I'm here in the closet, Oh, Lord, what shall I do?' Remember that one? Jesus. Thinking back, it seems like a nightmare. I can't believe myself what we were doing." He was trying not to grovel, not before Chris, and so he made a joke. "Doesn't everybody hide in the closet with a video camera while

220

their wives invite strangers up to their bedrooms?" He shook his head. "I guess we were just acting crazy, that's all," he added.

Chris was watching him exactly as he had all along.

"Well, I could hear the music going and I guess Cathy gave him something to drink." Leigh resumed his walk around the room. "All I know is, after about twenty minutes they came upstairs and Cath made her way over to the bed. Right from the start she was playing her role perfectly. She kind of lay down on top of the covers and asked him to come over and sit with her."

Leigh stopped pacing and raised his eyebrows. "He does that all right. But that's about all he does. He's sitting there looking around like he's being strapped in an electric chair or something, and Cathy's playing with his hair, rubbing his shoulders. She starts whispering to him to relax, and the more she tells him, the more tense he gets. You can actually see it on the tape."

"You've still got the tape?"

"That's what I've been building up to. I'd kind of like it if maybe you'd just watch it instead of making me tell you any more."

"You're asking me to look at the tape of Cathy and this guy?"

Leigh nodded.

"You got it with you?"

"It's at home."

"You want me to go there with you?"

"Will you?"

"When?"

"Now."

Chris threw up his hands. "If that's what you want."

Leigh breathed a sigh of relief. "In that case," he said, "I better call Cath and tell her you're coming. She's not going to want to be there."

221

CHAPTER TWO

It was a brass bed covered with a white satiny comforter. The woman lying on the bed was wearing a gorgeous sea green robe. She was on her side, but from the knees down her legs were scissored and the robe was open, exposing the bareness of her shins, her ankles, her feet. The middle third of her body was blocked by the figure of a young man sitting on the edge of the bed. He was not looking at the woman, even though she was obviously touching him, even though every so often the tips of her fingers would creep over one of his shoulders and massage it fore and aft with a gentle sculling motion. The young man sat rigidly, as though he was waiting for the woman's fingers to find the boundaries of a wound he knew was there.

His hair was corn yellow. It was long enough to fall down over his eyes, but he wore it swept to the left, just above his brow, in the exact place it would have been had he combed it using nothing more than his right hand. His cheekbones were high and prominent. His eyes were rather small and light in color. His nose had a slight hook below its bridge, but otherwise it was very straight. It was long without being big. Strong without being thick. His skin was smooth and unmarked. The young man was quite good-looking in an unfriendly sort of way.

The woman behind him had his hair between her fingers. She eased his head back until his chin stuck out and his throat bulged. He let his mouth hang open, he let his eyelids close.

"Just relax, Bobby," the woman said. She sat up. Seeing her eyes was like seeing two little specks of cloth left in the wake of her robe. They seemed to show the same vivid green color, drawing attention away from all her other features.

She got on her knees and began rubbing the base of the young man's neck with the palms of both her hands. She leaned down and whispered in his ear, and when she did so the top of her robe fell open, exposing part of her shoulder and a thin white strap of material.

The young man laughed and brought his head forward again. He was still smiling, but he did not look happy. Now the woman, her head next to his, draped her arms down his front, dangled her hands until they came into contact with his belt. The young man seemed to stiffen. His eyes became as alert as those of a wild fox.

"Ooh, you're so strong," the woman said, running her hands back up his stomach to his chest and then down again.

The young man seemed to gain some measure of succor from what she had told him. His shoulders lifted: it could be seen in the way her head moved, the way she had to reach further to slide her hands beneath his belt.

She had hold of the hem of his maroon knit shirt and she was raising it slowly. He lifted his arms over his head to help her as she took it off him and then he sat very still while she caressed every inch of his exposed skin. It invited caressing. His pectoral muscles were like little plates, each marked with a small unobtrusive nipple hardly larger than a mole. The hairless skin between the pectorals flowed sharply, smoothly, evenly. It formed a ravine-like channel that gradually flared into a wishbone line of demarcation between his rib cage and his abdomen, setting off his stomach like a carved door panel.

The woman stood him on his feet, made him turn around, pressed her lips to his skin. She undid the belt to her robe and let the robe slide off her. Beneath it she was wearing a lace corset designed not so much to support her breasts as to set them off in a gauzy film. Below her naked belly was a white G-string, covering each side of her with a heart of smooth cloth no larger than a playing card. She bent lower. She was mumbling something; it couldn't be heard distinctly. "Such a beautiful body," she seemed to be saying.

The young man's back was blocking her as she went lower still, moving her mouth downward until it could have been no higher than his navel. He seemed not to know what to do with his hands. He laid them on her, took them away again, and then finally eased the garment straps off her shoulders.

She stopped what she was doing and knelt upright. The corset was supposed to come off by going over her head, not down her arms. She

223

took it off herself, a smile of bemused acceptance on her lips. Her breasts rose, swollen targets with broad pink bull's-eyes, and then they fell back, quivering in perfect synchronization. The young man reached out and stroked down one breast, and when he got to the end he turned his wrist and started to stretch his fingers beneath it. And then he pulled his hand back as if he had been burned.

The woman pulled away, too, but almost immediately a sensuous, sultry look returned to her face. She lay on her back, her knees raised above the satiny comforter. Now she kept her eyes fixed on the young man as she slipped her thumbs under the floss-thin sides of her G-string and slowly eased it down the length of her thighs.

"Holy shit," Chris Cage said, and the color that rushed to his cheeks indicated that he had not meant to speak out. He had meant to watch the whole tape clinically, without comment or judgment, and the words had escaped on their own with the unexpectedness of what he had seen on the television screen.

"It's shaved," Leigh Rossville said, "that's all." Then, as they watched her kick the string away, move her legs apart, and very briefly touch herself with the tips of her fingers, he added, "It was something we did one night and we just sort of kept it that way for a while."

On the screen, Cathy Rossville had taken the young man's hand and was guiding him around to the other side of the bed so that the front of his body was now facing the camera. His belt was undone and his zipper was partially down, but his pants were still clinging to his hips. He was staring, almost transfixed, at the unnatural bare spot between Cathy's legs.

She rolled onto her side, her legs coming together. The camera caught her blond-brown hair tumbling in waves that broke on her shoulders. It caught the sweep of her back, it caught the swell of her buttocks and the slender lines of her thighs and calves.

She was touching the crotch of the young man's jeans as he stood with his head rolled back and his arms hanging straight down by his sides. The touch brought his zipper the rest of the way down and soon she was tugging at his jeans. There was a flash of white from his cotton underwear, but the young man made no move to help her. She went to her knees once again, this time holding herself up as straight as she could, placing her hands on each side of his face, guiding his lips to hers.

It was a strong, feverish kiss, meant to draw life out of his mouth and into hers. When she broke away she went directly below his waist, forc-

224

ing down his jeans and his underwear as though they were obstacles in her path. The expression on the young man's face was almost one of alarm. A slurping, sucking noise came over the sound track and the expression of alarm became one of helplessness. Cathy's head was going back and forth like a piston and the young man was looking down at her with the same uncertain panic that one could imagine in a novice cliff diver. He bounced briefly on the balls of his feet, perhaps trying to get in rhythm with the movement of Cathy's head, and then something happened to make his face cloud, his lip curl. He stopped bouncing and she stopped moving back and forth.

As Cathy drew away from him the camera caught his penis hanging shrunken and flaccid. His pants and his underwear were bunched at the top of his legs, making him look truncated, a carved body arising out of a block pedestal.

"Do it again," he ordered.

Cathy dragged the back of her hand across her mouth. "Maybe we better wait a little bit," she said.

He grabbed his crotch so that his penis stuck out between his thumb and his forefinger. "Do it now," he said, pointing it at her.

Cathy's head spun and for an instant she looked directly into the camera. She looked back to where the young man was still holding himself, still trying to get her to return to him. "I don't think this is going to work out," she said loudly.

The young man's lips disappeared from sight while his face flushed red. "What do you expect?" he shouted. "You don't hardly got any nipples. You shave your thing. How am I supposed to get off on somebody like you? You'd look like a little kid's doll if you weren't so fucking old."

He switched hands on his crotch and grabbed for her hair. Cathy shrieked and drew her knees to her chest for protection, but he had hold of her and was pulling her toward him.

"Leigh," she screamed.

The camera was apparently bumped at that point because the picture on the screen was suddenly tilted at a crazy angle. A cacophony of loud noises came over the sound track, the picture rocketed across the room, taking in a wall, the ceiling, a corner. Half the screen was dark and then the darkness disappeared and in its place the young man was striding toward the lens. His jeans were pulled back into place, but his face was a twisted mask of fury. A door swung shut on the screen, bringing darkness with it again. For barely a second the darkness seemed to be moving and then there was a sharp crack as the camera lens hit the floor and now there was only a blank screen and a sound track: Cathy screaming, a man shouting, a bang, swinging hinges, another shout, and then a soft but powerful sound that went *fluuutte* and was immediately followed by a strangled, gurgling cry. There were more bangs, more bumps, more scrapes, but there were no more words that came out of the videocassette recorder.

After a moment or two, Leigh Rossville got up and shut off the machine.

The Rossvilles' bedroom had been custom designed. It was located at the top of the staircase ascending from the first-floor level and it took up a good portion of the second floor all by itself. It had its own fireplace, it had an archway leading into what Leigh called the sitting room, and it had another archway leading into an oak-fixtured bathroom with a Jacuzzi tub, a separate dual-faucet shower, a double-basined sink and vanity table, and a long hothouse window.

As one entered the Rossvilles' bedroom from the second-floor hall, the brass bed with a matching brass reading light was immediately to the right. The wall to the left was made entirely of redwood and was lined with a series of full-length mirrors. One of the mirrors was the door to Cathy's closet, another was the door to Leigh's. There were no handles, nothing to distinguish these mirrors from any of the others. They were opened by pressing them along the left-hand edges. An astute person perhaps could tell by the fingermarks which mirrors were doors and which were not, but Chris Cage had no need to look that closely. The fact that a large rectangle of white wall-to-wall carpeting had been cut away from in front of one of the mirrors told him where Leigh had been hiding with his video camera. He scuffed at the exposed floorboards with his toe. "Hardwood?" he asked.

"Soft," said Leigh. "Pine."

"What did you do with this piece?"

"Cut it up into little pieces. Put them into big green trash bags with real garbage. Drove the bags over to San Rafael and dumped them in the Marin County dump. Scattered them around, you know?"

"Risky."

"What would you have done? The whole thing was soaked with blood. It had gone right through to the pad."

"Anything in the trash you put in with the pieces that might have

226

had your name on it? Or anything with the name of any stores you shop at?"

Leigh shook his head. "It was clean trash. Safeway brand names and that type of thing on some of the cartons, but that's about all. No, the bags were tied up tight and there was no reason why anybody would be looking inside them once they got to the dump."

"You'd be surprised."

Leigh contemplated the open spot on the floor. "I doubt it," he said. "I doubt I'd be surprised by anything at this point."

Chris looked out the door toward the hall. The bedroom carpet was the same as that which covered the entire second floor, the same as that which came up the stairs. "First thing I'd do," he said, "is tear this whole thing up. Buy some Orientals. Make it seem as though you just wanted a change in decorating. You've at least got to do it for this room. It's going to require buffing up the pine, maybe renting a sander or whatever they use to polish softwood floors, but then go out and buy a few rugs. Throw them down as fast as you can."

"Sounds like it's going to cost a fortune."

"Count on it. Count on everything costing a fortune." Chris opened the door to the closet and looked inside. It appeared innocent enough, a walk-in that ran laterally instead of deep. The pocket of space to the left was primarily taken up with skis and other athletic gear; to the right was five or six feet of galleyway, lined with double rows of hanging suits and shirts, jackets and slacks. In the center were built-in shelves and a large space for shoes. A light switch to the left of the door turned on a track of three shrouded lamps hanging from the ceiling.

Chris walked into the closet and squatted down. "You were here? You had the camera set up on a tripod?"

Leigh sighed softly. "See that little three-legged stool back in the corner? I was sitting on that."

Chris pulled the stool over and tried it. Using his hands to approximate where the video camera would have been, he framed the shot. It was an unobstructed view of the bed, at most twelve feet to the near side, another five feet to the far side. "This about right?" he said.

Leigh nodded. "Let me," he said, and he and Chris changed places. "I was here, you see? Only, the closet was closed more. The door was open enough that I could get the whole bed in through the lens, but I couldn't quite see the door to the hall. That's why I didn't start taping until they sat down. With the tripod spread out and everything, I had just enough room to get up and down from the stool by moving my feet

227

around. Otherwise, any movement I made would hit the camera. And notice how I am: I'm right-handed, of course, and sitting here with my right hand out, I can just reach past the skis and the poles and all this junk."

Chris looked. Leigh at that moment had his hand on a silver Scott ski pole. He was holding it by the saber grip and balancing it on its pointed tip.

"Then what?"

Leigh looked past his hand, into the pocket of the closet. "When I saw the trouble developing I wasn't quite sure what I should do. You know. I wasn't sure whether I'd make things worse by coming out at that point, or what. I suppose I was hoping it was all going to get worked out in a second or two and so I just sat there, not doing anything until Cathy screamed." Leigh swallowed. "What you don't see there, because that's when I hit the camera trying to stand up, is that as soon as Cathy screamed he hit her. Slapped her right across the mouth. I was trying to get out there so fast I got everything all tangled. It was like I couldn't get up. I fell back on the stool without managing to do much more than kick open the door." He demonstrated, his left foot flailing awkwardly around the now imaginary tripod. Then he sat still.

"You know, it's a funny feeling, Chris. I know I did everything I could to get out of here. I know I tried. I look at the tape, I see the whole thing lasted only a couple of seconds. Yet I remember sitting here, being almost paralyzed. Not scared exactly, but just being, like, unable to move. I keep thinking, you know, if I had just reacted a little quicker . . . if I had just shoved the camera through the door . . . I mean, what was I doing trying to save a stupid old camera? Why didn't I just knock the thing over and go flying out there the moment the kid grabbed her? But I didn't. I tried to get up and get out without knocking the camera over, and all of a sudden it's the kid who's coming toward me. Instead of me jumping out and surprising him, he's got me cornered in here, sitting on my ass on this crummy little milking stool. And the kid, I can tell by the kid's face he knows exactly what I've been doing. He's coming and Cathy's screaming and I just reach out and grab for anything I can get my hands on."

Leigh's hand moved from the ski pole. It reached deeper into the recess of the closet, groped for an instant, and then came out holding the three-foot black barrel of a pneumatic spear gun. Emblazoned in white on the barrel were the words "Mares Californian." Sticking out of the barrel was several inches of metal spear, its end rounded and tapering very suddenly to a sharp and vicious point.

"He saw I had it, Chris. By this time, somehow, I was on the floor. The camera had gone over, the stool had gone over, and the door had swung shut. I even had time to get the damn thing cocked . . ." Leigh got in position, lying on his right hip and elbow, cradling the spear gun between his body and his arm. ". . . and still he came in after me. I just pointed the gun up in the air and let it go."

Chris was silent. He looked back over his shoulder at the far side of the bed, the place where the victim must have been standing when he first noticed Leigh. He traced the path from there to the closet and his eyes came to rest on his friend, still lying on the floor, still vaguely pointing the loaded weapon toward the bedroom.

"You hit him the first shot, Leigh?"

"There is only one shot. It got him right in the side of the neck." Leigh rose to his feet, taking the spear gun with him. He assumed the position of the victim, hunched over the threshold to the closet, suddenly grabbing the right side of his neck, staggering backward in a small quarter circle that left him standing sideways to the closet, his knees slightly bent, his back slightly arched. "The blood was just spurting. It was getting all over him, but he kept trying to grab at the shaft. Leigh flicked the tip of the spear with his finger and a metal catch sprang out. "It wouldn't have done him any good," he said, "even if he could have held on to it."

Leigh sank to his knees, his hand again at the side of his neck. He pitched forward, his head getting almost, but not quite, to the floor. "He stayed like this, gagging, for a couple of seconds, and then he just fell over." Leigh toppled onto his side. He lay there looking up at Chris.

After a moment Chris nodded and Leigh got back to his feet. "Cathy, she's practically catatonic. She's kneeling there on the bed with the comforter stuffed in her mouth and she's just staring at this kid. And me, it's my gun, I'm the one who shot him and I can't think of a goddamn thing to say or do. One minute I'm sitting there making a movie and the next I'm a murderer. All I can think of is, No, this can't be, this can't really have happened. But I've got the body right there at my feet, still oozing blood. I'm trying to replay the past couple of minutes, trying to take them all back, trying to live them all over again so I can fix this thing, so I can get my spear out of this guy's neck, get him up off my floor and out of my bedroom. I'm thinking, Jesus Christ, how did this happen? I'm thinking I just have to have that one instant back when I pulled the trigger. I'll let him beat me, I'll let him kick my ass, I'll let him do anything he goddamn wants, just give me another chance not to pull the trigger."

"You made sure he was dead?"

"Oh, shit, Chris, he was dead. The guy was dead."

"And you were afraid the cops wouldn't believe it was self-defense?"

"I wasn't even sure it was self-defense. I mean, it was and it wasn't. What it was was a mistake. And what am I supposed to tell the cops? That I was sitting here in my closet filming this guy doing things to my wife until the guy went wild and I had to shoot him with a spear gun?"

"That's what happened, isn't it?"

"Look, if I could have thought of some plausible reason why this young man's in my bedroom with his shirt off and a spear through his neck, I would have called the cops immediately."

"It didn't have to appear plausible to anyone else. You had the film as proof."

"Right, Chris. I'm gonna show the cops the film. I'm gonna let half the police department and all of the DA's office see the porno film I made of my wife. You don't think that would get in the papers? You don't think Channel Seven news would pick that up? 'Prominent Bay Area attorney's sexual orgy ends in death.' So I beat the murder charge, I'm through as a lawyer. I'm through as a person and so's Cathy. And my father, what about him? And the firm?"

Leigh dragged his hand across his mouth. "I know what you're thinking. Believe me, I've thought it all myself. A person kills somebody, he's not the one who's supposed to determine if it was justified or not. Any killer can rationalize what he's done, I realize that. But this one . . . Jesus Christ, I'm no murderer. I was no more a threat to society the minute after I shot the spear than I was the minute before. Less, if anything. The world's not going to be a better place for investigating me. The only thing an investigation is going to do is provide thirty seconds of titillation to four and a half million people who follow the news."

Leigh stared at the exposed floorboards and Chris stared with him. They stared until Leigh said, "Getting the spear out was pretty easy. It's just a shaft, you know. I just reached around the back of his head and pulled it all the way through. Then I got an old blanket and wrapped him up in it. Carried him down to the garage and stuffed him into the trunk of the Jag. I lined the trunk with a bunch of garbage bags first, so there wouldn't be any fibers or blood or anything to show that a body had been in there. Then I went back upstairs and helped Cathy to get dressed. We had to get rid of his motorcycle, you see, and she had to help. We couldn't run the risk of somebody noticing it out in front of the house. So I took the bike and went out Tranton Park Lane one way. Cath took the car and went the other."

"Where did you go?"

"San Francisco. I took the bike back to McGuppers. Parked it where I had seen the kid park it before."

"You weren't afraid of being noticed?"

"It was almost two o'clock in the morning. I figured anybody was out in that neighborhood at that time of night couldn't see anything anyway. I just drove up, parked the bike like there was nothing unusual, like I was no different from anybody else, walked up to Union and a few minutes later Cathy drove by and picked me up. If anybody noticed me, I didn't notice them."

"Then what?"

"Then we drove over to the Oakland Hills. Drove along Skyline for a ways until we got to a pretty deserted spot, but where we could see pretty far in both directions. I didn't try to hide the body or anything. I just stopped, ran around to the trunk, grabbed it, and threw it out. It's what they always claimed the Hell's Angels did, remember? I figured whoever found him would just figure that's what happened to this guy."

"You didn't leave the blanket?"

"No. Took the blanket, took his shirt and jacket, and stuffed them all in the trash bags I had used to line the trunk. I put the shirt and jacket in a Goodwill box and I threw the blanket in a dumpster down in Fremont."

"Jesus, Leigh—"

"Hey," Leigh said sharply. "I'm no hit man. I hadn't planned this thing out. All I know is I've got to get rid of all the evidence. If I had a big incinerator I would have burned it all, but I figure what I'm doing, going around putting trash in with trash, is a hell of a lot smarter than burying things in the woods where animals can dig them up, or throwing them in the Bay and waiting for them to pop to the surface again."

"But you didn't get rid of all the evidence, did you?"

Leigh pointed to the closet. "You mean the spear? I did get rid of it. In the best possible place. The day after all this happened, Cath and I got on a plane and flew down to Cozumel. We took all our scuba-diving

231

stuff, everything we hadn't lent to the Goulds, and I managed to lose the weapon in about fifty feet of water. The shaft and the tip you see now, I bought those down there."

"You didn't go all the way to Cozumel just to—"

"Oh, shit, Chris," Leigh said, violently thrusting both his hands into the pockets of his suit coat. "Give me some credit, will you? We came back here Sunday morning after getting rid of the body, there's blood all over the place, Cathy won't even come upstairs. . . . She's supposed to go to work that day, but she can't. Neither one of us could even think of going to work. So I just called my secretary and told her that there had been a last-minute nonrefundable cancellation at Cathy's agency and that we were going to take advantage of it by flying down to Mexico for a few days. . . . Don't shake your head. I understand what happens when you get into these little lies, how they start compounding on you, but it's like what I said before—I hadn't planned on any of this. It was all on the spur of the moment and I just did the best I could."

Once again the two men stared at the pinewood planking. They might have been two winter fishermen looking down through a hole in the ice.

"It wasn't the spear I was thinking about," said Chris. "It was the videotape."

"I know," Leigh said grimly. "I've thought about destroying it a thousand times. But it's my ace. It's the only thing I've got if absolutely everything goes wrong that can go wrong."

"And is that what's happening now? Is everything going wrong that can go wrong?"

Leigh snorted. He took his hands out of his coat pockets, ran one of them through his hair, and then plunged both into his pants pockets. "What's happening now is like a bad joke." He tried a smile, but it came out looking more like a wince. "Up until this point, I've never so much as been contacted by any form of law enforcement officer. And why should I be? As far as I know, the cops haven't even identified the body yet. There's no reason to suspect me of anything." Leigh walked over to the bed and rested his arm on the brass rail. "I've got a lot of things to worry about, I admit, but the only thing that really bothers me is this old man who starts coming around the neighborhood, knocking on doors.

"At first he tells everybody he's doing a survey. At least that's what he tells me. Asks all kinds of questions about shopping and entertainment. Except he specifically asked me what we did the night of the . . . you know. And then he starts asking me about motorcycles and hunting weapons and all of a sudden things start getting a little too coincidental. Later, I come to find out through John Clarke Lane, the guy turns out to be a private investigator. How he traced the kid to this neighborhood I'll never know, but he did and what he was doing, see, was going around to every one of us trying to find out why the kid had been here and who he'd been visiting."

Leigh left the bed. He walked over to the sitting room and sat down in a Queen Anne chair with embroidered back and seat cushions. Neither the chair nor Leigh looked comfortable. He leaned forward, resting his elbows on his knees and clasping his hands. Then he sat back and folded his arms across his chest. He talked through the archway to Chris, who had taken his place at the bed and was leaning his body against the brass railing.

"Okay, so I answered his questions, just like everybody else did, I suppose. This was in March. A few weeks later he shows up at the door again. He says, 'Mr. Rossville, I just have one further question for you: Do you ever go to McGuppers bar on Fillmore Street in the City? I'm caught flatfooted. What can I do? Slam the door in his face? Tell him he's crazy? Deny I've ever been there? Hell, he's asking me because he knows I met the kid there. So I say, 'McGuppers? Sure. Great place. Why? Is that the type of business they're thinking of putting in around here?' You see, that's what his survey was supposed to be about when he first came around. The thing was, though, John Clarke had already busted him on that. He had already given John Clarke his card, showed him a picture of the dead kid, told him he thought the kid had been shot with a bow and arrow or something like that by someone here in T.P. And there I am, standing there at the door, standing there at the door like some idiot, still playing the game about the survey just as if I don't know who he is and why he's come."

"Did you tell him anything, anything at all, that could hurt you?"

Leigh shook his head. "Nothing that I can think of. How he got to T.P. and how he got to me in particular are mysteries as far as I'm concerned."

"Any chance he could be bullshitting? Any chance he and Reuben Wechsler are proceeding against anybody else besides you and Cath?"

Leigh put his legs out straight and drew them in close again. He put his head down so that his chin was nearly on his chest. "Last month he

233

came to my office. Walked right up to the receptionist, announced himself and said he wanted to see me."

"So you treated him just like anyone else without an appointment. You sent your secretary out to see what he wanted."

Half of Leigh's mouth lifted, half sank. "I saw him. I brought him into the office and I closed the door and I asked him what he wanted."

"You were taping him, right?"

Leigh nodded. "He could have had a recorder in his pocket, too. I mean, here it was April. Sun's shining, birds singing, and the guy's wearing a raincoat like it's December. An old, yellowish sort of raincoat that he probably hasn't had off since 1949. That's what his cards say, you know: 'Never A Day Off Since 1949.' "

"You still got your tape?" Chris asked, but Leigh waved him off.

"The tape's nothing. He's a smart old codger, he knows how to talk in euphemisms. 'I represent,' he says, 'the wife and daughter of a young man named Robert O'Berry, who died recently. We have reason to believe that Mr. O'Berry may have met his death while visiting with you or in your home. The death of Mr. O'Berry is going to cause a great deal of hardship for his family, financial and otherwise,' some bullshit like that. 'And,' he says, 'the reason I am here is to explore the possibilities of obtaining compensation for the family without the necessity of instituting legal action.'

"I'm hearing all this and I'm sitting there thinking the old bastard's trying to blackmail me. He's saying if I don't pay him off he's going to go to the authorities with whatever it is he's got on me. So I'm trying to find out how much he's got without admitting anything. . . ." Leigh's voice tailed. His left knee was bouncing up and down nervously, but he was trying to hold Chris's gaze. He was trying to read it, search it for reactions that would tell him how to describe what happened next.

"And?" said Chris.

"And nothing. The guy says he's not a lawyer and he's not there to discuss the pros and cons of liability. He's there to discuss whether I'm willing to pay compensation, that's all. I say, 'Look, I don't have any idea what you're talking about. I don't know anything about anyone named Robert O'Berry or how he came to die or even if he is dead. But I am a lawyer,' I say, 'and I know how much it costs someone to defend himself even if he hasn't done anything and is being wrongly accused.' I said, 'So if you've really got something against me I'd like to hear it so I can attempt to evaluate what it's going to cost me to prove your case is a bunch of crap.'

234

"The guy, his name is Owen Carr, doesn't answer me. He just says, 'The family has instructed me to inform you that they're willing to provide you with a full release in exchange for sixty thousand dollars.'"

The Queen Anne chair began to squeak as Leigh's leg bounced higher into the air, harder into the carpet. Suddenly he burst to his feet. "A," he said, "I don't have sixty thousand dollars. B, I don't know if this guy is bluffing or what. And C, I'm not about to start doing anything that's going to be construed as an admission. For all I know, this guy may be working with the police and this may be some sort of deal where I pay him the money and the cops show up the next day and haul me away in handcuffs."

Leigh Rossville began pacing the floor, walking rapidly from the sitting room to the fireplace; from the fireplace to the sitting room; the sitting room to the closet and back again. "So I try laughing at him. I say, 'Mr. Carr, you're out of your mind. If you have something that I should know about, tell me. But don't just come in here and try to extort sixty thousand bucks out of me.' You can understand what I'm doing, Chris. I'm practically pleading with him to give me an excuse to buy him off, but he doesn't seem to realize it. Instead, he just asks me what I'd be willing to pay for the release." Leigh stopped pacing. He held up both hands and spread his fingers wide. "This is where I might have blown it. I told him to get out of my office." He looked apologetic. "It seemed like the only appropriate thing to do. I mean, I couldn't just start throwing numbers at him."

"Did he leave?"

"He gets up. He says I've given him no choice, he's got to turn it over to an attorney. I'm thinking, He's the one who's given me no choice, but that's what he tells me. I tell him, 'Good. See you in court and then I'll see you there again when I sue you for malicious prosecution, abuse of process, and intentional infliction of emotional distress.' He looks about as concerned as if I said I would see him in church on Easter Sunday. He goes out the door and I don't hear another thing until this shows up." He slapped the pocket where he was carrying the complaint and summons he had earlier shown Chris.

Chris, blowing air softly out of his cheeks, said, "Sounds like you've got to talk to a good lawyer."

And Leigh, his face upturned, said, "What do you think I've been doing the past couple of hours, you big jerk?"

235

CHAPTER THREE

On its face, it did not seem so unreasonable. Now that it was out in the open, Leigh felt his anxiety disappear. He could count on Chris, he was sure; even if Chris's skin had gone white, even if his mouth had turned taut.

Chris, when he spoke, reminded Leigh that he was not a defense lawyer. That he only did plaintiffs' work. That the two sides employed wholly different approaches, wholly different strategies.

Leigh brought up the Johnson-Doheny case, the one where Judge Gifford had assigned Chris to defend the indigent nurse, and Chris, perhaps reacting more strongly than he intended, said that was exactly the problem. Hadn't John Gregory gone through the roof over that thing? Hadn't they palmed it off on Bill Bunton and wasn't that as good as throwing it away? Gregory wasn't going to let another case like that come into the office.

Leigh said he wasn't expecting them to do the case for free. He was planning on paying.

"I wouldn't know how to go about charging you," Chris said. His color, by this time, had returned. He was showing signs that he wanted to kid his way out of the situation.

"I've got ten thousand bucks," Leigh said. "That should help you figure it out."

Stung, Chris said, "You know how far ten thousand bucks would go in a case like this?"

Leigh did not know. He had thought it would be enough. "I can sell the rental unit we have. I can sell one of the cars, both if we have to." He could feel the surge of panic come over him again. He tried to fight it off with black humor. "Shit, as long as I keep my job I can pay you something every month for the rest of your working life." He reached out and poked Chris's shoulder. "Hell, I'll consider you a dependent. The child I never had."

But Chris Cage did not laugh. He took the poke as if he were being stabbed. "I don't want your money," he said as he recoiled. "I don't want ten thousand dollars or a hundred thousand dollars from you. I don't want to get rich off a friend and I don't want a friend's life riding on my shoulders." He spoke with an edge in his voice and a glare that was meant to cut off further argument.

Softly, Leigh reminded him, "You do it for strangers all the time."

And quickly Chris came back with his repsonse. "Exactly. And not like this, I don't. Look, you take a case for a stranger, you do the best you can. You win, you get paid. You don't, you feel bad, but you walk away. I take this case for you and I'll have to start living with it. I'd have to have it on my mind all the time. I'd be carrying it around with me, sleeping with it, knowing that one screwup on my part and my friend's not just going to have a civil jury return a verdict against him; he's going to have the criminal courts down on him, too."

"That's right."

"That's right," Chris repeated. "A civil jury finds you killed O'Berry and you're liable to end up facing an indictment. A murder trial. Prison. That's no kind of responsibility to put on a friend."

Chris's tone was pugnacious, fearful, accusatory; and Leigh, feeling as though he had just been punched in the stomach, shook his head in wonder. "Oh, boy," he said. "We've really got this turned around, don't we? A friend comes to you for help and you tell him if he were really your friend he wouldn't be asking for help."

"That's not what I'm saying."

Leigh stared hard into Chris's face and wondered why it looked so different to him. How long had Chris had gray hairs in his sideburns? When had he gotten that scar on his upper lip? Had his eyes always been so piercing? Why had he never noticed these things before? "It's funny," Leigh heard himself saying. "You know somebody for twenty years and then you find out you don't know him at all."

The look in Chris's eyes softened. The scar and the gray hairs stayed where they were.

"Maybe that's the way you feel about Cath and me, Chris. If so, then that's our fault, if what we did was so repulsive to you. But Jesus, you know, I don't think it was. If I'd been doing what I was with anybody besides Cathy you'd have probably thought it was hilarious. And if

237

you're shocked because Cathy and I were doing this thing together, well, I'm sorry; but we're still the same people we always were. We're still hurt, we're still scared, we're still desperately in need of some help. And you think about it, you put yourself in our position, who else are we going to turn to? My dad? God, he's one of the people we're trying to save from this situation. No. As far as I was concerned, you were the only person I could trust—"

"You can't trust me," Chris shouted, flinging himself further away from Leigh, trying to increase the distance between them. An idea seemed to come to him as he moved. He pointed a finger. "And what about all the other cases I have? Those people are trusting me, too, you know. I took your case, I'd be shortchanging them at every turn. What am I supposed to do—farm them off to Bunton because somebody I know wants me to do something for him instead?"

"Yes." The word dropped from Leigh's mouth and crashed to the floor between them. It remained shimmering in place, almost a physical presence whose circumference had to be negotiated before anything else could be addressed.

Chris ran his fingers through his hair and then stood with his hand still on the back of his head, while Leigh said, "It's not just somebody, it's your best friend. A friend's supposed to be someone you can count on, isn't it? Or do you disagree? Do you think a friend's just someone you enjoy going places with?"

Choosing his words carefully, Chris said, "I think that as your friend I don't want to work on this for you. I think that as your friend I can give you support, money, advice. I can share your losses and your victories. But if you're my client it won't be like that anymore. There won't be any more give-and-take in our relationship. It will be you depending on me and that will be it. You won't be able to call me an asshole or risk hurting my feelings or even arguing with me. You'll find yourself being careful about everything you say in front of me for fear it will affect my judgment. Worse, you'll start telling me things for the specific purpose of affecting my judgment. The whole exchange between us will become so cautious, so contrived, so fraught with reminders of what's at stake, that we won't even want to be around each other." Chris's hand came down. His face constricted into an anguished squint of appeal. "Do you understand what I'm saying?"

Leigh felt himself on the verge of a violent shiver. When he spoke he had to grit his teeth to keep them from chattering. "What I understand, Chris, is that even while you're talking to me about friendship, you're talking like a lawyer. What I understand is that you and I knew each other as human beings a long time before you became a lawyer and that's why I came to you today. I don't want you to take me on as a client. I want you to say, 'Holy shit, you're in trouble and this is what I can do to help.' It's like, it's like . . . if you need to borrow my house, my car, my ski cabin—whatever—they're yours. And if I need your legal talent, I expect you to say, 'Here, it's at your disposal.' One might be more serious than the other, sure, but they're both things that a friend should do."

From across the room, Chris said, "So as a friend, I automatically assume these responsibilities and forget all my other obligations—is that what you're saying? My obligations to my clients and my partners and the people who work for me? My job, my sanity, my own life. You know, Leigh, it may not sound like much to you, my little firm, my crummy take-home pay, and so forth, but it's mine. I've had to fight for every bit of it, I've done it all on my own, and that makes it worth something—even if it's only to me."

Leigh tilted his head so that he did not have to look at Chris when he spoke. "Hey, nothing's simple, is it?" And then, still not looking, he said, "Do you remember Dunkirk?"

Chris repeated the name as if it were somebody he thought they once had known.

"Dunkirk, in World War Two, when the Allied troops were beaten back to the beaches of France and every person in the south of England who owned a boat that could float went across the Channel to bring them home. I'm sure nobody wanted to do that. It was dangerous, it was time-consuming, it was probably even expensive for all the poor goddamned fishermen. But these were their people and they were helpless. If they left them there, they were going to get wiped out."

"Dunkirk?"

"Well, that's the way I feel about the position Cathy and I are in. We're in trouble. The biggest trouble we'll ever be in in our entire lives, because, you see, the fact is I killed that kid. I didn't mean to, and I believe in my own mind it was justified, but pleading that is not going to save our lives or our reputations."

Tears sprang to Leigh's eyes too quickly for him to fight them back. He tried swiping at them briefly with the heel of one hand. "What I want," he said, "is to prove it never happened. What I want is for you to change reality . . . just like you told me you could."

"I didn't say I could. I said litigation could. If you really want reality changed, you're going to need someone who's a better litigator than I am."

"We need you, Chris. Because outside of you, I don't want anyone in the world to know what actually took place. I don't want to have to tell another lawyer or a jury or a judge or anybody else that for at least one hour Cathy and I were crazy perverts or that for at least one second I was a killer. . . . Because while it may be true, it's also not true at all."

A long moment passed in which nothing more was said. Then Leigh mumbled ambiguously, "This is embarrassing."

Chris, one hand inside his coat and on his hip, one hand holding his forehead, said, "This is crazy."

A painful grin parted Leigh's lips. "I don't feel crazy," he said. "Stupid, yeah."

Chris snorted. His hand moved from his forehead to his nose to his mouth. He looked at Leigh over his fingers.

"Ah, go ahead and laugh," Leigh said.

"I'm not laughing."

"It was that damn spear gun. It was just the first thing I grabbed."

"Too bad you didn't grab the basketball instead, huh?"

This time it was Leigh who laughed, and the noise came out so suddenly that tears once again welled in his eyes. Immediately he tried to hide his face, but Chris was coming closer to him and as he attempted to turn away, Chris's arm went around his shoulders and pulled him back so that his face was against Chris's chest. He could smell Chris's skin, he could feel Chris's heart, and he could not keep himself under control any longer. A great noise burst out of his throat and tears washed down his face.

Chris's arm tightened around him. "It's all right," he said. "I'm here, okay? Whatever you need from me, I'm right here with you."

Roger Gifford

CHAPTER ONE

Roger Gifford almost got it to work. There had been hope for a while. Jeanine had rubbed it, squeezed it, pulled it, even put her mouth on it—something she never liked to do. Now she sprawled exhausted across the bed, her peach-colored nightie pushed into a wrinkled fold at the top of her thighs.

She still had good thighs after all these years. Smooth and thin and free of mottled surface veins, free of blemishes and visible cellulite. Giff caressed one thigh lightly and then slid his hand upward, under the nightie, until he touched her buttocks. They were soft now, not like they were when he first met her, when she rode horses every weekend. But that had been almost forty years ago. Two thirds of a lifetime spent with him, spent out of the saddle, and he couldn't expect the same things of her now that he had expected then. Just as she couldn't expect the same things of him.

Giff got up and used one foot to poke under the bed for his slippers. Glow-in-the-dark slippers, given to him by his thirty-two-year-old daughter for Christmas, an unintentional slur on his kidneys and his eyesight. He took his Scottish woolen bathrobe from the bedpost and glanced quickly at himself in the mirror over the dresser before he put it on. There was no sign of possible arousal, no encouragement to go back to bed and try one more time. Sighing, he headed for the kitchen to put on a pot of coffee before beginning his morning ritual in the bathroom.

The smell hit him when he was halfway down the stairs. Something burning that was not supposed to be burning. He quickened his pace, scurrying around the banister and down the hall. The kitchen was gray-dark, illuminated only by the sunless early morning light coming through the two rectangular windows. Giff saw the glow beneath the pot on the stove and ran to shut it off.

A red and white can of Campbell's soup, its top removed, sat in the middle of the pan. A yellowish, sluggish liquid, the consistency of cake batter, was rolling over the top of the can and down its sides to the bottom of the pan, where it formed a sea of frying, popping goo.

"Oh, my God," Giff said, jerking the pan off the burner. Quickly he spun around. His son Peter sat slouched at the breakfast table, unmoved by the smell, the *spack*ing noises of the frying soup, the flurry of his father's motions.

Giff forced the annoyance from his face. "Making soup, son?" he said, his voice unnaturally cheery.

Peter Gifford very slowly raised his eyes to the level of his father's and said nothing. He brought the stub of a cigarette to his mouth and tried to inhale, but it was no longer going. In fact, the end had been stubbed out and it was now splayed and bent.

"Easiest thing to do," Giff said, just as if they were having a conversation, "is to empty the can into the pan, keep the flame on low, and add whatever amount of water they tell you to." He looked at the can, holding it up in an effort to read the small print. "Let's see, this one says to stir in one can of water as you go. That's easy enough, huh? But just don't ruin all your mother's good pans, okay, son?"

Peter's head drooped and Giff got no answer. After a moment he acted as though Peter had enthusiastically agreed. "Good. Now how about a nice cup of coffee?"

Giff set about making it, getting out the coffee, the coffeepot, running the water. "Just getting in, son?" he called over his shoulder. "Or you been here for a while? Sunday night, there can't be that many places stay open. Where'd you go?"

"Nowhere."

Giff, facing the stove, his back turned on his son, gave Peter the chance to say something more. He waited what he thought was a long time before he repeated his son's one-word answer. "Nowhere," he said. He turned, wishing he had on his glasses so he could see the expression on Peter's face. He took a step closer, trying to see. Then he took another step and another. He grabbed his son by the front of his jacket and swept him to his feet. "Get the hell out of the kitchen, you little sonofabitch, before your mother sees you." Wrenching his wrists, he flung Peter toward the back pantry, toward the stairs leading down to the garage and the room Peter occupied behind the garage. "Get the hell down there and don't come back until you've cleaned yourself up, you stinking bum."

Peter, who had hit against the wall, hung there until he was able to push himself straight with his elbow and his shoulder. In a slow-motion huff he pulled at the lapels of his sateen jacket. Then, without so much as a glance at his father, he staggered back to the stairs.

He left behind him the Honorable Roger Gifford, breathing heavily, heart beating, pulse racing: ready for another day in court.

What kind of case was this? He flicked his fingers disdainfully at the file. Wrongful death. They were talking about a killing. Where was the reference to the criminal action? And look at this cast of characters. Rossville: this had to be the son of *the* Leigh Rossville. If he had killed somebody—what's it say—'with an arrow, or bolt, or spear, or knife, wouldn't it have been in all the newspapers? Wouldn't somebody be talking about it? Who was the settlement conference judge on this case? Why hadn't he said anything to anyone about it? A case like this, it should have been the talk of the courthouse. Was it because that lunatic Wechsler was involved? If this was another one of his crazy schemes, why the hell didn't the defendant bring a summary judgment motion? The judges of this court like nothing better than throwing Wechsler out. Judges here have more than enough to do without letting some marauding madman create new causes of action. What had his latest trick been? To sue the same defendant twice: once for negligence and once for preventing him from proving negligence by spoiling the evidence. Holy smoke, the defendant had been a department store. It had cleaned up the mess so nobody else would have an accident. Who is the defense attorney? Chris Cage. He should have known what little credibility Wechsler has around here. But what was Cage doing on the defense side in the first place?

Judge Gifford pressed hard on his buzzer and his law clerk practically sprang through the door. She was an eager little thing, he had to say that much for her. Pretty, too, despite her obvious misunderstandings about how to dress like a professional. It was, he resisted an impulse to tell her, not necessary always to wear a full blouse with some sort of massive bow on the front. But he frowned anyway.

"Lisa," he said sternly, "the PJ has sent us a jury trial to start in one half hour, are you aware of that?"

245

"Yes, sir." She looked at him as if expecting to be blamed for the presiding judge's action.

"I get the file delivered to me, there's almost nothing in it."

"That's all there was, sir."

"Oh, really?" The judge raised one great gray eyebrow. It soared above his eyeglasses and hung there as visible evidence of his question. "And where's the reference to the settlement conference?"

"There wasn't one, Judge. Defendant refused to participate."

"Lisa, this is a wrongful death case. The way I read the pleadings, our friend Mr. Wechsler—you know who he is, don't you?—has accused this Mr. and Mrs. Rossville of somehow stabbing to death one Robert O'Berry, who left as evidence of his brief stay here on earth one wife and one child. What does this case sound like to you, Lisa?"

"It sounds like . . ." she said, struggling, and the judge knew she was not going to come up with the right answer.

"It sounds like murder, doesn't it?"

"Yes, sir."

"But there's not one reference in this entire file to any criminal proceedings."

"There weren't any, Judge."

The judge turned to the row of shelves behind him and reached for his pipe. First bowl of the morning. He loaded up the tobacco, arranged it to his liking, and then set fire to it. "So," he said at last, "Reuben Wechsler claims there was a murder, the DA files no charges, the civil case is begun and proceeds to trial with no pretrial motions, no pleas for summary judgment, no settlement conference. That sort of makes me the court of first resort, doesn't it, Lisa?"

"Yes, sir."

He sighed. "Well, it's going to be interesting. It'll be just my luck it will run all month. All right, bring in the trial briefs as soon as counsel arrive. Tell 'em to sit tight until I've had a chance to read them."

The judge slammed the edge of his fist down on his desk hard enough to make his award from the Rotary Club bounce; hard enough to make the picture of his wife shudder. "Gentlemen," he thundered, "just what in God's name are you doing here?"

Reuben Wechsler sat unperturbed. He was a tall man who resolved his balding pattern by shaving his skull hairless. He wore gold-rimmed glasses and a thick mustache which he fashioned in an inverted U. He wore a large gold-nugget ring on his pinkie finger and a thick-banded gold wristwatch. His suit was a conservative gray-brown tweed, but his shirt was an off-pink color and his tie had purple in it.

By contrast, Chris Cage was dressed like Richard Nixon: dark blue suit, white shirt, red tie, polished black oxford shoes. Chris's hair was neatly parted, meticulously combed. He sat with military posture in his chair, his shoulders squared, his jaw firmly set. This was not the Chris Cage the judge had come to know through past experience. That Chris Cage usually had his hair falling over his forehead, his shoes scuffed, his suit well made but slightly in need of a good pressing. As it was, Cage's rigid bearing, his formal hairstyle, his conservative attire, all combined to give the judge a fairly good answer to his thundering question. Cage had something to fear from Wechsler's case.

The judge looked hard at Cage, trying to assess just how vulnerable he was, just how far he could be pushed in the interest of achieving a settlement before the jury was selected and the circus began. "You, Chris," he said, "you realize what your client stands to lose in this case?" The judge regretted the question as soon as it was out. It was a bad start. It was too condescending.

"You can't buy somebody off who accuses you of doing something you didn't do, Judge," Cage said evenly. "That would be extortion."

The judge made a humphing noise. He tried to make it seem as though he was displeased at being lectured on the law. In truth, he was disturbed because half a dozen of his best settlement arguments had just been swept away. He said, "Sometimes you make the best of a bad situation . . . Mr. Cage. Sometimes you find yourself inadvertently traveling on the wrong road and you decide to turn around and go back rather than hoping it will lead to where you want to go. Sometimes you buy a stock and the stock goes down and you sell it at a loss rather than run the risk it will go down any lower." He punctuated what he was saying with an arch of his eyebrows.

Chris Cage nodded.

The judge nodded back, confirming his own point. He glanced down at the trial briefs in front of him. "Now these people, the Rossvilles, are they related to the Rossville of Rossville, Dailey and so forth?"

"Leigh's a partner there. He's the son of the founding partner. . . . Right now he's on a leave of absence . . . self-requested."

"Hmmm," the judge said, peering at what Wechsler had written in his introductory description of the case. "Vulnerable situation for somebody of Mr. Rossville's stature." He read to himself.

247

"Mr. Wechsler, according to the papers he's filed with the court, says Mr. and Mrs. Rossville wrongfully caused the death of Mr. O'Berry. He says they disposed of the body, stripped it of identification and attempted to cover up their involvement. Mr. Cage, if I understand your position correctly, you simply deny everything Mr. Wechsler alleges. You say there is nothing to connect your clients with the body that was ultimately found and identified as O'Berry other than a bartender's testimony that Mr. Rossville invited O'Berry out to his house on the night he was killed—"

"The bartender didn't even go that far, Your Honor. In his deposition he said he saw the two of them talking and that after Mr. Rossville left the bar the kid he thinks might possibly have been O'Berry asked him some questions about Tranton Park."

"There were no 'thinks' or 'might possiblies,' Judge. The bartender made a positive ID." Wechsler's voice twanged with disgust. Before the judge could cut him off, he added, "And we've got a second witness who saw the kid go into the Rossvilles' house."

"All right, gentlemen, don't put the gloves on yet. We'll find out who said what fast enough. I'd just like to get a few preliminary matters straight. All right?"

"Yes, sir."

"Mr. Wechsler?"

"Sure."

The judge let his eyes rest an extra second on Wechsler, who did not seem to mind in the least. Then he turned his attention to Cage and said, "Mr. Cage, you seem to think that the circumstantial evidence which plaintiffs have is not enough for them to meet their burden."

"That's right, Judge. They've got no murder weapon, no motive . . . not a single thing to explain why my clients would or could have killed this guy. All they've got is two witnesses, one of whom is certifiably crazy and won't even come out of her house."

The judge turned a page and read something. "That's John Clarke Lane's wife?"

"That's right."

The judge leaned back in his chair. "I know John Clarke, you know. I used to know Mary Elizabeth, although it's been some years since I've seen her. If either of you thinks that might have any effect on my handling of the case, you better speak up now. Once the trial starts, it will be too late."

Wechsler said, "No problem with me, Judge."

Cage said, "I think it might be difficult for you, Your Honor."

The judge used his eyebrows. "You don't believe I can be fair in adjudicating Mrs. Lane's testimony?" He thought Cage was kidding.

But Cage hesitated. "I think it might add to what might already be a strained relationship, Your Honor."

The judge was genuinely surprised. "What do you mean?"

"I mean"—Chris Cage set himself—"I'm not sure you can be fair to me, and my client has too much at risk here for me not to bring that up."

The judge felt his neck begin to flush. Out of the corner of his eye he saw the stunned look on Wechsler's face, but he refused to exchange glances with him. He was not about to share with that man either his humiliation or his indignation. Slowly, controlling each word, he asked Cage to explain himself.

"Your Honor recalls the Kinsey case, I'm sure. Your Honor recalls that we had a disagreement over the use of jury challenges and that I filed a motion for new trial after the jury had come in against us."

"But," the judge said incredulously, "I ruled for you on the motion. I found juror misconduct and I granted you a new trial, didn't I?"

"The other side appealed."

"How unusual. I'd just taken a defense verdict away from them."

"And I cross-appealed on the grounds of legal error, just in case they won on the juror misconduct."

"Your prerogative."

Cage looked uncomfortable. "I thought you were mad about it."

Judge Gifford leaned forward so that his elbows and forearms were resting on the glass that covered his desk. He leaned so far forward that his haunches were off the pillow on his chair. "Are you saying that just because an attorney appeals one of my rulings, I'm going to be unable to perform my duties whenever he appears in my court again?"

Cage made a quick attempt to get help from Wechsler, and just as quickly changed his mind. Flicking his eyes back to the judge, he said, "You stuck me with that Doheny case just after the appeal happened. What was I supposed to think?"

The judge pushed himself back in his seat. He spun the chair sideways and began drumming his fingers on the glass. "My God in heaven," he said, and spun back again. "I sent you that case, Mr. Cage, for one reason and one reason only. I saw what I thought was a terrible injustice about to happen to Mr. Doheny. I felt he was being punished quite enough for what I considered to be a well-intended act of mercy

---

and I wanted to make damn sure he had competent counsel who would try to keep him from getting the bad end of the stick once again.

"I sent the case to you, Mr. Cage, because we had just finished the Kinsey trial and because I had been impressed by the care and concern you showed for your client. I apologize for not being aware that you found the task of representing an indigent so onerous. I apologize for my naïveté in not recognizing your real interest in the practice of law."

Wechsler smirked and the judge fired a look at him that told him to get the smirk off his face. Wechsler covered his mouth loosely with his fingers and looked away, fairly glowing with amusement.

From his seat directly in front of the judge's desk, Chris Cage made no effort to defend himself. Only the redness in his cheeks and the whiteness around his mouth revealed the anger he was feeling.

"What's the status of Doheny's case now?" the judge demanded.

Swallowing before he spoke, Cage said, "I'm afraid I can't tell you, Your Honor. That case has stayed with the firm I used to be with."

The judge pawed at the papers in front of him. "You're not with Gregory, Bunton anymore?"

"Not as of the start of this trial."

The judge held up the trial brief submitted on behalf of the Rossvilles. "What's this address you have on here? This a new office for you?"

"It's my home."

Judge Gifford looked over the top of the papers he was holding. Cage held his stare. The two men said nothing.

There was a knock on the door and the judge's secretary marched in, using the quick-stepped important stride that all judge's secretaries are taught the first day of their jobs. "The jury panel's here, Judge Gifford," she announced.

The judge picked up the file and held it out as an offering to either attorney. "Gentlemen, do we begin, or does either of you want to take this back to the PJ for reassignment?"

Wechsler, standing, said, "I'm here to try the case, Your Honor."

The judge inverted his elbow and directed the file toward Chris Cage. "Chris," he said, "it's up to you."

Another moment passed before Chris spoke. "Ready, Your Honor," he said, and did his best to smile. The judge nodded and did his best not to.

CHAPTER TWO

This time there were no problems with jury challenges. Each side was entitled to excuse six prospective jurors for whatever reason, or lack of reason, it chose. Both Cage and Wechsler started off following the standard plaintiff's personal injury line: Off went the Asians, off went the retired people. The two attorneys studied their jurors' biographies and asked their questions, but both were challenging on the basis of stereotypes and neither seemed to want conservatives in the box. It almost began to appear that they could choose a jury by consensus, and then on his fifth challenge Wechsler unexpectedly excused a Berkeley man who either was gay or should have been.

A new name was called and an obviously well-to-do older woman took the open seat. Cage huddle with his clients. Both attorneys asked the woman things that involved lengthy and complicated hypotheticals, and neither seemed pleased with her responses. Cage huddled some more, but the result of his conversation was to excuse a soft-spoken young black woman. The judge sat like a referee at a chess match and wondered at the apparent shift by both sides.

A plumber came up. He didn't want to sit. He worked by the hour and a long trial would be a financial hardship. The attorneys agreed to let him go. He was replaced by an overweight, acne-ridden gas station attendant who, when asked what he did for recreation, said he danced with blind girls. Everybody laughed, except the gas station attendant. Wechsler, looking concerned, asked for a bench conference and the judge summoned both attorneys to come up to meet with him.

"I think he's crazy, Judge," Wechsler said. "The court should excuse him for cause."

The judge cocked his eyebrows at Cage.

"He's not crazy at all," Cage whispered. "Somebody's got to dance with blind girls."

Wechsler made a noise and threw up his hands.

"Mr. Wechsler," the judge said, "are we annoying you?"

"No, you're not. But . . ." He looked at Cage and rolled his eyes.

"Mr. Wechsler, for all you know, this man belongs to a charity organization. Just because he does something that you wouldn't consider doing doesn't make him unfit for jury duty. I'm going to deny your request unless you can come up with something more substantive."

Wechsler went back to his table and addressed the juror again. "Sir, can you tell me how it is that you happened to . . . ah . . . become engaged in this activity?" The question brought forth a new round of titters.

"My sister's blind," said the juror. "And I escort her to the various dances that her school puts on."

In the end Wechsler had to use his final challenge on the dancing juror. There was too much likelihood that he had offended him.

A new name was called, that of Joe Gutierrez, a young, unemployed Chicano with long hair and a scraggly beard, wearing a leather vest over a white T-shirt. He answered all his questions "Yeah" or "Nah," and Wechsler clearly was uncomfortable with him, but there was no longer anything he could do. The last challenge was in the hands of Cage.

Once again Cage huddled with his clients. When the huddle ended he kept the Chicano and excused the older woman.

The clerk called the final name and a tall, thin man with a very short haircut and a full mustache took the last spot. He wore a shirt, a tie, and blue jeans that clung tightly to his slender hips. By the time he had settled gingerly into his seat, everyone in the courtroom who cared to think such thoughts knew that despite Wechsler's efforts the gay community was going to have a representative on the jury.

The judge surveyed the twelve panelists: a gay computer programmer; an unemployed Chicano; four blacks, including a housepainter, a postal worker, a grandmother, and a student; a divorced mother of three; a city clerical worker; a pharmacist; a newlywed housewife; a fast-food manager; and a Filipino golf caddy. Democracy in action, he thought, with ironic satisfaction. Had this been a criminal murder case, it would have been a defendant's dream to have this conglomeration sit in judgment. Had it been a civil suit against some corporation or governmental entity, it would have been a plaintiff's dream. As it was . . . well, time would tell.

Two alternates were quickly selected and then the judge turned to the people sitting on the back benches and gave his usual speech about how many are called and few are chosen. He thanked them all for coming and sent them back to the jury commissioner for further assignment. But of the dozen people remaining, only about half got up and ambled out of the courtroom. Those left behind included a plump, round-faced girl flanked by two behemothic men in slightly loud sport coats—one yellow, one red and gray. In the same row as this threesome, but sitting slightly apart, was a stoop-shouldered older man wearing a yellowish raincoat over a baggy suit, white shirt and polyester tie. In the far back sat a stocky, curly-haired man with handsome Irish features, wearing a dark blue blazer and holding a legal notepad in his hands.

The judge looked at each of these people in turn, and then addressed himself to the attorneys. "Gentlemen, are you ready to commence opening statements or do you wish to take a break first?"

"Ready, Your Honor," said Wechsler, bounding to his feet, clutching a sheaf of notes.

"Ah, Your Honor," Cage said, looking over his shoulder. "Could we have the usual ruling excluding witnesses from the courtroom until after they've given their testimony?"

"To get the usual ruling, as you call it, Mr. Cage, you have to ask for it."

Grinning boyishly, Cage dipped his head and said he was sorry, he wondered if he could have it now. The posturing had begun.

"All witnesses other than the parties themselves are to remain outside the courtroom until called to testify," the judge announced.

Nobody moved.

"Anyone who is present during the testimony of others will not be allowed to testify later. That's my ruling."

Wechsler got up and went back to talk to the old man in the raincoat. The old man nodded, gathered his briefcase and left the room. Wechsler returned to his seat. Cage looked at the three people in the front row, then he looked at the Irishman in the back. Then he looked at the judge and shrugged.

"Let's begin," the judge said.

* * *

253

Wechsler made the usual introductions. He identified the round-faced girl as being his client, Barbara O'Berry. He told about her little daughter, Roberta, "Bobbie," named after her dad. He said she wasn't in the courtroom today but they would be getting a chance to meet her as the trial went on.

He explained that what he was doing now was providing them with an outline to the case, a road map, as it were. He talked about the dead man, Bobby O'Berry, filled with hope and promise; known for his strength and his good looks. He produced a blowup of a picture taken for his high school yearbook less than a year before his death, and he paraded it back and forth in front of the jury box. "Catnip to the ladies," he said.

And then, just when it seemed Wechsler was going to describe Bobby O'Berry as a paragon of virtue, fatherhood and wholesome manliness, he suddenly began tearing him down. "The evidence will show that Bobby O'Berry, as handsome and capable as he was, was also immature, callous and self-centered . . . just the qualities you might expect in a boy eighteen or nineteen years old, suddenly thrust into the real world of marriage and parental responsibility. We will show that at this very early stage of his life, Bobby tried to shirk that role. That having readily met his obligation of marrying and giving his unborn child a name, Bobby tried to run away to California—our great state of opportunity, our magic little paradise at the end of the rainbow.

"But being just eighteen, untrained and inexperienced, knowing no one to call upon for aid, assistance, guidance—not yet having had the opportunity to benefit from those things that come from friendship, settlement in the community, age—Bobby began his existence here using his best asset . . . his looks."

Judge Gifford glanced at the defendants' table. Cage was busily writing down everything that was being said, his face impassive as he concentrated on the paper in front of him. But in the two chairs next to Cage, his clients were nervously shifting on their bottoms. Cage was going to have to lecture them on remaining as impassive as he.

"The evidence will show that Bobby O'Berry, in need of money like anybody else, attempted to get that money by making himself available for sexual encounters. With women."

Cathy Rossville's hand clutched the edge of the table. Her lips pursed. The judge looked from her to the jury and saw that all the jurors were watching Wechsler. They hadn't grown jaded enough yet to look anywhere else. But the judge had, and he liked what he saw in

254

Mrs. Rossville. That plain tan suit of hers was not hiding what appeared to be an astoundingly good figure. He wished he had seen her walk into the courtroom, or that he had noticed her more closely when she stood for him.

"Objection," shouted Cage, stirring the judge from his reverie. "He's arguing the case."

The judge looked at Wechsler without any idea what the attorney had been saying. "Don't argue your case, Mr. Wechsler. This isn't the time for that."

"Yes, sir," said Wechsler, and faced the jury again. "The evidence will show," he went on, "that the defendant Mr. Rossville met with Bobby in a bar over in San Francisco and procured his services—for what purposes, we do not know. Only Mr. and Mrs. Rossville truly know the answer to that—"

"Objection."

"Sustained. I don't want to have to warn you again, Mr. Wechsler. So just get on with your statement."

"Sorry, sir," Wechsler said unrepentantly. Using heavy emphasis on the next several words, he said to the jury, "But the evidence will show the types of activities in which the Rossvilles were engaged, and the evidence will show, moreover, that on the very night of his death, Bobby O'Berry was seen entering the home of Mr. and Mrs. Rossville . . . but he was never seen leaving it. Instead, the evidence will show, it was Mr. Rossville who was seen driving away from his home that night on Bobby's motorcycle . . . and when Bobby himself was next seen, he was dead and dumped by the side of a roadway."

Wechsler stared hard at each of the jurors, the twelve regulars and the two alternates, imparting significance to each one individually. Cage's chair scraped and he stood up. "I'm sorry," he said unctuously. "Is counsel done?"

"No, I'm not done," snarled Wechsler.

"Sit down, Mr. Cage," the judge said.

Cage, looking confused, sat down. Wechsler, glaring at Cage, resumed his talk, telling the jury that despite what they had heard so far, this case was not really about the victim but about the victim's survivors: his wife and his little girl. They, he said, were entitled to Bobby's support whether he was there or not, whether he stayed in California without them, sent home for them, or returned home to them. "The evidence will show," he said again, "that Barbara and little Bobbie were deprived not only of their man, but of their opportunity to ever have

255

their man return to them. The evidence will show that they are entitled to compensation for the loss of Bobby's obligation to support them, as well as the loss of Bobby's care, comfort and society—whatever time and circumstances would have allowed that to be. . . ."

Wechsler spun on his heel and went back to his seat. Chris Cage, this time, made no move to rise until the judge said, "Mr. Cage, are you planning on making an opening statement?"

Cage, pushing himself slowly into a standing position, holding half a dozen pieces of paper in his hand, looked puzzled. He spread the papers he was holding and then let them drop to his table. He turned to the jury and he smiled as though they were mutual participants in some small, vaguely unpleasant ordeal. "Ladies and gentlemen of the jury, as you all know by now, my name is Christopher Cage and it is my privilege to represent the defendants in this case, Leigh and Cathy Rossville. The Rossvilles, as you can well see, are people who have been fortunate in many respects. They're attractive, they're well educated, they have good jobs, nice cars and a beautiful home. God has not seen fit to bless them with any children, but they have a good strong marriage that has lasted for some twelve years. That's not very Californian, is it? Yet both are native Californians, born and raised and lived all their lives right here in the Bay Area.

"What does this all mean? It means, we will show as we put on our case, that Leigh and Cathy are target defendants. They are being singled out because they were available, convenient, because they appear to have some assets that somebody else wants. They are being singled out because it has been their misfortune to live next door to the wrong person at the wrong time.

"Our case will be, in a sense, a rebuttal. But we can only rebut what has actually been put into evidence by the plaintiff. We can't rebut innuendo and rumor and speculation. So do not expect us to. Look instead to the evidence. See what they have other than a very young woman who has given birth to a little girl." He paused as though paying homage to the enormity of the situation; and because he did not mock it, the jurors felt free to engage in their own de-emphasis.

Cage studied their faces, going from one to another.

"We will put on only a few witnesses, ladies and gentlemen," he said. "And when we are done, you will be able to answer for yourselves the question of why people have said the things they have said. We ask only that you wait until you have heard all the evidence before you attempt to provide that answer."

Then he sat down, taking everyone by such surprise that a very long time seemed to pass before the judge told Wechsler to call his first witness.

The old man seemed frail as he slowly took off his raincoat, folded it over his arm and carefully laid it down on one of the empty benches. "Which way?" he said to the bailiff, who was already trying to direct him to where the clerk was waiting in front of the witness box to swear him in. Wechsler sprang to the swinging door in the rail that separated the participants from the spectators and held it open long enough for Owen Carr to shuffle through.

"Right there?" asked the old man, pointing to the clerk.

The bailiff smiled. Wechsler smiled. Half the jurors smiled.

The clerk made him raise his right hand. She asked him if he swore to tell the truth. "I surely do," he said, and took his seat.

"Your name, sir?" asked Wechsler.

"Owen Michael Carr."

"Your occupation."

"I'm a private investigator."

There was a gasp from the jury box and the gasp brought giggles from three or four other jurors, who craned their necks to see who it was who had breached decorum. The judge frowned at all of them.

"What is your experience, sir?"

"I formed my own company in 1949, Owen Carr, Private Investigations, and I've been working at it ever since."

"Ever since?"

"Every day since. In fact, that's my motto—'Never a day off since 1949.' "

Several of the jurors shook their heads in admiration. The grandmother, sitting in the front row, let her lips drop into a downward smile and looked out at the audience. Barbara O'Berry and the two men with her smiled back.

"Have you been employed by the family of Robert O'Berry to investigate the circumstances surrounding his disappearance and death?"

Before Carr could answer, Cage objected. "Assumes facts not in evidence, Your Honor. There's been no proof that Robert O'Berry is dead. For that matter, there's been no proof that Robert O'Berry ever lived."

Wechsler was nonplussed. He fumbled with his notes. He stuck his hand in his pocket, adjusted his glasses, dragged his hand across his mustache.

The judge let him do all that and then he said, "I think he's right, counsel."

Wechsler looked at the witness. "Do you know who Barbara O'Berry is, Mr. Carr?"

"Oh, indeed I do. I was hired by her."

"Objection. Move that the last part be stricken as nonresponsive."

"It will be stricken. Just answer the questions, Mr. Carr."

Wechsler said, "Do you see her in the courtroom today?"

Owen Carr said, "Yes, I surely do," and he pointed to the round-faced young woman.

Wechsler asked Barbara O'Berry to stand and she did.

"Do you recognize the people with her?" Wechsler asked Carr.

"Yes. Those are her two brothers, with whom she lives. Terry and Billy are their names, I believe." He smiled at them and gave them a little wave.

"Were you, as a private investigator, asked by the Cochrane family, these three people whom you've just identified, to do anything for them?"

"Why, yes. I was asked if I could help them find out what happened to Barbara's husband. You see, she'd just had a baby and—"

"Your Honor—"

"Sustained. Confine yourself to the questions, please, Mr. . . . ah . . . Carr."

The witness looked suitably chastened.

"Mr. Carr," Wechsler said, "how is it you came to meet Barbara O'Berry?"

"Well, I found her myself. . . . I sort of traced her."

"You mean, like, tracked down?"

"Yes, exactly."

"And how did you come to do that?"

"I received word that the body of an unidentified young man had been found near a roadway here in Oakland. I went down to the coroner's and I viewed the remains."

"Can you tell us how the body was dressed?" Wechsler interjected. "When you first saw it, I mean."

"Yes," said the witness. "He was wearing blue jeans—Levi's, I believe they were—white underpants, socks—dark, I think they were—and a pair of what we used to call engineer boots."

"No shirt?"

"No shirt."

"Bare-chested?"

"Bare-chested."

"Go on."

"He had a hole in his throat right here." The witness craned his neck and demonstrated to the jury, pointing with his index finger. "And then," he said, turning, "another one coming out the other side, right about here," and he pointed to the back of his neck.

"Were you able to recognize the individual whose body you observed?"

"Never saw him before in my life."

"Were you able to observe any clues to his identity?"

"Just the underpants."

"Can you explain what you mean by that?"

"Well, they had a label on them. In the back, where it gives the size and everything. Said 'Filene's.' I figured that was the name of a store or something, because I'd never heard of a make like that. So I went to my library and I looked up Filene's in one of the stock reporting services. Sure enough, it was a store, all right. Stores in the New England area."

"So how did that help you in determining the identity of the body?"

"I figured if the underpants came from New England, chances are the boy did, too. Then I figured, if the boy came from New England, he had to get here some way and there was at least a possibility he had come here by motor vehicle. So I began checking around. Checked with Oakland police, all the surrounding communities. Every time I came across a record of an abandoned vehicle with New England plates, I looked into it, found out where they had picked it up, how long they'd had it, that sort of thing."

"Did you ever find a vehicle which assisted you in your determination of the identity of the body?"

"Sure did. I found a Honda 750 motorcycle, Mass plate KS1745."

"Mass?"

"Massachusetts."

"And where did you find that?"

"San Francisco authorities had towed it away from in front of a bar named McGuppers, just the same day as the body was found."

"So what did you do when you learned this?"

"So I went to McGuppers and asked around. Assistant manager there told me he'd had—"

259

"Objection. Hearsay."

The judge looked at Cage, who was on his feet waiting for a ruling. "I'm going to allow it, Mr. Cage. He's not testifying to the truth of the matter. He's explaining why he did what he did during the course of his investigation."

The witness continued. "The assistant manager told me he'd had the motorcycle towed away because it had been parked in front of the bar in an illegal zone since the night before. Saturday night."

"And what did you do when you found that out?"

"Showed him a picture."

Wechsler picked something up from his desk and showed it to Cage. Cage stared at it for a moment and then went back to his writing.

"I show you what's been marked for identification as Exhibit One," Wechsler said, handing the picture to the witness.

Owen Carr said yes, that was the picture he had shown.

"Did he recognize what was depicted in that picture?"

"No."

"Did anybody in the bar recognize it?"

"Yes. Another bartender did."

"Objection. Hearsay."

"Sustained."

Wechsler said, "We're calling that other bartender as a witness, Your Honor."

"Good. He can testify himself. Until then it's hearsay."

"But a minute ago—"

"Don't argue, Mr. Wechsler. I've made my ruling."

Wechsler, whirling dramatically, said to the witness, "Do you recognize what is depicted there?"

Owen Carr said, "Yes. It's a picture of the head and upper body of Bobby O'Berry after he was killed."

"Objection. No foundation. Move to strike."

"Sustained. The answer will be stricken."

"Who took that picture, Mr. Carr?" Wechsler said quickly.

"I did."

"And what did you take that picture of? Not who, but what?"

"Of the body I observed at the coroner's office, 480 Fourth Street, Oakland."

"And . . . on the basis of your showing that picture which you took to the bartender at McGuppers, what, if any, conclusions were you able to draw—"

"Objection. Compound question."

"Rephrase your question, Mr. Wechsler."

Wechsler, annoyed, snapped, "Were you able to draw any conclusions, Mr. Carr?"

"Yes."

"What?"

"That the person in this picture had been in McGuppers a few nights previous to his death."

"Objection—"

"Sit down, Mr. Cage."

"Now," said Wechsler, "you had the license number of this motorcycle. Did that assist you in identifying the person in the picture?"

"Yes. I called back to Massachusetts and had them run a check on the registration."

"And what did you learn?"

"Objection. Hearsay."

Wechsler said, "We have a copy of the computer printout, Your Honor," and he held up a large piece of paper.

"No foundation to that, Your Honor. No one here to certify its authenticity. No evidence of the chain of custody. For all we know, this paper could have come from somebody's home computer." Cage's handsome face was contorted in earnestness.

Wechsler was livid. "That's an outrageous thing to say and he knows it, Your Honor: accusing us of falsifying evidence. It so happens that we have a certified copy of this document and with it we've got an affidavit from the custodian of records at the Massatoosits registry of motor vehicles."

"Custodian of records at the what?" asked Cage.

"Mass—at the state registry back there."

"Gentlemen, please," the judge said. "Let me look at the document." A few moments later he said, "You moving this into evidence, Mr. Wechsler?"

"Yes, Your Honor. Exhibit Two."

"It'll be admitted."

Wechsler passed the exhibit to the witness. "Can you read what this says, please."

"It says the motorcycle was registered to Julius Sabatini of 74 Quarry Street, Portshead, Massachusetts. It says it was reported stolen a year ago last November, which would have been four months before I began my investigation."

"And you began your investigation how soon after the body was discovered?"

"Oh, within hours. He had only been dead a short time, Saturday night to Sunday morning."

"Objection."

"We have the coroner's report on that, Judge."

"Then we'll have to wait until that's brought into evidence. Objection sustained. Let's take a break, gentlemen."

Jeanine wasn't home when he called her. This was Tuesday, where would she be today? Was this art lessons or Oakland Historical Society? Or was this the day she worked with the cerebral palsy children doing that swimming therapy thing? Of course, she could be shopping. She seemed to be doing a lot of that lately, slipping cash out of his wallet and going out God knows where to buy God knows what. He'd like to see something she bought from time to time, just to find out what she was doing with the money.

He left a message on the machine to let her know he had called and then he turned to his pipe and the stack of papers he was going to have to read before his early morning law and motion calendar. What was this first one? Oh, Christ, a landlord-tenant dispute. First Wechsler and his cockeyed theories and now a landlord-tenant dispute. Would it never end? He should get away. Grab Jeanine and take off for a few weeks. Get out in the woods. Maybe go on a long trail ride. Get Jeanine back in the saddle. Get himself back in the saddle.

CHAPTER THREE

The same group of people assembled. Barbara and her two brothers and the curly-haired Irishman, all sitting in the audience. Wechsler alone at his table. Cage and his clients at their table. Freddy Wagner or "Vagner," as he liked to be called, seated at his little bailiff's table by the door leading to the jury room. Gerta, the court reporter, perched in front of the bench with her knees spread around the tripod that held her little machine, on which she took down everything said in the courtroom. Next to her, ensconced like a race car driver in her own three-sided, high-bordered desk, was Myrna, the secretary and court-room clerk; Myrna the indestructible; Myrna, who had come with the courthouse and who probably would remain until the bricks and the mortar collapsed. And off to the side, hidden for the most part from everyone else, was lovely little Lisa, with her blouse and her bow. The judged looked down from his elevated platform and gave the signal to Freddy to go out and get the jury.

Owen Carr was already back on the stand when the jurors resumed their positions. Wechsler, standing in the middle of the floor with his hands clasped behind his back, said, "Now, Mr. Carr, speaking only in terms of your investigation—why you did what you did and so forth—I want you to tell us what happened when you learned—"

"Objection."

"Strike that. When Mr. Sabatini's name came to your attention."

"I had my Boston associate, Dan Gleason, interview Mr. Sabatini. Then I had Mr. Gleason go to Mr. Sabatini's high school with a picture of the, ah, dead person—"

"The picture we have marked as Exhibit One?"

263

"Exhibit One, yes, sir."

"And what did Mr. Gleason report back to you?"

The judge quickly waved Cage down before he could rise for his objection.

Owen Carr said, "That the decedent's name was Robert O'Berry. That his address was listed as 21 Water Street, Portshead, and that he was marked as having died the previous November."

"November. You mean four months prior to you seeing the body at the coroner's?"

"Yes, sir."

"Did you obtain a copy of the school record for Mr. O'Berry?"

"I did."

Wechsler showed a file folder to Cage, Cage waved it off, and Wechsler handed it to the witness. "I show you what's been marked as Exhibit Three."

"That's it."

"Move it into evidence, Your Honor."

"No objection."

"It'll be admitted."

Wechsler waited until the judge and the clerk had written down the admission. Then he said, "Is that file stamped 'Deceased'?"

"It is."

"How do you account for that? I mean, if Mr. O'Berry died in November, why do you think you saw his body in March? His recently deceased body, that is."

"I had Mr. Gleason go to the local newspaper in Portshead and obtain a copy of the obituary. I think that explains it."

"Do you have that copy with you?"

"I do."

"I show you Exhibit Four; is that it?"

"Yes."

"No objection," called out Cage in an unexpected move.

"It'll be admitted," answered the judge and, once again, he and the courtroom clerk busied themselves recording the admission.

"Would you read what this clipping says, please, Mr. Carr."

Clearing his throat, Carr read: " 'Missing, Presumed Drowned. Robert Michael quotes Bobby close quotes O'Berry, eighteen, of 21 Water Street, Portshead, disappeared while on a midnight swim in Lake Winnipesaukee in New Hampshire last Saturday night and is presumed drowned. Mr. O'Berry, who was on his honeymoon, had just been married that afternoon to Barbara Cochrane O'Berry, also of Portshead.

" 'Mr. O'Berry, a June graduate of Portshead High, was employed as a loading dock worker at Tyco Transmetics, where his father, John quotes Jack close quotes O'Berry has been employed for many years. The younger O'Berry left his job with Tyco last Wednesday in order to get married, his father said.

" 'According to a statement given by Barbara O'Berry to New Hampshire police, she and her husband had arrived at the L'il Bit of Heaven lakeside resort earlier in the evening and after getting settled into their cabin, Mr. O'Berry had decided to go for a moonlight swim. She told police that they had been drinking champagne in celebration and that she had been unable to talk him out of the idea. Mrs. O'Berry herself had not gone in because, she said, the water was too cold.

" 'The manager of L'il Bit of Heaven, Drew Lewis, was awakened by Mrs. O'Berry's screams at approximately eleven-forty-five P.M. He stated that he did not immediately investigate the screaming because he knew the O'Berrys were on their honeymoon and, he said, they were a long way away. When the screaming got closer, he went out with a flashlight and found Mrs. O'Berry, clad only in a towel, in a state of uncontrolled hysteria. Mr. Lewis then returned to his own lodgings and called police. There were no other guests at the resort at that time.

" 'A search by patrol boats was carried on throughout the remainder of Saturday night and all day Sunday, but no sign of Mr. O'Berry or his body was found. Yesterday New Hampshire authorities declared him missing and presumed drowned.

" 'In addition to his wife and father, Mr. O'Berry is survived by his mother, Patricia, and his sisters, Rita and Roxanne. A memorial service will be held for him at a time and place as yet undetermined.' "

Owen Carr put the newspaper clipping down. "That's it."

The judge glanced at the jury. Young Mr. Gutierrez was grinning from ear to ear. The newlywed was staring at the rail in front of her. The computer programmer had his fingers steepled beneath his chin and looked as if he were being called upon to make a decision at that very moment. In the upper row of chairs, the housepainter leaned back with his arms folded, looking as comfortable as if he were watching television; but the caddy and one or two others looked confused.

Down on the floor, Wechsler was pacing back and forth. "To your knowledge, Mr. Carr, has any sign of Mr. O'Berry's death ever been found in or around Lake Winnespowkokee?"

"Winnipesaukee. No, sir. As of yesterday, when I checked with Sergeant LeCount of the state police, there was no record of any evidence of his death other than his disappearance."

"All right. Did you, for purposes of your investigation, assume that Mr. O'Berry had not drowned in Lake . . . whatever it's called?"

"Winnepesaukee. Yes, sir. I and Mr. Gleason took the picture I had taken, Exhibit One, and went to the home of Barbara O'Berry."

"And what did you discover there?"

"I discovered that she had a little baby."

"Yes. But what did you discover with respect to the identity of the person whose picture you had?"

"That it was Mr. O'Berry."

"She identified the picture for you?"

"Yes," said Owen Carr. "Everybody identified the picture. Mrs. O'Berry, her two brothers. They all said it was Bobby O'Berry."

Chris Cage slowly pushed himself to his feet. "Your Honor," he said. "We will stipulate that the person in the picture taken by Mr. Carr is Robert O'Berry, that it is the same Robert O'Berry who married this woman back here in the audience"—he gestured behind himself—"and that Mr. O'Berry did not drown in Lake Winnipesaukee, as he led everyone to believe."

"I ob-ject, Your Honor," Wechsler hollered. "I object to counsel's last characterization."

"Well," said Judge Gifford, trying not to show his surprise at the sudden turn of events, "you don't have to accept the stipulation, then."

Wechsler took off his glasses and used them to extend his pointing arm at his opponent. "I'm wondering, Your Honor, why it is that counsel waited until now to offer his stipulations. He's known what the evidence is for months—"

"Did you send him a request for admissions on those points?" the judge cut in.

Wechsler stopped ranting. "No, I don't think so."

"Then I don't see where you have any room to complain. Want to discuss this outside the presence of the jury?"

"Yes, I do."

"Fine. Freddy, take the jury out."

Two minutes later, with both attorneys leaning their rear ends against the front of their tables, the judge asked Cage why he had waited so long to offer the stipulation.

"Because we had no idea how they would present their evidence," Cage said.

"You had a chance to take discovery, didn't you? Civil attorneys are supposed to know everything about both sides of a case before they start trial."

"Yes, sir. But we didn't know if Reuben was going to try to present the dead boy as some kind of hero, or if he was going to try to hide the fact that he had abandoned his new wife and unborn child—"

"He knew, Judge. We went back to New England and took the depositions of the boy's mother, of his friend Sabatini, even of the guy up at the honeymoon cabin. . . ."

Cage, waiting until he was sure Wechsler was finished, shrugged. "I didn't know if he was going to be able to get the connection before the jury. I've been objecting my tail off—"

"So I've noticed," Wechsler commented.

"—trying to keep some of this stuff out. I mean, if he couldn't show that the guy who was killed was Barbara O'Berry's husband, I'd be that much better off, wouldn't I? But now it's in, so let's establish what a creep the guy was and let's get on with it."

"Eat shit," said a voice in the back.

Everyone before the bench froze. Freddy, Gerta and Myrna were all looking to the first row of the audience. Slowly Chris Cage turned and looked with them. Wechsler threw a quick peek and then studied his pant cuff.

"Who said that?" the judge demanded.

Nobody answered.

The judge motioned to Freddy, who was sitting closest to Barbara O'Berry and her two brothers, and told him to come to the bench. He whispered with his bailiff for a second and then said, "You with the yellow jacket, stand up."

One of the brothers stood.

"What's your name?"

"Terry Cochrane."

"Mr. Cochrane, you so much as open your mouth in my courtroom again and I'll throw you in jail. You understand?"

Terry Cochrane nodded.

"Say it out loud. I'm making a record here, Mr. Cochrane. This court reporter sitting in front of me heard what you said and she took it down. Now I want her to take down your acknowledgment of what I've just told you. So say it out loud, Mr. Cochrane."

"I understand."

"Good. Let's have no further outbursts from anyone. And as for you,

267

Mr. Cage, this family has had to undergo a great tragedy. It appears they've undergone it not once, but twice. They may have to listen to you disagree with their version of what happened and they may have to listen to you disagree with the extent of their loss. But they do not have to listen to you gratuitously insult their loved one. Is that clear?"

"Yes, Judge."

"All right, now this is what I propose. It's almost four o'clock. I think we should send the jury home for the night and you two counsel should sit down and figure out what it is you agree to and how you want the stipulations worded. Then we'll start off fresh tomorrow. Okay? Freddy, bring the jury in and I'll read them the usual instructions about not talking to anybody and so forth. Mr. Cage, Mr. Wechsler, we'll resume at ten. Mr. Carr, you'll return then."

She gave the answer he expected: "Shopping, dear." He asked her where she had shopped. "Oh, here and there, hither and yon." He asked her what she got. "Oh, nothing much. But I saw some beautiful things." He asked her why she didn't buy anything and she laughed, the notes trilling together. Finally he asked about Peter. "I don't think I've seen him at all," she said. "He was still asleep when I went out and he was gone when I came home." Giff wanted to know where he went and Jeanine didn't have much of an answer for that one, either: "Wherever boys that age go, I suppose."

"Like in *Pinocchio*, is that what you mean?" he called to her as she busied herself in the kitchen.

"That's right, dear," she called back, but he knew she was not really paying attention.

He poured himself another Scotch and sat down to watch the evening news. A wife who spent her days shopping for nothing and a grown son who spent his nights going nowhere. He might as well be living in a boardinghouse.

268

CHAPTER FOUR

Could it be, or was his mind playing tricks on him? Had the Cochrane brothers actually switched sport coats? The one with the hair and the flat nose had worn the yellow coat yesterday. Surely. That was how Freddy had identified him when Giff had asked who had cursed. But today the balding one had it on, and Terry had on the red and gray check that his brother had worn yesterday. And there was the Irish kid, back once again, this time sitting behind the Cochranes. What was his interest?

The Irish kid caught him looking and smiled. The judge averted his eyes and looked at the attorneys. "Gentlemen, are you ready?"

With all the jurors in their assigned places, the judge took up the paper that Cage had handed him earlier. "Ladies and gentlemen," he said, "the attorneys for both sides have met together and agreed on certain facts. You are to treat these facts as having been established and you are to make your decisions in this case in light of these facts, if you find them relevant. They are as follows: One, that the person depicted in Exhibit One is, or was, Bobby O'Berry; two, that Bobby O'Berry was legally married to Barbara O'Berry; and three, that Bobby O'Berry disappeared on his wedding night and was declared missing and presumed drowned after having last been seen swimming in Lake Winnis-pesky in New Hampshire.

"Is that the sum of your stipulations, counsel?"

They agreed it was.

The judge looked over the stipulations curiously and wondered who they benefited. Cage had thrown away a possible defense of mistaken identity, but he had established that the decedent had abandoned his wife and unborn child. Still, that would have come out anyhow. Had he kept pushing Wechsler, kept challenging him, the best Wechsler could have hoped to do was establish that Bobby O'Berry had faked his own drowning and run away to California. And there was always the chance that the jury would not have believed him. Maybe they wouldn't have believed O'Berry had survived his little swim, or that he was the same person whose body had been viewed by Owen Carr. From what Giff could see in the file, there was not going to be any production in evidence of the actual body, nor was there going to be any matching of fingerprints or other identification. No, he would have to give the advantage to Wechsler on this one. In the background, Wechsler was speaking.

"Good morning, Mr. Carr," he said, just as if he had not spent half the day's waking hours reviewing his testimony with him. "Once you had identified the body as being that of Bobby O'Berry, what did you do next in your effort to find out what had happened to him?"

"Well, what I had learned at McGuppers was that Mr. O'Berry had been seen talking at length to a well-dressed man, that the well-dressed man had given him directions to—"

"Your Honor."

"Yes, Mr. Cage?"

"Allowing this man to testify as to the course and scope of his investigation is one thing. But this is blatant hearsay testimony which, even if you think it fits within a hearsay exception, should be excluded as inherently unfair under Evidence Code section three fifty-two. I mean, this man says somebody else told him that somebody else said something to somebody else. That is inherently unreliable testimony, Your Honor, and whether it is offered for the truth of the matter or not, it stands a very real chance of prejudicing this case in that it could lead people to believe it's the truth. The fact that this man claims he was doing some sort of job doesn't make what somebody told him that somebody else said any more reliable."

The judge looked at Wechsler for rebuttal.

"Look, Judge, we could take this man off the stand temporarily and put the bartender on in his place, if that's what Mr. Cage wants."

Cage said, "I don't know if that's going to cure the hearsay. It just reduces it."

The judge said to Wechsler, "You got the bartender here now?"

"Out in the hallway."

"Well, let's see what he has to say. Mr. Carr, you may step down for the moment. Wait outside and we'll call you when it's time to resume the stand."

Carr left and was replaced by a short-legged, barrel-chested, bearded young man who had his sunglasses perched on top of his head. "Hi," said the young man after he had been sworn in and Wechsler had said good morning.

The judge, without looking at him, said, "Take your sunglasses off," and the witness slapped around his head until he found them. The jury laughed lightheartedly.

The witness identified himself as being Arnold Gross, also known as Goose. He said he had worked as a bartender at McGuppers for three years, that he was a college graduate, and that he was twenty-eight years old.

Yes, he recognized Owen Carr as the man who had just walked out of the courtroom. Mr. Carr had come into his bar one afternoon and asked him if he recognized an individual in a photograph Mr. Carr had with him. Yes, that was the photograph, Exhibit One. And yes, he recognized the person depicted. He was somebody who had been in the bar just a couple of nights previous to Mr. Carr. Big, tall, good-looking guy. Goose had been afraid he might be a troublemaker, the way he kept looking around the place, and Goose had kept a special eye on him. But no, he wasn't a troublemaker at all. In fact, he spent most of his time drinking beer with and talking with a shorter man in a three-piece suit. Yes, Goose saw that other man in the courtroom here today, and he pointed to Leigh Rossville.

Did they involve Goose in their discussions? Well, not really, but the big one did ask him for a pen and paper so he could write down directions. He didn't remember when he asked, but he was sure it was to write down directions. Where to? To Tranton Park. That much he was sure of, because after the shorter guy had gone, the guy in the picture asked him if Tranton Park was a place where rich people lived and Goose thought that was a real strange question to ask. What did he say? He said it had to be a place where rich people lived, because that was where Roarke Robinson had just bought a house.

Goose finished his direct testimony looking rather pleased with his deductive ability. Cage, who hadn't objected to any of Wechsler's questions, got to his feet for cross-examination.

"Mr. Gross . . ."

"Yes?"

"Goose . . ."

271

"Yes, sir?"

"How did you get that name . . . Goose?"

"I don't know. 'Cause I look like a goose, I guess."

Cage waited until the laughter died down. Then, his face drawn in serious lines, he said, "Isn't it because you're in the habit of going around goosing girls?"

There was a distinct silence for a second or two and then Wechsler was screaming, "Outrageous. He should be censured, Your Honor."

"Both of you," the judge said, thrusting his thumb in the air, "come up to the bench."

The judge waited until their faces were looming over the high edge of his desk and then he said, "What the hell kind of question was that, Mr. Cage?"

"It goes to his credibility, Judge. I'm trying to establish if this man is a practical joker. Let me just get the answer to my question and then you can decide where it goes from there."

The judge thought about it. "I'm going to let it go this time, Cage. But don't push your luck on questions like that. You hear me?"

The lawyers went back to their battle stations. The judge told the witness to answer.

"No," said Gross. "It wasn't like that at all. I went up to Chico State, see, and my older brother was there before me. His nickname was Goose, so everybody who knew him started calling me Goose, too."

"Goose Two, huh?" said Cage.

"Yeah. I mean no. Goose, also."

"So tell me, Goose Gross, when was the last time you saw Mr. Rossville? Saw him in person, I mean, prior to coming here for trial."

"I just saw him that one time."

"Just that one time. And would you have remembered him at all if Mr. Carr hadn't come into your bar asking about him?"

"Objection," said Wechsler. "Calls for speculation."

"Sustained."

"All right, then. Did you remember him at all—Mr. Rossville, I mean—between the time you saw him . . . the one and only time you saw him . . . and the time Mr. Carr came in and asked about him?"

"Well, obviously I remembered him—"

"Had you thought about him at all since the time he had left your bar?"

"No."

"Do you remember what he was wearing when he was in your bar?"

"A three-piece suit and a silk tie."

"What color suit?"

"Don't remember that."

"No. Well, were you able to describe him to Mr. Carr . . . other than saying he was in a three-piece suit and a silk tie?"

"No, I don't think so."

"Mr. Carr asked you to describe him, didn't he?"

"Yeah, I guess."

"And you couldn't."

"Just the suit."

"But you come here today and you recognize Mr. Rossville right away, a year and a half after the only time you ever saw him."

"Yes."

"You recognize the man who is sitting here . . . in a three-piece suit . . . at the defendant's table. . . . The man who's on trial?"

Goose pointed, but his arm did not extend all the way. "Yes. That man."

"You ever remember me being in your bar, Mr. Gross?"

The witness hesitated. He glanced at Wechsler in confusion, and Wechsler, clearly struggling to come up with an objection, jammed a pencil into his mouth. "I don't know," said the witness. "You look kind of familiar."

"Do you recall what I was wearing anytime you saw me before?"

"I don't know that I ever did see you before," replied the witness, and he looked at Wechsler for approval of his clever avoidance of an obvious trick question.

"Ah, Mr. Gross . . ."

"Yes, sir?"

"I took your deposition, didn't I?"

The witness's face fell. "Oh, yeah."

"What was I wearing that day?"

After a moment Mr. Gross admitted that he could not remember. Mr. Cage, shaking his head, told him he had nothing further.

Owen Carr resumed the stand. He said that after he had been informed that Bobby O'Berry had asked about Tranton Park, he went to that neighborhood and began his own house-to-house investigation. He

273

did this by conducting a survey. He told each person to whom he spoke that he was trying to ascertain the needs and interests of the people of Tranton Park.

"And were you, really, trying to ascertain the needs and interests of the inhabitants of Tranton Park, Mr. Carr?" Wechsler asked, his voice brimming with confidence.

"Yes, I was."

"For what purpose?"

"For the purpose of trying to determine if those needs and interests would provide any clues as to who Bobby O'Berry was visiting and what he was doing."

"Did you tell anybody you were looking for clues?"

"Mr. Lane. He was the last person I surveyed. Oh, and Mrs. Robinson was present, too, as I recall."

"Did you lie to anybody about what you were doing on your survey?" Wechsler made the word "lie" seem a euphemism for excrement.

"No."

"Well, what were you looking for in your survey?"

The old man nodded as though he had been waiting for the question. "For example, in a roundabout way I was hoping to find out what people were doing on the night Mr. O'Berry was killed. Whether there were any parties, that sort of thing. I was trying to find out if there were any sportsmen in the neighborhood who might have had access to the type of weapon that brought about Mr. O'Berry's death. I was trying to find out if anybody had any interest in motorcycles, because I knew Mr. O'Berry had one. Things like that."

"You mentioned the weapon. Did you have any idea as to what kind of weapon caused Mr. O'Berry's fatal injury?"

"Yes, sir. By the size and shape of the entrance and exit holes, by the fact that there were no other discernible wounds on the body, I initially assumed that it was an arrow or some sort of spear or crossbow bolt. Something like that."

"Objection," called out Cage. "No foundation. Calls for speculation. This man hasn't been certified as an expert witness qualified to give his opinion as to the source of wounds."

The judge looked to Wechsler for a response. Wechsler looked at some papers. "Your Honor," he said, "we have the autopsy report and we have the autopsy surgeon standing by."

The judge asked, "Who is the autopsy surgeon?"

"Dr. C. K. Richards."

Giff nodded. "And is he here in the courthouse?"

"No, but he's just across the street and could be here shortly."

The judge looked at the courtroom clock high on the wall above the jurors' heads. It was not yet time for a break. He said to Wechsler, "Do you need Dr. Richards to get the autopsy report into evidence?"

"Not if Mr. Cage will stipulate to its admissibility."

"Have you seen the autopsy report, Mr. Cage?"

"I have, Your Honor."

"Any problems with its authenticity?"

"Ah, no. Not really."

"Any reason why it can't be admitted at this time so that we don't have to keep taking this witness off and putting him back on again?"

"Judge, I just don't want this man testifying as to what caused the holes in the decedent's neck. I don't believe he's qualified to do it."

"He wasn't, Judge," Wechsler whined. "He was just testifying as to why he went around asking questions about certain kinds of weapons."

Giff suddenly felt irritated with both lawyers. "The autopsy report will be admitted. . . ."

"Exhibit Five," sang the courtroom clerk.

"Mr. Carr may make reference to it if he has relied upon it, but he is not to give testimony as to his own opinion of what weapon was used and the jury is instructed that it is not to assume that any assumption made by Mr. Carr in his investigation was fact. All right? Let's get on with it, gentlemen."

Wechsler, wearing a contemplative look, asked, "Were you able to find out if anybody in Tranton Park owned a bow and arrow?"

"Nobody I asked knew anybody who owned a bow and arrow."

"Objection. Hearsay. Move that the answer be stricken as not being responsive to the question."

The judge thought about it. "He's right, it seems to me, Mr. Wechsler." He turned to Mr. Carr. "Answer the question yes or no, if you can."

The question was read back by the court reporter. Carr stared at the floor. "Well, I can only tell you that from everything I was able to find out, nobody in Tranton Park—"

Cage interrupted him, drowning out the last of his words. "There he goes again, Your Honor. If he can only testify as to what various people told him about various other people, then the answer is clearly 'No. I was not able to find out if anybody in Tranton Park owned a bow and arrow.'"

"The answer will be read as 'no,' " the judge said.

Wechsler asked for a recess.

Giff finished his pipeful of Borkum Riff, swallowed the last of his coffee, and told Myrna to tell Freddy to get the jury. He stood up and buttoned his robe, wondering why it was that Jeanine was not home now. It was only eleven o'clock in the morning. And why hadn't Peter answered the phone? Surely he had come in by now. Was he asleep in that foul-smelling dungeon of his? There was an extension down there and the answering machine did not kick on until the phone rang half a dozen times. Even Peter should have been able to pick it up by then.

Giff opened the door to the courtroom expecting to see the jury in the box and expecting to hear Freddy call out the familiar "All rise." But the jury was not there and Freddy still stood with his hand on the door leading to the jury room. He was looking to the back of the court, where Reuben Wechsler was gesticulating wildly to a tight circle of people including Owen Carr, the two Cochrane brothers, and the grieving young widow.

"Freddy," said the judge sternly.

Freddy jumped.

"Of these weapons which you believe could have caused the wounds you saw in the body of young Mr. O'Berry, were you, Mr. Carr, able to ascertain if anyone in Tranton Park owned any of them?"

"Yes, Mr. Wechsler," the old man said, resting one hand on the rail in front of him. "I wasn't able to find out if anybody owned a bow and arrow or a crossbow or a conventional-type spear, but I was able to find two people who owned a spear gun of the type used in underwater diving."

"And who are those two people, Mr. Carr?"

"That was Mr. and Mrs. Rossville," he said, looking directly at them.

"In your survey, did you interview either Mr. or Mrs. Rossville?"

"Yes, sir. I interviewed both."

"When?"

"Well, I interviewed Mr. Rossville the first time at his door on Saturday, the week following Mr. O'Berry's death."

"And Mrs. Rossville?"

"Two days after that. At her travel agency."

"When did you start your investigation . . . Strike that . . . your survey?"

"On the Tuesday morning following Mr. O'Berry's death."

"Why didn't you talk to the Rossvilles sooner?"

"I tried. There was nobody ever home at their house between Tuesday and Saturday."

"How do you know? How many times did you try?"

"About three."

"About three. And when you finally caught up with Mr. Rossville, did he tell you where he had been?"

"Objection. Hearsay."

"Or what he'd been doing?" shouted Wechsler over the objection.

"Objection. I had an objection, Your Honor."

"Withdraw the question," declared Wechsler with a flourish. "I have nothing further of this witness."

The announcement seemed to take Cage by surprise. His smooth jaw tensed. His blue eyes flicked to the clock. The judge looked up from the book in which he was noting the time at which Wechsler's direct examination had ended, and said with exaggerated patience, "Mr. Cage, do you have any questions of this witness?"

Cage tugged at the knot in his tie, glanced disinterestedly at a note handed him by Leigh Rossville, and began, "Mr. Carr, how many houses are there in Tranton Park?"

"Thirty-six."

"And how many did you call upon in the course of conducting your survey?"

"All of them."

"Oh, you did?" Cage said, his voice rising in wonderment. "You called upon the Artinians, did you?"

"I called upon them. They wouldn't talk to me."

Impressed by the old man's unflappability, Giff took a moment to examine him closer. He was wearing a slightly out-of-date brown suit, a brown-striped white shirt that could have used some collar stays, cordovan shoes, and brown socks that bunched around his ankles instead of staying up on his calves where they belonged. His tie was more than a little too wide and, with its brown, yellow and green floral pattern, more than a little flamboyant, but it somehow enhanced the air of genuineness which the man had about him.

The witness noticed the judge staring at him and he glanced up, but he showed no more interest than a subway rider who just happened to

277

see an overhead poster for Chiclets gum. His liver-spotted hands were folded neatly in his lap, his back was curved into the arch of the chair, and he sat as though he were a guest at tea, a participant in small talk and polite conversation.

With a sudden sense of alarm, Giff realized that Chris Cage was not aware of what he was up against in this seemingly harmless old man. Giff himself did not know the source of his own feeling of recognition, but he did not question it. After almost eighteen years on the bench, he was confident of his instincts in sizing up witnesses and he knew, as surely as he knew his own name, that Owen Carr was the person who was really running this case. He leaned a little further forward, anxious to get just that much closer to the drama.

Cage, one arm crossed in front of his stomach so that he could support his opposite elbow while he held his fingers to his cheek, stood behind his table and said, "So, Mr. Carr, how many other households in Tranton Park were you unable to interview?"

"I interviewed thirty-one out of thirty-six."

"Well, isn't it possible, Mr. Carr, that there was at least one person in at least one of the houses you didn't get to who was, say, an avid crossbow hunter or bow-and-arrow hunter, or even underwater fisherman?"

"No."

Giff turned his face toward Cage, waiting for him to stick his head into the trap that the old man was setting for him. How do you know? Giff was sure he was going to ask; and then the door would be open to all sorts of hearsay that the old man would be able to relate. Except it didn't happen. Chris Cage stood as still as a statue, and then he smiled enigmatically and sat down.

CHAPTER FIVE

"I don't understand it," Giff said, scooping more rice onto his plate and covering it with the ersatz Chinese amalgamation of beef and beans and celery and water chestnuts that Jeanine had whipped up in the wok their daughter Donna had given her for a sixtieth-birthday present. "The whole thing is screwy, if you ask me."

The wok was nothing Jeanine had wanted. She was no fan of Chinese food and was certainly not very adventurous when it came to cooking. But the wok, even though in all likelihood purchased on the spur of the moment at a Macy's overstock sale, had been a gift from her child and so it was kept in a place of honor and dutifully hauled out from time to time.

Jeanine took the serving bowl from her husband and ladled a few of the more select morsels of beef onto her son's plate. "Why's that, dear?" she asked.

Peter, for his part, sat crossways to the table, resting his ear in the palm of one hand while a cigarette burned unnoticed between the fingers of the other.

"First of all, it's a civil murder case without an attendant criminal case. Whoever heard of such a thing?"

"Not me," Jeanine said.

"Secondly, it involves Reuben Wechsler, and any case that involves Wechsler has got to be screwy. You gonna eat, Peter, or are you just going to sit there ruining my view?"

"Hush, Roger, he's thinking. Aren't you, Peter?"

"What's he got to think about? More importantly, what's he got to think with?"

"Roger. Don't start that again." Jeanine turned toward her son.

279

"Come on, Peter, pull up to the table and eat while the food is still hot."

They ate in silence for a while, Giff's eyes on Peter, Peter's eyes on his plate, Jeanine's eyes on the center of the table. Eventually Giff began to talk again. "But the funny thing is, Wechsler's putting on a relatively straightforward case. He's got nothing but circumstantial evidence against these defendants, but he's presenting it methodically and reasonably, and if you follow what he's doing, it all hangs together. It doesn't quite make sense, maybe, but it all hangs together."

Jeanine buttered a piece of sourdough bread. "Why doesn't it make sense?" she asked, and put the buttered bread on Peter's plate.

"You've got to see the people he's after. Rossville: remember I told you—"

"Yes. Old Leigh Rossville's son. But rich people can commit murder just like anybody else can, can't they?" To Peter she said, "Do you need a fresh glass of milk?" She touched the one he already had. "Has yours grown too warm?"

Giff curled his lip. "Of course they can. But the question is, why would these two people, of all rich people, if that's the way you want to look at it, murder this particular boy? Young Leigh, Leigh junior, the one who's on trial, has everything in the world going for him. He's a partner in a major law firm, he's good-looking, he's got a home in Tranton Park, his wife is beautiful— You should see her in that court. Tasteful, attractive, expensive outfits, all nicely tailored, all subdued. She never says a word, never looks at anybody but the witness. If you didn't look at her you wouldn't even know she was there. But when you do look, when you look closely, she's the picture of understated elegance. That's what she's like, a picture, a painting on somebody's wall that you pass by a half-dozen times before you happen to see how exquisite it really is." Giff stopped, slightly embarrassed at finding himself speaking with such ardor.

But Jeanine was more interested in what Peter was drinking. "You prefer ice water, honey? There's still some beer in the fridge, if you want that."

"You're not listening, Jeanine. I feel as though I'm talking to myself."

"I am so. You were telling me how fabulous Mrs. Rossville is, only it sounds to me as though her attorney has her well in hand. Presenting her as the silent young sophisticate who couldn't possibly have done what she's accused of."

Giff wiped his mouth with his napkin and assessed the food remaining, trying to decide if he needed another serving. "Maybe," he said. "But that's another screwy thing. The defense attorney is this Chris Cage you've heard me mention before. Young guy, comparatively speaking. He could talk the leaves off the trees when he wants to. Eloquent, witty, good-looking . . . that whole side of the table is good-looking. I mean, from what I saw of Chris Cage the last time he tried a case before me, that's his strength. He stands up there and he smiles at all the women jurors, his cornflower blue eyes twinkling boyishly for all the older ones and sexily for all the younger ones—and at the same time he comes off as not too threatening to the male jurors. I mean, his eyes twinkle at them, too, in a conspiratorial sort of way. You know what I'm trying to say?"

"Oh, yes." Jeanine took the decision out of Giff's hands and put the remainder of the wok food on his plate.

"But," Giff said, "this trial's been going on for days now, and so far Cage has shown about as much charm as a water buffalo. You'd think he's the one on trial, for God's sake. Which, in a sense, he may very well be. I mean, he's left the firm he was with and he seems to be devoting himself exclusively to this case— Peter, Jesus, don't light another cigarette until I'm done with my dinner, okay? First day, I look at the trial brief, all of a sudden Cage is operating out of his house, if you can believe that. I don't know. I'd love to get the story on this whole thing."

"Well, I'm sure you will, Roger. After all, that's the whole purpose in having trials, isn't it?"

Giff chewed what he had put in his mouth. "Supposedly," he said. He swallowed. "I don't know what the hell's coming out of this one. I see Wechsler's story unfolding and I see it being this masterpiece of detective work by this private investigator named Carr, who looks like a slovenly old bum but who seems to be a degree or so smarter than all the rest of us put together.

"Wechsler puts on Carr, first witness. Carr tells about seeing the body, traces him to a bar in the City, and from there to Tranton Park. Wechsler puts on the autopsy surgeon, old C. K. Richards—remember him?"

"Oh, sure. How's his wife, Bernice?"

"I didn't ask, Jeanine. It wasn't relevant."

"A bit tubby last time I saw her. I hope she lost some weight."

"You want to hear what C.K. had to say, or not?"

"Yes, of course. I always wonder what such a cherubic-looking man

281

could be doing cutting up bodies and things." Her shoulders twitched. "Oooh, it gives me the shivers just thinking about it."

"How about you, Peter, you want to hear?"

Peter said, "Yuh," and slouched over his dinner.

Giff grunted in satisfaction at having gotten a response. Then, deftly clearing a space between two teeth with his thumbnail, he said, "C.K. gets on and identifies the holes he observed in the neck of the deceased. Describes them, draws little pictures of them. He says, 'The remarkable thing about these holes is that there is nothing in or around them. No residue left behind by whatever caused them. Therefore,' he says, 'I can rule out death by gunshot. The holes were not made by a bullet. Plus,' he says, 'in addition to there being no powder marking, the fact that there is no grease or dirt around the borders means that in all likelihood these holes were not made by anything organic like a wooden arrow. Something,' he says, 'passed through these holes, caused extensive hemorrhage and brought about rather sudden death. This something was then removed from the neck, from the two holes, without causing any additional ripping or tearing of the skin.' "

The lecturing, somewhat skeptical tone Giff had been using suddenly changed. He grinned and looked around the table. "What," he asked his wife and son, "do you think it was?"

"Well, I'm sure I don't know," said Jeanine. "What do you think, Peter?"

"A rocket."

Giff's grin faded. "A rocket," he repeated sadly.

"Was that it? Was it a rocket?" said Jeanine, clapping her hands.

"No, it was not a rocket. What Wechsler did was he pulled out a spear from a spear gun." Giff spread his arms. "About thirty-six inches at least. At the end it's got this tip, looks like a sharpened bullet. Screws right off. The idea being that when you shoot a fish, the speartip goes through it and then this little catch comes out on the far side of the fish so that the spear can't slip back the way it went in. You want to get the spear out, you either pull it all the way through or you unscrew the tip and pull the shaft back out."

"You're not saying . . ." Jeanine put her hand to her mouth.

Giff nodded. "Wechsler says to him, 'Could this spear have made the holes you observed in the neck of the decedent?' C.K. makes a big show about looking the spear over, inspecting the tip. Then he says, 'Yes, it could. In fact, I believe those holes were made by a weapon very much like this.' 'Why's that?' Wechsler says. 'Because,' says C.K., 'I took this weapon down to Groveland Hospital, where they had just done a leg amputation—' "

"Oh, no."

"Oh, yes. '—and I put this spear through that amputated leg and when I was done I had holes of the identical size and shape as those which I had observed in the neck of Robert O'Berry.' "

"Oh, no." Jeanine repeated.

Peter's elbow slipped from the table and his face dropped straight down to within a few inches of his plate. He managed to hold it there while his parents watched in horrified silence, and then he picked up his fork and slowly began shoveling the Chinese food into his mouth.

"Don't slurp, dear," Jeanine said gently.

CHAPTER SIX

Giff was annoyed. He was sure he had had thirty-five dollars in his wallet when he threw it on top of the dresser the night before, and now there were only a five and three ones. He hadn't had any ones. He had had three tens and a five; he would almost bet his life on it. If Jeanine had taken the three tens, why had she put the three ones in there? And why was she always taking his money without telling him? Suppose he had gone to lunch someplace that didn't take credit cards? How would that look, Judge Gifford unable to pay his bill? It was just a good thing he had stopped at the blind man's this morning to get a paper and a sweet roll. It was just a good thing he had opened his wallet and seen what she had done.

Cage was objecting again. Cage was going to set an international trial record for objections. This time he was claiming that the testimony being elicited was irrelevant.

The judge studied the witness. Bert Gould had taken the stand wearing a Hawaiian wedding shirt and old blue jeans covered with intricately embroidered patches. He said he had an MBA from the Wharton School and had been an investment counselor for twelve years, specializing in arranging for and raising venture capital. Now he was a poet. Specializing in computer poetry. Yes, he realized it was a new field, but he felt it was a very viable one. Not only did it produce art for its own sake; it also could prove scientifically beneficial. If we could teach machines the feelings of words, the nuances, the connotations, then we would be taking a major step forward in our efforts to make machines think—as opposed to reproduce.

The judge said, "I agree. I think this testimony is objectionable, Mr.

Wechsler. What's the witness got to say about the matters at hand, that's what I want to know."

Wechsler said to the witness, "Mr. Gould, where were you on the night of March three of last year?"

Gould caressed his reddish beard and studied the ceiling. "That's the night Marietta and I returned from Maui, I believe."

"What were you doing in Maui, Mr. Gould?"

"We were, essentially, reexamining our lives. It was, in some ways, a transcendental experience for us."

Mr. Gutierrez in the front row of the jury box snickered. Gould's response was to smile serenely at him. Mr. Gutierrez tapped his fingers on the arms of his chair and looked away.

Visibly annoyed with this little exchange, Wechsler walked directly over to the jury box, did a smart about-face, and addressed the witness in a very loud voice. "Mr. Gould, what activities did you and your wife engage in while you were in Maui?"

"Oh," Gould said offhandedly, "the usual beach things."

Wechsler, his voice still booming, said, "Did you snorkel, Mr. Gould?"

"Snorkel? Why, yes, I believe we did."

"And where did you get the snorkeling equipment, Mr. Gould?"

"Well, we have our own, Marietta and I."

Wechsler's fists clenched at his sides. "But then, back then, whose equipment were you using?"

Gould looked puzzled. He rolled his eyes toward the ceiling.

"Do you want me to read from your deposition to refresh your recollection, Mr. Gould?"

"Why, no, I don't think that will be necessary. I was just trying to think. . . ."

"You borrowed it from the Rossvilles, didn't you, Mr. Gould?"

"That time? Well, yes, I guess we could have."

"You in fact traded the use of that equipment for use of your video camera, didn't you?"

Gould put a finger alongside his face and said, "Yes, I believe we did."

"And that was masks and snorkels and fins, wasn't it?"

"Yes, I suppose it was."

"And they not only borrowed a camera, but they also borrowed a tripod, didn't they?"

"Yes, I guess they did."

285

"And when did you return those masks and snorkels and fins and get back your video equipment from the Rossvilles?"

"I don't know."

"It was not the night you came home, was it?"

"No."

"Nor the following day?"

"Um . . . I don't think so."

Wechsler, his breathing tight, his temple throbbing, wheeled around and went back to his seat. Just before sitting down, he fired off one more question. "So as far as you know, Mr. and Mrs. Rossville still had your video camera and tripod on the night of March three?"

Bert Gould said, "What do any of us really know?"

She took the stand in the afternoon. A vision of loveliness in a jonquil-yellow dress with just a touch of black at the cuffs and the neck and on the buttons that ran down her front. She wore no jewelry except her wedding ring. Her heels were medium in height, but almost businesslike in appearance. She took her seat coolly and looked at no one other than her questioner. Had she looked at the judge, she would have received a smile of assurance, but her eyes never strayed.

Catherine Rossville. Age thirty-six. One hundred twenty Tranton Park Lane, Tranton Park, California. She lived there with her husband. No children. They had lived there almost nine years.

Self-employed. Travel agent. She owned the agency. Venture Forth Travel in Tranton. Yes, she issued tickets to herself and her husband from time to time. Yes, they had been to Cozumel together on several occasions. Yes, the tickets Mr. Wechsler was showing her had been issued by her agency in the names of her and her husband. Yes, they were for travel on Sunday, March fourth. Yes, they had been issued on Sunday, March fourth. It was a spur-of-the-moment decision. Why? Because Saturday the third was her birthday, her thirty-fifth, and midway into their second bottle of champagne they decided the best way for her to embark on middle age was to do something totally spontaneous. Yes, like go to Cozumel.

What had they done there? They had scuba dived, among other things. Equipment? They had their own. Yes, they had loaned equipment to the Goulds. No, they hadn't gotten it back before they flew off. Mr. Wechsler, they had been scuba diving all their adult lives; they had more than one set of snorkels and masks and fins.

Why did they come back on a Friday? Because it had just been a lark to go there in the first place. Her busiest days were on the weekend and she had to get back to the agency.

Last question. Yes? . . . Why, yes, they did trade with Mr. Gould for his videotape equipment.

Last question never means last question to a lawyer; and all the participants in the proceeding acted accordingly as Wechsler continued to appraise Mrs. Rossville from his standing position across the room.

Did you have anybody over your house on the night of your birthday? . . . No, we celebrated alone. . . . Did either of you go out that night? . . . Oh, it's hard to remember. But no, not unless it was to the 7-Eleven or something like that.

Then why, Mrs. Rossville, did you and your husband borrow the Goulds' video camera? . . . Well, originally Leigh wanted it for his tennis game. I was supposed to tape his serve and so forth, so he could see what he was doing wrong. But then we decided on the Cozumel trip, so we never got around to using the camera. . . . Never? . . . Never.

Thank you, Mrs. Rossville. . . . Oh, Mrs. Rossville? Just one thing more . . . Did you happen to tear up some of the carpet in your house shortly after March fourth? . . . Orientals, hmmm? For your birthday . . . Another birthday gift . . . Ah, what room was that? . . . The bedroom, I see. In that case, I guess I really am done.

Mr. Cage? No cross-examination? Fine. Mr. Wechsler, your next witness, please.

Giff rested his Scotch and a splash insecurely on the arm of his overstuffed reading chair, folded his hands behind his head and said, "Today the Colossal Brothers showed up in matching black leather coats with epaulets on the shoulders. They both had long-sleeved knit shirts, one green, one striped, and they looked for all the world like a pair of dockside hoods."

"And what about the girl, dear, their sister?"

"Well, actually, she's kind of . . . what would the word be? Innocent, I suppose. She just sits there looking suitably stunned by the entire proceeding."

Jeanine Gifford was trying to do needlepoint. She kept a frame and pattern jammed between the cushion and arm of her favorite chair and whenever she sat down she would make a few more stitches. She never, ever, sat down just to do the needlepoint, but it was always there when

287

she did sit down. Now, with her eyes on her work, she said to her husband, "And what did she wear?"

The question irritated the judge. He had mentioned the dress of the Cochrane brothers only as a very minor anecdote, not as the preface to a discussion of sartorial splendor in the courtroom. If she wanted to discuss his work with him, she really, by this time, should know what was relevant and what wasn't. Sighing in exasperation, he said, "She's quite heavy and everything she has tends to look the same on her. She's given to wearing those loose blouses that are designed to hide your shape, you know the ones I mean? Those are fine, but then she tends to wear these stretch slacks and she's got a bottom that you could use for a fry stove, it's so big."

"Oh, Giff."

He took a sip of his drink. "Despite all that, she's actually kind of cute. Appealing, I guess you'd say. I think some of the jurors feel sorry for her, the way they keep looking at her. Then they look at her brothers and their eyes sort of shrivel up." Giff shriveled his own eyes, but Jeanine didn't notice.

"Say," Giff said suddenly, "did you take some money out of my wallet this morning?"

Jeanine held up her design and studied it critically. "No," she said. "Why would I do that?"

"Because I know I had thirty-five dollars in there last night and today when I got to the blind man's I only had eight."

"Did you stop at the store on the way to work?"

"Jeanine . . . goddamnit." Giff bit down fiercely on his lower lip and then gulped another swallow of Scotch.

"Yes?" She looked at him with concern.

"You ever feel as though we're living on different planets? I mean, physically we're all here, you and Peter and I—even Donna, when she's around—but we all seem to be functioning in different time zones. You ever notice that?"

"Not really." Jeanine returned to her work. "I think we all get along just fine. I do wish, though, that you would make more of an effort to talk with Peter."

"I do. He never answers."

Jeanine put on her all-will-be-well-in-no-time voice. "I think he's mixed up about what life has to offer him."

"Oh, really? You didn't notice that when he dropped out of Colum-

288

bia after spending fifteen thousand dollars of my money and not getting a single complete grade?"

"New York City wasn't for him. He told you that."

"He told me he was going to go to UC Santa Cruz. Two months after he's supposed to have started there, we get a collect call from La Paz, Bolivia, where the boy has discovered himself stranded without a wallet or a passport."

Jeanine finally put down her needlepoint and focused her attention on her husband. "Those people down there took advantage of him, you know that, Giff. He saw what he thought was going to be a good business opportunity, to go down there and get all those lovely sweaters and bring them back. And then he got sick from the water and those terrible men he was doing business with ripped him up."

"Off. Ripped him off, Jeanine."

"There. You've admitted it. What could a nineteen-year-old boy do when he finds himself sick and broke in a strange country?"

"I think he got rolled while he was curled up with a bottle of beer someplace."

"He calls his family, that's what," Jeanine continued.

"That's the problem with families. You're forced on each other even when you don't have anything else in common."

"Nonsense. I think you and Peter would find you have a lot in common if you would only take the time to sit down and have a talk with him."

"Well, I'm here now, aren't I?" Giff threw up his hands. "I've got the time now. So where is he?"

"He's out, dear."

The fourth day of testimony. Wechsler wanted to call someone named Tricia Van Valkenberg and Cage wanted to have an argument about it. In chambers.

The judge looked around the courtroom. The jury had been sent out. The only people besides the courtroom personnel who were still there were the Rossvilles, the Cochranes, the old man, and the ever-present smiling Irishman. But Cage was insistent. All right, Gerta, bring your machine.

"Unfair surprise," Cage declared when they were set up behind closed doors. "We don't even know who this person is."

"They had a chance to find out, Your Honor. But they never asked about witnesses during discovery."

"We did too."

"That was over a year ago, when we didn't have this witness."

"You're supposed to update answers to interrogatories."

"We are not."

"Gentlemen, would you two cut the crap? You sound like a couple of schoolkids."

"Well, I've about had it with his sneakiness."

"Who you calling a sneak?"

"Hey, cut it out. I won't have this, do you understand me? Next one who starts anything I'm going to find in contempt." The judge glared hard at both attorneys until he was sure he had their compliance. "Now who is she, Mr. Wechsler?" he said.

"She owns Village Videos. It's a videotape rental store patronized by the Rossvilles."

"What's the relevance?"

"It's run like a club. You pay annual membership dues and you're given a club number. Then every time you want to take a tape, they tap your number on a computer and put the name of the tape down next to it: when you took it out, when you brought it back."

"The relevance, Mr. Wechsler. All I've heard so far is a big 'so what?' "

"The computer records show that for ten weeks prior to the third of March, the Rossvilles rented an X-rated movie every Saturday. Returned it every Sunday. The third was a Saturday. It also was Cathy Rossville's birthday. She testified they stayed in that night. But they didn't rent a movie, Judge."

Chris Cage's mouth dropped open and hung that way for effect. "Big deal," he said. "So they watched a few dirty movies. Don't you read the papers? That's what all the Yuppies do when they first get a VCR. Then they get bored with them and they stop."

Wechsler said, "That's a point of argument, Judge. We think this is extremely relevant evidence because it goes to motive. The Rossvilles paint themselves as your average professional suburban couple, when all the time they've got this secret life going on, watching porno movies and doing God knows what other kinds of sexually deviant acts."

Cage bristled. He took a menacing step toward Wechsler, and Wechsler, who was taller but much thinner, turned, snarling, to confront him.

The judge, thrusting himself from his chair, shouted, "Hold it right there," and both attorneys thought better of what they were doing.

"This evidence you have, Mr. Wechsler," the judge said, coming around the desk and positioning himself almost incidently between the two men. "I think it's awfully weak if that's all you've got to prove motive. But that's only my own opinion. If you want to put it in and argue about it, fine. It's certainly going to be left wide open to the type of response Mr. Cage has just given us. But I'm not going to tell either one of you what to put in and what not to. So if Mr. Wechsler still wants it, I'm going to allow it."

"Good," said Wechsler, smiling triumphantly.

"Mr. Cage, you look like you're still having problems."

"Judge, you know the old saying about you can't unring a bell? Well, that's exactly what will happen here. He damns my clients with something that could be offensive to certain members of the jury, regardless of whether it has any relevance to the facts of this case whatsoever. And what if it doesn't have any relevance, Judge? Why should their privacy be invaded in this whole other area? I mean, they can be cleared of the murder charges; that's what this trial's all about. But they're not going to have a chance to be cleared on charges about their sex life. That's just going to remain out there in front of these strangers forever. And their sex life isn't what this case is all about."

"I disagree with you there, counsel," Wechsler snapped. "Their sex life is exactly what this case is all about."

Cage looked at Wechsler. Then he looked at the judge. "I don't know what he's saying."

Judge Gifford retraced his steps and returned to his chair on the other side of the desk. He fixed a troubled expression on his face and looked at Wechsler. "He's got a point there, Reuben."

Wechsler reacted by flinging his hand out in front of him and pulling at his long fingers one at a time as though he were dealing cards. "First," he said, "I show defendants have these sexual proclivities. Second, I show the kinds of movies they were renting—where there was three-way sex, that sort of thing. Third, I show they borrow a video camera *and* a tripod on the one week they don't rent a video movie. Fourth, I show on that same night they bring this stud over to their house—"

"There's no proof he's a stud, Judge," Cage said, interrupting.

"All right," the judge said, cutting off any further argument. "I see what you're both getting at and I'm inclined to agree with Mr. Cage

291

about the unringing of the bell. So for the time being I'm going to re-serve ruling on Miss Van Valkenberg's testimony. At the moment I think it's too speculative to outweigh Mr. Cage's very legitimate con-cerns. But we'll see how plaintiff's case goes and I'll withhold my final decision until after we learn what else Mr. Wechsler has to offer. If you can establish O'Berry was working as some sort of stud, as you call it, Reuben, then the videotape evidence may be relevant after all. If you can't, then I think the dirty movie stuff is too prejudicial to be allowed in. Okay? Now I want the two of you to go take a nice long walk and meet back in the courtroom in fifteen minutes. That's it, let's go off the record.

"We off, Gerta? Good." The judge pointed his finger first at one man and then at the other. "One more thing. Either of you lose your temper again like you did a while ago and you're going to wish to God you hadn't. Got me? You'd better, because so far you're both acting like a couple of douche bags as far as I'm concerned."

CHAPTER SEVEN

"Your mother thinks it would be a good idea if we had a litle talk, Peter. What do you think?"

Peter shrugged. He looked around the living room for escape.

"You want a drink?"

Peter shook his head.

"All right, well, I've got one. I'm just going to sit here and sip on it, smoke my pipe, and try to tell you a few things that have been on my mind. You, you can stand there like you're doing, you can sit down, smoke, get a beer, or walk out. Whatever it is you want."

Peter sat. He sat at first on the very edge of his mother's chair. Then he leaned back into a slouch so that his head was resting halfway up the back cushion.

"You're twenty-one years old now, Peter. Not a very advanced age, to be sure, but an age which is something of a milestone. You're supposed to be assessing your preparation at this point. Wrapping it up, deciding if you've had enough, if you want more, maybe even if you need a rest. It's not the time for irrevocable commitments, but it is the time to make sure you don't get irrevocably shut out of opportunities that may appeal to you later in life."

Giff drew on his pipe. Peter covered his brow with his left hand. Giff decided he had been pontificating and made an effort to shift gears.

"The great thing about being twenty-one"—he smiled—"is that you can afford to try anything. As long as it's a positive effort. For example, you want to start a business venture and you find you don't like it? Well, that's fine. At least you've gained some experience. Say you want to go to graduate school, but you get there and the program is not what you want. No problem. Go do something else. But what you've got to make sure you don't do, Peter, is nothing. You can't do nothing." Giff pointed the stem of his pipe at his son and waited in vain for a reaction.

"Yeah. Right. Okay. Are you with me, Peter? Are you still there? Am I talking to myself?"

"I hear you. You just haven't asked me any questions yet."

"This isn't really a question period. This is a talk. You see, what your mother and I are concerned about is that you didn't really reach the plateau we had hoped you would reach at this age. We thought you'd be in your third year of college. You haven't completed any. You still can, of course, but you're already out of sync. The high jinx, the camaraderie, that most of us experienced by going through school with people of our same age is probably already lost to you. If you came to us and you said, 'Mom, Dad, one more year of school and I'm going to take off for a while. Go skiing in Aspen, surfing in Australia,' I'd say, 'Good, live it up. C'mon back when you've decided what you want to do.' But you, Peter, you haven't earned that right yet. And now, well, you're hardly living it up, are you? So what good is any of this doing anybody? You're not enjoying yourself—" Giff cut himself off before he could say, "and we're not enjoying having you around," but Peter, had he been listening, would have understood the words unspoken.

Giff, shifting in his chair, tried to inject new enthusiasm into his voice. "On the other hand, Peter, not everybody's cut out for going to school, I realize that. Judge Burford's boy dropped out of law school and now he's a carpenter and very happy, I understand. Of course, you've never had any interest in carpentry or working with your hands. But you used to like going camping, so maybe you'd be interested in being a forest ranger or river guide, or something like that." Giff shrugged and drank some more, the ice cubes snapping in his glass.

"The problem I'm having is I can't see that you have any interests in anything anymore, except going out at night and sleeping all day. You don't even seem to have any friends, except the occasional silly cretin who calls up and won't leave his name: 'Duh, Peter there?' and then he hangs up as soon as you tell him no."

Once again Giff had to stop. He could hear the nastiness that had crept into his voice and he needed a moment, and another sip of drink, to eradicate it.

"So all I can do," he said, "is share with you a few of my own life fantasies, the things I would be interested in if I had it to do all over again." Giff pushed his glasses up onto his forehead and leaned back into his chair. "Turn on the TV, go to a movie. There are hundreds of actors out there, thousands of them. Faces and names you've never heard of before. Plenty of them are your age and younger. Sure, they're the lucky ones. For every person you see working, there are ten who aren't. But the point is, some *are* working and all of them had to come from someplace. Somewhere they had to start out in some little theater or school production, maybe they even had to work their way into that. Somewhere they had to show up the first day. At some point they had to learn something they didn't know before, they had to do something they didn't want to do. The good ones survived that first step and passed on to the second. No reason why you couldn't be one of those good ones, Peter, if you only applied yourself. Set your mind to it.

"You could pursue any of these high-profile jobs that people have. The key word there is 'people.' They're all people. They don't spring full-blown into their magic personae. If they can get where they've gotten, no reason you can't do the same."

Giff's pipe had gone out. He propped its bowl in an ashtray, arranging the stem so that the ashes wouldn't spill. "As I look back from the vantage point of my sixty-odd years, I realize that most people fall into their careers in one way or another. They happen to be somewhere or they know somebody doing something and all of a sudden they're working at what's been made available to them rather than what they really wanted to do, until one day they look around and they say, 'I am a teacher,' or 'I am a refrigerator repairman,' or a bartender or a judge or whatever. That can be okay, too. Some people have been very fortunate in becoming, say, a lawyer because their father was a lawyer, or in becoming a waiter because they were short on rent money one month. But what I'm here to tell you, Peter, is that there's another way you can set the course of your life, and that's by deciding what it is you want to do and then, by God, going out and working at it. What I'm saying is that at this stage of your life there's almost nothing that's too farfetched for you. All it takes is effort. All it takes is for you to get out there and try."

Unintentionally, Giff had ended on a high, forceful note that made his speech sound like a locker room pep talk. For a moment he feared that Peter would scoff at him or mock the feeling with which he had spoken. But there was only silence from Peter's corner of the room.

Without his glasses, Giff could just make out that his son's hand was still covering his brow and that he had not moved from the slouch he had assumed several minutes before. A stream of angry thoughts entered Giff's mind, but he said nothing more. Instead, he pushed himself to his feet and, without lowering his glasses, headed for the kitchen to make himself another drink. He chose to interpret Peter's silence as meaning that his son was thinking over what he had just heard. He chose to interpret it that way because if he had discovered Peter had fallen asleep he would have felt compelled to brain the boy.

Friday morning's fight was over Mary Elizabeth Lane. Wechsler wanted to present her testimony by reading from her deposition. He said she suffered from something called agoraphobia and was too ill to come to court and give live testimony. Cage said that she was only a few miles away, well within subpoena range, and that if she was too crazy to appear live, her testimony should not be given any credibility.

"To allow Mr. Wechsler to put some sane, rational person on the stand to read Mrs. Lane's answers from her deposition transcript would add a whole veneer of respectability to what amounts to hallucinatory ramblings by a severely disturbed woman," Cage contended.

"She's not severely disturbed," Wechsler argued back. "She just can't come out of the house."

Cage said, "I know what this woman claimed in her deposition, Judge. The jury is entitled to assess the speaker and not just the speaker's words when a person says the things that she said."

The judge drummed his fingers on the top of his desk. "You," he said, speaking to Wechsler, "you have a statement from this woman's doctor saying she can't come down here to testify in person?"

Wechsler, looking as though he were poised to argue that a doctor's opinion was not the issue, shook his head one time. Then Cage spoke up.

"She doesn't have a doctor. She says right there in her deposition that she hasn't been to any sort of counseling at all."

Wechsler, licking his lips, getting his tongue briefly caught in his mustache, said, "She's so agoraphobic she can't get out to get counseling."

The judge flattened his fingers and brought the palm of his hand down on the desk. "No doctor's report, no excuses. She appears live or her testimony doesn't come in."

Wechsler asked for a recess to see if he could talk her into it.

* * *

The jury was waiting. Cage, with his chin tucked, was sitting with his pen hovering over the black plastic binder that served as his trial book. The judge was looking at Wechsler expectantly.

"Plaintiff calls Leigh Rossville," Wechsler suddenly announced.

The defendant slowly got to his feet, glancing at his counsel for confirmation. Cage smiled and nodded him toward the witness chair.

Rossville was not a large man, but he looked fit and trim and he carried himself well. His hair was graying at the temples and there were crow's-feet at the corners of his eyes and permanent lines in his forehead, but he had an easy, youthful look about him. His mouth, sealed tightly now, had a looseness to it as though it were experienced in the art of grinning. His eyes had a brightness that made the seriousness with which they adhered to Wechsler seem all the more sincere. He looked like the student body president being called upon to explain the sins of his classmates.

Wechsler trotted Rossville through some identification questions and then asked him what he owned for motor vehicles.

"A three-year-old Jaguar and a four-year-old BMW 733."

"Ever own a motorcycle?"

"No."

"Ever ridden one?"

"Sure."

"Were you riding one the night Bobby O'Berry was killed?"

"No."

"Did anyone come to your house riding one that night?"

"No."

"No? No, you did not even see a motorcycle in your driveway that night?"

"No."

"I see." Wechsler looked confused. He looked as though he had boarded a plane to Birmingham and ended up in Binghamton. "Uh, Mr. Rossville, your wife has testified that she did not go out of the house that night—"

"Objection. She said she could have driven to the all-night store."

"And I object to that, Your Honor," Wechsler said, momentarily losing his composure. "She didn't use those words, 'all-night store.' "

"She said the 7-Eleven," the judge said. "Let's move along." But in a corner of his mind he held an inch of admiration for the way Cage had subtly sneaked a new fact possibility before the jury.

297

"Did you go out of the house that night?" Wechsler demanded edgily.

Leigh Rossville shifted slightly in his seat so that he could lean over and put his lips right next to the witness's microphone. "No," he said, and sat back again.

"Did Bobby O'Berry come to your house that night?"

"No."

"Did you ever meet Bobby O'Berry?"

"No."

"No?" Wechsler said, his voice rising in indignation. "Did you hear what Mr. Gross said? On this stand? Under oath?"

"Mr. Gross was wrong," Leigh Rossville said calmly.

"Well, are you denying you've ever been to McGuppers?"

"No. I've been there lots of times."

"Lots of times. Were you there during the week preceding March third?"

"I may have been. I don't remember."

"Is it possible you don't remember meeting Bobby O'Berry there?"

"Objection. Calls for speculation."

"Sustained."

Leaning forward, Rossville said, "I'd like to answer that if I could. If I did meet Bobby O'Berry, I certainly don't remember it. But I most definitely never gave him or anyone else in McGuppers directions to my house."

"Mr. Rossville." Wechsler drew himself up to his full height and paused until he was sure he had the complete concentration of everyone. "Did you kill Bobby O'Berry?"

Once again Leigh Rossville shifted slightly in his chair. He looked at the end of the microphone and then lowered his mouth to it. "No," he said softly, but his voice filled the courtroom. He raised his eyes until they met Wechsler's and the two men held each other's gaze for nearly a quarter of a minute.

"Did you," Wechsler said, his mouth twisting scornfully, "rent any"—and then he came down loudly on the next word—"video movies on the night he died?"

The judge turned to sustain Cage's objection, but none was offered. At that point Wechsler betrayed his own success by looking surprised.

The witness said no. He said it simply.

Wechsler pushed. "Were you in the habit of renting video movies, Mr. Rossville?"

"Not on my wife's birthday," was the prompt reply.

Wechsler stared unseeingly at his notes. "Did you," he said without looking up, "make any video movies that night?"

"Make them?" Rossville's face wrinkled in confusion. "Make them?"

"Make your own, with Bert Gould's video camera?"

The wrinkles of confusion stayed in place long enough for Rossville to look at his wife. Then they gave way to what amounted to a shrug. "No," he said.

Wechsler snapped his notes down to his side. "I have no further questions of this man at this time."

"Mr. Cage?"

"Nothing, Your Honor."

"The witness may be excused."

"Subject to recall, Judge?" Wechsler asked.

"Subject to recall. Mr. Rossville will be here, as, I'm sure, will Mrs. Rossville, throughout the course of the trial."

The defendants, realizing the judge was looking at them, gave brave smiles of confirmation. Right you are. Yes, sir. No doubt about it.

CHAPTER EIGHT

The thought that passed the judge's mind when Mary Elizabeth Lane walked into the courtroom was that the look on Chris Cage's face deserved to be immortalized. If it could have been preserved, it could have taken its place next to the traditional theatrical masks. Comedy, Tragedy, Shock. But Cage quickly regained his composure and even as the judge was watching him he grabbed a pen and began writing feverishly in his trial book. The judge was reminded of a drawing he had once seen of Gladstone penning his letter of resignation to Queen Victoria while Parliament rioted around him over his supplantation by archrival Disraeli. Where had he seen that? It had been on the wall of a London pub famous for its breakfasts. The Albert, was that what it was called?

"Your Honor, plaintiff calls Mary Elizabeth Lane."

She had come in on the arm of her husband, wearing a navy blue suit and carrying white gloves and a white purse. John Clarke had walked her to the swinging gate and then more or less passed her to a beamingly attentive Reuben Wechsler. Before taking a seat in the first row on the side opposite the Cochranes, John Clarke had sought out Judge Gifford's eye and given him a curt and worried nod. The judge had dipped his head in return and then had welcomed Mrs. Lane by name.

She had gotten markedly older in the years since he had last seen her. Surprise, surprise. But it had not been that many years, and surely her hair had never been that gray or her skin that white.

The judge leaned down from his elevated position and said softly, "Anytime you want a break in the proceedings, a drink of water or anything like that, you just let us know."

She ignored him. She stared at Wechsler, silently commanding him to fire away.

"Your name, please?"

"Mary Elizabeth Lane."

"Your address?"

"One two four Tranton Park Lane, Tranton, California."

"Mrs. Lane, is there a one twenty-two Tranton Park Lane?"

Silence.

"I ask that, you see, because Mrs. Rossville testified that she and her husband live at one twenty Tranton Park Lane. Is there a house in between yours and theirs?"

"No."

"Okay. I guess they just left the gap in numbers in case there ever is. In case things get even more crowded in the Bay Area so that we all have to squeeze that much closer together."

It was meant to be taken lightheartedly, but it fell flat. Mrs. Lane stared and her hostility kept the jury from so much as smiling.

"Yes. Well. Mrs. Lane, how long have you lived next door to the Rossvilles?"

"Eight years."

"You know them pretty well?"

"I know them. I know who they are."

"See them in the courtroom today?"

Immediately Chris Cage beckoned both his clients to lean over and talk to him so that none of them was looking directly at Mrs. Lane when she said yes.

"Ah, Mrs. Lane . . . where were you on the night of March third, last year?"

"I was home."

"What were you doing at home?"

Mrs. Lane delivered a visual message before she answered out loud. The visual message told Wechsler that she thought his question was stupid. Then she said, "I fixed dinner for my husband and me. I read a book. I took a bath. I went to bed."

"What were you doing at eleven o'clock?"

"Reading."

"Where?"

"Downstairs. In my living room."

"Does the living room have a window?"

___

301

"Of course. It has many windows."

"Were you sitting in such a way that you could look out one of them?"

"I was sitting next to one of them."

"And where was your husband?"

"He was in his study."

"Is that also in the downstairs portion of your house?"

"It's in the back. Away from the road."

"Did you notice anything outside your window at around this time?"

"Yes."

"What?"

"I noticed a motorcycle go slowly by my house."

"Was that unusual, Mrs. Lane?"

"Yes."

"Why?"

"Because it is a small neighborhood we live in and there is no reason to be on our portion of Tranton Park Lane unless you are going to one of a dozen or so houses, none of which, until recently, has had a motorcycle."

"Someone has a motorcycle now?"

"The Butler boy. Across the street."

"How do you know no one had a motorcycle as of the night in question?"

"Because I am at home a lot, Mr. Wechsler. If there had been a motorcycle in the neighborhood, I would have seen it. I would surely have heard it, just as I see and hear the Butler boy's."

"This motorcycle that you saw on the night of March third—did you see where it went?"

"It turned into the Rossvilles' drive."

"You saw it do that?"

"I saw it."

Wechsler walked up and down, forward and back, across the courtroom. When his journey was finished, he said, "When did you next see the motorcycle?"

"About one o'clock in the morning."

"Where were you then?"

"I couldn't sleep. I was sitting on the lounge in my bedroom, staring out the window."

"Staring in which direction?" Wechsler turned his body while leaving his feet locked in place.

"Toward the Rossvilles."

"And what did you see with respect to this motorcycle?"

"I don't understand the question."

Wechsler stroked his mustache, swirling his fingers to make sure the ends were pointing straight down. "All right. First of all, where is your bedroom located?"

"On the second floor."

"And the window you were looking out—does that face the Rossvilles' house?"

"It does."

"You could see their garage?"

"No."

Wechsler reacted quickly. "But you could see their driveway?"

"Yes."

"At or about one o'clock A.M., could you see the motorcycle in the Rossvilles' driveway?"

"I saw it rolling out of the driveway."

"Rolling . . . You mean being driven?"

"It wasn't making any noise. The person seated on it was pushing it out with his feet."

Wechsler got into a semi-squat and held his fists out in front of him. "You mean there was a person in the seat who was propelling the bike forward by pushing off the ground with his feet?"

"Yes."

Wechsler straightened up and nodded as though it were all suddenly clear to him. "And you could see who this person was?"

"It was Leigh Rossville."

Almost every single juror turned and stared at the defendant. Wechsler gave them a few seconds and then he said, "Did you ever hear the motorcycle start up?"

"No."

"Mrs. Lane, if one were looking for the fastest way out of the subdivision in which you live, and one were leaving the Rossvilles', which direction would one take—left or right?"

"One," she said, heavily emphasizing Wechsler's word, "would turn left and go past our house."

"And what does the road do in front of your house?"

"It slopes downward."

"It goes downhill."

"Yes."

303

"Thank you, Mrs. Lane." He smiled. "Oh, Mrs. Lane . . . did you see any other activity at the Rossville house after you saw the motorcycle leave?"

"Yes. A short time after that, I could tell the garage door opened because the end of the driveway was suddenly bathed in light. A few moments later the Rossvilles' Jaguar drove out. Was driven out."

"Had you ever seen the Jaguar driven by the Rossvilles before?"

"Of course."

"Did you notice anything different about it this time? As compared to the other times you had seen it, I mean."

"Yes."

"What?"

"The trunk appeared to be very low, as though—"

Cage burst to his feet. "She's answered the question. Your Honor. Anything else is pure speculation."

The judge agreed. "That's sufficient, Mrs. Lane. You've answered the question."

She pressed her lips together angrily and there was an instant of almost explosive tension. The jurors, mystified, looked on. The judge and the attorneys waited for some cue to tell them how to respond. And then the moment passed and everyone relaxed.

"That's all I have. Thank you very much, Mrs. Lane," Wechsler said, and sat down.

Mary Elizabeth Lane gathered up her purse and gloves and prepared to leave the stand. The judge reached out his hand to try to direct her to stay put, but still she was halfway to her feet before she noticed Chris Cage standing in front of her, his hands stuck casually in his trouser pockets.

"Mrs. Lane?"

"Yes?" she said in the same voice she would have used if Cage had been a panhandler asking her for a quarter.

"As you know, I represent Mr. and Mrs. Rossville, and there are a few questions I'd like to ask you, too."

The judge could see Mrs. Lane look to her husband and he could see John Clarke fold his arms across his chest and slide the base of his spine away from the back of the bench on which he was sitting. Mrs. Lane continued to clutch her purse and her gloves, holding them to one side as though she would not be detained long. "Yes?" she said again, resuming her seat.

"You, ah, you didn't tell us who it was you believe you saw riding up to the Rossvilles' house at about eleven o'clock in the evening of March three."

"I don't know who it was."

Cage walked to the clerk's desk and whispered to Myrna. He returned to the witness stand and handed Mrs. Lane what Myrna had handed him. "This is Exhibit One, a picture of Mr. O'Berry. Is he the person you saw drive up on the motorcycle?"

She studied the picture for an inordinately long time. "I don't know," she said, holding it out to Cage to take back.

Cage turned and walked away from her without taking it. "Well, what do you know about the person riding the motorcycle? Can you tell us anything about what he . . . or she . . . looked like?"

"It was a he, Mr. Cage, I can tell you that."

"Could it have been Mr. Rossville?"

"No."

"Why not?"

"It just wasn't, that's all."

"It was a man, but it wasn't Mr. Rossville, and you don't know if it was Mr. O'Berry. Is that all you can tell us about the motorcycle rider you saw at about eleven o'clock?"

"He was riding very slowly, as though he were looking for an address."

"That's your own impression, is that right? That he was looking for an address?"

"Yes."

"But you couldn't see what he looked like?"

"It was dark, Mr. Cage," she snapped.

"Of course it was, Mrs. Lane."

A panicky look entered Mrs. Lane's eyes. "I want a drink of water," she said.

The judge abruptly stopped the proceedings.

The jury had gone out and come back. During its recess the judge had stayed in the courtroom and watched the mingling of the various people involved.

John Clarke Lane had gone immediately to his wife's side and put his arm around her shoulders. She, with her purse slung over her wrist, her white gloves caught in the crook of her hand between thumb and fore-finger, both hands gripping a white paper cup full of water, had asked him to take her to the hallway.

Wechsler had gone to the back of the room and spoken with Owen Carr. After a minute they were joined by the young Irishman, who approached them tentatively, his pen and paper in hand. Soon Wechsler was speaking animatedly and the Irishman was rapidly jotting down notes.

At the defendants' table, Cage and the Rossvilles sat silently. None of them talking, none of them writing. They barely moved until Freddy brought back the jury, and then all three sat up a little bit straighter.

"Freddy," said the judge, "get the witness, would you, please?"

Freddy went to the door and stuck his head out. He looked both ways and then glanced back at the judge. The judge waved his hand at him and Freddy left the courtroom. Time passed. The jurors began to stir and then they began to whisper among one another.

"Mr. Wechsler," the judge said, and then the door opened and Freddy and the Lanes reentered. Head down, still holding on to her gloves, Mrs. Lane walked to the stand and took her seat.

The judge nodded at Cage.

"Are you all right, Mrs. Lane?" Cage said with great concern.

"Yes," she said, dragging out the s sound and finishing the word with clenched teeth.

"You were telling us how dark it was at eleven o'clock. It was still dark at one o'clock, wasn't it?"

"Yes." Same sibilance. Same clenched teeth.

"It was dark, you couldn't see the Rossvilles' garage, but you could see their driveway. Could you see all of it?"

"No."

"No. Did you know there was a motorcycle in that driveway . . . I mean, could you see a motorcycle in that driveway before you saw it move at, ah, about one o'clock?"

"No."

"No. Let's see now. It was one o'clock in the morning. You were sitting up in your chair in your bedroom looking out the window. Where was your husband, Mrs. Lane?"

"I assume he was asleep."

"Didn't you know?"

"No."

"Why was that?"

"Objection. Irrelevant."

The judge tilted back his head and held out his hand to keep counsel quiet while he thought about it. The gesture did not work with Wechsler.

"I don't think there is any need to invade marital privacy, Judge. This witness—"

But Cage, raising his voice, shouted over him. "Mark those words for future reference, Your Honor."

Gerta, the court reporter, called out that she couldn't record both men at once.

The judge said, "I'm going to allow the question."

Wechsler threw up his hands and sat down.

Cage stared at Mrs. Lane until she said, "My husband and I have different rooms."

"Different bedrooms?"

"Yes."

"And you in your bedroom were sitting up, looking out the window, looking at part of the Rossvilles' driveway, looking at it in the dark . . . and suddenly you saw a motorcycle move and you saw Mr. Rossville sitting on it . . . pushing it with his feet . . . at one in the morning?"

Mrs. Lane's face twisted with hate. "Oh, that's very clever, Mr. Cage. Break down everything I say into little parts and try to make it sound stupid. Well, you're the one who sounds stupid, Mr. Cage, because that's exactly what happened."

The courtroom fell silent. The judge was not sure at whom he should look and so he kept his eyes on his notebook and he waited for Cage to respond. Cage, however, only let the embarrassment grow. Then, obsequiously, Cage said, "Would you like another break, Mrs. Lane?"

Wechsler, calling out from his seat, said, "I think it's Mr. Cage who needs the break, Your Honor."

Someone in the jury box laughed.

The judge said, "There'll be no further breaks at this time. Do you have any other questions, Mr. Cage?"

"Oh, indeed I do, Your Honor. I expect to be here the rest of the day with this witness."

"As long as it's relevant," said the judge.

Cage went back and consulted the hard-plastic black binder that seemed to be the very embodiment of his knowledge of the case. He turned a few pages of notes and then he glanced up quizzically at the witness. "You said in answer to one of Mr. Wechsler's questions that

307

you know your neighbors the Rossvilles. You wouldn't consider yourself friends with them, would you?"

"We're friendly."

"Oh, really? Ever been inside their house?"

"No."

"They ever been inside yours?"

"Not"—she paused—"that I know of."

Again someone from the jury laughed. Without looking, the judge
had a fairly good idea who it was.

"When was the last time you spoke with either one of them, Mrs.
Lane?"

"I don't recall."

"Have you ever spoken directly to either one of them?"

"I don't recall."

"Yet you've lived right next door to them for how many years?"

There was no answer.

"They have neighborhood parties from time to time in Tranton Park,
don't they, Mrs. Lane?"

"I suppose so."

"You ever been to one?"

"I don't recall."

"Yet your husband goes, doesn't he?"

Once again there was no answer.

"Why does he go and you don't?"

Wechsler objected on the grounds of relevance and Cage did not
even wait for the judge's ruling. He went right to his next question.

"Do you work outside the house, Mrs. Lane? . . . No? . . . Belong to
any clubs, engage in any activities, participate in any volunteer work,
get any exercise . . . go to any functions?"

Turning her head very, very slowly, Mrs. Lane looked at the judge. "I
would like some more water now, please," she said tautly.

Judge Gifford tapped his pencil while he read the clock over the
jurors' heads. "Freddy," he called out, "would you please get some
water for Mrs. Lane."

When she had swallowed most of the cupful that Freddy brought her,
Cage asked if she was ready. He waited and then he asked again. "I said,
are you ready, Mrs. Lane?"

The judge told him to go on.

"I want to know just what is it you do with your time, Mrs. Lane."

"I work around the house. I read. I tend my plants. I take care of my husband. I live, Mr. Cage."

"Do you ever go outside the house for any purpose?"

"I'm here now, aren't I?"

"Touché," said Wechsler.

"How many other times have you been outside your house this past, oh, four weeks?"

"I prefer to stay home."

"Isn't it a fact that you are afraid to go out, Mrs. Lane?"

"No."

"Isn't it a fact that you suffer from agoraphobia?"

"No."

"Have you ever sought counseling, Mrs. Lane?"

"No."

Cage ran his fingers through his hair. His hard-edged approach was not working. The judge could tell from the sympathetic looks in their eyes that the jurors were not enjoying Cage's baiting tactics; and he could tell from the look on Cage's face that he was not unaware of the dangers of his approach.

Tugging gently at the lapels of his coat, Chris Cage lowered his voice to the point where the judge had to tune his ears to make out what he was saying. "Despite the fact that you prefer to stay at home, Mrs. Lane, despite the fact that you cannot remember if you have ever even spoken to him, you have testified that you recognized my client Leigh Rossville maneuvering a motorcycle in the dark. And you recognized this from how far away?"

She did not answer his question. Instead, she lifted her head and tilted her chin toward the courtroom, a gesture imperious in nature, and said, "One of the things I spend a great deal of time doing when I stay home, Mr. Cage, is looking out my window. I have seen Mr. Rossville from the distance of my window on literally hundreds, perhaps thousands, of occasions."

"And this . . . experience . . . you have had in looking out the window allows you to say with certainty that you saw Mr. Rossville in the dark, across half your yard and all of his? It allows you to say that that was definitely Mr. Rossville you saw on a motorcycle at one in the morning?"

"It allows me to say not only that it was definitely Mr. Rossville on the motorcycle at one in the morning, but also that it definitely was not

Mr. Rossville whom I saw on the motorcycle at eleven o'clock in the evening."

By now it was clear to everyone that Cage was getting slaughtered. His clients were grimacing, moving about uneasily in their seats, and Cage himself was retreating to his black binder, where he thumbed a few more pages and then made a move to sit down.

Suddenly something caught his eye and he popped back up again. He extracted an object from his binder and unfolded it. From its size and its distinctive green color, it was obviously a page from the *San Francisco Chronicle*'s sports section, "The Sporting Green."

"The night we're talking about," he said, "it's the night of March three to March four, right, Mrs. Lane?"

"That's right."

"The evidence, such as we have it, says Bobby O'Berry died the night of March three."

"Yes? So?"

Cage held up the sheet of newspaper. Without making direct reference to it, he said, "Do you know your neighbor Roarke Robinson?"

"I'm aware of him."

"You're aware that he is a very famous baseball player, aren't you?"

"I don't follow baseball. But yes, I'm aware that he is a baseball player."

"I have here the sports page from Monday, March fifth." His eyes scanned it. "Were you aware that Roarke Robinson reported to spring training in Arizona on Sunday, March fourth?"

"No," she said.

"Your Honor," Cage said, "I'd like to have this sports page marked as defendants' next in order. The headline says, 'Robinson Reports to Camp.'"

The judge turned to Wechsler, anticipating his objection, but Wechsler, leaning back in his chair, simply waved his hand and said it was all right with him if Mr. Cage wanted to use some hearsay newspaper article.

"It'll be admitted."

Cage handed the exhibit to Myrna and strolled slowly back to his desk. Looking toward the audience, he said to the witness, "Mrs. Lane, you see this man sitting there in the raincoat and the pinstripe suit? The older gentleman? You recognize him?"

"Yes."

"That's Mr. Carr, isn't it? Did he interview you?"

"Yes."

"Mrs. Lane, when he was on the stand, Mr. Carr testified that the last people he . . . 'surveyed' was the word he used, I believe . . . were Mr. Lane and Mrs. Robinson. Were you present when he surveyed them?"

The answer was rolled around her mouth and then spit out: "No."

"Hmmm." Cage looked contemplative. "Did you know your husband and Mrs. Robinson were together at that time?"

"Objection. Irrelevant. Misleading."

Cage shrugged and moved on. "Mr. Carr also testified that he interviewed Leigh Rossville on Saturday, March tenth. If the last two people he interviewed were your husband and Mrs. Robinson—"

"They weren't. He interviewed me after he interviewed my husband."

"Oh, really? All right. Well, let's assume that Mr. Carr's statements were otherwise correct. That would still mean that he interviewed your husband and Mrs. Robinson together on or after the tenth. And yet this sports page just admitted into evidence indicates that Mr. Robinson was off in Arizona as of the fourth. How do you account for your husband being alone with Mrs. Robin—"

"Ob-jection. This is vicious, irrelevant character assassination, Your Honor. Has this man no decency whatsoever?"

The judge was trying not to show his incredulity, but Cage's attack seemed so gratuitous that he was almost inclined to join in Wechsler's denunciation. "At the very least," he said, staring, "the question calls for speculation."

Cage said, "I'll withdraw it, Your Honor." He turned to the witness and said, "Thank you, Mrs. Lane. You've been very kind. Last question, though. Your husband, is that the gentleman sitting right behind me? The fellow over here in the dark blue suit? It is? Thank you, thank you very much." And he dropped into the chair grinning as if he had just gotten Mary Elizabeth herself to confess to the murder of young Mr. O'Berry.

The judge said, "Mr. Wechsler, any redirect?"

"No, sir."

"Next witness then, please."

"Ah . . . that's all we have for today, Your Honor. I thought I heard Mr. Cage say he was going to go all afternoon. . . ."

"Then we'll be in recess till Monday morning. Ten o'clock. Counsel, I want to see you both in chambers, so don't run off anywhere."

The judge had removed his robe. He had his vest unbuttoned and hanging loosely from his shoulders. He had his shoes off and his feet stuck in some stocking-like slippers he had once been given on a transatlantic flight. He had his pipe filled and fired. It was Friday afternoon and his week's responsibilities were behind him. He had two demandless days ahead of him and he would have liked nothing better than to start preparing for those days with a good fistfull of Bell's Scotch. But first he had to take care of the two gentlemen seated before him.

"You ever feel, you finish a week in trial, it's like emerging from a coal mine? I have this image in my mind of those guys coming up into the sunlight, their faces all sooty, their bodies weary, suddenly getting a good breath of fresh air and having the intensity of all they've been doing just vaporize away from them."

The judge grinned. Wechsler grinned. Cage looked as if he had been poleaxed.

The judge returned his pipe to his mouth, transforming his grin into a teeth-gritting grip on the stem. "The reason I asked you guys in here," he said, the bowl bouncing up and down with his words, "is I just wondered if maybe we hadn't reached a point where one or both of you would be willing to talk settlement. I'm not getting in the middle of it, mind you, not unless you ask me to, but I just thought I'd throw the idea out."

"We've always been willing to talk settlement, Judge," Wechsler said.

The judge cocked his eyebrow at Chris Cage, who sat immobile, as though he weren't even involved. "How about it, Chris? It seems to me that we might have developed enough information so that Reuben's going to get his case to the jury. I'm not telling you he's entitled to a directed verdict or anything like that, you understand; I'm just telling you what my impression is at the moment."

"You haven't heard my case yet," Chris said, his voice a monotone.

"Oh, no, no, no. I realize that. I just wonder, you've got this attractive, seemingly well-off couple with everything in the world to lose, and we all know that just about anything can happen when twelve average citizens go into a jury room. Hell." He stopped to chuckle. "Ain't nobody knows that better'n you after our last little fiasco with Mr. . . . ?"

"Kinsey."

"Kinsey, yes. Look, Chris, I don't want to tell you how to run your case, God knows. But this woman here who just testified, Mary Elizabeth, she might be crazy as a loon, I'm not arguing with you. But this jury, they don't know her like you and I might. They know what they see on the stand, and I'm telling you, I thought she did a pretty good job."

"It's all circumstantial evidence, Judge. Some guy named Goose says O'Berry went to Tranton Park. A doctor says O'Berry might possibly have been killed with a spear gun. My clients live in Tranton Park and own a spear gun. Some suburban hermit says she saw somebody drive a motorcycle to my clients' house and later on she saw Leigh Rossville push the motorcycle away. You think that's probable cause to believe the Rossvilles killed that kid?" Cage's unblinking blue eyes cut highways through to the judge.

"All I'm saying," the judge answered, fighting back the urge to remind Cage to watch his tone of voice, "is that Mary Elizabeth is probably the key witness in this case, and I think the jury is going to find her credible. Maybe you've got something to offset her, I don't know. But if you don't, you may wish to sit down with Reuben— Tell you what: I don't have anyplace I have to go the rest of the afternoon; I can wait for you to do just that. Why don't you two go have a cup of coffee together?"

Chris, without taking his eyes off the judge, said, "I'd rather choke on my own vomit."

The remark was greeted with silence, but the rage it generated was almost palpable. Wechsler, playing with the coins in his pocket, stared off at a wall covered with the judge's licenses and certificates. The judge himself studied Chris Cage as though he were some incomprehensible lout who had just upset his dinner table. Then he slowly withdrew his pipe from his mouth and held it a few inches away from his face. "Then I guess," he said softly, "we have nothing more to discuss."

It was, everyone knew, more a pronouncement than an observation.

As far as bailiffs went, Freddy Wagner was about the best of the lot, his affectation of the name Vagner notwithstanding. For the first two years he had worked for the judge he had pronounced his name the same as everyone else; in fact, he had even referred to himself as Daddy Wags from time to time. The nickname had been appropriated

313

from a baseball player who once had occupied a good deal of Freddy's quota of daily concerns. Then he had gone to see a movie about the nineteenth-century German composer (he had gone for no reason other than the fact that they spelled their names the same way) and he had returned with the message that he would henceforth be known as Freddy Vagner.

Freddy, who was about ten years younger than the judge, actually served very little function in the courtroom. Unlike their counterparts in San Francisco and most other California counties, the bailiffs in Alameda wore neither weapons nor uniforms. Their primary function was to serve as messengers, and this Freddy did quite well. He showed up for work religiously, he did what the judge told him to do, he controlled the jury, he kept relatively closemouthed in discussing courtroom matters, and every now and then he served as Judge Gifford's eyes and ears.

The judge, while not being manic about Freddy's value, found him particularly useful at times like this; and Freddy, who was always looking for ways to make himself seem indispensable, derived tremendous pleasure from his ability to provide the judge with bits and pieces of information.

"Do you know, Freddy," the judge asked as he propped his stockinged feet up on the desk, "just what the hell is going on between these two guys?"

Freddy's brow furrowed. He so hated not having answers to the judge's questions that he occasionally made things up. But he couldn't do even that until he understood the question.

"Wechsler, of course, is a screwball, but he's acting like Prince Charming compared to Cage. I'm trying to figure out what's gotten into Cage. When we did the Kinsey trial he worked hard and he did his best to win, but at least he'd lighten up and act like a reasonable human being when the occasion called for it. This time, my God, he's acting like it's his own life on trial. He comes in here just now, I suggest that maybe he and Wechsler ought to sit down to discuss this case, he comes out with some remark about how he'd rather puke, for Chrissakes. I felt like busting him in the chops."

"There's some nasty feelings out there, Judge. I hear them Cochrane boys talking about what they'd like to do to Mr. Rossville, what they'd like to do to Mr. Cage. . . . They're bad characters, Judge. Maybe that's what's bothering Mr. Cage."

The judge was interested. "Like what do the Cochranes say?"

"Oh," Freddy said, his voice rapid and enthusiastic, "they gather

314

around Mr. Wechsler during the breaks and I hear them saying the f-word this and the f-word that, calling Mr. Cage an a-hole and calling Mr. Rossville a little squirrel."

"They call them these things to their face?"

"They say 'em sometimes so they can hear 'em. Like out in the hall. The brothers be leaning against a wall and Mr. and Mrs. Rossville come walking down the corridor and the brothers say things like 'Good morning, Killer,' or 'How's it going, Killer?' "

"I want you to tell them not to do that anymore."

Freddy's eyes widened. "Me?" he said, covering his chest with his hand.

The judge thought better of it. "Tell you what. Next time you observe this or anything like it, you tell me right away. Okay?"

"Okay," Freddy said with relief.

"Now, what else have you heard out there, Freddy? Anything which gives you an indication whether these people did it or not?"

Freddy grabbed his chin with his right hand and propped his elbow in his left palm while he screwed up his face in a thoughtful pose. "I think they did it. What that lady said who was just on—"

"Where was she, by the way? Why did it take you so long to get her back to the stand?"

"She was way down by the elevators, Judge. Her and her husband. She wasn't coming back. Saying she had to get out of the building and all that. Her husband, he holding on to her arm, telling her she had to go back. Telling her she started this and now she was going to have to finish it. 'Just tell the truth,' he says. 'Look right at Mr. Cage and pretend it's just you and him talking and there's no one else there.' Then she gets out this little package of Kleenex, pats her eyes and nose, and comes walking back to the court smart as you please."

"So you think she was telling the truth?"

"I do, Judge. Yeah."

"So do I. I'm just not sure what her testimony means, that's all."

"Well, the way I see it, this Mr. Rossville, he meets this boy in the bar and he invites him home to service his wife as sort of a birthday present to Mrs. Rossville. He got the video camera, see? He's gonna film the whole thing." Freddy held his circled fingers to one eye and made a rotating motion with his free hand just as if he were cranking an old-fashioned movie camera. "Only something went wrong. Maybe they were doing something kinky with the spear gun or something. Maybe she didn't like the idea and the boy wouldn't leave. Maybe they just wanted to get rid of the boy afterwards so he couldn't tell nobody what they'd been doing."

The judge took his feet off the desk and stabbed around for his shoes. "I think you're getting pretty close with that last theory, Freddy, weird as it sounds."

Freddy smiled and spread his hands. "Hey, we see weird things all the time, Judge. Weird don't mean it isn't so."

The judge showed his agreement with a grimace and a little twist of his head. He was about to dismiss Freddy when a new question occurred to him. "Say, any idea what that Irish-looking fella is doing out there?"

Freddy went blank and the judge suspected that the concept of a person looking Irish or Italian or Swedish or Polish was something that Freddy simply did not employ.

"You know," the judge said, patting the top of his head, "the young guy with the smile and the curly hair."

"Oh," said Freddy, "you mean Mr. Gilhooley."

"Gilhooley?"

"From the DA's office. He's been assigned to follow this whole trial, try to see if there's enough evidence to bring criminal charges against the Rossvilles."

A tingling sensation swept across the judge's back. "Does Cage know who Gilhooley is, what he's doing here?"

"Oh, indeed he does, sir."

"Ah," said the judge, "well, that sort of casts things in a whole new light, doesn't it?"

"It sure do," Freddy said agreeably.

CHAPTER NINE

Giff was having a dream. He had gone to bed with four healthy glasses of Scotch under his belt and the dream was a little disjointed. It was, nonetheless, very intense.

He was being chased across fields by scantily clad African natives. There were many of them and they were all carrying spears. At first, when he looked back over his shoulder, he could see only black dots, which he assumed were their bare chests, and shiny silver objects that looked like radio antennas. Then, as the chase went on, as they raced over rock-strewn plains and through thigh-high grass, the natives closed distance on him and he could see that the native in front was not African black at all. He was white and he was wearing a pair of Jockey shorts and Giff knew, without being able to make out his face, that it was Bobby O'Berry who was after him.

The thought filled Giff with panic. It soaked him with perspiration until he realized, all of a sudden, that he, too, had a weapon. He, too, had a spear. Except that it wasn't the same kind of spear the natives had. His was attached to him. And it was between his legs.

He stopped running. He turned to face the native Bobby O'Berry with his penis-spear in his hand. Bobby O'Berry kept coming straight on toward him, but Bobby, unlike the other natives, had no spear of his own. He had nothing with which to attack Giff but his scream. And he was screaming. He would scream and then stop. Scream and then stop.

Giff woke up. The telephone was jangling on the bedside night table. His body was clammy. His head ached. And his hand was on his semi-hard penis. He wanted to wake Jeanine, who still lay with her back to him, but the phone kept up its piercing ring and he had to reach over to get it. The time on the clock radio said six-nineteen in digital numbers.

"Judge Gifford?" a man's voice asked.

"Yes.'

"This is Sergeant Malthus, the booking officer down at the county jail."

Off-hour phone calls from police officers usually came only when they wanted an emergency warrant issued. In Giff's befuddled mind he could not figure out why a booking officer would be calling about a warrant. "Yeah?" he said warily.

"Do you have a son named Peter Gifford?"

Giff's head cleared instantly. Now it only throbbed. Jeanine was stirring next to him. Her eyes took a second to focus and then immediately became filled with concern.

"Yes," said the judge.

"I come on at six, Judge. I'm dealing with a booking problem and, uh, his name has come up."

"Is it the same Peter Gifford?"

"Oh, my God," moaned Jeanine.

"I don't know, sir. His car is registered to a Jeanine Gifford at your address. But I was hoping you could check, maybe you could tell me if it really is your son."

Giff covered the mouthpiece of the phone loosely and said, "Jeanine, go down quick and see if he's there." But he knew, as soon as he said the words, that she would not find him in his room. He waited until he heard footsteps on the stairs and then, gathering his courage, he said, "What's the charge?"

"We caught him in the middle of a purchase, Judge. Cocaine. Apparently it was a fluke thing. An off-duty officer was walking through a parking lot in Berkeley and saw the exchange take place in the car."

It took Giff several moments to catch his breath.

"Judge . . . ?"

From two stories below he could hear his wife's wail. His voice a broken whisper, he said, "Could it have been a mistake?"

The sergeant hesitated. He might have been looking at his records. "The other charge, Judge, freebasing paraphernalia. It was found on his person. He was only the buyer, but . . . well, it looks like your boy's a user."

"A user," Giff repeated, still whispering.

The officer hurried on. "The guys who took him in, obviously they didn't know, Judge. Boy didn't say anything about who he was, either.

318

Problem now, we got it on the books, press guys may have been through it already, I don't know. That and the other kid. The other kid's the son of some doctor or something and his mother's been down here screaming at everyone since before I came on. Telling us how important her husband is and trying to blame the whole thing on your boy. She's saying it has to be your son's drugs because her son doesn't do things like that. . . ." The officer's voice trailed off. When the judge said nothing, he added, "Thing is, it would be awful difficult to let your boy fly without the other kid, and . . . frankly . . ."

"I understand, Sergeant."

"You want me to have the DA give you a call?"

"Um, yes . . . Jesus, I can't think."

"There may be some things he can do."

"Yes, please. Have Gary call me. And, um, thank you . . . Yes, thank you very much."

Giff's Scotch seemed as raw as vinegar. Its effect was as flat as water. Jeanine's sat untouched on the coffee table, the original pouring swelled by melted ice. She held her hands in her lap and he, when he wasn't drinking, kept his hands hooked over the arms of his chair.

They had been sitting like that for most of the evening, staring at an empty fireplace. Neither consciously realized that that was what they were doing. The conversational exchanges, such as they were, always were started by Giff.

"I keep asking myself," he said at one point, "if he did this somehow to get back at me for something. To punish me. I think, what better way to humiliate a judge than to have his son get arrested for something like this? I mean, it's not like when Judge Swoboda's daughter got booked for that antinuclear demonstration. I could almost understand that. But this, this is just dirty business."

"I don't think he did it to get back at you, Giff. I think it was a cry for help."

Giff had raised his drink to his lips, but now he held it there untasted. "A cry for help," he said. He spoke the words as if they were in pig latin and required deciphering. "Just what the hell does that mean, Jeanine?"

Jeanine Gifford unfolded and then refolded her hands. Talking slowly and choosing her words with infinite care, she said, "I don't think Peter's life has been quite as easy as you seem to imagine."

319

Giff twisted violently in his chair. The drink he was still holding sloshed onto his pant leg. "No, it must be very difficult deciding whether or not to get up before noon, what radio station to listen to, what nightclub to go to. The boy's living at home for free, for heaven's sake. He doesn't go to school, he doesn't work, he doesn't cook or clean or keep house. He couldn't live a less demanding existence if he were in outer space."

"Don't you think that's a bit unusual, Giff? Especially given the way he was before he went away to college, always working so hard at everything he did."

"I think it's damn unusual, but what can I do about it? I've tried being patient, hoping he's going to snap out of whatever this thing is he's going through. I've tried sitting him down and talking to him—"

"He told me about your talk."

"It was like speaking to a brick wall."

"He told me you want him to become a movie star."

"A movie . . . oh, c'mon, Jeanine, this is some sort of joke, isn't it? You told me the kid was mixed up about life, so I tried to show him what it had to offer. I tried to give him some advice—some ideas about what I might do if I were in his shoes, that's all."

"I don't think telling him to become a movie star was very realistic."

"I wasn't . . . Will you listen to me, Jeanine? Why doesn't anybody in this house ever understand what anybody else is saying? I was just giving Peter examples of what's out there. You can be anything you want to be, I was telling him. The world's your oyster. You see, at the time I didn't know all he really wanted to do was sit downstairs smoking drugs he got with money he stole from me."

"Maybe taking the drugs was just his way of escaping from all the pressures you've put on him, Roger."

"Pressures?" Giff shouted. "What pressures?"

Jeanine's eyes stayed on the empty fireplace. Her hands stayed clasped in her lap. "There are a lot of pressures that come from being a judge's son."

Giff kept himself from shouting again by filling his voice with anguish. "Jeanine, will you please tell me what you're talking about? Please? If you want to blame me for what's happened to Peter, let's get it out in the open and stop talking around in circles."

But Jeanine would not be rushed. "I think," she said slowly, "that a judge has to have certain ways of presenting himself in the courtroom

320

and I think sometimes he may unintentionally carry those ways over to places where they're less appropriate, like the home."

"I don't believe this," Giff muttered. "You are blaming me."

"No," Jeanine said, but there was a second's delay before she said it. Her face, at least that side Giff could see, took on a look of simple understanding. "I'm just saying that there's so much involved in being a judge, Giff, there are so many demands put on you, that it's extremely difficult to change roles when you walk out of the courtroom. You've been on the bench ever since Peter was born and he's never really had the opportunity to know you as anything but The Judge."

Giff found himself seething. He seethed at the pauses and inflections in his wife's voice, at the message she was delivering. When he looked up and saw the slump of her shoulders he seethed at that, too. "What about you, Jeanine?" he asked sarcastically. "Am I The Judge to you?"

Jeanine did not respond until Giff started to speak again, and then she softly cut him off. "I've learned to cope."

The answer stunned Giff. He took a vulgar gulp of his drink and then gulped it again until it was gone. The ice cubes banged against his nose and then toppled back to the bottom of his glass. "Just what is it—" he said, but he choked and had to start over again. "Just what is it you've had to learn to cope with?"

Jeanine smiled sadly.

Glancing first toward the back of the house, toward the stairs that led down to their son's room, Giff leaned onto the arm of his chair, drawing himself as close to his wife as he could without actually getting up and moving. "The only adjustment I've seen you have to make is with this sex thing. Other than that, you live the way you please. You go to all these functions, you belong to all these organizations I know nothing about—" And then he stopped, because she wasn't listening.

"Do you remember back when we were kids, Giff, just dating? And everything we'd do we'd do together?"

Giff hung on the arm of his chair and wondered why he had opened himself up the way he just had.

"Do you remember that time we went to the rodeo in Salinas and you lost the only keys to your father's car and it was Sunday and we had to hitchhike home? Remember how awful it seemed then?" Jeanine's eyes, staring into the past, were fixed and unblinking. "I think about that sometimes, even now. I'll be washing pots and pans in the sink and looking out the window and all of a sudden I'll get this picture in my

---

321

mind, or this feeling will come over me, and it will be just like we were back there. And all I can think about is how much fun it was."

Giff slid back into his seat cushions.

"Remember," Jeanine said, "the party we went to, I think it was my cousin's wedding party, where you had too much to drink and you got dancing so hard you fell through the window?"

Giff said, "Goddamnit, Jeanine, you want to wax nostalgic about things that happened thirty-five or forty years ago, that's fine. If you liked me better back then, I'm sorry. But times have changed. I've changed, you've changed, and I doubt you'd find my little foibles quite so amusing now. I doubt you'd be quite so pleased with me if I got drunk and fell through a window at this stage of my life."

Jeanine turned, at last, to face her husband and he could see that the skin on her neck was mottled red. "The point is, Giff, I can hold all these memories of the silly things you did in my heart and they can help me distinguish between Giff and The Judge. Peter's never seen that side of you, though. To him you've always been a very austere figure. He never saw The Judge make mistakes and he never saw where there was any room for him to make mistakes, either. If he played Little League, he had to hit a home run. If he played in the school band, he had to be first trumpet. If he went to college, he had to go to the Ivy League. Anything less than the best was failure. And finally the burden just got to be too much for him. Finally he just rebelled against the whole struggle by avoiding any situation where the possibility of failure might come up. So he drops out of Columbia; so he doesn't go to Santa Cruz, so he doesn't look for a job . . ."

"You know, Jeanine," Giff said wearily, "I have to listen to garbage from real psychologists all year long in my courtroom. I don't see why I should have to come home and listen to it from you, too."

But Jeanine edged forward so that she was only half sitting on her chair. "Think about it, Giff," she urged. "Don't you avoid situations where you might fail? I mean, if that's what you're really afraid of. Like, well—you mentioned it yourself a few minutes ago—this sex problem we've been having—"

"I'm not avoiding sex with you, Jeanine, if that's what's running through your mind. What's happening to me is a natural occurrence for men my age."

"But if it's a problem you don't go around flaunting it. You tend to avoid the whole situation, don't you, instead of making yourself miserable?"

322

"Look, Jeanine. I'll repeat, what's happening to me is natural. What's happening to Peter is not. You want to say the whole thing is the fault of my being a judge, fine. I just want to point out to you that we didn't do such a damn good job with Donna, either, and I was in private practice during most of the years she was growing up. So you better have a whole new excuse as to why she ended up the way she did, living with some semiliterate bum and having babies by him without ever getting married."

The eagerness with which Jeanine had pressed her theory a moment before evaporated. On her face appeared an expression, first, of uncertainty, and then of such utter defeat that Giff felt his own anger drain out of him. "We could only take them so far, Jeanine," he said quietly. "Once they got out in what we call the real world they were on their own and all we could do was hope for the best."

Jeanine moved back within the arms of her chair and resumed her watch on the fireplace. "Then we should have prepared them better for it," she said, her voice as quiet as his.

Giff lifted his glasses to his forehead and rubbed his eyes with the fingers of both hands. He rubbed for a long time and then he said, "Maybe that's what I thought I was doing, all those years when you say I was being too austere. Maybe . . . maybe, if you think I've changed, it's because of what I've seen of the real world since putting those robes on. You, Jeanine, in all fairness, you've lived a very sheltered existence. You've basically only known people like yourself. But there are others out there who think differently than you do . . . who live by different codes than you do, than your friends do, than your neighbors do. Not everyone believes in the Ten Commandments, the benefits of work, home, family, a night in front of the television, and a two-week vacation every year. Not everyone even believes in life and death, I've found. In fact, there are people out there who are born so far on the outs from mainstream society, they're so . . . what's known as disaffected that in a sense they actually believe it's moral to disrupt life for other people."

In the silence that followed, noises in and around the house took on an added dimension. A car went by outside, the refrigerator hummed on in the kitchen, the minute placards inside a digital clock on a bookshelf in the corner of the living room flipped from a 7 to an 8.

"Is that," said Jeanine, "what you think happened to Peter? That he fell in with those kinds of people?"

Giff tilted his head back on the cushion. "I don't know. I really don't. The boy he was arrested with, the one who was selling him drugs, is ap-

323

parently the son of some doctor. That doesn't sound very disaffected, I admit, but the rich are perfectly capable of developing their own codes of thinking, just like the poor—their own ideas that what's right for them at a particular moment is all that counts. On the other hand, maybe that boy fell in with the wrong crowd, or maybe his father was mean to him, or maybe he's afraid of failure. To tell you the truth, Jeanine, I suddenly feel as though I don't have the slightest clue as to what's going on anymore."

"I wonder if we should try to get in touch with his parents."

"Whose?"

"The other boy's. Maybe they're sitting there just like we are tonight, trying to figure out where they went wrong. Maybe if we got together and talked we could see we made the exact same mistakes."

"And then maybe we could all go on the talk show circuit and explain to America the precise reason why her sons and daughters go on drugs."

Jeanine closed her eyes, a silent statement of suffering. Her eyelids were rough and lumpy. They had been smooth once. All of her had been smooth.

"Look, I'm sorry," he said suddenly. "But you don't want to call up these people. According to what the police said, they're already trying to blame the whole thing on Peter. It was his car, they're arguing, they had to be his drugs."

"Did you get their name?"

"The only thing I got was the boy's name. I didn't ask anything else."

Jeanine nodded. Her eyes opened. "What is it?"

"Jeanine, don't call them. Everybody's going to be far too emotional to accomplish anything."

"I won't call them. I just want to know his name, that's all.

Giff sighed. "It was Butler," he said. "Arthur Butler."

CHAPTER TEN

"Plaintiff calls ... Strike that. We call plaintiff Barbara Cochrane O'Berry."

She had been sitting, as always, between her two brothers. Now she stood up and looked about uncertainly, just as if she had never noticed the steady stream of witnesses who had made their way to the stand over the course of the trial. She was wearing a black and red checkered dress which had enough cinch at the waist to differentiate top from bottom, but which otherwise hung straight to her knees. Her brown hair fell in thick waves around her shoulders, framing and emphasizing the roundness of her face. An unnatural pink color marked each of her soft, smooth cheeks, and moist reddish-brown lipstick accentuated her already oversized mouth. She looked, Giff thought, as though she had come ill prepared for a school dance; you wanted to strip her down, throw her in the shower, re-prepare her from the ground up. Yet she also looked heartbreakingly vulnerable and, strangely, almost appealing.

"Step right up here, young lady," he said gruffly.

She took her oath and then sat exactly as if she were taking a seat in a stranger's formal living room. Her glance toward the jury was half fear and half apology for intruding on their busy schedules. The black grandmother liked her, and smiled encouragement. Barbara O'Berry nervously fluttered her darkened eyelashes and smiled back. Then, perhaps feeling she should not be even silently communicating with one of the jurors, she swiveled her head and sought out her counsel.

"Would you please state your name?"

The words got lost in her throat. When they came out they were jumbled, sounding run together. "Barbra Cockleberry."

She gave her address. Yes, she was married—she had been married. Yes, she had one child, Roberta. She was here today, in the courthouse.

At a signal from Wechsler, Billy Cochrane, who had moved to the last row of benches, got up and pushed open the swinging doors that led out to the hallway. A smiling gray-haired woman entered with a bonneted young girl riding on her hip. Barbara O'Berry beamed. She inched forward in her chair and waved. Yes, that was her little girl, and her mother, too. Mum had been taking care of her while Barbara was in trial.

In the jury box, young Mr. Gutierrez surveyed the scene without any apparent interest. The golf caddy stared blankly. The pharmacist studied the little girl as if looking for clues of ancestry. The housepainter barely bothered to look. But the rest strained and grinned and moved their heads from side to side, trying to see as much as they could, just as friends and families do at christenings. At the defendants' table nobody even turned to see what all the commotion was about.

Over the course of the morning session, Reuben Wechsler masterfully walked his client through descriptions of herself, her late husband, their tragically brief marriage, his disappearance, her attempts to cope, her confidence that he would come back. . . .

"Didn't you accept the fact that he was dead?"

"I nevva believed it. Not for a minute."

"But you held a memorial service."

"That was for Bobby's mutha and the rest of his family."

"Where did you think he had gone?"

"I didn't know. I just knew we had nevva found the body and I was nevva going to accept him as dead until we did. He could have been hurt someway-uz, he could have hit his head and suffawed amnesier."

"Did you consider the possibility that he could have run away from you?"

"Oh, yes. I considered that a real likely possibility."

"You did? But why did you think he would do a thing like that?"

"First, I hoped that's what he had done. Because that would have made him all right, you know? That would have meant he was still alive and could still come back to me when he got his head togethuh."

"What do you mean by that—when he got his head together?"

"Well, assuming, you know, that's what he did, that he ran away. I could unduhstand that almost, because while Bobby and I really loved each other and all that, we hadn't really planned on getting married at the time we did. . . . I mean, you know, we had to get married."

x

326

"Who said you had to get married?"

"Who said? Well, he did, really. I mean, I told him I was pregnant, what should I do? And he really wanted to do the right thing. Get married, you know? Give the baby a name. He said he didn't want a child of his to be a . . ."

"Bastard?"

"Yeah. I mean, yes."

"Yet you felt even though Bobby wanted to do the right thing, as you put it, he could still have run away that night, after he had given you and the baby his name."

"He coulda. Like I said, you know, he wasn't really planning on getting married and I always thought maybe there were places he wanted to go, things he wanted to see befowwa he settled down."

"But you still had hope he would come back and settle down?"

"Oh, yeah. I mean, like, Bobby was that way. I mean, nobody said he had to get married, but he did because it was the right thing. And I just knew that when he heard he had a baby, well, then he'd do the right thing then, too."

"Had you heard from him in all the time he'd been gone?"

"He hadn't been gone that long."

"What, four months?"

"About that. I was waiting till the baby was due. I figyuhed then, if I didn't hear from him when the baby was bonn, then I'd know he really drownded in the lake."

"And what day was the baby born?"

"Mahch fifth."

"Two days after . . ."

In all the time Reuben Wechsler was questioning his client, Chris Cage never once objected. In fact, the judge noted, Cage barely ever raised his head from the trial book in which he was scribbling. It was almost as if what she had to say was of no particular interest to him.

The judge's mind was wandering. He was vaguely aware that Chris Cage was struggling as he tried to home in on Barbara O'Berry's conviction that her husband would have returned to her as soon as he heard that she had the baby.

"He woulda at least been in touch with me, I know that," she said.

"And how is it you know that, Ms. O'Berry?"

"Because Bobby was like that. I mean, he had his wild streak, like a lotta kids do, but he knew when to do the right thing."

"You keep saying that, Ms. O'Berry. What is it you mean by the right thing?"

"I mean, sometimes you gotta do what you gotta do. I mean, sometimes things are sorta beyond your control, but you have to do them even though they're not your first choice. You have to do them because, well, that's what you're s'posed to do. Because they're the right thing, that's all."

The judge was thinking about trail riding again. He was wondering if it wouldn't be better to take Peter instead of Jeanine. Get him out in the wilderness. Get him alone where they would have no choice but to talk to each other. Just the two of them, with nobody else around, maybe they could get to know each other all over again. Of course, the whole idea behind a pack trip was to get Jeanine on a horse. He didn't care about horses, and he couldn't image that Peter did. . . . Maybe they could just go hiking. Backpacking on the John Muir Trail. . . . The important thing was to get out in the forest, where all that mattered was finding water and a level campsite.

"Your Honor . . ." Wechsler's voice was pained. He had made an objection and he was demanding a ruling.

The judge, with no idea as to what the objectionable question might be, looked down at Chris Cage. "Well," he said, "what do you have to say in response, counsel?"

"The objection's absurd, Judge."

"I wonder if you have a slightly more legal basis."

Through clenched teeth, Cage said, "Of course the question's relevant. I mean, it goes to the very heart of what this lawsuit is allegedly all about. Doesn't it?"

This was getting the judge nowhere. He turned his gaze on Wechsler and said, "And what do you have to say to that?"

"He's already stipulated to the child's paternity. The matter's no longer in issue—"

"I never stipulated to any such thing, Judge. I stipulated to the fact that the O'Berrys were legally married, that's all."

Wechsler hesitated. His eyes rolled. "Well," he said, dragging out the word. "Now he's asking a question about what might or might not have happened before they were married and it doesn't make a darn bit of difference. I don't even know what the answer to his question is, but it seems to me that he can't have any reason for asking it except in the hopes of embarrassing my client."

The judge became acutely conscious of the anxiety on Barbara O'Berry's face as she watched him and waited for his decision. Her expression was so childlike, so devotional and dependent, that he had a momentary vision of her clapping her hands and saying something like "Oh, goody," if he ruled she did not have to answer the question.

The judge rubbed his nose and thought about having the reporter read back the objection. Then he had a new idea, "I'm going to sustain the objection, unless you can come up with a better foundation, Mr. Cage."

Cage rocked back on his heels and pantomimed disbelief. Then, quickly, he terminated his act with a shrug. "Mrs. O'Berry," he called out, "when did you first meet your husband?"

"I knew him all through high school, but we didn't really know each other well until the very end."

"End of your senior year?"

"Yes."

"June?"

"I guess. Around then."

"And that was, what, nine months before your baby was born?"

"About."

Cage paused. He slipped his hands into his pockets. "And you had intimate relations with Bobby O'Berry in that month of June, is that right?"

Barbara nodded. "Yes," she said softly.

"And my question to you is"—Cage cast a look of significance toward the bench—"did you have intimate relations with anyone else?"

"Objection," roared Wechsler, but the judge waved him back into his seat. Wechsler took the direction, but kept on shouting: "Overbroad. Irrelevant."

The judge said, "I'm only going to allow the question if you limit it as to time."

"June," said Cage, not taking his hands out of his pockets, but simply raising his shoulders as he spoke.

Barbara O'Berry drew her lower lip between her teeth and sucked on it for a moment as she leaned forward in her chair. "Not at that time," she said, her voice catching as though she were congested.

"May?" asked Cage.

"Objection," said Wechsler.

"Overruled," said the judge.

Barbara looked out to the audience, to where her big brothers sat with their arms folded. "I think, maybe, once, before I met Bobby. I mean, before I really got to know Bobby." Again she spoke as though she needed to clear her throat.

"Just once?" Chris Cage asked gently. "With one other person?"

She did not answer right away. She could have been trying to remember. She could, possibly, not have heard the question.

"I asked you if it was just once, Ms. O'Berry."

She nodded her head.

"All right, Ms. O'Berry," Cage said with just a hint of disbelief.

He began turning the pages of his trial book, running his ballpoint pen down columns of notes. He seemed not to be able to find something. With his head down, still flipping pages, he said, "So you became intimate with Bobby O'Berry in June and you married in November, is that right?"

"Yes."

"You saw each other throughout the summer?"

"Yes."

Had Cage been looking at her instead of his trial book, he would have seen her eyes dart between her brothers and her attorney before she answered. As it was, Cage was barely listening. There was a particular thing he was determined to find in his notes and he was simply filling time until he came across it.

"How often?"

"Not as often as I woulda liked."

"Uh-huh. Did you go out with anybody else that summer?"

"No," she said firmly.

At the bench, the judge noted her answer by writing the word in capital letters and underlining it twice.

"Did he?"

Wechsler squirmed in his seat, but kept his mouth shut.

"I don't think so."

"Uh-huh." Cage found something and stopped his questioning long enough to read it. Apparently it was not what he wanted.

"When did you discover you were pregnant?"

"I figyuhed it in July."

"When did you know for sure?"

"Late August."

"When did you tell Bobby?"

"Septembuh."

Cage stopped again. He skipped back to another page and compared two notes. "Whose idea was it to get married?"

"Both of ahs. We discussed it and we decided to do it togethuh."

Cage bent at the waist and began writing something down, glancing back and forth between the two pages he was holding. "And how were you going to support yourselves?"

The judge's mind was beginning to drift again. He casually stroked in the features of a cartoon face on his blotter.

"Bobby was going to work for my brothers."

Without looking behind him, without even straightening up, Cage pointed toward the audience with his pen. "That's these two gentlemen over here, is that right?"

"Yeah. I mean, yes."

The judge saw her look at her brothers and giggle self-consciously. She immediately covered her mouth and her eyes flicked toward the judge to make sure she had not done something wrong, but the judge merely returned to his blotter doodling.

"So," said Cage, still scribbling on his note, "you got married in November. . . . Where? In Portshead?"

"Yes."

"And then you went on your honeymoon up to New Hampshire."

"Yes. Lake Winnipesaukee."

"And that," he said, at last finishing whatever it was he was writing, "is where you consummated the marriage." He stood up, waiting for her answer so that he could get on to whatever he had been developing.

But Barbara O'Berry was not answering. Her brow was knotted. She was staring at him in confusion. "That's where we what?" she said.

Cage appeared almost to have forgotten the question himself. He hesitated, thinking back. "Consummated the marriage." He spread his hands. "That's where you first made love as husband and wife."

The wrinkles in her forehead disappeared, but she still did not answer.

"You did, didn't you?" asked Cage. "I mean, before Bobby disappeared."

"Well, not really."

There was not a sound in the courtroom. Cage's mouth moved, attempting to phrase another question. But before he could say anything more, Barbara spoke again.

331

"We tried," she said. She spoke almost cheerfully, as though she wanted to be helpful and alleviate her questioner's obvious bewilderment.

"What happened?" asked Cage.

Barbara tilted her head slightly to the left and brought it back again. Her mouth lifted at one corner. "It didn't work," she said.

"What didn't work?"

"His . . ." She pointed to her lap. "You know, his thing."

"You mean he didn't get an erection?"

Barbara seemed shocked that he would use that term in a courtroom. She sat back in her chair and looked at her lawyer. Wechsler was leaning on his elbow, his hand covering the lower half of his face, the overhead lights gleaming off the lenses of his glasses. His silence told her she had just gone beyond his help and it made her flustered. "We tried," she said, "but it didn't work."

Cage read the note on which he had labored for so long, and then slowly crushed it into a ball. "Thank you very much, Ms. O'Berry," he said. "I have no further questions."

CHAPTER ELEVEN

They held the argument in open court, outside the presence of the jury. Wechsler started off calmly, confidently, unsure as to how much he had been damaged by Barbara O'Berry's admission. He found out soon enough.

Wechsler raised his voice. He began punctuating his statements by thrusting his hands into the air. His demands became more forceful, his claims more insistent, his inferences more personal.

Giff was unmoved. He was, in fact, barely following what Wechsler was saying. He was aware of the tone of Wechsler's voice and he understood his message, but all he felt was a fortification of his own resolve. The idea that he was letting Wechsler carry on this way actually occupied his thoughts more than did Wechsler's contentions. He tried to analyze why he was not putting Wechsler in his place, but the concept was too abstract. Why was it too abstract?

Giff looked up from his desk. They were all staring at him: Wechsler, Cage, Freddy, Myrna, Gerta, even little Lisa. They were all silent. They were all expectant.

"It seems to me," the judge said, "that one does not enter a regatta unless one has a boat."

Nobody reacted. Not a single person changed expression.

The judge spread his hands. "You can use any analogy you want. You don't play tennis without a racket. You don't agree to take a job digging a hole if you're not going to have a shovel." He could not understand why they were not comprehending. It was only out of deference to little Lisa that he was not being more explicit.

"Look," he said, thrusting himself forward so that he was leaning on his desk. "If you've got a problem, it seems to me that you don't go around inviting situations where the problem is going to arise."

"Or not arise," Cage deadpanned.

The judge shrugged. It was what he meant. Freed by the judge's reaction, Freddy and Myrna laughed out loud.

The judge went on. "You've argued that the decedent was some sort of stud, or working as a stud the night he allegedly went over to the Rossville house, Mr. Wechsler. But you haven't shown me any evidence that he was a stud then or at any other time in his life. Indeed"—he spread his hands—"the single piece of evidence we have on the subject shows he wasn't qualified in that regard. And I, personally, can't believe that he would allow himself to—"

The judge sat back suddenly. He had said enough. It was time to rule. "I'm not going to allow the evidence as to the renting of X-rated videotapes. The fact that Mr. and Mrs. Rossville may have been in the habit of renting such tapes for viewing in the privacy of their home does not in my mind correlate with Mr. Wechsler's still unsupported theory that this particular victim would have had any sort of sexual purpose for going to the Rossville house. As far as I'm concerned, based on what I have before me, such evidence would not do anything other than cast a prejudicial shadow over the proceedings. It will not be admitted and Miss Van Valkenberg will not be allowed to testify.

"Now with that, gentlemen, the court will be in recess for fifteen minutes. Maybe longer, if I feel like it."

Chris Cage announced the name of his first witness. "Defendants call Ann Robinson."

The jurors were not trained actors. They were observers, as comfortable as a family now, after days of being together. The men straightened up when they saw her. The women inspected her from head to foot, searching, perhaps, for flaws, as she walked the length of the aisle. Ann Robinson had the undivided attention of every last one of them.

She answered the questions put to her without elaboration or expansion. Yes, she was married to Roarke Robinson, the outfielder for the Oakland Athletics. They had two children. No, she didn't work outside the home. She just tried to raise the kids and keep everything running right because Roarke traveled so much.

Yes, she recalled the night before Roarke went to spring training last year. She remembered it very well because it was Roarke's first season with the A's and he was worried about how he was going to be accepted by some of the veteran ballplayers whom he didn't know; what with all the publicity about his contract and so forth. He was also worried about what was expected of him, if he was supposed to be a superstar right away, if they still expected him to be the ballplayer he was ten years ago. They had talked about these things. Yes, some people had come over that night to say goodbye: Jay and Janice Butler and their son, Arthur.

"What?" said Giff. He had been watching more than he had been listening. He had heard what she had said, but he wanted to make sure he had heard it.

Mrs. Robinson stopped cold. It was as though she had not even realized the judge was there and now he was glowering at her, his great bushy eyebrows tunneling his vision.

"Jay and Janice Butler," she said hesitantly. "And their son, Arthur."

"This Jay Butler, is he a doctor?" the judge demanded.

"A dentist."

"This boy Arthur, how old is he?"

"I don't know. He must be about eighteen or nineteen."

"And the Butlers are friends of yours?"

"In a way." Ann Robinson lowered her eyelids.

What else was she going to say? She had given such an equivocal answer, what had she meant by it? The question of whether there was something wrong with the Butlers was formulating on the tip of Giff's tongue, but Cage, intent on his interrogation, was already speaking again.

"Other than the Butlers, did you see any of your neighbors at all—" Cage caught the judge's fierce glare and stammered on his last words: "—that night?"

Mrs. Robinson looked to the judge and the judge, his mind working furiously, held her in silence for so long that Gerta turned from her stenographic machine to see what was going on.

"Oh, answer Mr. Cage's question," he said at last, and sank back into his chair. He told himself this wasn't the time or place to be pursuing the identity of Arthur Butler, and that no matter what she told him, it wasn't going to do him a damn bit of good anyway. With an irritable sweep of his hand, he motioned to Cage to go ahead.

No, she didn't remember seeing any other neighbors at any time that

---

night. What time had they gone to bed? Quite late. There was a lot of packing to do, and she had to do most of it. Roarke was downstairs in his music room, recording tapes for his portable cassette player.

Yes, she knew the Rossvilles. Yes, she knew what vehicles they drove. No, she didn't remember seeing either drive by at any time that night. That's it? That's all? She could be excused now?

There was no cross-examination. Mrs. Robinson left the stand, her blue designer dress clinging to her hips, her long shapely legs conquering whatever spaces were randomly hit by her high heels, sucking attention away from everything else that was going on in the courtroom.

"Defendants recall Owen Carr."

Olivier could not have made a better production out of stumbling up to the stand. Obviously, neither Carr nor Wechsler had expected this to happen, and yet here he was. Yes, he told the judge, he realized he was still under oath.

"Mr. Carr," Cage asked, "how is it you managed to get in touch with Mary Elizabeth Lane when you were doing your interviews?"

"I went to her house."

"You rang the doorbell?"

"I think she had a door knocker."

"And she let you in?"

"Yes."

"The first time you went there she let you in?"

"No. The first time she did not."

"How about the second?"

"I don't recall."

"How about the third?" It was, given Carr's last answer, something of a trick question, but it got by.

"I don't remember."

"Could you have gone more than three times before she let you in?"

"I could have."

Cage moved in closer to the witness stand. He stood at an angle facing the jury, his head tilted to look at Owen Carr, who now sat like a shriveled leaf, his shoulders curved forward, his neck bent: a poster model of the vulnerable senior citizen.

"Given what both you and Mrs. Lane have testified to already, I gather that you first spoke to her after you had spoken to her husband. Am I correct?"

"I think you are, sir."

"You had already told her husband what you were doing?"

"Yes, sir."

"Tell me, Mr. Carr, after you told her husband what your real purpose was for being in Tranton Park, going around from one neighbor to another, who called whom? Did you call her again . . . or did she call you?"

Carr thought about it.

"Come, come, Mr. Carr," Cage argued. "Your memory has been superlative on every other point."

"I believe she called me."

"She called you, knowing you were a private investigator, knowing you were trying to find out about people riding motorcycles and hauling away bodies in the middle of the night, isn't that right, Mr. Carr?"

Wechsler leaped to his feet, nearly tipping over his table, definitely scattering most of his papers. "Speculation, Judge. Calls for the witness to testify what was in somebody else's mind at the time."

"The witness can only answer what he knows," said the judge.

"Did she indicate to you any knowledge of what I've just said, Mr. Witness?" Cage fired.

"She told me her husband had told her who I was and what I wanted."

"And why was she calling you, Mr. Witness?"

"To tell me she had some information that I needed."

"And what is it she wanted from you in exchange?"

Wechsler, who had never resumed his seat following his last objection, now objected again.

"What grounds?" the judge asked.

Wechsler did a little dance and moved out from behind his desk. "Attorney-client and work product privileges," he said.

Cage responded quickly. "I think he's going to have a tough time establishing Mr. Carr was working for any attorney at the time he made this contact, Judge. And besides, if Mr. Carr won't answer"—he looked over at Wechsler delightedly—"we can always recall Mrs. Lane."

The judge looked at Wechsler. Wechsler said nothing. "Answer the question, Mr. Carr," the judge ordered.

"What is it she wanted from you, Mr. Carr?" Cage repeated.

Carr picked up the bottom of his unfashionably wide tie and flopped it over his palm and then over his forefinger. "She wanted to tell me about the Rossvilles."

Cage smiled at the evasiveness of the old man's answer. "She hadn't been willing even to talk to you before she found out what you did for a living, though, had she?"

"I hadn't talked to her, no."

"Yes or no, Mr. Carr: Was there anything that Mrs. Lane wanted you to do in exchange for telling you the story about the Rossvilles?"

Carr's tie flopped up and down. He looked thoughtful, perhaps trying to calculate how much Cage knew, but taking a fatally long time to answer a yes-or-no question.

"Do you have the question in mind, Mr. Carr?" the judge said, leaning over to get a better look at the witness's face.

"Yes, sir."

"Then what is the answer, please?"

"We discussed . . . the possibility . . . of me watching her husband for her. Which I never did do." Carr hooked his arm behind the chair and swung himself toward the bench. "That was why I hesitated, Judge. In the end she decided that she didn't want me to do that, after all."

"I see," said the judge, and busied himself writing the answer in his notebook.

But Cage was not yet through. "Mr. Carr . . . did Mrs. Lane's request have anything to do with you catching her husband alone with Mrs. Robinson?"

"Object to the word 'catching.'"

"I'll rephrase the question. Did it have anything to do with you seeing Mr. Lane alone with Mrs. Robinson?"

Owen Carr resumed his shriveled-leaf position, but when he spoke, his voice was pure and steady. "I don't know, Mr. Cage. How could I possibly know what's in another person's mind?"

"Objection," called Wechsler belatedly.

"Your Honor, for our last witness, defendants call Patricia O'Berry."

Wechsler started. He looked to the back of the room, but there was no one there except Gilhooley, the DA's man, his pen jabbed into his mouth, his brows knitted.

"Unfortunately," Cage continued, "the decedent's mother lives in Boston, or near there, and she's not susceptible to subpoena. Now, two months ago, Mr. Wechsler and I went back there and took her deposition. I'd like that published now and I'd like to read a portion of it, beginning at page seventy, line twelve, and ending at the end of my examination."

The judge was handed the original deposition transcript and slowly read through the designated material. Wechsler tore through his bags until he found his copy and then started shuffling through it from the beginning. "All right," said the judge. "You can read that portion. If he wants, Mr. Wechsler has the right to have the entire transcript read into evidence. But we'll take that when it comes. Who do you want to read the part of Mrs. O'Berry, Mr. Cage?"

"Mrs. Rossville."

"So be it."

Cathy Rossville had been sitting with her eyes downcast, her hands folded in her lap. Now she looked at her counsel with alarm. He was motioning her to get up and she did, but she did not seem to understand what to do next.

She was wearing a tan pleated skirt, a white blouse, a sleeveless brown sweater. It was schoolteacher's dress, dignified and youthfully conservative. Giff looked at her, looked away, looked at her again. Cage was handing her a copy of the deposition transcript, explaining what he wanted her to do, directing her up to the witness box. Slowly, reluctantly, she went.

" 'Mrs. O'Berry,' " Cage read, his voice loud and clear and strong, his copy of the deposition held out in front of him as if it were an actor's script, " 'did your son ever speak to you about the possibility of not going through with the wedding?' "

Cathy Rossville sat looking at Cage in silence. Gently, he motioned to the testimony until she looked down and found her place. " 'Not once they decided to do it,' " she said softly.

" 'Who's they?' "

" 'The kids. Bobby and Barbara.' "

Giff told her to speak up. She read the words again, her tone curiously flat.

Cage read, " 'What about before the date was set? Did he ever talk to you about alternatives to getting married?' "

" 'Like what?' "

" 'Like not getting married.' "

" 'He never said anything about that.' "

" 'Did you tell him he didn't have to get married?' "

" 'I never said anything one way or the other.' "

" 'Did you ever discuss with anyone' "—Cage came down hard on the word—" 'the possibility of him not getting married?' "

There was no response from the witness stand. But this time Cathy Rossville was looking directly at the page before her. She appeared to be concentrating on it, she appeared to know what she was supposed to read, and still nothing came.

"Cathy?" Chris Cage said.

She lifted her chin. To Giff, her eyes looked watery. " 'My priest,' " she answered.

Cage lowered his copy of the transcript. "Do you want a cup of water?" he asked quietly.

She shook her head. Myrna got up from her three-sided desk and handed her a tissue. "I'm all right," she said, but she dabbed at her face with the tissue anyway. She tried to smile and then quickly covered her nose and mouth with what was left of the tissue.

"Can you turn to page seventy-one, Cathy?"

She did as she was asked. A crinkling of paper came from where she sat, from the judge's bench, from Wechsler's table. The jurors moved their heads from one side to the other.

" 'Did you have any idea before the wedding that Bobby might choose to leave Barbara after the ceremony?' " Cage read.

" 'Not really.' "

" 'You say not really. Does that mean you had some inkling to that effect?' "

Wechsler stood up. "Just a minute, please, Mrs. Rossville. Judge, I think this next answer is both without foundation and speculative."

Giff examined the answer. Then he read on. "It'll be allowed," he said.

Wechsler sank slowly back into his seat as Cathy Rossville, her speech losing power once again, said, " 'I knew he didn't really want to marry Barbara.' "

" 'Did he indicate to you in any way that he might leave after the wedding?' "

" 'Not really.' "

Cage cleared his throat and, perhaps as a hint, spoke louder than necessary. " 'You did it again, Mrs. O'Berry. That answer makes me think that there was something he said or did which gave you the impression that he might leave. Was there?' "

" 'Not really.' "

340

" 'Okay, Mrs. O'Berry. Were your surprised when you found out your son had disappeared on his wedding night?' "

" 'I thought he was dead.' "

" 'Did you have any reason for thinking he wasn't dead, that he had just disappeared?' "

" 'Well, he never said anything to me about doing that.' "

" 'Did he ever contact you after he was reported missing?' "

" 'No.' "

" 'Were you surprised to learn that he had been out in California?' "

" 'Yes, of course I was.' "

" 'Did you have any reason to believe he was still alive after he was reported missing?' "

" 'Just a mother's instincts.' "

" 'You had a feeling he was still alive?' "

" 'Yes.' "

" 'Do you know how he managed to get out to California?' "

" 'No.' "

" 'Do you know if he had any money he could have used to get there?' "

" 'There could have been.' "

" 'Pardon me?' "

" 'I had given him something.' "

" 'For what purpose?' "

" 'It wasn't discussed.' "

" 'In what context did you give it to him?' "

" 'We were talking about what we would do if we had our lives to live over again.' "

" 'And what happened?' "

Cathy Rossville stared at the transcript page. In the jurors' box, a chair scraped as somebody shifted position. And then she said, " 'I gave him the money I had been saving.' "

" 'How much?' " came the question.

Again the answer came slowly. " 'All of it.' "

" 'And how much was that, Mrs. O'Berry?' "

Cathy's hand was between her lips. Her eyes squeezed shut.

"You have to read the line, Cathy," Cage said.

Her eyes never opened. She simply spoke the words she knew were on the page. " 'Three hundred dollars.' "

And then a single loud sob escaped from her lips.

For several seconds she was the sole object of attention for every person in the courtroom; and then Cage was at her side, blocking her off from the jurors and the spectators, slipping the transcript from her hand, whispering across the two feet of space that separated them—whispering words that only Giff was in a position to hear: "It's all right, Cath. It's all over now. You've done what you had to do."

Then Cathy Rossville, without so much as looking at Cage or anyone else, got up and walked directly out of the courtroom.

CHAPTER TWELVE

Wechsler began his closing argument strongly, fortifying the testimony of his eyewitnesses, extolling their virtues, remarking on the inability of defense counsel to rebut their claims. He glossed over his own failure to establish a motive by hinting broadly at nefarious activities behind the impenetrable facade of the Rossville home; and he parlayed this into a general denunciation of the Rossvilles, their lifestyle, their attitudes, their social position. He called them people who thought they could get away with anything and he asked the jurors to send them a message: to tell them they were no better than anyone else, despite their material acquisitions; to tell them that human life was not theirs to trifle with; to tell them that if they brought harm to others, whether negligently or purposefully, they had to pay recompense for that harm. In this case, he argued, based on a forty-six-year work expectancy for Bobby O'Berry, that recompense had to be in the form of at least one million dollars.

Wechsler ended his argument expressing confidence that the jurors would carry out their responsibilities, live by their oaths, and ensure that his clients, Barbara O'Berry and her little girl, little Bobbie, were properly compensated for the loss they had endured at the callous hands of the Rossvilles. Then he sat down as though he were waving goodbye to a lover, reluctant to let them go, but knowing that he had to nonetheless.

Giff's eyes shifted to the defendants' table, where Cage sat alone with Leigh Rossville. He wondered if Cage needed a break before launching into his own argument. He expected he would be wanting to bring in Cathy Rossville, who had not returned to the courtroom since giving her rendition of Mrs. O'Berry's testimony. But Cage was pushing himself to his feet, making one last pass through his trial book, and clearly readying himself to speak.

"Mr. Cage," Giff called out. "Would you come up here for a second?"

Cage, surprised, glancing over at Wechsler, complied.

"Don't you want the other defendant to be here?" Giff asked him.

Cage hesitated. He looked back at Cathy Rossville's empty seat for a long time before answering. "Mrs. Rossville's not up to another appearance, Your Honor," he said. Then he tried a smile which could have meant any number of things. Giff chose to interpret it as a plea not to be put on the spot.

Speaking to the jury, Giff said, "Ladies and gentlemen, we will proceed directly with defendants' closing argument," and then with the mere flick of an index finger he signaled Cage to go ahead.

Chris Cage had worn a brand-new suit of a tan color so light as to hint at being white. He began slowly, and predictably enough, repeating his opening statement claim of the Rossvilles' being target defendants, people whose lives might seem at first blush to be so enviable they aroused hatred in those who didn't even know them. Deftly, almost happily, Cage picked up on one of Wechsler's themes and began talking about the haves and the have-nots. He accepted the Rossvilles as being in the haves category and compared them with unknown persons whose lives had been so unhappy, so unsuccessful, perhaps so misbegotten, that they wanted to lash out at, hurt, punish, strip the dignity from anyone who might appear better off than they. He matched the Rossvilles against people who were looking for a fast buck, people who were trying to beat the system, people who had failed within the system. He spoke of the legal process as being part of that system and then he spoke with obvious distress about people who attempt to misuse the legal process for their own monetary gain. He spoke of those who were willing to go along with misuse of the legal process for their own purposes; and then he looked directly at Owen Carr and said, "And of course there are those who see in our legal system a chance to do nothing more than create work for themselves."

Unlike Wechsler, Cage used no lectern. He needed none because he had no notes. Positioning himself directly in front of the jury box, he said, "And what of those folks who are seized on, used, exploited by these people I have just mentioned? What of a nice, innocent person like that bartender, Goose? Not the brightest guy in the world, maybe, but a nice guy, one who means well. Who better to support a case you are creating out of whole cloth? 'Hey, Goose, you're a bartender in one of the most popular spots in town. You see thousands of people a month. Ever seen this guy? Sure you have, Goose. And it would help a whole lot if you could give me the name of someone he was talking to while he was in here. No name? How about an address? A neighborhood? A city? Anything that will help me get someplace where I can start asking people if they've seen a motorcycle and a dead body being hauled out in the middle of the night.'

"And so, in our quest for work, we get to Tranton Park, home of the seemingly well-to-do, home of people who would not like to have their names linked with any sort of scandal and who might very well pay plenty to see that it doesn't happen. Problem now, we have to get somebody in this neighborhood to talk about somebody else. What do we have—thirty-six houses? And in thirty-six houses surely there is one unfortunate soul suffering some sort of emotional impairment. Out of thirty-six houses we find one person who fits this description and, lo and behold, she is the one person out of thirty-six houses willing to tell us what we want to hear. She's so willing to tell us that she actually calls us up. And when does she call us up? After we have told her husband exactly what it is we want to hear."

Holding his hand between his ear and his mouth as if he were talking into a telephone, Cage said, "Hello, Mr. Carr, I understand you're looking for a motorcycle and a dead body. Why, I could see a motorcycle and a dead body right outside my window . . . if only you'll do something for me. I know you'll do this thing for me, Mr. Carr, because you're a private detective and in all my years of reading books and watching television I've developed a pretty good idea of the type of things private detectives do. They spy on people. And I'd like you to spy on my husband. . . . I can't do it myself, you see, because I never leave the house. . . . Why do I want you to spy on my husband? Because I think he's cheating on me. With whom do I think he's cheating? Only with the most beautiful woman I've ever seen. Only with a woman who is married to one of the world's greatest athletes, a man who is truly a legend in his own time."

Cage discarded his imaginary phone and ran to the clerk's desk. Shuffling through exhibits, he pulled out the green sports sheet that had noticed Roarke Robinson's arrival at spring training camp. Turning the page over, pointing to an article on the reverse side of the one he had referenced during his cross-examination, he said, "Only with a woman whose husband is currently earning over eight hundred thousand dollars a year." Throwing the newspaper back on the clerk's desk, Cage said, "Talk about delusions of grandeur. Talk about delusions. Ladies and gentlemen, you saw the man Mrs. Lane identified as her husband. You saw Ann Robinson. Do you believe your own eyes or do you believe the suspicions of some poor, aging, troubled, unhappy woman who has nothing to do with her time but stare out windows and create fantasies in her head?

"Do we, ladies and gentlemen, assume that this one time Mrs. Lane was telling the truth? We remember that the house directly next to hers is the Rossvilles'. We remember that the house which her bedroom overlooks is the Rossvilles' and we remember that at one o'clock in the morning most people are in their bedrooms; so that if Mrs. Lane is to see anything at all, she has to see it at the Rossvilles' house. A house at which she just happens to be looking at one o'clock. By herself.

"And what, we ask ouselves, if we accept her testimony, was Bobby O'Berry doing at the Rossvilles' house in the first place? Remember what we were saying about the haves and the have-nots. The Rossvilles, we say, are haves. Poor Bobby O'Berry, eighteen–nineteen years old, married and about to become a father, unemployed and just out of high school, riding around on someone else's motorcycle, is most definitely a have-not. For heaven's sake, his mother gave him everything she had, and that amounted to a grand total of three hundred dollars. What, if you please, was Bobby doing at the Rossvilles'? At eleven o'clock on a Saturday night he wasn't there to work, that's for sure. Did they lure him there to kill him? The Rossvilles? A corporate lawyer and a travel agent? They were planning on leaping on this muscular kid and killing him? What, was Cathy going to hold down this six-two two-hundred-pounder? Or what else? Were they going to have wild sexual orgies? Was that it?"

Giff's head lolled back. Cautiously, he eyed the jurors. Their expressions revealed nothing other than total immersion in what Cage was saying. Cage had gotten away with it. He had defused Wechsler's undeclared implication and Wechsler, by the way his lower lip was jammed between his teeth, well knew it.

"Not," Cage said, drawing himself up straight, "very likely, given what we know of Bobby O'Berry's background.

"Let us consider that background. Indeed, let us consider Bobby O'Berry. He is, of course, not here to defend himself, but no one need fear he needs defense from me. In my opinion, Bobby O'Berry was a victim of the very same forces now at work on Leigh and Cathy.

346

"What do we know of him? We know he led a short and, in the end, very tragic life. We know he married Barbara. We know that they were high school classmates. We know that they married when she was several months pregnant. We know that on his wedding night Bobby was not able to peform his spousal duties. Not unheard of, perhaps, but it is all we really know about Bobby's sex life.

"But what of Barbara? you say. And I return the question to you: What of Barbara? A nice girl. A very nice girl. But Barbara, by her own admission, was sexually active in high school. By her own admission she was experienced before Bobby. By her own assertion she was not intimate with Bobby until the very last month of their very last year of high school. This is the girl who suddenly found herself pregnant in late August. This is the girl who says Bobby was the father. Was he the father? Whose word, besides Barbara's, do we have on that?" Cage paused, looking from one juror to the next, as though actually expecting an answer. "We don't even have a blood test to prove paternity in this case. You must ask yourselves why we don't. You must ask yourselves why better evidence was not offered in this case."

He shook his head. "Bobby's gone. He can't tell us the truth anymore. He was, in fact, gone on his wedding night. Was he telling us something then, when he faked his own drowning? When he disappeared? Bobby O'Berry, who could not perform on his wedding night. But why did he marry her, you ask, if he wasn't the father of her child? And I say to you: Two reasons. Two very big reasons."

Chris Cage walked away from the jurors. He walked to the railing that separated participants from spectators and he looked directly at the Cochrane brothers in their first-row seats. "Two big reasons named Terry and Billy Cochrane.

"Commendably, they wanted their baby sister to be taken care of. They wanted her child to have a name and a father. In the face of such fraternal desires emanating from two such formidable sources, what option would Bobby O'Berry have had? What option did he have?"

Twin sneers twisted the faces of the Cochrane brothers and only their sister, sitting between them and squeezing their legs, seemed to be restraining them from doing anything more. Cage waited longer than he needed to wait, giving them every opportunity to react, and then he turned back to the jury. "Maybe Bobby O' Berry did make love to Barbara Cochrane. Maybe he did spill his semen inside her. Maybe he did impregnate her. But others had slept with her, had spilled their semen inside her. Why single out Bobby? I'll tell you precisely why. It's the same reason Barbara gave over and over again. Because Bobby could be counted on to do the right thing."

Cage sat on the edge of his desk, his arms folded, one foot on the floor. "So now," he said, "Barbara has his name. Her child has his name and Bobby is gone for good. He was gone before, of course, but Barbara could always dream he would come back. Was he coming back? His mother had given him her last cent. His friend had given him his motorcycle. He was on the other side of the continent and even the people who claim they saw him don't claim he was asking for directions back east. Well, we'll never know now. Not now. But if you're Barbara and you're in Barbara's position; if you're her brothers and you're in their position—heck, why not claim it? What have you got to lose? Why not claim the only reason he's not coming back is because the Rossvilles killed him? Why not? They appear to be rich."

Chris Cage got off his desk and unfolded his arms. "You, ladies and gentlemen, know why not. . . . Because it just isn't so."

He swung around and looked at Wechsler. "Your reply, counsel." His voice was calm and even, and only the half moons of dampness under the arms of his tan suit gave evidence as to the strain of his efforts.

To Giff, Wechsler looked like a basketball player with the ball at half-court, two seconds left and his team down by a point. It was entirely possible that to the jury he looked completely different. To them he might have been a tower of strength and patience, rising above a storm of babble. But it was his burden, as plaintiff, to prove what was more likely than not; that was why he got to go first as well as last, giving his closing argument, and to Giff's legal mind Wechsler was just going to have to let fly with a long shot and pray that it dropped through the hoop.

For a while he spoke urgently, a wounded expression on his face, the hurt creeping into his voice as he tried to come to grips with the terrible things Mr. Cage had said about all those who were trying to tell the truth in this case. If someone says something that Mr. Cage doesn't like, well then, apparently that person is crazy, or a liar, or worse. It was clear that Wechsler felt sorry for Mr. Cage and his dementia.

It took expert detective work by a dedicated man like Owen Carr to identify the remains of Bobby O'Berry. It was not mere happenstance that such detective work led him, as well, to the Rossvilles. This was not done by serendipity. Owen found the motorcycle. The motorcycle led him inside the bar. The bartender had seen Bobby get directions to Tranton Park. Mrs. Lane had seen Bobby's motorcycle arrive in Tranton Park and she had seen it go away without him on the night he was killed.

And then Reuben Wechsler let fly. "As for what Bobby was doing there, well, it's really no secret, is it? Heck, Mr. Cage came so close with his various aspersions that I thought for sure he was going to come right out and say what, unfortunately, must be obvious to all of us." He paused. He looked at each of the jurors. "Bobby was there to rob the place."

Wechsler's face grew long and sad. As such, it was in marked contrast to the faces of the Cochrane family, all of whom were in plain view of the judge. All three were gaping: Barbara in disbelief, the two brothers in outrage.

"How else do you suppose Bobby had been supporting himself for all those months with nothing but the three hundred dollars his mother had given him as a wedding present? He had, after all, stolen his friend's motorcycle. And now he had run into this smart-looking fellow in a San Francisco bar and what had happened? Had Leigh Rossville, in the course of a few drinks, said too much? Had he mentioned he wouldn't be home on Saturday night? Had he and his wife changed their plans and not gone out because they had decided to go off to Cozumel the next day? Had Bobby just gotten the day of Leigh's departure wrong? No matter. The fact is, Bobby went there; and whether he should have been there or not, they shot him. Killed him. And who knows? Maybe they just couldn't accept what they'd done. But the law does not allow you to kill a person, even one who's trespassing on your property. And the Rossvilles knew that, him being a lawyer and all. And so they tried to cover it up, to deny what they had done.

"After you jurors return with your just verdict, there won't be room for them to deny it anymore."

Freddy reported they were arguing out in the hallway, actually raising their voices and yelling. He had tried to get them to quiet down and the big one had told him to leave them alone. He had used the f-word.

Barbara, he said, was crying. She was over against one wall trying to smoke a cigarette and hold herself up at the same time. The brothers were standing on each side of Wechsler and he was waving his arms around, looking like he was trying to get away from them. Finally the old man, Owen Carr, had pushed his way into the middle and gotten Wechsler out of there by keeping his own body between the attorney and the two angry brothers.

The jury came in exactly at five o'clock. That was usually a bad sign for one side or the other. It meant that somebody had compromised; some juror, perhaps wanting to get home, had capitulated in order to achieve the nine votes that were needed for a verdict.

They had been out since eleven o'clock, not a lengthy period of time, yet longer than would have been expected if they were going to return a straight defendant's verdict. They had been out long enough to decide not only liability, but damages as well. And they wouldn't have needed to get liability unless they had decided in favor of the plaintiff.

"Mr. Foreman," said Giff, "I understand you've reached a verdict."

The pharmacist stood up. "We have, Your Honor."

"Would you hand it to the clerk, please."

Myrna went over and took it from him. She passed it to the judge and the judge, before opening it, glanced once more around the courtroom. The twelve jurors were in their places, the two alternates gone. Cage and Leigh Rossville sat gripping the edge of their table with their white-knuckled hands. Next to them, gaping as though it were a missing tooth, was the empty chair of Cathy Rossville. Giff's eyes paused longer than they should have at the open space, and then he shifted them to Wechsler's table, where Wechsler sat alone, his fingertips pressed into his forehad.

Freddy, at his little desk just inside the railing, just next to the door leading to the jury room, leaned forward eagerly. On the other side of the railing sat the two Cochrane brothers, each in a cardigan sweater: Billy in gray, Terry in red. Their sister, her legs crossed, her head down, sat a few seats removed from them. Gilhooley was nowhere to be seen, but in the far back, his arm draped over the bench behind him, his raincoat across his lap, sat Owen Carr.

The judge opened the verdict and read it. Immediately he wanted to look at Barbara Cochrane, but he was afraid of the expression he would see on her face. He glanced at Wechsler, but Wechsler's eyes were downcast, and so his gaze went to Owen Carr while he handed the verdict form back to Myrna. Carr understood. He nodded once and stood up. Before Myrna unfolded the sheet of paper, he was pushing his way through the courtroom doors. He was in the hallway before she read: "We, the members of the jury in the captioned case, vote nine to three for the defendants Leigh and Cathy Rossville, and against the plaintiff Barbara O'Berry on behalf of herself and the Estate of Robert O'Berry."

Chris Cage let out a scream of joy. He and Leigh Rossville collapsed into each other's arms, their heads falling on each other's shoulders. The noise of Chris's voice, so uncontrolled after so long a period of formality and decorum, caused one of the jurors to begin to clap. Then several others joined in. Cage and Rossville turned, each with an arm about the other, each with an arm extended toward the jury, and the jurors responded by rising from their seats. They were trying to get to the defendants' table and the judge was trying to restrain them. He was banging his gavel, calling to them, telling them to stay where they were.

"Please," he shouted. "Ladies and gentlemen, please remain in your places. You are not through yet. Freddy, get them back. Mr. Wechsler, do you want the jurors polled? Do you want them polled?"

"Yes, sir," Wechsler shouted back.

And then there was a roar, a deep, inhuman eruption of pain and anger, and all other sounds ceased. Heads turned. Faces froze.

The noise was coming from Terry Cochrane, and Terry Cochrane was standing on his feet, with his clenched fists held out from his sides. "You idiots," he cried. "These lying, scummy bastards get up there and they lie and lie and lie, and you, Judge, you let them. You let them keep lying and lying."

"Sit down, Mr. Cochrane," the judge commanded. His great gray eyebrows were gathered together threateningly. His voice was severe.

"Sit down?" Terry Cochrane said incredulously. "Why don't I just fall down like you, you worthless old buzzard, let this prick stomp all over me?" He threw out his hand in the direction of Chris Cage.

"Freddy," the judge said, not taking his eyes off Cochrane, "summon the sheriff's deputies."

Freddy, who had been in the jurors' box trying to carry out the judge's last directive, took one step toward his desk. In the next moment Terry Cochrane's hand went beneath his cardigan sweater. "Don't you move," Cochrane said, and suddenly there was a semiautomatic pistol in his hand. It had been in his belt, the judge had watched it come out, and now it was being waved around the courtroom.

It swept from Freddy to the jurors, and the jurors cried out and tried to duck behind each other, their shoulders raised high and their faces scrunched. And then the semiautomatic came to rest on the judge, pointed straight at him, seemingly aimed directly between his eyes.

There was a button beneath Giff's desk. He only had to shift his knee to press it. But he had not reacted fast enough when the gun had first appeared and now, with the gun trained on him, and even though his knees could not be seen by anyone, he felt incapable of making the move. His legs were too feathery. They would not respond. There was a liquefying feeling in the pit of his stomach. He was going to let loose, everything was going to let loose, if he didn't get control. "Put the gun down, Terry," he said, and the sound of his own voice filled him with confidence. It came out strong and authoritative, like that of a minister who speaks directly to God and is passing along His messages to the congregation. "Put that down and at least allow your lawyer to finish doing his job. He can ask for a judgment notwithstanding the verdict. He can ask for a new trial." The judge started to come forward in his seat, started to slide his knee.

"Don't move," screamed Terry. He was hunched over now, both arms outstretched, both hands on the grip, and the gun was quivering. It swayed and then it swung. The judge hit the button. It would be sounding in the deputies' office on the first floor. They would be running for the stairs, for the elevator. But it was after five o'clock; how many would be there? Would any of them be there?

The gun was on Wechsler now and Wechsler slowly raised his hands and tried to smile beneath his mustache. "Hey, Terry," he said, "I'm a loser, too. I'm not even going to be getting paid, remember?"

Terry swung his arms and the barrel of the gun went from Wechsler to Leigh Rossville. There was one long second in which the two men stared directly into each other's eyes and then Terry shifted the gun just a few more degrees and blew off the top of Chris Cage's head.

The gun went *whap* and *whap* again, and Chris Cage flew backward into the defendants' table. He hit with his back, his arms spread, his legs staying straight, and then he slid to the floor. All around the room people were shrieking in terror and diving to the floor, until only the three Cochranes were left standing and only the judge was left sitting in his chair.

Terry was in the middle of the aisle now. The gun was being pointed from wall to wall, from person to person, but he was backing up, making his way toward the door. His brother Billy had jumped out in front of him like a pass blocker protecting a quarterback. Billy's knees were bent, his huge shoulders were curved, his forearms were held chesthigh and his bulging eyes were sweeping the room. Off to one side stood Barbara in a semicrouch, both hands to her face. She was saying, "Please don't, please no, please stop," but all the words were coming out as one long incomprehensible wail.

On the bench, the judge sat so motionlessly he might have been a statue. His hands were out in front of him, his knee was wedged against the trouble button, and he was breathing only enough to keep his prayers running through his mind. And then he saw the face in one of the porthole windows of the courtroom doors. It was an old, weathered, almost yellowish face, and it wasn't recoiling from what it saw.

The brothers continued backing up, looking everywhere but behind them, knowing that the doors would be there soon. Terry released one hand from the grip. He began feeling the air behind himself. Billy, still positioned between his brother and the rest of the courtroom, was simply following the sounds Terry was making as they inched over the carpet.

Terry's hand touched the door just as it was shoved from the outside. It smacked him in the back and Terry lurched forward. The gun went off so quickly he seemed not even to realize it. Three times it sounded before he could get his finger away from the trigger, and by then his brother Billy was on his knees, slowly pitching forward, slowly toppling onto his face as blood spurted out of the back of his head.

Owen Carr was pressed up against Terry's chest, his face tucked into Terry's chin. "Whoops, Terry," he was saying, "whoops, sorry." It was a comic routine that got them more and more entangled with every attempt to get away. Terry's gun hand was pointed straight toward the ceiling because Owen was nestled into his armpit, keeping him from lowering the arm, all the time saying, "Oh, sorry, Terry, sorry. Let me out of the way." Then Owen's voice changed and he was speaking softly, almost crooning, telling Terry he loved him, saying his brother loved him and needed his help; and Terry was staring down incomprehensibly at the heap of his brother's body on the floor, at the fountain of blood that was arcing out of his brother's head.

This was how they were when the doors flew open and three uniformed sheriff's deputies, two men and a burly woman, charged into the room. Without breaking stride, the three deputies nailed Terry

353

Cochrane and a still clinging Owen Carr in a gang tackle that brought everyone crashing down in a huge writhing pile of bodies.

Reporters had come in almost on the heels of the deputies. One of them had a camera and was taking pictures indiscriminately, in the expectation that anything in this courtroom was going to prove newsworthy. One had a tape recorder and was busily thrusting the microphone into people's faces, demanding comments, explanations, observations, anything people would say. All of them descended on the judge before he had managed to leave his raised platform.

"Would you care to tell what happened, Judge Gifford? In your own words," the one with the microphone shouted.

Giff looked over the reporters' head. Leigh Rossville was on his knees, bent over the body of his lawyer, his hands, his suit, even his face splashed with Chris Cage's blood. He seemed to be trying to put Cage back together again. Beyond him, on the floor, the deputies were still grappling with Terry Cochrane. They had him handcuffed from behind and they were trying to get something around his ankles. And in the far back stood Owen Carr, putting on his raincoat and buttoning it to the neck as though he were leaving a business appointment. He had somehow managed to slip away from everyone else and now he was going out the door and no one was trying to stop him. Giff wanted to call out, but there was too much noise. The reporters were all hurling questions: "Who's the lawyer who was killed? Was he anybody famous?"

Giff felt he should answer. He needed to tell them something about Chris Cage so that they would know that he was not just a body, not just a sensational murder victim, not just a dead lawyer.

The reporters sensed that he was about to say something important and pressed in closer. "What was he like?" they said. "Did he have a family?"

Giff hesitated, trying to think of what he really knew about Chris Cage, trying to come up with something to tell them that would transcend the courtroom.

"He was," he said, "a most honorable man."

They had expected more. He could see it in their faces.

"But . . . but," one of them said, "the person on trial, was that *the* Leigh Rossville? The San Francisco attorney?"

And another shouted, "Juror Gutierrez says the case was all about

354

Leigh Rossville shooting an impotent burglar. Would you care to comment?"

"Is it true that Mr. and Mrs. Rossville were engaged in sexual orgies, Judge?"

"Were there drugs involved?"

Roger Gifford shook his head mutely and began to push his way toward his chambers. If he could only get through the door and into his own office, it would be all right. It would be cool in there. Quiet. Like the forest.